PRAISE FOR MARIAH STEWART

THE LAST CHANCE MATINEE

"The combination of a quirky small-town setting, a family mystery, a gentle romance, and three estranged sisters is catnip for women's fiction fans."

—*Booklist*

"A good read, with a nice blend of mystery, family drama, and romance. Readers will look forward to the next installment."

—*Library Journal*

"Mariah Stewart has blown me away with her new series featuring the Hudson sisters. . . . *The Last Chance Matinee* is a multifaceted story of family and what happens when you put three sisters together to bring their father's dream to reality."

—*Lovey Dovey Books*

"You know those books that are just easy to read? The kind where you want to know what happens next and want to sneak off to read just a few pages more? This was one of those books for me."

—*I Wish I Lived in a Library*

"A heartwarming read, full of surprising secrets, humor, and lessons about what it means to be a family."

—*That Book Lady Blog*

THE CHESAPEAKE DIARIES SERIES

"The town and townspeople of St. Dennis, Maryland, come vividly to life under Stewart's skillful hands. The pace is gentle, but the emotions are complex."
—*RT Book Reviews*

"If a book is by Mariah Stewart, it has a subliminal message of 'wonderful' stamped on every page."
—*Reader to Reader Reviews*

"The characters seem like they could be a neighbor or friend or even a co-worker, and it is because of that and Mariah Stewart's writing that I keep returning again and again to this series."
—*Heroes and Heartbreakers*

"Every book in this series is a gem."
—*The Best Reviews*

"Captivating and heartwarming."
—*Fresh Fiction*

A DIFFERENT LIGHT

"Warm, compassionate, and fulfilling. Great reading."
—*RT Book Reviews*

"This is an absolutely delicious book to curl up with . . . scrumptious . . . delightful."
—*Philadelphia Inquirer*

MOON DANCE

WONDERFUL YOU

DEVLIN'S LIGHT

MARIAH STEWART

the last chance matinee

POCKET BOOKS

New York   London   Toronto   Sydney   New Delhi

Pocket Books
An Imprint of Simon & Schuster, Inc.
1230 Avenue of the Americas
New York, NY 10020

This book is a work of fiction. Any references to historical events, real people, or real places are used fictitiously. Other names, characters, places, and events are products of the author's imagination, and any resemblance to actual events or places or persons, living or dead, is entirely coincidental.

First Pocket Books paperback edition December 2018

POCKET and colophon are registered trademarks of Simon & Schuster, Inc.

For information about special discounts for bulk purchases, please contact Simon & Schuster Special Sales at 1-866-506-1949 or business@simonandschuster.com.

The Simon & Schuster Speakers Bureau can bring authors to your live event. For more information or to book an event, contact the Simon & Schuster Speakers Bureau at 1-866-248-3049 or visit our website at www.simonspeakers.com.

Manufactured in the United States of America

10 9 8 7 6 5 4 3 2 1

ISBN 978-1-5011-9658-4
ISBN 978-1-5011-4491-2 (ebook)

To Loretta Barrett,
who believed in me before I believed in myself.
You are missed.

ACKNOWLEDGMENTS

Ask any writer and they will tell you that, yes, it does in fact take a village to get a book out of the murky recesses of the author's mind and into the hands of the reader. This time around, the village may have been on both sides of "the veil." I need to acknowledge my late mother's role in writing this story. While she wasn't happy about the fact that her own father had kept so much hidden for so many years (and she was absolutely positive that her mother never knew anything about his other life), she readily shared with me everything she had discovered. Her openness cracked the code to tracking our family's story in a way we never would have been able to do otherwise, since the name my grandfather went by—the name he passed on to his children—wasn't the name he was born with. I definitely felt my mom's amused presence while I was writing this story (so different from what really happened, but the spirit was certainly the same).

My thanks to Sandra Koehler Lee, the daughter

of my cousin Peg West Koehler, for her efforts to compile a complete genealogy. It's a long, winding road she has followed to help us find the truth.

The entire team at Gallery Books has been wonderful in putting together all the pieces necessary to turn this story into a book. My grateful thanks to publisher Jennifer Bergstrom and publicist Melissa Gramstad for their support. Thanks also to the art department for a cover that accurately reflects the spirit of my fictional Art Deco theater. Many thanks to the production crew and the copyeditor who worked on this manuscript and caught my flubs and stumbles. I can't say thank you often enough to editorial assistant Elana Cohen for all she does.

Special thanks to fellow author Victoria Alexander, lifelong friend Jo Ellen Zelt Grossman, and the Writers Who Lunch (Terri Brisbin, Cara Marsi, Gwendolyn Schuler, Gail Link, Kate Welsh, Martha Schroeder, and Georgia Dickson) for their encouragement.

I owe the deepest of debts to my wonderful, incredible, hardworking editor, Lauren McKenna, who not only loved the story I proposed but who beat me unmercifully—figuratively, speaking—until I got it right. I am so blessed to have an editor with such clear vision, endless talent, sheer love of story, and respect for the author's process. I may whine and complain, Lauren, but I truly do love you to the moon and back, and I know that every book we've worked on together has been infinitely better for your touch, my characters so much stronger for your insights. There are no words to express how much I appreciate you.

PREFACE

Everyone is familiar with the adage "write what you know"; it's a saying that has dictated much of my decades-long career in publishing. But this time, it was what I (or rather, my mother) *didn't* know that formed the basis for this first book in my new Hudson Sisters series.

When my mother was in her mid-forties, she received a letter from a woman named Alice, the wife of her recently deceased cousin Bill. Alice thanked my mother for the sympathy card she'd sent her, and finished her note by saying, "You do know that Bill was your half brother, right?"

Ah, no. She did not.

Before she could sing the opening bars of "Poppa Was a Rolling Stone," my mother had Alice on the phone. The story Alice told my mother was almost too crazy to be true.

Almost.

My grandfather was in vaudeville from around 1906 to 1915, and during that time struck up a romantic relationship with a woman named Trudy. In 1910 Trudy gave birth to a son, the aforementioned "cousin" Bill. Three years later, Trudy had a daughter, but both she and the baby died. Shortly thereafter, in 1913, my grandfather gave Bill to his sister, Bess, and her husband, who were childless. And a few years later, my grandfather met and married my grandmother, none the wiser to his partying ways, at least to the best of our knowledge.

Bess and her husband ultimately adopted Bill, who was never told that the man he called "uncle" was actually his *father*. After Bill passed away, and sometime before her own death, Bess finally came clean to Alice, who shared the story with my mother, who then shared it with me.

Of course, I was fascinated. My grandfather died when I was four or five years old, and I have very little memory of him other than his deep, hearty laugh. I've been thinking for years that this foundation of a love child and secret siblings would make a great story, but not knowing all the facts, I was free to fill in the blanks—and so I did. Years passed before I felt I had the right story in my head. This is that story.

I hope you enjoy my version of what *could* happen under such circumstances.

Best,
Mariah

Disclaimer (intended for my cousins, should they wonder if someone's been holding out on them): *The Last Chance Matinee* is total fiction. There is no theater, no Hollywood wife, no yoga studio in Devlin's Light, New Jersey (and no Devlin's Light, either), and definitely no fortune waiting to be distributed. The sisters were not based on anyone we know, and sorry, but there are no secret relatives living in a Victorian mansion somewhere in the Poconos.

PROLOGUE

◆

Cara

The bell rang halfheartedly over the door of the only bakery in Devlin's Light, New Jersey (the self-proclaimed "best little town on the Delaware Bay"). Cara McCann's eyes met those of the proprietor and her best friend, Darla Kerns, and they both laughed.

"I know," Darla said. "The bell sounds anemic. I have to get a new one. It's on the list."

"Some days the list is longer than others." Cara went to the counter to make her morning's selection from the freshly baked muffins.

"So what's it going to be?" Darla rested her arms on the thick countertop.

Cara scanned the case. The selection of her one high-calorie treat of the day deserved serious thought.

"The chocolate zucchini muffin is new," Darla pointed out. "As is the raspberry lemon." Before Cara could even ask, she added, "Lemon muffin with raspberry cream filling. Divine, if I do say so myself."

"That does sound good. I think I'll try—"

"Amber, listen to me. You need to make a decision and make it fast. You don't have all the time in the world." The voice from the back boomed as it came closer.

"Help," Cara begged Darla.

Darla opened the case and grabbed a raspberry lemon muffin and placed it in a small white bag. She was handing it to Cara when the stout woman behind the loud voice emerged from the back of the store.

"I'll call you later." The woman dropped the phone into her pocket and greeted Darla with a big smile. "Good morning, boss."

"Morning, Angie."

"And Cara, how's it going this morning?" Angie Hoff slipped on her white apron and tied it around her waist.

Not bothering to wait for Cara to respond, Angie launched into her usual morning down-to-the-last-detail recitation of her daughter's wedding plans as if they were dying for an update. As if Amber Hoff hadn't been one of Cara's best friends, once upon a time. As if Amber's fiancé, Drew McCann, wasn't Cara's ex-husband. As if Amber hadn't moved in with Drew and gotten pregnant while he was still married to Cara.

"So the florist calls my daughter and says she can't get peonies for the bouquets and the centerpieces after all. Something about a frost somewhere

where they grow this time of the year. Did you ever hear of such a thing? A florist can't get something their client wants? Amber's crying, she's a wreck. It's ruining her vision, she says. She needs peonies. Has to have white peonies." Angie looked from Cara to Darla. "Either of you girls know where we can get white peonies? I mean, they have to be in season somewhere, right?"

"Sorry, I don't know anything about flowers," Cara muttered, and went to pay for the muffin.

"Me either. I just bake." From behind the counter, Darla made a shooing motion with her hand. "Just go," she mouthed.

"Thanks. See you later." Cara waved as she left the shop, her exit marked by the barely audible ring of the soon-to-be-retired bell.

She stopped at the storefront three doors down and unlocked the door. Once one-third of a hardware store that dated from the 1890s, Cara's yoga studio had been the first section sold when the previous owner had succumbed to the big chain store that had opened right off the highway outside of town. Using the proceeds from her late mother's life insurance policy, Cara had worked hard to repurpose the space. Back then, Drew had fully supported the venture and had worked by her side to make her dream a reality. He'd laid the black and white tiles in a checkerboard pattern on the floor, and helped her paint the walls in a soothing lavender. He'd taught her basic carpentry skills so she could help hang drywall and frame out the walls for her office. He'd helped the electrician install the sound system and changed the locks on the doors.

And somehow, while he was doing all that, he'd found the time to fall out of love with her, and into love with Amber Hoff.

Cara picked up the mail that had been pushed through the slot earlier that morning and went straight to her office. She tossed the mail onto her desk and plopped down in the chair. The voicemail light on the phone was flashing but she ignored it.

She was so tired of hearing about Drew's upcoming nuptials, tired of pretending she was okay with it when she was anything but. Tired of hearing about the names he and Amber were considering for their baby boy due in May. Tired of wondering why he was seemingly so happy about his impending fatherhood when he always swore he'd never have children. It had been the one thing he and Cara had seriously argued about.

She should have listened to her mother when Susa tried to tell her that having or not having children was a fundamental issue and needed to be addressed before the wedding. But Cara had been so sure that Drew would change his mind once they'd been married for a while.

"Oh, Mom." Cara sighed. "What I wouldn't give to have you here with me now."

Susa would understand that the hurt she covered with a smile went deep. Cara liked the way she'd seen her life's path playing out. Being blindsided by someone you loved and trusted and being forced to change direction had shaken her to the core. Most days she could cope. Today she felt every emotion and every ounce of betrayal all over again.

She heard the door open and the voices of her students for the nine o'clock class trickled in, and she smiled. Most had become friends, and she loved them. Loved the calm that surrounded her when she focused and freed her mind, and loved that she could teach others how to obtain that same sense of peace and well-being. Her students brought her joy daily. They had sympathized with her plight, readily offering comfort when the news trickled out that Drew had left her for one of her oldest friends. Not that most of them hadn't known about the affair before she did. Everyone in Devlin's Light had apparently figured it out before Cara.

That was one of the drawbacks of living in the town you grew up in. Everyone knew all your business, and yes, sometimes you were the last to know because no one who knew you wanted to be the one to spill the beans and break your heart.

It would've been nice if Drew and Amber had moved to, say, Cape May, or Somers Point after they started to cohabitate. But no. Now that they were expecting, Amber had to be within shouting distance of her mother and her two sisters.

Don't dwell on it, Cara could almost hear her mother say. *Move past it and greet each new day as an opportunity to bring fresh joy into your life. Look beyond today to the future and trust the universe to bring you what you truly need.*

That was Susa. Always the optimistic flower child she'd been raised to be by her hippie parents. Even as she lay dying, she'd smiled and held Cara's hand. "Don't cry, sweetie. I've never been afraid of what happens next. Why, there's a secret to life, to all this and what comes after, and I'm now going to find out what it is. . . ."

"Mom, please . . ." Cara had pleaded. "Don't . . ." The words had stuck in Cara's throat.

"Tell your father that I know." Susa's voice had begun to fade as she slipped away. "Tell him I've always known, and it's all right . . ."

"You know what?" Cara had clutched her mother's hand. "You've always known what?"

Susa had passed quietly then, an enigmatic smile on her face. It had fallen to Cara to call her father and tell him that he was too late. The heart attack had been fatal. Susa was gone before he boarded his plane in L.A. As heartsick as she'd been, her father had been broken. He'd sobbed through the services they'd held graveside and was still sobbing a week later when he left Devlin's Light to fly back to California, where he worked and lived for part of the year. Cara had forgotten to give her father the message her mother had wanted her to pass on. As many times as she'd reminded herself, it always seemed to slip her mind.

It had been Susa who, years ago, introduced Cara to yoga, and following her mother's death, Cara had come to appreciate even more the feeling of inner peace, of contentment, the connection to Susa she found in her studio. Even today, with visions of

Amber's wedding flowers dancing in her head, Cara could lead her students in an hour of contemplation and gentle motions with a heart that was at peace. Susa would have expected nothing less.

Looking forward to the class, Cara rose to join her students. "Time to embrace my inner goddess."

She managed to maintain that lightness for the rest of the day, but while walking home late that afternoon, she had a niggling sense that something wasn't right. All in all, it had been a good day: Her classes had been full, and she'd had a surprise visit from an old friend of her mother's, who'd stopped in to say hello. She'd even laughed out loud when she'd received a text drawing from Darla showing Amber chasing giant white peonies with cartoon faces that fled along the beach. So why did her heart suddenly feel so heavy?

Susa would've said that her uneasy, unsettled feeling had been the universe's way of preparing her for news she wouldn't want to hear. Susa somehow always knew about such things.

Cara was just about to start clearing the table after dinner when the phone rang. She glanced at the caller ID and smiled.

"Uncle Pete. How are you?" she said. Peter Wheeler was her father's best friend since childhood as well as his lawyer.

"Not so good right now, honey." She could hear the tension in his voice, and the earlier feeling of unease returned.

"What's wrong?" she asked.

"Honey, I want you to sit down. . . ."

"What's going on?"

"Cara, I don't know how to tell you this, so forgive me if I just lay it out there." Pete took a deep breath. "Fritz passed away early this morning."

For a moment, Cara sat still as a stone, as if she had not heard.

"Cara? Honey?"

"My . . . my *dad* . . . ?" Cara stumbled over the words, her mind trying to grasp the unimaginable. "What happened? But I just spoke with him a week ago—he was fine. *What happened?*"

"Six weeks ago, your father was diagnosed with terminal cancer. The doctors gave him a month. He managed to hang on a little longer, but there was nothing anyone could have done for him. He didn't want you to know."

"But there are treatments. . . ."

"Not when the disease has progressed as far as his. Trust me. He went to a half dozen different doctors but they all told him it was too late. I'm sorry, Cara, but there wasn't a treatment that could have saved him."

"But . . ." Cara began to weep softly.

"I know it's a shock, honey, and I'm so sorry that I had to be the one to give you the news."

"But he told *you*, didn't he? How could he tell you and not me?"

"He had to tell me. I'm his lawyer. He had affairs that had to be taken care of, and he knew he could trust me to do everything exactly as he instructed."

"Where is he now? I'll have to have him brought back here—he'd want to be with my mother." Even in her shock, her mind began to organize the tasks to be done. "How do I arrange to have him transported? And I'll have to call the little church here to set up the funeral and ask how to—"

"Cara, there won't be a funeral."

"What?" Surely she hadn't heard correctly.

"There isn't to be a funeral. He's already been cremated, Cara. It was his wish and part of the explicit instructions he gave me."

Cara's throat threatened to close and she couldn't hold back the sobs.

"Cara, I'm sorry. I'm so sorry, but Fritz was adamant that everything be done this way."

"Why? Why would he do this? How could he do this?"

"He had his reasons."

"What reasons?"

"Cara, you're going to have to trust me for a while. Things'll be as he wanted, and it's my duty as his lawyer, the executor of his estate, and his friend to make sure that everything is done to the letter."

"So we just have a memorial service and that's it?" Cara tried to wrap her mind around the situation.

"No memorial, either. He specifically nixed that."

"No memorial," she repeated. "You can't be serious. What about all the people who will want to pay their respects? What about his friends? What about his clients?" Cara protested. *What about me?*

"In accordance with your dad's wishes, there's to

be no service of any kind," Pete said firmly. "As for friends and clients, I'll contact every one myself. I wouldn't put that burden on you."

"What about his"—she swallowed hard—"you know, his ashes?"

"The urn holding his cremains will be sent here to my office. I'll hold them for you."

"Why not just have them sent directly to me? I'm his next of kin, his only living relative."

He paused for a long moment. "Again, it's what he wanted, Cara. I have to respect his wishes, and you're going to have to trust me."

"I don't understand, Uncle Pete. I can't think of one good reason why he wouldn't have told me he was dying. Why wouldn't he want to say goodbye to me, to give me a chance to say goodbye to him?"

"What can I say, honey? You know your dad could be a stubborn coot when he got something in his head. In any case, we can't change things now. We can only move forward." She heard a rustling of paper. "So as soon as things are in order, I'll contact you and you can come into the office and we'll talk over the terms of his will."

"Terms?" She frowned. "What terms?"

"We'll discuss all that when you get here. I'll be in touch, Cara. I have to go, but call me if you need anything. You know I'm always here for you."

"But . . ." She realized he'd hung up.

She disconnected the call and gave in to her need for a good cry. There were so many questions speeding around inside her head. Why hadn't her father told her he was ill? Why had he wanted Pete to wait until after he'd been cremated before breaking the news of his death? She was certain Pete knew exactly what her father had been thinking when he'd issued his instructions. Pete knew her father better than anyone. So why wouldn't he share that information with her? Her father was dead. Whatever his reasoning had been, surely it no longer mattered. So why keep it a secret? Cara had lost her father under unusual circumstances, to say the least, and she'd been denied the chance to say goodbye. What could possibly be worse than that?

Allie

Los Angeles, California

One stray stone had somehow landed on the otherwise pristine path that led to the front door of Allie Hudson Monroe's equally pristine abode, and she kicked it onto the lawn, where it belonged. Today was not a good day to get in her way. She unlocked the door and kicked off last year's Manolos with the same ferocity with which she'd attacked the stone.

From the moment she first saw it fifteen years earlier, she'd loved this house, known in the neighborhood as the cottage because of its rustic appearance. She'd begged her then-husband, Clint, to buy it, but wanting something grander, he'd balked, until he realized how much "grander" was going to cost in the Los Angeles suburbs. Over the years, they'd added on: a larger kitchen and family room on the back, a sunroom on one side, an office on the other. There were still only two bedrooms upstairs, but the first-floor renovations had provided for a more spacious second floor, two baths, several walk-in closets, and a sitting room.

It was killing Allie to have to sell it, but the TV show on which she'd worked as assistant director had been canceled two months ago, and the résumés she'd sent out to everyone she knew had failed to produce so much as a *thanks but no thanks*. The house represented the bulk of her divorce settlement, but the increase in property taxes over the last two years combined with her lack of a steady income had taken a huge bite out of her shrinking savings. She'd tried not to panic, but as weeks went by without even the prospect of an interview, Allie could no longer pretend not to see the writing on the wall. Hence the FOR SALE sign out front, which she tried to ignore. It made sense from a practical viewpoint, but still. She loved the place, and every time she thought about giving it up, she found herself pissed off at her ex all over again.

This afternoon she'd attended a cocktail party hosted by Ivan Corrigan, actor turned director who'd once shared the silver screen with Allie's late movie star mother, Honora Hudson, and who, if rumors were to be believed, had carried a flaming torch for her right up until her death three years ago. At Honora's funeral, Ivan had cried on Allie's shoulder, and before he left, he'd handed Allie a card and told her to call him if she ever needed anything.

She'd called Ivan two weeks after her show folded, and again two weeks after that before his secretary returned her calls with an invitation to the party that would kick off his latest sure-to-be-a-hit show. She'd tried not to get her hopes up, but even so, she'd been disappointed when he'd introduced her by her sister's name to his latest protégé.

"It's Allie." She'd tried to smile good-naturedly after he'd called her *Des* for the second time.

"Right. Right. Des was the one who had the hit series that ran so long. How's she doing, by the way? She ever mention wanting to get back in the business?"

Before Allie could respond, he'd turned to his girlfriend and said, "You remember her sister, Desdemona Hudson? Had that show years ago, *Des Does* . . . something, I forget the name. Great little actress, that one. So much talent for so young a girl."

Allie had gritted her teeth to the point her jaw hurt.

As if that hadn't been bad enough, he'd patted Allie on the back and said, "Tough about your show, but you know, that time slot never seems to work for drama." He'd put his arm around his girlfriend, leaned over to kiss Allie on the cheek, and said, "Listen, give me a call if there's anything I can do for you."

That's why I'm here, you bonehead, she'd wanted to say, but he'd already moved on.

She'd known she'd have a tough time finding another job, and she knew she had no one to blame but herself. But even so, Ivan throwing her sister in her face had made her want to grab him by the collar and hold him still while she poured her drink over his head. The last thing she needed right now was the reminder that her sister had been the talented one, the successful one, the one who'd had her own series from the time she was nine until she turned sixteen.

Reliving the party made Allie's jaw hurt all over again. She went into the kitchen and poured herself the evening's first scotch. Gold bangles jangling on her arm, she sorted through the mail she'd dumped earlier and simultaneously listened to her messages, one each from her sister; her attorney; her friend Blair, with whom she shared dinner and gossip, though little else, every other Wednesday night; and Nikki, her daughter, in that order.

She called Nikki back first.

"Hi, sweetie. It's Mom. What's up?"

"Would you be upset if I didn't stay with you on Friday?"

In this respect, Nikki was exactly like her father. No reason to beat around the bush, just come right out and say whatever was on her mind.

"What's happening on Friday?" Allie lowered herself slowly into a nearby chair.

"There's a big dance at school—"

"That's fine. I can pick you up after," Allie told her.

"But . . . see, there's a sleepover at Courtney's after the dance, and I really want to go." Nikki paused. "*Everyone* is going. All my friends. I can't be the only one who doesn't go."

"I don't know, Nik. We missed last weekend because of the soccer tournament."

"That wasn't my fault," Nikki protested. "I had to go. I'm a *starter*."

"Don't you have an away game this Saturday as well?"

"Yes, but Courtney's mom said she'd drive us all and take us for pizza after."

Allie fell quiet, deliberating whether it was worse to insist that her daughter spend the weekend with her and risk the silent treatment, or to be the cool, understanding mom who let her daughter have her way even if it meant Allie had to spend more than half her custody weekend alone.

"Mom?"

"I'm thinking."

"Please? I don't want to be the only girl in the class who doesn't go to Courtney's. Pretty please?" Nikki pleaded. "I don't want everyone talking about me."

"What do you mean?"

"You know, someone always talks about the girls who aren't there."

"If they're talking behind your back, they're not really your friends, Nik."

"*Mom.*"

Allie sighed. She wouldn't be any more successful in winning this one than she had been last weekend, or the weekend before, when Courtney's mother had taken three of the girls to a beach house in Malibu for a few days of fun in the sun. Allie often wondered what Courtney's father was doing while her mother shuttled the kids everywhere.

"All right." Allie silently cursed her ex-husband. It had been his idea to enroll Nikki in Woods Hall, the tony private school that was four blocks from the spacious new house Clint had bought after the divorce was final, and twenty-seven miles from Allie's. Nikki had made a whole new circle of friends at Woods Hall, most of whom Allie couldn't have picked out of a lineup. At the neighborhood school, Allie had known every kid in Nikki's class, and most of their mothers. Just one more reason to hate that man.

"I'll pick you up . . . where should I pick you up?" Allie couldn't remember where Courtney lived.

"Courtney's mom can drop me off at Dad's and you can pick me up there."

Swell.

"All right. Give me a call when you get to the pizza place and I'll get on my way then."

"Thank you, thank you, thank you!" Nikki squealed. "You're the best mom ever! Love you!"

"Love you more."

Best mom ever. Allie toasted herself and tossed back the scotch after Nikki hung up.

It was all Clint's fault. Their original custody agreement provided that their daughter spend weekdays with Allie and weekends with Clint. That had worked for the first year, but it'd started to crumble one night last summer when Clint brought Nikki back from a weekend with him. Nikki had run straight up to her room, and Clint had proceeded to blindside Allie with a brochure from Woods Hall.

"Nikki deserves the benefit of a private school education," Clint had said solemnly. "Don't you want her to have the best?"

"Of course I do," Allie had snapped. "But what's wrong with the junior high she went to last year? It's only a few blocks away."

He made a face. "Really, there's no comparison, Al. Woods Hall has small classes, an excellent art program, music, athletics, more of everything she likes. Oh, and their language program is second to none."

Allie tried to come up with a retort but couldn't. The arts and athletic programs at the local public schools had been cut drastically over the past two years, and the only language they still offered was Spanish. Nikki had taken French for two summers at camp and had loved it, and several times she'd grumbled about the fact that she couldn't continue her study during the school year.

"Besides, she's already met some of the girls who'd be in her class, and—"

"Oh? And how did that happen?"

"One of my neighbors has a daughter Nikki's age, and Nik spent a lot of time with her over the summer when she was visiting me. They've become friends, and when Nikki expressed interest in Courtney's school, I made an appointment for a look-see. We went on a tour yesterday, and Nikki fell in love with the campus. It goes without saying that academically, it's head and shoulders above her old school. You know how bright she is. Think about how much more Woods Hall has to offer." Clint had remained calm in the face of Allie's gathering storm of emotions, as he always had. It never failed to drive up the drama. "So what do you say, Al? Give her the best, or be content with the rest?"

"I really hate when you say things like that."

Clint had shrugged. "What we like or dislike about each other has already been established. Right now, we're talking about our daughter's future. About her *life*."

"How much is the tuition?"

"It's been taken care of." Realizing he'd tipped his hand, he'd tried to smooth it over by saying, "It's refundable if you decide you don't want her to go. But there was only one spot left in her class and I didn't want her to lose out."

"Sounds as if this really isn't a discussion about will we or won't we, but whether or not I'm going to be a bitch and ruin her life by saying no, she can't go to this exclusive, wonderful school that her daddy has offered to send her to." Allie folded her arms across her chest.

"I knew you'd get into a snit over this." He'd tossed the brochures onto the coffee table and stood to leave. "Let me know what you decide."

"You know how far it is from here to there. And you also know that I have to be at work by seven." Allie followed him to the door. "How am I supposed to get her to school in the morning and get to my job on time?"

"I'm sure you can work something out." He opened the door. "Think it over, Al. Think of what's best for her, not what's convenient for you."

He'd quietly closed the door behind him. She'd wanted to slam it, but he hadn't given her the chance.

Allie had caved, but insisted on paying half the tuition.

The school year had begun with Allie driving Nikki every morning, which had been an enormous pain, but it'd worked, mostly because Allie'd negotiated a later starting time at work. Of course, a later start meant a later finish, which meant most days Nikki went to Clint's after school to wait for her mother, but more often than not, the rush hour traffic increased Allie's drive time to the point that Nikki was eating dinner with her father every night. By mid-October, even Allie had to admit that the arrangement simply wasn't working. And Nikki had joined the soccer team, which practiced every day after school and often had Saturday games. When Nikki begged Allie to let her live with Clint during the week and stay with her on the weekends, effectively reversing the custody agreement, Allie couldn't think of a good reason to refuse. She hated losing those five days with her daughter, but as Clint reminded her every chance he got, it was all about what was best for Nikki.

It had broken Allie's heart to watch Clint's car drive away with the only person in the world she truly, deeply loved in the passenger seat. After the car had disappeared around the corner, Allie had gone into her daughter's room and sat on the edge of the bed to cry. Nikki had left her old quilt but had stripped the room of just about everything else. It had felt empty, a ghost room, a place that had lost its heart. Even now, Allie would stand in the doorway and stare at the mural she'd painted on the wall, a happy forest scene with all of Nikki's favorite animals frolicking together. It had taken two months to complete, but Nikki's delight when it was finished had made every minute worth it.

The first Monday night that Nikki was gone, Allie had parked herself in front of the TV with a bottle of wine. They'd always watched *Castle* together. Watching the show alone had taken the fun out of the evening. It had come as a shock to her the next morning when she realized she'd fallen asleep on the sofa, with the empty bottle on the floor next to the remote, and she was late for work.

Fallen asleep sounded so much better than *passed out*.

After that, wine and a few game shows became Allie's nightly routine. She'd come home from work and, too lonely to fix something to eat alone, she'd pull the cork on her favorite pinot grigio. Before she knew it, it'd be morning, and the pain and loneliness she'd tried to smother the night before would surface again. Somehow she made it through work until it was time to go home and pull another cork.

Then Allie discovered scotch, and she pretty much forgot about wine. Scotch had been Honora's drink of choice, a choice that had led to the once popular actress being fired from more than one film when she proved incapable of remembering her lines, or showing up on time, or filming an entire scene. After a while, the roles had stopped coming, and the humiliated Honora bought a ranch house far in the Hollywood Hills, where she could ignore the gossip, and had replaced her husband and daughters with two parrots and a cockatiel. The entire family seemed to splinter then, with Allie and Des going their separate ways and their father, Fritz, seeming to fade from their lives.

Long before her death, Honora had ceased to be a presence in her life, but tonight, for some strange reason, Allie felt the loss acutely.

We should've been closer. I should have tried harder to understand what she was going through. I should have been kinder. Less judgmental. Especially since I seem to be following in her footsteps, Allie thought wryly as she tossed a few more ice cubes into her glass and poured another two fingers of the amber liquid.

Of course, I'm nothing like Mom. I'm a good mother. A great mother. I'm always there for Nikki when she needs me. I've earned a drink or two after a long day to help me relax.

She remembered the earlier message from her sister, and wondered if Des had the same regrets where their mother was concerned. If she did, she'd never shared them with Allie, which, Allie acknowledged, was her own fault. Des had tried over the years to reach out to her, but Allie had never been able to set aside her resentment of her younger sister.

I should call her back before it gets too late. . . .

Allie went out to the patio and peered over the stone wall that surrounded the rose garden she'd planted five years ago. Clint had laughed when he came home from work and found her sweaty and dirty after having dug and planted and watered all day, and had told her she smelled like a field hand, but she'd been pleased with the effort and taken much pride in the many buds that had bloomed. She hated the thought of someone else picking her roses, making pretty arrangements for the front hall or the dining room, but inevitably, someone else would.

Mostly, she hated Clint for having turned her world upside down. The roses were just one more thing she loved that she'd have to give up because he "just wasn't feeling it anymore." She hated feeling bitter, but there it was.

"Clint, is there someone else?" she'd asked.

Clint had rolled his eyes, and his face wore that expression she hated most. The one that said, *Oh, please,* in an exaggerated tone of exasperation. "Really, Allie, you're such a cliché. You can't imagine that I could fall out of love with you without having fallen in love with someone else. I've already told you. I just don't feel it anymore."

And just like that, her marriage—her life—had crumbled.

Inside the house, the phone was ringing, and she hurried inside to answer it. Maybe it was Nikki calling to tell her Friday's party had been called off. . . .

"Hello?"

"Allie, it's Uncle Pete. I'm afraid I have some bad news. . . ."

Des

CROSS CREEK, MONTANA

"You're going to have such a great life. Your new family is going to spoil you like crazy. You are one lucky little doggie, Sasha."

The small white pit-mix female sat on the front seat of the big SUV as if she owned it, and thumped her tail.

Des Hudson followed the GPS to the lakefront home of Jim and Mary Conner, the couple who'd soon become the proud owners of Des's latest foster dog via the Cross Creek Animal Shelter.

"Here we are, Sasha." Des parked at the foot of the driveway. "Let's get this leash on you. Yes, you are so pretty in pink."

The little white dog jumped into Des's lap and planted a dozen sloppy kisses on her face.

"Now, be a good girl, just like I taught you," she whispered. "You remember your manners and be sweet, okay?"

Des gathered the dog and her bag and got out of the car. She set Sasha on the ground and took a deep breath. This was always both the happiest and the hardest day for her, when all her efforts to prepare a dog for a new home paid off. Like so many dogs before her, Sasha had come to Des after having been abused and abandoned, in need of love and a gentle hand. Sometimes it took longer than others, but by the time Des was ready to turn over her charge to its new owners, she knew for certain that dog would be the best pet they would ever have.

Des loved fostering, loved being the one who helped the animals find their new homes, but still, it nearly killed her every time to hand over a dog she'd come to love, and she'd loved every one she'd taken into her home over the past five years.

Now it was Sasha's turn to get her happily-ever-after.

"There's your new mom and dad," Des told Sasha. "Go get 'em. Turn on the charm. Go on, Sash. Time to fly."

"Oh, she's such a sweetie." Mary Conner knelt down as Sasha ran up the driveway, her pink leash flying behind her. She scooped up the dog and hugged her. "You're such a pretty girl."

Jim Conner followed his wife, beaming like a new dad.

"We can't thank you enough," he called to Des, who stood at the end of the driveway, a lump in her throat. She knew she shouldn't get so attached, knew that each dog would only be with her for a short time, but she couldn't help herself.

"You're welcome." Des removed the dog's crate and a bag of treats from the backseat. "She's used to this crate, so I thought you might want to have it. Her favorite blanket and her toys are in here along with some of the food she's accustomed to."

The Conners walked toward Des, Sasha dancing along between them before taking off after a leaf that blew across the lawn.

"And these are her favorite treats." Des handed over the supplies.

"Thank you, Des. We're so grateful to you for bringing her to us."

"There's a sheet in the crate with her history, her shots and that sort of thing. Of course, there's only one vet in town and Doc Early has all of this on record, but you never know."

"Thanks," Mary said.

"Well, I guess that's that." Des watched the dog prance on the lawn. "Call me if there's anything. . . . Oh, did I tell you she's afraid of loud noises?"

"You did, yes, when we met before." Mary turned and called the dog. "Sasha, come say goodbye to Des."

"Oh no, that's . . ." Des started to protest, but Sasha was already running to her, tail wagging, ready to be picked up and put into the car. "Not this time, little girl." Des knelt down on one knee. "You're home now."

She wanted to say more, but the words stuck in her throat, so she bent her head to let the dog lick her chin one more time, then stood and handed the leash to Mary. "Call if you have any questions."

"We will," Mary said. Des got into her car.

Through the window, Des could see Sasha straining at the leash as the car pulled away. The tears she'd been holding back began to run down her cheeks.

"Damn."

She cried all the way home, and again when she went inside her empty house. But she knew that tomorrow another dog that needed her soothing voice and gentle ways would be joining her. A six-year-old beagle running loose in the woods had been found by a hiker and brought into the shelter the week before. He'd been cleared by the local vet, but he was wary and fearful and malnourished, spending much of his time huddled in the back of his crate.

"The poor thing is scared to death. He was brought in wearing a collar without a tag. Looks to me like he's someone's pet who got loose somehow and took off to explore and couldn't find his way home. Might've been wandering awhile, which would account for him being so thin. We've gotten him cleaned up and will be putting his photo out in all the usual places. Doc says he isn't chipped, and there's always the chance that someone abandoned him. He's a skittish little guy, so of course I thought of you right away," Fran, the shelter's long-winded director, had said, barely pausing long enough to take a breath. "No one has a way with a frightened animal like you do. Will you take him, see what you can do to bring him around while we try to find his people? If we can't send him back home, we'll need to try to adopt him out."

"Of course. I'll pick him up on Wednesday. I'm dropping Sasha off at the Conners' on Tuesday afternoon."

"That was a good placement," Fran said. "The Conners will take good care of her."

"They'd better, or she comes back to me."

"Des, we've never had to pull one of your dogs and bring them back."

"I know. Just sayin'."

Des turned on the TV to break the silence. She stood in the middle of the living room and listened to the weather report for the upcoming week. Clear and cold the next two days and a chance of snow on Thursday. In Montana, winter came early and stayed late. It'd taken Des some time to get used to, especially coming from Southern California, but she'd acclimated. She stocked her pantry and her woodpile, made sure her generator was in good working order, and prayed she had enough books to see her through the worst of the season.

It had been her dream to live in a log cabin from the time she was six. Her mother had had a role in a film that was supposed to have taken place in the Wild West, and Des had played on the log cabin set in between takes. She'd been bitterly disappointed when filming ended and the cabin had been dismantled. Five years ago, she'd visited some friends who'd built a home in Montana, and she'd fallen in love with the town and the state. When a few acres with a log house on the edge of town became available, Des had jumped on it. That first year had been hard, the winter harsh and seemingly never-ending. She'd survived it with the help of her friends, but had promised herself that she'd never be caught unprepared again.

She turned off the TV and went into the kitchen, picked up Sasha's water bowl and washed it. It was almost six o'clock, which meant she had one hour to shower and dress. Tonight was book club—dinner and conversation with a group of women who met every other Tuesday night. Usually Des looked forward to going. She really enjoyed the company and the discussions, but tonight for some reason she wasn't her usual enthusiastic self.

She paused on her way into her bedroom to look at the array of family photos on the wall over the fireplace that stood opposite her bed: her mother in several of her film roles, back when she was breathtakingly beautiful, before alcohol had taken its toll; her sister, Allie, as a child, and later as a mother, holding her daughter, Nikki, as a newborn; Nikki through her childhood; and Des's father, Fritz. *What a rogues' gallery.* She shook her head. *Mom's gone and Allie, Dad, and I almost never speak.*

That thought had been niggling at her for the past week or two, so much so that she made a mental note to call her father and sister in the morning.

She headed for the shower, and forty-five minutes later she was dressed and out the door, her book under her arm and the apple cake she'd made for dessert in hand. Blessing her heated seats and heated steering wheel in the frigid temperatures, she slipped a CD into the player and sang along with Katy Perry all the way to Jenny Sander's house two miles down the road. By the time she arrived, her mood had lifted and she was ready for a great dinner with good friends and a lively discussion of a book she'd enjoyed.

Des picked up Paolo the beagle at two, and spent most of the afternoon sitting with the sad little dog in her backyard, talking softly about anything that came into her head, to get Paolo accustomed to her voice. When the sun began to drop behind the hills, she told him, "That's it for today, pal. It's getting colder and this California girl has reached her limit. Time to go inside."

She held the leash and the dog rose on shaky legs but followed her inside.

"Come on, Paolo. Let's see if you're hungry now." She offered the bowl of food he'd only sniffed at earlier. She turned to hang up her coat, and when she turned back, he was taking a few tentative bites. "Good boy," she said approvingly.

She pulled off her boots and left them by the back door. "Don't even think about chewing those. I'll be in the next room. Feel free to join me when you're feeling sociable."

She changed into a pair of stretchy knit pants and a tee and went into the family room, where she popped in a DVD. For the next thirty minutes, along with the perky twenty-year-old on the screen, Des stretched—downward dog, hare, half moon, half cobra—while she tried to clear her mind and relax. Movement from the doorway caught her attention. Paolo had taken a few cautious steps toward the room. Des ignored the DVD and sat on the floor, motioning for the dog to join her. It took a few unsure moments, but eventually, he lay next to her, and before long, his head was on her leg.

"Good boy," she crooned, scratching behind his ears until his eyes closed and he fell asleep. Des leaned back against the sofa, and had just closed her own eyes when her phone rang. She reached behind her and grabbed it off the table.

"Hello?" she said softly.

"Des?"

"Hi, Kent." Her current . . . what? Not boyfriend. Hopeful boyfriend? Prospective boyfriend? She hadn't decided how to categorize him.

"Why are you whispering?"

"I picked up a new foster dog today. He fell asleep with his head on my leg and I don't want to wake him."

"Lucky dog."

"Ha-ha. His recent past hasn't been so lucky, but I have high hopes for his future."

"You're really into the whole rescue thing, aren't you?" He made it sound as if maybe it wasn't such a good thing.

"I am. Someone needs to step up. Why not me?"

When he didn't respond, she sighed. "It's my thing, Kent. It's what I do."

"I get it." As what seemed to be an afterthought, he added, "I like dogs, too."

His declaration aside, he obviously didn't get it.

Des didn't feel like going into all the reasons why her efforts at the shelter were so important, why it meant so much to her to be able to make a difference in the lives of the animals she fostered as well as in the lives of those who adopted her fosters. The reasons behind her efforts were none of Kent's business. There were some things Des didn't share easily.

"Well, can you leave the dog long enough to maybe catch dinner on Friday? Saturday, if that's a better night for you?"

"I have something on Saturday, but Friday would be fine." She tried to ignore the slightly sarcastic tone of his voice. She'd enjoyed the few dates she'd had with him and wasn't ready to cross him off yet. She'd been told by several friends that she'd been too quick to toss other guys in the past, and one of her new resolutions was to be more open-minded and less judgmental.

"The Campfire Inn okay with you?"

"Of course. It's one of my favorites."

"Seven?"

"I'll be ready."

For the next fifteen minutes she was treated to Kent's recitation of that afternoon's golf outing, hole by hole, green by green, putt by putt. She sat back, her head against the sofa, the dog snoring on her leg, and half listened with her eyes closed. It wasn't that he was boring. It was more that he was . . . well, yes, he was boring, in a self-absorbed sort of way. Truth be told, she couldn't care less about golf and had probably as much interest in his game as he had in her fostering efforts. Which didn't say a whole lot about their future prospects. But maybe if she kept an open mind and got to know him a little better, she'd feel differently. Everyone said what a terrific guy he was, and really, she was trying hard to see it. But when she heard the click that indicated she had a call coming in, she was almost grateful to put him on hold.

"If I lose you, I'll call you back," she promised. Before Kent could respond, she hit the hold button and said, "Hello?"

"How's my favorite hearty pioneer girl?"

"Uncle Pete!" She laughed quietly. "I'm hanging tough in my log cabin. How're things there?"

"Not good, Des." He cleared his throat. "I'm afraid I have some really bad news, honey."

She frowned. She'd never heard that dark note in his voice before.

"It's about your dad. . . ."

CHAPTER ONE

Peter J. Wheeler sat at the shiny Honduran mahogany desk in his high-rise paneled law office in Center City Philadelphia rehearsing what he would say to the beneficiaries of his best friend's will once they arrived. There'd be no easy or pleasant way to get through the next few hours, and if he hadn't loved the deceased like a brother, he would've killed Fritz Hudson with his own two hands for putting him in this position. Over the years, Pete had been called upon to clean up a good number of messes on Fritz's behalf, but this . . . this was . . .

Cowardly. There was no way around it. Fritz was an out-and-out coward. He'd gone ahead and died and left his old buddy Pete to do his dirty work. Not that Pete didn't owe Fritz—he'd be the last person to deny that—but still. Weren't there limits to repaying a debt?

"Mr. Wheeler, Ms. Monroe and Miss Hudson

have arrived," Marjorie, the firm's receptionist, announced through the intercom.

Send them away. Far, far away . . .

"Send them in."

Pete stood and adjusted his cuffs for something to do with his hands, mentally preparing for the reading of the will—and the breaking of the news.

The door opened and Fritz's daughters, Allie and Des, walked in, smiling and offering hugs and kisses on the cheek. It wasn't a secret that their father's estate was quite substantial, and Pete had no doubt the two women were already mentally spending their shares.

"Allie, Des. Great to see you girls," he said, before reminding himself of the somber reason for their presence. He cleared his throat and assumed a solemn expression. "Again, my condolences to you both."

"And to you as well." Des gave his hand a squeeze. "Since you were closer to Dad than either of us, I suppose you'll miss him more than anyone else."

"I'd give anything to have him here with us today." *So I could wring his neck the way I should have when he was alive. Or at the very least, if he were here today, he could do his own dirty work.*

"I'm sure." Allie looked around the office. "New décor? I like it."

"Thanks. All that leather and those prints of English hunting dogs were starting to get to me." He smiled to himself.

Six months ago, Fritz had stood in the middle of Pete's office with his hands on his hips. "Don't you think it's time for all that tired old 'tally ho!' stuff to go, Pete? I'm pretty sure that style went out in the nineties."

I should've tied him to a chair right then and there, dialed the phone, handed it to him, and not let him up until he'd come clean with his kids. All his kids.

"Allie, how's Nikki doing? The new school working out for her?" Pete offered a chair to the tall, slender blonde, who seemed a bit on edge.

"She's doing just fine, thank you."

"And you?"

"Oh, I'm great." The sarcasm in Allie's voice was unmistakable. "Except that the TV show I was working on was canceled and I'm going to have to sell my house because I can't afford the upkeep and my half of Nikki's private school tuition. Other than that, I'm just swell."

"I'm sorry things aren't better for you right now. But you have a lot of directing credits, right?"

"*Assistant* directing," she corrected.

"Still, you have a recognizable name. I'm sure someone will call." He tried to be encouraging, but could see by her expression that she wasn't buying it.

"Well, once Dad's estate is settled, you'll be able to turn things around." Des, who was three years younger and four inches shorter than her sister, hadn't waited for a chair to be offered before she sat. "That's what this is all about, right, Uncle Pete?"

"Ahhh . . . well . . . yes, but . . ." he stammered. No rehearsal would have been adequate to prepare him for what was ahead this morning.

It was then that Allie pointed to the third chair in front of the desk.

She frowned. "Is someone joining us?"

Before Pete could respond, Marjorie tapped on the door, then opened it. "Mr. Wheeler . . ."

"Ah . . . yes." He walked around the desk as a petite woman with curly light auburn hair entered the office. "Cara. Come in, please." He embraced her as he had the others. "Have a seat."

With puzzled expressions, Allie and Des turned to face the newcomer.

"Allie. Des. This is Cara McCann." He took a deep breath and prepared for the shit storm that was about to occur. "Your half sister." He turned to Cara. "Cara, meet Allegra Monroe and Desdemona Hudson. *Your* half sisters."

The silence that followed could not have been more intense. The three women stared first at Pete, then at each other for what seemed to be an eternity.

Finally, Allie cleared her throat, and with a death stare aimed at Pete, said, "What the hell, Uncle Pete?"

"The *hell* is that your father lived a double life. On the West Coast, he had Nora and the two of you," he said, addressing Allie and Des. Turning to Cara, he added, "And on the East Coast . . ."

"He had Susa and me," Cara said quietly, her face white, her hands clasped tightly in her lap, and her eyes on him. "Obviously, that's the short version. Surely there's more."

"The long version isn't much different. It's just a matter of filling in the blanks."

"Then I suggest you do that." Des folded her arms across her chest, an *I'm waiting* expression on her face.

"This is why he didn't want a service or a memorial of any kind," Cara said. "He wanted a quick cremation so we wouldn't meet at his graveside."

"Sad but true. When he realized how close he was to the end, he added a codicil to his will that he'd be cremated immediately and that you would not be notified until after the cremation."

"Start from the beginning," Allie said, still glaring. "And maybe at some point you could toss in an explanation of why Dad kept this secret to himself."

Pete sighed deeply. "If I told him once, I told him a thousand times that this was a stupid way to live. That he needed to come clean, to tell Nora that he was going to go through with the divorce. That he'd met someone who made him happy." He glanced at Cara, his voice softening. "Your mother made your father very happy, Cara."

"So you're saying he didn't love our mother and she made him miserable?" Allie snapped.

"Well, of course she did." Des turned to her sister. "We both know that. Come to think of it, she made both of us pretty miserable, too. How long can you love someone who makes you feel sad, inadequate, and unloved all the time?"

"That's our *mother* you're talking about, Des. The woman who gave birth to us."

"And regretted that she did. Let's face it. Mom liked the *idea* of children way more than she ever liked actually *having* children. When she could whip us out in front of a camera to smooth out her image after she'd been on a bender, we served a purpose. Other than that, she really didn't have much use for either of us."

Before Allie could respond, Cara leaned forward and said, "Wait . . . back up. I think I may have missed something. Go back to the part where you told Dad he had to tell . . . the other woman he was going through with the divorce."

"Careful, missy." Allie trained a lethal glance in Cara's direction. "That 'other woman' is our mother. And since she and Dad were never divorced, I believe it's *your* mother who's 'the other woman.'"

"Is that true, Uncle Pete? Was Dad still married to their mother when he married mine?" Cara's stare ate right through him, and he knew that one of the moments he'd dreaded most was upon him.

He walked around his desk to sit on the right corner opposite Cara's chair. "Well, technically . . . yes."

"What does that mean? Either he was divorced or he wasn't when he and Susa were married." Cara's eyes bored into Pete's. "Was my father divorced from his first wife when he married my mother?"

"No."

"Did my mother know that?"

"I . . . I can't say for sure . . ." Pete mumbled. God, how he hated Fritz at that moment.

Unexpectedly, Cara laughed. "Of course you can. You knew everything about him."

"I think he *meant* to tell her, in the beginning.

But he fell so hard for Susa that as time went on, it became harder and harder to tell her. He wanted to make her happy, wanted to marry her." He shrugged. "So he did."

"How could he have married her mother when he was still married to ours?" Des asked. "Don't you have to apply for a license? Aren't there some sort of checks or something?"

Pete shrugged. "I honestly don't know how he got around all that. He just showed up one morning with a bottle of champagne in one hand and two glasses in the other. Asked me to drink a toast to his new bride." Pete paused. If he closed his eyes, he could still see the light in Fritz's eyes. There was no doubt that he'd been happier than Pete had ever seen him, and definitely head over heels in love.

"And you said . . . ?" Allie gestured for Pete to get on with it.

"I don't remember exactly what I said, but I'm sure it was something to the effect of . . . well, to quote you, Allie, 'What the hell?'"

"Did you ask him about Mom? Did you ask him when he had filed for a divorce?" Des asked pointedly. "Though I would suspect that as his *lawyer*, you should've had a hand in that."

"I did ask, and he hemmed and hawed, the way he did when he didn't want to talk about something." He glanced at each woman before adding, "I think you all know what I mean."

The three women nodded.

"So what you're saying is that he was a bigamist."

Cara was on the verge of tears. "How could he have done something like that to my mother?"

"*Your* mother?" Allie snorted. "What about *our* mother?"

"Did Mom know, Uncle Pete?" Des asked quietly.

"As far as I'm aware, he never told her."

"Probably because they rarely spoke to each other." Allie leaned back in her chair. "So can we cut to the chase? What does this all mean in terms of Dad's will?"

"We find out that Dad had another wife and child and all you can think about is how this news is going to impact your inheritance?" Des asked.

"Of course it's going to have an impact, assuming that Dad's named her in his will," Allie replied. "And I'm assuming he did, or she wouldn't be here and there'd have been no need for this big revelation. Which, frankly, I couldn't care less about. So Dad had a mistress and they had a kid together and—"

"She wasn't his mistress," Cara snapped, whirling to face Allie.

"Where I come from, if a woman cohabitates with a married man—"

"She didn't know he was married. She couldn't have known. She never would have . . ." Cara stood. "She wouldn't have . . ." She choked back tears. "You didn't know my mother. You don't know who or what she was."

Allie stared out the window behind Pete's desk. "Oh, I have a pretty good idea of what she was."

"Allie, stop," Des exclaimed. "Don't go there."

"Why not? What would you call her? She was sleeping with another woman's husband and had a child with him."

"Drop it, Allie," Pete said simply. More gently, he said, "Cara, sit down. There's more you all need to know."

All three women turned to him as if on cue.

"Wait, don't tell me," Allie said dramatically. "There's a third woman out there. . . ."

Would it surprise him if there were? Pete pushed the thought from his head, returned to his chair, and took a deep breath. "Let me start by saying the three of you are the beneficiaries of Fritz's will, with one—"

Allie interrupted. "*Equal* beneficiaries? *Her* too?"

"Yes. Equal." He rested his forearms on the desk. "It's a three-way split, and that is ironclad. I know because I wrote your father's will. So get over it."

When Allie opened her mouth—apparently not ready to let it go—Des said, "Oh, for crying out loud. Dad was pretty well-off, Al. He'd been a well-known entertainment agent and manager in Hollywood for years. One-third of his investments alone would keep even you in Jimmy Choos for a long, long time." She glanced at Pete. "Right, Uncle Pete?"

He nodded. "Yes. Your father left a large estate. The sum you're each going to inherit will be significant. Assuming that you meet the rest of the conditions."

"What conditions?" Cara asked warily.

Now came the hard part. Pete cleared his throat again and launched into the part of the disclosure that he'd rehearsed over and over.

"Your father loved all of you very much. I know he didn't always go out of his way to show it." He directed these remarks to Allie and Des.

"That's an understatement," grumbled Allie. "If you call an occasional phone call proof of how much he loved us." She tossed a dagger at Cara. "Of course, now we know why he was so preoccupied."

Cara started to protest, but Pete raised a hand. "Trust me, there will be plenty of time to snipe at each other later."

"That sounds ominous," Des said.

Pete continued on with his speech. "As I said, your father loved you all. He wanted more than anything for you to know and love each other."

"Which is why he kept *her* a secret." Allie pointed in Cara's direction.

"He didn't tell me about *you*, either," Cara countered.

"Ladies. Please." Pete placed a hand on the top of his head, a habit once intended to smooth back his hair, which was now pretty much gone.

"If it was so important to him that we know each other, why didn't he tell us himself?" Cara asked.

"Because at his core, he was a coward." There. He'd said it. "He just couldn't face you. I think he believed it didn't matter so much because Nora was gone. Cara, after Susa died, he couldn't face you with the truth. So he let it go and was convinced that the right time would present itself. As you know, it never did."

"So what comes next?" Des asked softly.

"Your father wanted you all to share in not only his wealth, but in his life."

"A little late on that score," Allie scoffed.

"Something he came to very much regret at the end, believe me. He became obsessed with wanting you to know each other. Which is why he left a challenge for the three of you. If you're successful, you inherit his entire estate. If you fail, you get nothing."

The pronouncement was met with silence and blank stares.

Finally, Allie said, "Please tell us you're kidding."

"I assure you, I'm not. Nor was this my idea, by the way," Pete told them. "Believe me. I did everything I could to talk him out of this. But he'd gotten it into his head that this was the way to—"

"What kind of challenge?" Cara blurted.

"Something along the lines of the twelve labors of Hercules would be my guess." Allie folded her arms over her chest.

"Close, Allie. He wants the three of you to restore an old theater in his hometown. Together."

"Wait, what?"

"Say that again?"

"Restore a theater? Had he lost his mind?"

Pete let the three of them vent for several minutes.

"If you've finished with your rantings, I'd like to continue." He glanced from Allie to Des to Cara and back again. When it appeared they'd settled down, he continued. "The theater was built by your great-grandfather Reynolds Hudson. It's an Art Deco treasure and belongs on the National Register of Historic Places."

"What if the owner doesn't want it restored?" Cara asked.

"Fritz owned it. It's now part of the estate you stand to inherit. As I said, his grandfather built it, and the family still owned it up until about twenty years ago. The new owner had plans to completely renovate it, but grossly underestimated the cost and ran out of money before he could finish," Pete explained. "When it was slated for demolition about a year ago, Fritz bought it back. He felt he'd let his father and grandfather down by allowing the building to pass out of the family in the first place. The fact that the building itself has fallen into its present state bothered him right to the end because it's part of his family legacy."

"Why did he sell it in the first place, then, if it's so important?" Des asked. "All I ever heard was that when he was young, he worked in a theater and he met Mom there."

"I never heard about it at all," Cara added. "And he never mentioned his family to me."

"Me either, come to think of it," Des said. "Allie?"

"Nothing."

"Time for a little history lesson, girls." Pete settled into his chair. "The Hudson family was instrumental in settling Hidden Falls, a small town in Pennsylvania. Fritz's grandfather owned several coal mines in the area back when coal was a big deal. Reynolds made a fortune and felt it was his responsibility to put his money into the town for the benefit of everyone who lived there."

"So he built a theater?" Allie asked.

"Among other things. He also gave money to build the county's first hospital, and a college in the area that was free for the children of his miners. The local elementary school was built on land he donated. The family always took pride in the fact that the Molly Maguires stayed out of Hidden Falls when so many other mines were targeted for attacks by the group protesting the conditions the miners had to work and live under."

"So he was quite the philanthropist," Cara said thoughtfully.

"He was. The mines have been closed for a long time, and the family fortunes took a dive during the 1930s, but Fritz's father—your grandfather, also named Reynolds—kept the theater going. Ran films once every other week, invited everyone in town to come for free. His wife got her friends together and started a local theater group for adults and kids. Times were pretty grim, but the theater gave people something fun to do. Every month they could see a new play, always free. Oh yes, the theater was an integral part of the town." Pete paused. "I remember my dad talking about going as a child with his whole family all dressed up for an enchanted night out. The Sugarhouse—that's the theater—holds a very special place in the town's history."

"No wonder Dad felt like he'd dropped the ball." Des nodded.

"So you understand where your father was coming from. He really did have all intentions of restoring the theater himself, went so far as to begin to solicit a few estimates for the work that would need to be done and actually did begin the work on some of the mechanics. I don't know how far he got with that, because it soon became apparent that he wasn't going to live to see the project through." Pete hesitated, remembering the last days with his friend. He waited for the lump in his throat to ease a bit before continuing. "So perhaps you'll understand why he made it a condition of your inheritance that the building be restored and returned to use as a theater again."

"It must've been the meds he was on. They made him delusional," Allie said. "He obviously wasn't thinking straight."

"Oh, believe me, he knew exactly what he was doing. We talked it through, every which way," Pete assured her.

"Then why didn't you talk him out of it?" Allie demanded.

"What can I say? You know your father: He was never going to be talked out of this. He thought this was the way to kill two birds with one stone. You get to know each other and the Sugarhouse gets restored. It was win-win."

"Ignoring the obvious problems with that, how did he expect us to accomplish this?" Allie asked. "Surely he didn't expect . . . Where is this place again?"

"Hidden Falls, Pennsylvania," Pete replied. "You

know your dad and I grew up together in Pennsylvania, right?"

"I knew he was from somewhere in Pennsylvania, but Dad never wanted to talk about his childhood. Is Hidden Falls anywhere near Philadelphia? Or Pittsburgh?" Des inquired.

"Or any civilized city?" Allie held up crossed fingers.

"It's in the Poconos. Population . . ." Pete paused. "Actually, I have no idea what the population is these days, but it probably isn't much."

"The Poconos? Aren't they mountains?" Allie wrinkled her nose in obvious distaste. "Wait. Not the place with all those tacky heart-shaped bathtubs?"

"That's right." Pete smiled. "The honeymoon capital of the world."

"Well, I have no intention of playing this silly game." Allie turned to the other two women. "Either or both of you can play along, but I for one—"

"Will inherit nothing," Pete cut in. "As a matter of fact, none of you will inherit anything. The money will then go to charities of my choosing."

Allie wheeled around, ready to explode. Before she could speak, Pete said, "If any one of you refuses, or leaves before the theater is restored, none of you will inherit a dime."

"All for one and one for all," Des muttered.

"You said 'leaves,'" Cara said cautiously. "Leaves where?"

"While you're working on this project, you'll live together in your father's family home, the house your great-grandfather built."

"No way."

"Not gonna happen."

"You cannot be serious."

"Couldn't be more serious," Pete told them.

"Live with *her*? You can't mean it." A clearly horrified Allie glared at Cara.

"Which means *I* would have to live with the two of *you*," Cara replied. "Frankly, I think I'm getting the worse end of the deal."

"Okay, let's say we agreed to do this," Des pondered aloud. "How are we supposed to pay for this renovation? I'm assuming if the building had been on someone's demo list, it must need a lot of work. Where's the money coming from?"

"From the estate. Your dad put money aside for the project in a special account. Might be a good idea to choose one of you to be in charge of the checkbook, because if you go over what he projected, it'll be up to you to come up with the rest of the funds." He pointed his pen in Des's direction. "Des, that might be a good job for you. Your dad told me many times how well you've handled the money you made from your TV series. How wisely you invested."

Cara frowned. "What TV series?"

"Long story," Des told her. "Apparently we'll have lots of time to catch up."

"So Dad just expected us to waltz out of our lives to do a job he should have done." Allie voiced what the other two clearly were thinking. "We have lives, you know. What about my daughter? This is outrageously inconvenient and thoughtless of him."

"Your daughter can live with her father until school is out." Pete's patience was nearing its end. "As for you, you're unemployed, with no immediate prospects, and on the verge of losing your house. So if you ask me, it's a plenty convenient time for you." She started to object, but Pete cut her off.

"Des, you're living off your investments and don't have to work, and you won't be leaving much behind this time of the year except the Montana winter."

He turned to Cara. "You own your business and have a remarkably qualified assistant who's been begging to buy in for the past year. Now's a good time to see how she'd do as a potential partner." He looked around at the three of them. "There's no real hardship involved for any of you, when you get right down to it. This is your father's last wish. Complying is all that stands between you and your inheritance."

"I still can't believe he's serious." Allie turned to Des. "Why don't we get our own lawyer and contest it? There has to be a way around this. I can't believe you'd do this to us, Uncle Pete."

"I'm not doing anything but what your father wanted. He was my best friend, and I do see there was a method to his madness. But suit yourselves." Pete opened a desk drawer and removed three envelopes. Handing one to each of the women, he said, "Here's a copy of the will. Please feel free to take it to the attorney of your choice. But you'll be wasting time and money. When I said the will was ironclad, I meant it."

The three women stared at the envelopes, but none opened theirs.

"I still don't understand why he did this," Cara said.

"Well, I've tried to explain it all as best I could." Pete reached into the open drawer and took out a small device. "Now it's time you hear directly from your dad."

"What?" Cara asked.

"Your father left an audio letter for you. He wanted me to play it after I'd gone over the terms of his will." He clicked a switch and sat back. A moment later, the women heard their father's voice.

"Is this thing on? Pete, is it on?"

"It's on, Fritz. Go ahead."

"Okay. Well, girls, if you're listening to this—and if old Pete here has done his sworn duty to me—I'm ashes in a jar, and the three of you have just been hit with a bombshell. I owe each of you an apology, for things I did and didn't do. There isn't time enough for me to go into every way I've failed you, but please know that I am sorry to my soul for not being the father you all deserve. Know that I love the three of you more than anything in this world . . . this world, the next world. Whichever world I land in." He chuckled at his attempt to make a joke, then coughed.

A moment passed before he resumed. "I want you to understand that I loved your mothers, both of them, in my own way, and in their own time. Don't think for a minute that any of my actions were the result of anything you did. Allie, I'm talking to you especially here. You just remember that last conversation we had and remember what I told you." He paused and coughed again. When he resumed speaking, his voice was a bit weaker. "Des, I'm sorry for not standing up to your mother when you needed me to. I shouldn't have let her bully you into doing things you didn't want to do." More coughing. "Cara Mia, I'm sorry for the lies. Sorry that I let you and Susa live a lie for all these years. Sorry that I . . ." *Cough, cough.* "That I left all this in Pete's lap." The voice grew faint, as if Fritz had turned from the recorder. "Pete, you're the best friend a guy ever had. I love you like a brother. . . ." Again a cough, longer, harsher this time.

Then, Pete's voice. "Fritz, that's enough."

"No. I need to tell them about the theater. Why it matters."

"I'll tell them."

"But—"

"I promise. I'll tell them." A heavy sigh from Pete. "Say goodbye, Fritz."

An even heavier sigh from Fritz. "Goodbye, girls. Be good to each other. Trust each other and yourselves. Do what I ask you to do, and all will be well in the end. I promise. Love you. Always."

Pete wiped his eyes and turned off the recorder. The only sound in the room was the sniffling of the three women as tears ran down their faces. He handed Cara a box of tissues. She took several and passed the box on to Des, who shared it with Allie.

When they finally all composed themselves, Cara pointed to the now-silent recorder. "When did he make that?"

"The afternoon before he died," Pete replied.

"When did he tell you that he was sick?" Des asked.

"The same day he found out," Pete admitted. "He had very little time to put his house in order."

"What happened to his ashes?" Cara asked.

Pete pointed to a large, shiny silver urn on the top shelf of a bookcase across the room.

"You mean he's here?" Allie's eyes widened. "He's been here this entire time?"

"In a sense, yes." Pete watched in amusement as all three women turned and stared at the urn. "I know this has all come as a huge shock to you, and I know that what your dad asked of you is . . . well, unusual, to say the least. But once the theater is up and running again, you'll bury his cremains in his family's cemetery next to his parents. Then you'll all be free to go about your lives and you'll never have to see each other again."

He waited for someone to comment. When no one did, he continued.

"Okay. Also inside your envelopes, you'll find directions to the house in Hidden Falls. Your father gave you each one month from today to arrive at that address. I remind you that all three of you must arrive on that date, or none of you will get a dime. If any one of you leaves before the theater is finished, the money goes to charity. I hope I made that clear." He stood, feeling satisfied. He'd kept his final promises to his old friend. "Any last questions?"

No one spoke.

"Good. Well, don't hesitate to call if you think of anything. Otherwise, I expect you'll all comply with your dad's wishes."

Again, silence.

"All righty, then." Pete walked to the door and opened it. "Keep in touch, girls. Let me know how it goes."

Pete hugged each of the three women and planted a kiss on their heads as they filed wordlessly out of the office. He walked them to the elevator, pushed the button for down, and stood aside as the three silently entered the car together. When the door slid closed, he walked back to his office, relieved that his part in Fritz's mess was, for the time being, over.

"How'd it go?" Marjorie asked as he passed her desk.

Pete rolled his eyes.

"As we suspected," she replied. "Well, it's certainly going to be interesting to watch this play out."

"Oh yeah."

"You think they'll be able to do it?"

"Once they come around to the idea, sure. Whether or not they can without killing each other . . ." Pete shrugged.

"Did you tell them about Barney?"

"Nope. Left that part out." Pete entered his office, adding over his shoulder, "There should be something for them to discover on their own."

Chapter Two

"Tell me everything." Darla burst through Cara's back door and into the pretty blue and white kitchen, a bunch of daffodils in one hand and a bottle of wine in the other. "Start from the beginning and don't leave anything out. Spill."

Darla opened the bottle and tossed the cork toward the stainless steel sink, where it landed with a ping.

Cara spilled everything.

A wide-eyed Darla hung on every word.

"And that's how I found out Dad had three daughters, not one. And two wives. Could've been one wife and one who may or may not have been married to him. I'm still not clear on that."

"This is just beyond . . . beyond . . ." Darla searched for words. "Just *beyond*. Your father . . ."

"I know. I still can't believe it." Cara filled a vase with water and absently arranged the flowers.

"And you never suspected . . . ?"

"Why would I? Who wonders if their father has another wife and kids—a whole other family—hidden somewhere?" Cara placed the flowers on the counter. "Of course, in our case, I suppose *we* were the hidden family."

"This is going to sound inane. I mean, I hate to sound like one of those TV reporters who thrusts a mic at someone and demands to know, 'So how does it feel to be shot in the face?'"

Darla poured wine into both glasses and handed one to Cara. "But how *do* you feel?"

"I don't know if I can find the right word. I don't know if there *is* a right word. Bewildered. Sad. Betrayed. Angry. Hurt. For me and for my mom." She tapped her fingers lightly on the side of her glass.

"Did she know?"

"I'm not sure." Cara thought back to her mother's dying words. "Maybe. I asked Uncle Pete, but I didn't really get a straight answer. Susa could have known and just didn't care. She didn't always care about things that mattered to other people. She was such a free spirit."

"Well, free spirit or not, it's all good, as long as you're happy with your life. Susa seemed happy. I don't remember ever hearing her complain about anything."

"She always said she loved her life, so yeah, she was happy. She had her shop and her yoga and her gardens and her knitting." Talking about her mother was so much easier than talking about her father.

"She always said if you talk about negative things, you're inviting negativity into your life. Better to look for the good, find things that would bring joy."

"Like all her craft projects," Darla reminded Cara. "Remember when she taught us to tie-dye?"

"We had red fingers for weeks from the dye, which of course, being Susa, she made from scratch." Cara laughed.

"I think of her every time I see a beet."

Cara rested her chin in her hand, her elbow propped on the table. "I always thought it was so cool that my mother wasn't like everyone else's. She always had time for me. She never shooed me away or talked around my questions. She was such a gentle soul. Open and honest. All those things—her gentleness, her honesty, her uniqueness, her love of life—those were the things that my father loved about her."

Cara stared into her wine for a long, quiet moment. "I can't reconcile what I learned today with the father I knew. I know he loved me, I know he loved my mother. Sometimes I felt they were so in love that they didn't need anyone else, even me. Dar, I just can't come to grips with the fact that he had another wife, other daughters."

"What are they like? Your sisters?"

"Half sisters," Cara corrected. "I was only with them for about forty-five minutes, so I really don't know what they're like."

"First impression?"

"The older one, Allie, seems bitter. Brittle. The

younger one, Des, didn't come across as hard as Allie did." Cara rolled her eyes. "But seriously, who names their kids Allegra and Desdemona?"

"I'm guessing the same guy who named you Cara Mia Starshine."

"The 'Starshine' was Susa's idea."

"Well, *duh*."

"I know they were both as stunned as I was, I'm sure of that. Especially Allie. She wasn't very nice. Actually, she was kind of bitchy about the entire thing."

"It's hard to blame her." Darla quickly added, "Not that I'm defending her or anything, but Fritz was married to her mother first, right? So maybe she feels that you and Susa took something from her. Like she was there first, and . . . and oh crap, I don't know what I'm saying." Darla covered her face with her hands. "Forget I said that."

"No, you're right. He *was* theirs first. I don't know what transpired between Dad and their mother, or why or when he left her—actually, now that I think about it, I don't really know if he ever left their mother. I got the impression that they didn't see him very often. If I had to guess, I'd say he was more invested in Susa and me, judging by the time he spent here, but then again, he made all those trips to the West Coast every month." Her voice dropped. "At least now I know why he kept his business out in California and Mom and me out here in New Jersey."

"I doubt Susa would've moved even if he'd asked her to."

"She loved living in this small town and knowing everyone and having her little shop and her friends," Cara said, as a faint smile crossed her face.

"Wasn't he lucky?"

"Lucky, yes, but he knew Mom well enough to know that she never wanted to visit L.A., even when he invited her along for a weekend. She hated to fly, and she always said she had about as much interest in his business as he had in hers."

"So what did they look like?"

"Allie is tall and thin. Like, model thin. Sleek. Very chic. Designer clothes for sure, though I couldn't tell you who the designers were. Long, straight blond hair. She just had that look, you know? Pulled together and hip and really beautiful. Lots of nice jewelry."

"Real?"

Cara shrugged. "I didn't get that close. But she looked the way I picture a Beverly Hills housewife to look."

"And the other sister?"

Cara thought for a moment. "Des is very different from Allie. For one thing, she's shorter and rounder. And more cute than beautiful. Hair a lot like mine, only darker and curlier and shorter. I'd guess a more casual lifestyle—tall leather boots and nice jeans, a great sweater, good leather jacket and gorgeous leather bag. Everything about her said relaxed and cool and expensive, but totally down-to-earth. She was as surprised as Allie and I were, but she didn't freak out."

"How'd you leave it with them?"

"I rode in the elevator with them, but no one said a word. When the doors opened, Allie just walked away as if she didn't know either of us. Once we got outside, Des said something like, 'So I guess we'll see each other in Hidden Falls next month.'"

"What did you say?"

"Something like, 'Sure, see you there.' Funny, but I don't think they were together. Strange, huh? I would've expected them to come together, but Allie went to the parking garage and Des walked across the street and got into her car."

"Maybe they live in different parts of the country."

"Possible. But still, if it'd been my sister, I'd probably have wanted to grab lunch with her afterward to talk about the bombshell that had just been laid on us. But Allie took off and Des didn't even react, like she wasn't surprised or she didn't care." She paused. "If she were my sister . . ."

"She is," Darla reminded her. "She *is* your sister."

"One would never know by the way she acted that she was related to Des or to me. She just . . . boom. Gone."

Cara swirled her wine before taking a long sip.

"I thought I knew my dad so well. I knew what made him laugh and what books he liked—history, books about presidents and other historic figures. His favorite authors—Jon Meacham and Doris Kearns Goodwin, Pat Conroy and James Lee Burke. His favorite movies—car chases and shoot-'em-ups. Maryland crabs over Alaskan, clams but never oysters. I knew summer was his favorite season and that he preferred beer to wine and liked his steak rare. He loved lilacs and hated the scent of gardenias, liked big dogs and big cars. I knew he liked to walk on the beach in the early evening and that he loved reality TV." She shook her head. "And yet I didn't know him at all."

"So what are you going to do?" Darla lifted her glass and drained it.

"Right now, I'm going to make that dinner I promised you." Cara topped off her glass, then refilled Darla's.

"I meant—"

"I know what you meant. I'm going to talk to Meredith about taking over for a while—she's been wanting to buy into the studio, so this would be a good way for her to find out if it's what she really wants. Then I'm going to go to Hidden Falls, Pennsylvania. Coming on the heels of Drew's big announcement and his wedding—not to mention the impending birth of his child—I'm not unhappy to have an excuse to get away for a while. By the time I get back, the wedding will be a done deal, and the gossip should've died down. I'm sick of hearing about it. I'm confident that by then, the fact that Drew McCann dumped wife number one in favor of wife number two will be a distant memory."

Cara tapped the rim of Darla's glass with hers. "So here's to Hidden Falls, and whatever I may find there."

They each took a sip; then Darla put her glass down. "What do you hope to find?"

Cara slumped against the island.

"My dad," she said simply. "I want to find out who my father really was, because he obviously wasn't the man I thought I knew."

Cara sat in front of 725 Hudson Street, her car in park, the engine running, the heater blasting against the cold March wind, and stared at the large Victorian that seemed to grow out of the front lawn. She checked the address against the information Pete had supplied in the envelope. This was definitely the place. This was her father's family home, the place he'd grown up, this imposing giant sitting off by itself on a lot that took up the entire first block of Hudson Street.

She hadn't expected anything quite like this, nothing quite so grand, with its wraparound porch and turrets that rose three stories, its exterior of pinkish brick and white trim that seemed to mound like whipped cream over the turrets and the windows. There was gingerbread trim everywhere trim could have been added, and a porte cochere stretched from the right side of the house across the driveway to what was probably a carriage house. The drive was lined on one side with ancient pines and with tall trees on the other, all still leafless, so she wasn't sure if they were maples or oaks. Cara had suspected her grandparents had been well-off, judging by what Pete had told them about their philanthropy, but still, she hadn't expected their home to be so ornate. Cara tried to picture her father here. Had he played ball with his father or with his friends on the front yard?

The property appeared well maintained, the grass and shrubbery neatly trimmed. The tall trees had no dead or hanging branches that she could see. Who, Cara wondered, had been caring for the property? Had Fritz kept a crew on retainer to keep up his boyhood home?

She turned off the car radio, bracing herself to get out. Moments later, a car went by, making a leisurely pass, and Cara wondered if it might have been Des or Allie, but the car continued to the corner before making a left turn. The key to the house hung from the same ring that held her car keys, but Cara couldn't bring herself to walk up the drive and unlock that massive front door.

She also didn't want to be the first to arrive, didn't want to be the one to open the door to greet the others when they got there, and, for some reason, didn't want to be alone in the house. She was nervous enough about meeting her half sisters again, especially under such bizarre circumstances. Cara had promised herself to remain open-minded, to do whatever she had to do to get along with the other two, even to try to get to know them as her—*their*—father had wanted. She wasn't naïve enough to think it was going to be easy.

None of this was going to be easy.

She hadn't eaten since breakfast, and while Darla had sent her on her way with a whole bunch of muffins and a batch of brownies, Cara wanted a meal. A big veggie burger, maybe, and a really good salad. She made a U-turn and headed toward Main Street, two short blocks away. She'd passed both the Hudson Diner and a small restaurant on her way through town. Either would suffice tonight.

She parked in the small municipal lot, got out of the car, and headed to the diner, but not before drawing her down coat around her and lowering her head against the wind. March was, indeed, coming in like a lion in Pennsylvania.

Where was the theater? she wondered as she glanced up and down Main Street. How soon could they explore it? How would they assess the repairs, and how would she and the other two be able to tackle the job and complete the task Fritz had left for them? Would they get along? How awkward was this first night going to be?

She wondered if the other two would arrive together.

That was answered fifteen minutes later while Cara sat in a booth rereading the letter Pete had sent reminding her and the others of "the rules of the game," as he called them.

"Excuse me, Cara, but would it be okay if I joined you? Would you mind?"

Startled to hear her name spoken in this place where she knew no one, Cara looked up. "Oh. Hi, Des."

"If it'd make you too uncomfortable, it's okay. There are other booths available, and I can—"

"No, no. It's fine. Really. I was just surprised to see you."

"I thought I'd grab a bite to eat before I went to the house," Des explained. "I did go over there, but I just couldn't . . . I didn't want to be the first one there. I didn't want to go into that empty place alone."

"I did the same." Cara gestured for Des to sit. "I was hungry after the drive and I doubted there'd be food in the house. I guess we'll have to go food shopping after we get settled in tonight."

"I hope something will be open. This place looks like 'Rolls up the sidewalks at eight p.m.' could be their town motto."

Cara slipped the letter back into the envelope, but not before Des saw what she'd been reading.

"I just reread my copy, too." Des slid into the worn bench seat and placed her bag and jacket next to her. "I don't know about you, but I'm finding this whole thing curiouser and curiouser."

"It's . . . well, yes. It's strange. Everything about this is strange."

"Think we'll be able to do it? Last long enough to do what he wanted?" Des laughed softly. "Leave it to him. Restore a theater! Like it's something we'd tackle over a long weekend."

"I don't think he thought it'd be easy. If all he'd wanted was to have the theater repaired, he could've hired someone. I think he wanted to challenge all three of us. Make us work together."

"To force us to get to know each other?" Des

shook her head. "There has to be an easier way than making three strangers live together and hoping we'll bond over the experience."

"I'm the only stranger," Cara reminded her.

"Allie and I hardly have a sisterly relationship. We never see each other and rarely even speak on the phone. You might have noticed that she walked away after the meeting at Uncle Pete's as if she didn't know *either* of us."

"So I'm assuming you didn't make the trip together?"

"I called her to suggest that we time our flights so that we could meet up at the airport and rent a car together, but she didn't pick up. I left a voicemail but she never called me back. Typical Allie. I don't let it bother me anymore." Des looked longingly at the tray a passing waitress carried to the next table. "Did you order yet?"

"A veggie burger and a salad." Cara flagged down their waitress and asked for a menu for Des.

"You're a vegetarian?"

"Mostly. I'm not crazy strict about it, though. Once in a while I'll eat eggs and dairy, and occasionally I'll eat fish, but no red meat ever. Never anything with fur or hooves."

The waitress was back in a flash and handed the menu to Des, who glanced over it quickly.

Des folded the menu and handed it to the waitress. "I'll have a burger also, but beef for me, please. Well done. Mushrooms and Swiss cheese, red onion, no tomato or lettuce. And an unsweetened iced tea."

The waitress wrote down the order and headed for the kitchen. Now that they had exhausted the initial make-nice chatter, a strained silence followed.

Finally, Cara said, "So do you think she'll show? Allie?"

"Nothing she does surprises me anymore. But unless her financial status has changed drastically over the past month, she'll probably be here. She needs the money from the estate. She won't be nice about it and she'll be an absolute pain in the ass the whole time she's here." Des paused. "Don't take any of that personally."

"I won't. But it's funny she didn't even call you to ask how you felt about the whole thing."

"How I feel about things is the farthest thing from her mind, I'm sure." Des leaned back as the waitress served her iced tea. "Like I said, we're not really close. She can be a bit testy at times. You probably noticed when we were at Uncle Pete's."

"She didn't seem to take the whole thing— meaning me—very well."

"Allie doesn't take anything well that doesn't benefit Allie."

"We were all blindsided that day. The last thing I expected when I went to Pete's office was to find out my whole life had been one big—"

Des interrupted her. "If you're thinking of saying 'lie,' don't. Don't go there. I've been giving this a lot of thought. I've tried to be rational and look at this through Dad's eyes. I'm trying to be fair."

"How's that working for you?"

"It wouldn't be truthful to say I understand. I really thought I knew him, but now . . ."

"I thought I did, too." Cara stirred her iced tea and tried to ignore the sick feeling she always got now when she thought about her father's tangled life.

Des thought for a moment. "I think we each just knew a piece of him, whatever it was he wanted each of us to see. For us, he was the high-powered entertainment agent who was always flying off to meet with a client, the dad who had little time to spend with us, but always managed to buy some big splashy gifts that made your friends almost faint from envy. I know he loved us, though: I don't mean to imply that he didn't. It was just his way."

"That was never his way with me. He always seemed to have time. My mother wouldn't have encouraged him to do the big-splashy-gift thing, though there were times when he did. My mom was so low-key. She didn't believe in throwing money around."

Des laughed. "As far as my mother was concerned, you couldn't throw enough of it."

"Funny he was so different with us," Cara said. "It sounds like he took his cues from the women he was with. Low-key Susa, low-key life."

"High-ticket Nora, high-ticket life." Des nodded. "Interesting."

The waitress appeared at the table with Cara's veggie burger and salad.

"Your burger will be up in another minute or so," she told Des.

"Cara, go on, eat. Don't wait for me. You look like you're starving."

"I am. Thank you." Cara took a bite of her burger. "So what, you think Dad thought up this whole crazy business because he wanted us to put the pieces together?"

"It's hard to know what he was thinking. Uncle Pete said it had occurred to Dad toward the end that he should've been up-front with everyone years ago."

"I'm not sure how that would have gone over with your mother. Mine was pretty much a free spirit, but still, there's a good chance she might have objected."

"Once my mom died, he could've told your mother the truth and that might've worked out."

"I don't know. What could he have said?" Cara lowered her voice. "'Oh, Susa, by the way, did I mention that I was married to someone else when I married you? But she passed away, so we don't have to worry about those pesky bigamy laws.'"

"Maybe he meant to tell her. To tell us." Des sighed. "Oh hell, there's no point in speculating, since they're all gone."

"I think Pete was right. Dad was a coward and he couldn't face any of us with the truth." Cara picked at her salad. "He made Pete break the news and now he's making the three of us complete this cockamamie renovation."

"I wonder if the theater's really as bad as Uncle Pete made it sound. Maybe it's not really that big a project." For a moment, Des looked hopeful. "Then again, if it'd been an easy fix, he probably would've done it himself."

"We're all smart and capable, right?" Cara said. "We'll figure it out."

"I like your positive outlook." Des smiled for the first time since she sat down. "I think I'm going to like getting to know you."

"I think I'll like getting to know you, too." Cara almost added, *And I think I might even like having you for a sister.* But she took another bite of her burger instead. One conversation does not a sister make.

The two finished eating and continued to make small talk until the waitress stopped at the table to ask, "Dessert, girls?"

Cara looked across the table at Des. "I have homemade brownies in the car."

"Oh, well, then. No dessert for me," Des told the waitress.

Once out front, Des stopped on the sidewalk. "I'm parked across the street."

"I'm in the lot behind the diner. I'll see you at the house."

"I could wait for you if you like," Des offered.

"Thanks, but I have to stop for gas. I'm driving on fumes."

"I noticed a gas station another block or two up. I'll go on to the house, but I'll wait for you in my warm car in the driveway." Des looked a little wary. "I wouldn't be surprised if that place was haunted."

Cara laughed and walked around the building to

the lot, her head down against the wind, and got into her car.

The gas station was on the next block, between the police station and a bar. Cara pulled next to one of the two gas pumps, rolled down her window, and waited for the attendant to come out. While she waited, she took a credit card from her wallet and a long drink of water from the bottle she'd left in the cup holder, and checked her email. From time to time, she looked toward the office. She could see through the windows that an older woman was behind the counter, and two men stood together talking, one of whom appeared to be wearing a police uniform. Several moments passed, and still no one came out to wait on her.

After a full five minutes Cara got out of the car. Cop or no cop, she needed to get on her way.

Cara walked quickly to the building and opened the door, the wind whipping her hair around her face.

"Excuse me," she said. "Sorry to interrupt, but I need to buy gas." She pointed behind her in the direction of her Subaru. "Is there an attendant on duty?"

Three pairs of eyes turned to settle on her.

One of the men was, as she'd suspected, a police officer. The other had thick, straight blond hair and wore jeans and a sweatshirt with the sleeves ripped off at the elbow in spite of the cold. He made no effort to conceal the fact that he was blatantly checking her out with a mixture of interest and curiosity.

"Did you need change?" the woman behind the

counter asked. She slipped on her glasses, and it appeared she was trying to get a better look at Cara.

"No, I'm using a credit card," Cara replied. She could feel her face beginning to color even as she tried to ignore the stares.

An odd silence followed. For a moment, no one moved. Finally, the guy in the jeans said, "I'll take care of it, Sally."

He held the door open for Cara, then followed her to the car.

"What's it take?" He opened the gas tank cover.

"Regular." She slid behind the wheel, uncomfortably aware that his eyes were boldly following her. "Fill it, please." She rolled up the window against the cold and turned up the heater.

The police officer came out of the office and waved. Cara heard him call, "See you in the morning."

The attendant waved back, then unscrewed the cap from the gas tank and filled it until the pump clicked off. He removed the nozzle and closed the gas cap with a twist, then walked to her window.

"That'll be thirty-five dollars even," he told her.

Cara handed him the card.

"Be right back." He went into the office to swipe her card. The woman behind the counter said something and they both laughed. He was still chuckling when, a minute later, he came back out and handed Cara the credit slip to sign.

"Thanks," Cara said.

"So you're from Jersey." He leaned casually on the driver's-side door.

Cara looked up into very blue eyes and nodded. "Let me guess. The license plate gave me away?"

"Nope." He shook his head, his eyes still fixed on hers. It struck Cara that up close, his face appeared more interesting than handsome. He had the kind of high cheekbones and long, thick lashes that most women would kill for.

She hated to admit it even to herself, but the combination of those pale, crystal-blue eyes and that blond hair was arresting, and totally masculine. His face might have been pretty if it weren't for the flat place high on the bridge of his nose that might have been on the wrong side of someone's fist but which did nothing to detract from his appeal. If anything, it enhanced it.

"So what was it then?" Cara forced herself to look away to sign her name, then handed the slip back to him.

"Did you know that New Jersey's one of only two states where by law an attendant has to pump your gas? Oregon's the other one, in case you're curious." He took the slip and stepped away from the car. "Everywhere else, it's self-service. Like here, in Pennsylvania." He smiled. "Where everyone pumps their own."

She stared at him dumbly, her face growing red.

"You have a nice night now." He gave her a receipt and lightly slapped the hood of the Subaru before walking back to the office, his stride long and easy.

Her cheeks burning, she drove away and headed

for Hudson Street. Had she known that Pennsylvanians pumped their own gas? She'd lived her entire life in New Jersey and had never had to operate a gas pump.

No wonder they'd been laughing. She tried to work up some indignation at the fact that they'd been laughing at her, as well as the fact that he'd been so obviously checking her out. Her indignation lasted only until she reminded herself that she'd checked him out just as closely.

Cara pulled into the driveway behind Des, thinking she was going to have to nurse this tank of gas for a very long time.

When Des saw Cara, she got out of her car, opened her trunk, and started to unload her bags.

"You weren't kidding about not going inside alone," Cara called to her.

"No way am I going in there by myself." Des pointed to the house. "But look—there's a light on in one of the back rooms."

"Probably left on by whoever takes care of the property," Cara replied. "Got your key?"

"Right here." Des held up her hand just as another car pulled in behind Cara. "That must be Allie."

Both women had started toward the third car when a police cruiser pulled over and stopped at the foot of the driveway. The officer who got out was the same one Cara had seen at the gas station. He walked up to Allie's car and motioned for her to roll down the window.

"Uh-oh," Des whispered. "That doesn't look good."

"I think we should wait here," Cara said. "That doesn't look like a social call."

They watched as Allie handed over her license and registration.

"Oh crap, what's she done?" Des muttered.

The officer returned to his car and got in. A few minutes later, he walked back to Allie's window and handed her something. It appeared he and Allie exchanged a few words. He turned to walk away, and Allie got out of her car just as the front door of the house slammed. All eyes turned toward the house, where a tall, trim woman with blond hair, wearing a plaid flannel shirt and jeans, trudged across the lawn to join them.

"You causin' trouble here, Benjamin?" she called to the officer.

"No, ma'am. Just a polite inquiry." He turned to her, his hands on his hips.

The woman stopped midway between Des and Cara, and Allie and the officer, a smile on her face. "Inquiring about a pretty face you didn't recognize?"

"No, ma'am. I didn't know until I pulled her over that she had a pretty face." He touched what would've been the brim of his hat, had he been wearing one. "'Night, ma'am." He nodded to Cara and Des. It seemed he said something to Allie under his breath, because she turned abruptly and started taking things out of the backseat of her car.

"You be sure to tell your grandma I said hello," the woman called after him. "I'll see her at bingo on Wednesday."

"Will do," he called back.

"Well, that was a nice welcome to town, I'm sure." She turned her attention to the three young women. "Grab your things and come on up to the house. I just started to fix dinner, if any of you are hungry."

"Could I ask who you are?" Cara asked.

"I'm your aunt Bonnie," the woman replied. "But you can call me Barney. Everyone does. Now hurry along before we all freeze in this wind."

Chapter Three

The three women exchanged blank glances with one another.

Finally, Cara asked, "Did you two know . . . ?"

"No," both Allie and Des responded. "You . . . ?"

"Dad never mentioned he had a sister," Cara said.

"Dad never wanted to talk about his family." Des looked as confused as the others.

"Maybe she's really just a family friend," Allie suggested. "You know, like the way we call Pete *Uncle* Pete."

"Yeah. I'll bet that's it." Des nodded.

"Sure," agreed Cara. "That has to be it."

They gathered their bags and hurried up the driveway to the house, the cold driving them forward.

"Or maybe she's been taking care of the house for us until we could get here," Allie said.

"Maybe." Des was obviously doubtful.

They filed up the front steps one by one.

"Should we knock?" Des whispered.

"She knows we're here. She's expecting us to come in." Allie leaned past her sister to push open the door. "Hello?"

"You can leave your bags in the hall and come on out to the kitchen," a voice called from the back of the house.

"Would you look at this place?" Cara murmured, feeling almost as if she'd fallen down a rabbit hole as she took in the spacious foyer with its handsome staircase that wound all the way to the third floor, the carved walnut wainscoting, and elaborate crystal chandelier. She pointed to the portraits painted in oils that hung in heavy frames on the walls. "Who do you suppose they are?"

"Relatives of Dad's would be my guess." Allie glanced from one picture to the next. "They all look so dignified. So . . ."

"Rich," Des said softly. "Check out the emerald necklace on the woman third from the right."

"I wonder who she was." Cara stood in front of the painting.

"I wonder where that necklace is now." Allie stood behind Cara, her arms crossed over her chest.

"There sure are a lot of them," Des noted.

"Girls, come on back. You can hang your coats right there in the closet unless you're still warming up. You can have a full tour later, or tomorrow morning, if you're tired." Aunt Bonnie—Barney—appeared in the kitchen doorway. She'd slipped on a dark blue apron, and in the light, Cara could see that her hair, chin-length and bluntly cut, was blond streaked with gray that could've almost passed as highlights. "I have some chicken noodle soup that I made earlier. I wasn't sure who'd be arriving when, so I thought I'd make something that could be warmed up whenever you got here. Didn't come together, I see. Shame you all had to rent cars on your own."

She disappeared back into the room.

Cara looked at the others, shrugged, and followed. Des and Allie trailed behind. For its age and size, the house felt surprisingly warm.

The kitchen was a large square room, and while it looked like it had been updated, it fell short of being contemporary. Wood cabinets painted ivory, some with glass doors, wrapped around two walls. Yellow Formica counters were flecked with green and gray. Hardwood marked by years of living covered the floor, and the walls were painted white with stenciled arms of green ivy vines climbing toward the ceiling. A breakfast nook, built into a bay window along the side wall, was painted to match the ivy. The appliances were all white but appeared to have been purchased in different decades. A large butler's pantry served as a bridge between the kitchen and the adjacent room, which Cara assumed would be the dining room, and a large fireplace, embers burning, stood along the inner wall. The table was round, the chairs an eclectic mix of styles. Still, the room had an air of cheerfulness and warmth. Where the foyer with its wall of formal portraits was imposing, the kitchen offered a welcoming and much-needed hug.

"Need something to drink? There are sodas in the fridge. Iced tea made this morning. And of course good old-fashioned water from the tap," their hostess said. She stood with her back to the room, stirring a pot on the stove. "There's coffee in the pot and water for tea on the stove if you'd rather something hot."

The scent of something delicious, something savory, wafted through the room. Even though the soup was made with chicken, Cara found herself wishing she hadn't already eaten.

"Glasses and mugs in the cabinet on the end there and ice in the freezer."

Cara was the first to speak, the first to move. "Something hot would be great. Thank you, *Barney*," she said as if trying out the name; she still wasn't exactly sure who this person was and how she fit into their lives, but she'd obviously been expecting them.

Cara went to the cabinet for a cup, trying not to appear as awkward as she felt. The bottom shelf was filled with ceramic mugs, each adorned with the picture of a different species of bird. She picked the first one her hand touched, the Baltimore oriole, then had a quick flashback to going on the Cape May bird count one year with Susa.

Turning to the other two, she asked, "Des? Allie? Glass or mug?"

"A glass, please," Des replied.

"For me as well," Allie said.

Cara handed out the glasses and Des went to the freezer and tossed several ice cubes into her glass. She passed the ice cube tray to Allie before grabbing a can of Diet Pepsi from the fridge for her sister and filling her own glass with iced tea.

"I prefer tea to soda, too, Des," Barney said.

Cara poured coffee into her mug, then added a bit of sugar from a nearby bowl and a splash of cream from a small pitcher.

Des took a sip, then asked, "Barney, how did you know I was Des and not Allie or Cara?"

"You look a lot like your father. Fritz always said you favored him. Allie, gosh almighty, I'd have known you anywhere. You look so much like Nora when she was in her prime. Though to be truthful, I see a little of myself in you, too. Of course you all have the Hudson blue eyes. Blue as an October sky, everyone used to say." She turned to Cara. "By process of elimination, you have to be Cara. Susa's girl."

"Right again." Cara took a sip of her coffee and found it as delicious as it was fragrant. "So you knew we were coming today?"

"Oh, sure. Pete's kept me in the loop. I know all about your father's will and why you're here. And in case you haven't figured it out, I'm your father's sister. Your only living relative—on the Hudson side, anyway. Don't know anything about Susa's family, but Allie and Des, you have some cousins on your mother's side around somewhere."

"Why didn't we know about you? Why haven't I ever heard of you before?" Cara pressed. "If Dad had a sister, wouldn't he have told us? I mean, it's really strange that he would have a sibling that he never bothered to mention."

A frowning Barney turned to her and leaned back against the counter, her hands on her hips. "Stranger than him not bothering to mention that you have *two* sisters? Frankly, I think that trumps not telling you about me. But you're welcome to see my driver's license."

"I'm sorry. I didn't mean to insult you. But Dad would never talk about his family or his childhood, other than to say that it was so unhappy he couldn't bear to think about it, and that—" Cara began but Barney cut in.

"What are you talking about?" Barney demanded. "Who had an unhappy childhood?"

"Dad. He told us that talking about his childhood only brought up bad memories, so we never pushed him about it." Des looked at Allie, who nodded.

"I guess that's why he never brought us here or talked about Hidden Falls," Allie said.

"That's the biggest crock of . . ." Barney laughed. "Total bull. For the record—the real record—we had a great childhood, and I never once heard him complain about a damned thing. He didn't want to talk about it because sooner or later, you'd have asked to come here, and there were conditions to his coming home that he didn't want to meet."

Before anyone could ask what those conditions were, she continued. "Allie, you've been here before. Spent almost a month with me after Des was born."

"No, I'm sure I've never been here. We've never met. I'd have remembered." But as she spoke, Allie appeared hesitant, unsure.

"You were only three, so I think you were probably too young to remember, but I have pictures somewhere. The camera doesn't lie, girl. I looked for them when I heard you were coming, but I can't seem to put my fingers on them. I can look again, if you're interested."

The room was so quiet, Cara was certain she'd hear a pin drop.

Finally, to break the silence, Barney said with forced enthusiasm, "Well, now that we all know who we are, who's ready for soup?"

"I stopped for dinner in town on my way here," Cara told her.

"Me too. I'm sorry," Des told her. "I didn't know anyone was here, and didn't think there'd be food."

"Oh, goodness. No need to be sorry." Barney brushed the apology aside. "Where'd you stop?"

"The Hudson Diner," Cara replied.

"I stopped there as well," Des said. "We ran into each other there, so we shared a table."

Allie turned to her sister. "You had dinner with *her*?" She yanked a thumb in Cara's direction.

"She has a name, Allie," Des reminded her.

Allie rolled her eyes and shook her head almost imperceptibly.

"Seems to me you're going to need each other a lot over the next year or however long it takes you to do what you have to do," Barney noted. "Might be a good idea to be cordial. Maybe save your energy for what really counts."

"The next *year*?" Allie's eyes widened. "Are you *kidding* me?"

"I'm not a contractor, but I know when things are in bad shape and need a lot of fixing. Of course, I could be wrong. I haven't been inside the theater in a while. Could be things magically got fixed on their own." Barney shrugged.

"I can't stay here for a year," Allie exploded. "I have *responsibilities*. I have a *child*."

"She's welcome to visit anytime," Barney assured her. "Maybe she'd like to spend her summer vacation here."

"Oh my God." Allie collapsed on one of the window-seat cushions and put her head in her hands. "I could kill Dad for this."

"I'm afraid you're a little late." Barney took two bowls from the cupboard. "Soup, Allie?"

Allie shook her head, got up, and started for the door, muttering in a shaky voice, "I need to call Nikki."

"You're in the last room on the right side of the short hall upstairs." Barney turned to Des and Cara. "You each have your own room and bath, but since there's no maid service here, you'll have to pick up after yourselves. I do have a cleaning service every other week but they're not my maids. There's an extra set of sheets and an extra blanket at the foot of your beds and towels in each of your bathrooms. Anything else you need to know about the accommodations?"

Des and Cara both shook their heads.

"Des, your room is right opposite Allie's, and Cara, you're next door to Des. I thought it'd be best to let you all stay in the same part of the house." Barney ladled soup into one of the bowls, then placed it on the table.

"How many bedrooms are there?" Des asked.

"Seven, not counting the third floor. I remember my dad telling us that they had live-in maids back when he was growing up and they lived on the top floor, but those days are long gone. The third floor is all storage now. Neither my mother nor my grandmother could ever part with a darned thing. Sooner or later, everything, furniture, clothes, you name it, all ended up upstairs."

"It sounds like a fun place to explore," Cara said.

"You're welcome to poke around anytime." Barney opened a drawer and took out a spoon. "Girls, are you sure you don't want to join me?"

"I'm really full from dinner, but it smells wonderful," Des said.

"Our former cook's recipe, refined for modern living." Barney sat, then motioned for the others to join her at the table. "Unless you have someone you have to call, too."

"No, I'm good," Cara told her as she sat on one of the other chairs.

"Me too." Des sat on the window seat her sister had vacated.

"So who was on the register at the diner tonight?" Barney asked.

"A woman with frizzy red hair," Cara replied.

Barney's laugh was deep and hearty. "That would be Kim. She's one of my early-morning walking partners."

"You walk in the mornings?" Des settled back on the cushion.

Barney nodded. "Every morning. Some days it's tougher than others to get out there, but I gotta do what I can to keep the creaks out of my knees. Don't always like it. This year the cold's lingered a little longer than last year, but by the time March rolls around, I'm used to it."

The room fell silent. Finally, Cara repeated her earlier question.

"Barney, why didn't our dad tell us about you? You must know why."

Barney held soup on her spoon for a moment to let it cool.

Finally she said simply, "I didn't approve of some of the things Fritz was doing."

"What things?" Allie came back into the room, her phone still in her hand.

"She means me. Me and my mom." Cara rested both arms on the table and leaned forward just a bit. "Right?"

Des turned to her. "Why would you assume that?"

"She"—Cara tilted her head in Barney's direction—"said she had Allie here for a few weeks right after you were born. So Dad was coming here then and bringing his family. I was born almost two years after you, but Dad didn't bring either of us here. So what happened after Allie's visit?" Cara put her hand over her heart. "Susa happened. I happened." She turned to Barney. "I'm right, aren't I?"

Barney put her spoon down quietly. "I never met

your mother, so it isn't that I didn't like her, and I don't judge her. It's that I didn't like what Fritz was doing. When Pete told me that Fritz had had a 'private wedding ceremony' on a beach somewhere in New Jersey, I was horrified. I said, 'He and Nora just had another baby not so long ago. When did he have time to find another woman and get a divorce?' When Pete told me the whole story, well, you could've knocked me over with a feather. Fritz called and said he wanted me to meet someone, but I said, 'Did you take her to meet Nora?' and of course he hadn't. So I said, 'You make it right with your wife—the legal one—and I'll be happy to meet the new one.'" She got up and poured herself a glass of water and took a long drink. "I said, 'Did you tell this woman you had a wife in California?'"

"Did he?" Cara asked.

"He never answered. He just said that he met the love of his life, his *soul mate*, and he couldn't take the chance of losing her." Barney took another drink, then returned to the table. "I told him to let me know when he'd decided to act like a man and come clean with both women, but until then, I didn't want to see him."

"And you never saw or heard from him again?" Des asked.

"Oh, he called me every year on my birthday, and I'd say, 'So, Fritz. Did you have that heart-to-heart with your wives?' And every year, he'd say, 'I'm still working on it.' And I'd say, "'Okay, then. Talk to you next year.'"

"So he never told them." Cara thought it through. "And you never saw him again?"

"He called me after he found out he was sick. Then when he found out just how sick he was, he had Pete drive him up here. Said he wanted to see me one last time, see the house, the town." Barney wiped away a tear with her fingertips. "He went all over town those two days. I don't know what all he saw or did—Pete took him around—but he seemed at peace at the end of the second day. Before he left, he told me what he'd set aside to keep this house going, so we could keep it in the family, and for a minute I thought, 'There's the old Fritz.'" She raised her eyes to the ceiling. "And then he told me what he'd put in his will about the three of you, and I said, 'And there's the Fritz who never met a harebrained idea he didn't like.'"

"So obviously you know all the details of his will and the stipulations." Cara tapped her fingers on the side of her cup.

"Oh, I told him. I said, Franklin Reynolds Hudson, for the love of all that's holy, just call those girls and tell them the truth while you still can. But no. He thought he was clever, kill two birds with one stone, he said. Get the girls to know each other and their Hudson heritage while the theater gets fixed up." She glanced from Cara to Des. "Either of you have construction experience?"

"I know how to use a few tools," Cara told her. "I worked on the renovations at my yoga studio. But real construction?" She shook her head.

"Nothing at all for me," Des said.

"Allie?"

Allie raised her eyes from her phone and met Barney's gaze.

"As I thought." Barney ate a little more soup, then asked, "Do you have a plan?"

"Not yet," Cara said. "But we'll work on one."

Barney finished her soup, then touched her napkin to the corners of her mouth. "Mind if I toss out an idea?"

"Not at all." Des glanced at Cara, who nodded in agreement.

"First things first. Find out what the building needs and what it's going to cost," Barney told them.

"Since none of us knows how to assess the extent of the renovation or to estimate construction costs, we're pretty much stuck on square one," Cara pointed out. "Obviously we'll need to get a professional opinion on just what has to be done."

"I have a friend whose grandson is a contractor. We can get him to take a look, tell you what needs to be done, how much it's going to cost. I'm guessing Pete told you that your father put money aside for the renovations."

"He mentioned that, but how did Dad know what it would take?" Des asked.

"There's a bank account with an amount he estimated the renovations would cost, but once it's gone, it's gone. You'll have to decide between the three of you how to spend it, and who will hold the purse strings. It isn't going to be me. I'll open my home to you—it's your home as well. I can offer suggestions, but I can't do any of the work."

"Can't or won't?" Cara asked.

"I promised my brother I wouldn't interfere, that I'd let you all figure it out for yourselves. But if I can make phone calls, point you in one direction or another, I'm happy to help where I can. So if you want me to call my friend . . ."

"Yes, please. The sooner we start, the sooner we'll finish," Cara said.

Barney smiled. "I like your positive attitude."

"We came here to do a job," Cara reminded her. "We didn't come here to fail."

"Well, then." Barney stood and took her empty bowl to the sink. "Who's ready for a tour of the old family homestead?"

All three rose and followed Barney through the butler's pantry, with its glass-doored cabinets that went almost to the ceiling, which had to be at least eleven feet high. The counter was an unbroken slab of marble, and the sink was old soapstone. A quick peek as they traveled through revealed china, glasses, and serving bowls and trays behind the glass doors. Cara would have to revisit those lovely things later. She adored old china.

If the china in the pantry had drawn her interest, the cabinet in the dining room mesmerized her. The piece was almost seven feet tall, made of solid walnut, with roses carved across the top. A large silver tray on the equally impressive sideboard held a cutglass decanter and several small matching glasses.

The dining table could easily seat twelve, but extra chairs set around the room hinted that leaves could be added to increase the number of guests. The large crystal chandelier hung from the center of a plaster medallion covered with painted roses woven around plump cherubs. Underfoot was a dark Oriental rug that looked like the real thing. A fireplace with an ornate mantel stood along the wall adjacent to the kitchen and the wainscot was shoulder-high, of dark wood. But the most stunning feature in this grand room was the mural painted above the sideboard.

"Barney"—Cara pointed to the wall—"the mural . . . it's . . ."

"Yes, exquisite. I agree." Barney stopped in the doorway, where she'd been about to move into the next room, apparently without planning on commenting on what Cara considered the focal point of the magnificent room.

"The colors . . . the greens and the blues . . ." Des stepped forward for a closer look. "The waterfall is so realistic."

"Those are the falls the town was named for," Barney told them with a surprising lack of interest or enthusiasm.

"Who painted this?" Even Allie appeared awed as her eyes swept from one side of the mural to the other.

"Alistair Cooper," Barney replied.

"*The* Alistair Cooper?" Cara asked.

"Who's Alistair Cooper?" Des wondered.

"He was a well-known landscape artist. I read about him in an art history class I had," Allie replied.

"Yes, he was very well known. He spent some time here in the early 1930s. He'd met my great-aunt Josephine at college and fell head over heels in love with her. Of course, a penniless artist wasn't cutting it with her parents. When my grandparents were abroad on vacation, Alistair painted the mural to prove to them how talented he was."

"What happened when they came back and found he'd painted their dining room wall?" Allie asked.

"He and Josephine were married in the backyard, with her parents' blessing."

"It must be very cool to have dinner in here, with the fireplace and the chandelier and candles all glowing," Cara said. "I'll bet when you have dinner parties the mural is the topic of conversation."

"I don't have dinner parties. I don't use this room at all. If the mural hadn't been done by a famous artist, I'd paint over the damned thing so I would never have to look at it again."

The three young women stood in stunned silence even as Barney walked through the arched doorway into the next room. "This is the sitting room. The small one, actually. The larger one is on the other side of the hall. . . ."

"How weird was that?" Des whispered to Cara as Barney's voice faded and Allie followed their aunt.

"That she hates the mural? Yeah. Strange. You'd think if you had a mural painted by a famous artist on your dining room wall, you'd want to show it off," Cara replied.

". . . and my mother liked to sit here by the fire-place and do needlework. Which is probably why she was damned near blind by the time she died."

"It's a pretty room," Cara noted as she and Des caught up. "Those two dark pink chairs and the green loveseat and that fancy lamp on that white table make the room feel so feminine."

"Well, I've never thought of it that way, but yes, I see what you mean." Barney appeared to be looking at the room through new eyes.

"This room is so sweet and cozy," Des said. "I'd sit in here and read if I lived here."

"For the time being, you *do* live here," Barney reminded her, "so feel free to sit and read anytime. Now, let's move on to the main parlor."

The larger parlor across the hall was furnished in the same Victorian style as the other rooms they'd seen, the pieces heavily carved, the upholstery on the chairs and settees dark blue velvet, and the tables topped with marble. Paintings on the walls were of landscapes, dogs, and still lifes with dark backgrounds. Another dark Oriental rug covered the floor.

In contrast, the front parlor was strictly contemporary in décor.

"This is my living room," Barney announced as she swept aside the heavy pocket doors. "I preserved most of the other rooms as they were when we were growing up. Mostly because it would've been a pain in the ass to try to lug the dining room pieces up to the third floor, and I couldn't face selling them. The furniture in the main parlor isn't especially comfortable—I've had it redone so that at least the seats aren't filled with horsehair—but still, none of it was made for curling up with a good book, watching TV, or chatting with friends."

"Wow. It's like a Pottery Barn showroom," Des exclaimed as they filed into the living room.

"They have a decorating service that was most helpful," Barney said.

"You have lovely views from here," Cara noted. The side windows faced the woods on the other side of the driveway.

"This sofa is very comfy." Allie sat on the end cushion of the off-white sectional. "I'd spend a lot of time here if this were my house."

Barney smiled and led them into the library, which had floor-to-ceiling bookcases, a huge brass chandelier, a solid oak mantel over the fireplace, and lots of leather seating.

"My dad furnished this room," Barney told them, "and I've never been able to bring myself to change a thing."

"Why would you?" Cara ran a hand over the buttery leather of a deep brown chair. "It's just how I'd picture the library in an old house. The bookcases, the fireplace, the leather sofas, the perfect lighting." She paused, then added, "The portraits."

"Who are all these people?" Allie asked. "These and the ones in the front hall?"

"Relatives," Barney replied with a grin. "Lots and lots and lots of relatives. Don't worry, before too long, you'll know them all and you'll know their stories.

But we'll do the ancestor thing another day. You girls must be tired from traveling."

"I don't know about you two, but I'm exhausted," Allie said.

"Wait, what's through this door?" Cara pointed to the door that stood next to the fireplace.

"Oh, that's the office." Barney opened the door and turned on the light. "My grandfather's, my dad's, now mine."

This room, like the others, had a fireplace, tall windows, and dark wainscoting. The oversize desk was oak, and behind it stood an imposing high-backed black leather chair that, while not shabby, looked as if it had seen plenty of use.

"Did you work, Barney?" Des asked.

"Yes, for a long time." She walked into the room and re-arranged some papers on the desktop. "I've been retired from the bank for about five years now."

"What did you do there?" Des asked.

"I was the president, like my dad and my grand-dad and my great-granddad."

The revelation took Cara by surprise. Judging from the looks on Des's and Allie's faces, they hadn't expected that news, either.

Barney moved to the door, her hand on the light switch. "Are we done here? We can talk more in the morning."

Allie tossed her bag on the double bed in her designated room and tried to calm herself. It was bad enough that she was here—that she'd driven from the airport not in the nice-size sedan she'd specifically reserved but in a tiny economy model that barely held its own around the treacherous mountain curves on the drive to Hidden Falls. Whoever had designed that road was insane: In some places there was barely a foot between the guardrail and the edge of the cliff on that last leg into town. And the town! Hidden Falls was barely a blip on her GPS. The shopping district was a joke. She hadn't seen one store she'd be interested in checking out. There'd been no cute boutiques, no pretty little café, no spa, no upscale anything. There wasn't even a nail salon, and she needed one immediately. She'd broken the tip of her index fingernail trying to lug her suitcase up that endless stairwell.

She really could kill her father for this ridiculous scheme. If he thought spending however long here would make her like or even accept Cara when she barely liked her *real* sister, well, he was just proving himself to have been crazier than she'd ever suspected. She couldn't bring herself to even consider the timeline Barney had suggested. Spend a year in this place? Not gonna happen. And what grown woman called herself *Barney* when she had a perfectly nice name like Bonnie?

And then there was the cop. He'd been on her tail since she left the Bullfrog Inn, a hole-in-the-wall bar but apparently the only place in town to get a drink. God knows she'd needed one once she'd driven past this house and thought about what awaited her. Des.

Cara. A ramshackle theater that stood between her and her inheritance. One shot of vodka had somehow become three, and when she left the bar, the cop was leaning against his cruiser watching her walk to her rental. When she got into her car, he got into his, and when she started the engine, he'd done the same. When she pulled away from the curb, so did he. He'd followed her all the way to Hudson Street. Of course, she'd driven slowly, trying to make damn sure he didn't have a reason to pull her over. If she hadn't been so focused on watching him in her rearview mirror, she never would've blown that stop sign.

When she got to the house, she'd parked as far up in the driveway as she could, mostly to establish her right to be there. He'd parked across the entrance to the drive as if to block any attempt she might make to escape. Before she even had a chance to remove the key from the ignition, he was standing at the side of her car.

He'd made a rolling motion with his right hand, and when she lowered the window, he'd asked to see her license, registration, and insurance papers.

"Have I broken any laws, sir?" she'd asked with a calm she didn't feel. Of course she knew she had.

"Your license, registration, and insurance information, please, ma'am."

She opened her wallet and removed her license and handed it over. She'd learned a long time ago that when a law enforcement officer asked to see your license, you could save yourself a whole lot of headache by simply handing it over.

"The car's a rental," she told him as she opened the glove compartment. "The papers are in here. . . ."

She handed them over as well. He took them back to the cruiser and got in. Meanwhile, Cara and Des had both gotten out of their cars and were watching.

Of course they were.

When the cop walked back to her car and handed over her paperwork, she asked, "Why did you follow me?"

"Just wanted to make sure you got safely to your destination, ma'am."

"Why would you think I wouldn't?"

"Three shots in twenty minutes, and you blew the stop sign at the top of the street."

"How do you know how many drinks I had?"

"Small town. One bar. Woman comes in alone and tosses back shots like that, someone's going to notice."

"And someone's going to call you?"

"If she's jangling car keys and headed out looking like she's planning on driving, yes, ma'am. Someone will call me. Every time."

Allie put her head in her hands and willed herself not to cry. "Okay, so you're going to give me a ticket for the stop sign. Just get it over with, Officer"—she looked at his name tag—"Haldeman."

"It's *Chief* Haldeman, and I'm going to let you off with a warning this time. Don't make me regret it." He lowered his voice, and his eyes narrowed and darkened, quietly threatening. "And don't ever drink and drive in my town again."

Before she could thank him for letting her off

easy, Barney had appeared and yelled at him, and he'd turned his attention from Allie.

All in all, it'd been one hell of a start to what she was certain would be an ugly chapter in her life. How annoying that someone had actually tattled on her, as if they were in kindergarten. Then to have the cop—sorry, the chief of police—follow her as if she were some kind of criminal. It was doubly annoying, because under other circumstances, she was pretty sure she'd have taken a second look at chief of police Benjamin Haldeman. True, he wasn't her usual type—that rugged look had never really been her thing—but there was something about him that might've appealed to her if he'd been just a guy and not a smirking cop who'd chided her about having had a few drinks and then driving a mere block.

And then there was that threat: "Don't ever drink and drive in my town again." The tone of his voice and the look in his eyes told her very clearly that it would not go well for her if she did.

God. Deliver me from small-town cops. Even— especially—ruggedly handsome ones with brooding dark eyes.

Allie plopped on the bed next to her luggage, pulled her phone from her pocket, and swiped at Nikki's number in the directory. The phone rang several times before her daughter's voicemail picked up. "Hi, you've reached Nikki. Leave a message and maybe I'll call you back."

Allie took a deep breath and left a variation of the message she'd left many times before.

"Nik, it's Mom. I just wanted to let you know I arrived safely, and I'm here in Hidden Falls, at my dad's house. You'd love this place—it looks like one of the Victorian mansions you see in movies or magazines. I'll take some pictures tomorrow when it's light and send them to you. Anyway, I'm here and I'd love for you to call me. I know you have a test to study for tonight, so tomorrow is okay. 'Night, sweetie. Love you . . ."

Allie disconnected the call, feeling worse than she had before she'd made it. She could picture Nikki at her desk in her pretty room at Clint's house, her history book open in front of her in case her father peeked in, her phone in her hand as she and her friends exchanged texts. For a fourteen-year-old girl, trading gossip with your besties always trumps a phone call from Mom.

She found the brown bag in her suitcase and took out one of the two bottles she'd purchased at the liquor store in a shopping center on the edge of town, opened it, and took a quick sip. The vodka trickled down the back of her throat, familiar and reassuring. Another sip; then she curled up in the chair that sat in the bay window overlooking the backyard, and waited for the tension to abate. She felt miserable and sorry for herself. She was someplace she didn't want to be with people she either didn't know or didn't like, to do something she didn't want to do.

Wrapping herself in the colorful throw that had been left over one arm of the chair, most certainly by Barney, Allie took in the room she'd been assigned. There was the double bed with the carved high head- and footboard, covered by an off-white matelassé spread, and a chest that stood almost six feet tall. The dresser had a marble top and a mirror that was as wide as it was tall. The rug was another ancient Oriental—the Hudsons apparently had a thing for those—and the drapes were a slightly faded damask. As in every other area of the house Allie had seen so far, the moldings around the heavy chestnut door were wide and elaborately cut. An earlier poke into her bathroom had revealed a claw-foot tub in perfect condition; a pedestal sink over which hung a large mirror in a gilded frame; a toilet; and a closet, in which she found extra towels and some cleaning supplies. All in all, while not the fanciest place she'd ever stayed—not by a long shot—the room was lovely and elegant in its own way.

Still staring out the window, Allie wondered why it was so hard for her to think like Des, to find something good in the situation. But right at that moment, she couldn't come up with anything that even seemed remotely good. Except that if they were able to complete this asinine task, she'd inherit a lot of money, with which she could buy a house closer to Nikki's school and could have Nikki back on their original custody schedule. That would be very good, she reminded herself.

She thought for a moment longer.

Just last week, the Realtor had found a renter for her pretty house, so at least for now, Allie wouldn't have to sell it. That was good, too. Once the estate was settled, she could put it on the market, if she decided that was what she really wanted to do.

Oh, and just a little while ago, the cop hadn't given her a ticket for going through the stop sign, so that counted as a plus as well. Of course, she was aware that was most likely due to the fact that apparently his grandmother and Barney were friends, but the reason didn't matter. Allie had thought of three good things to balance out the nightmare she felt closing in on her. She toasted herself with a long swig from the bottle. Maybe tomorrow she'd see if she could dig up an ice bucket and a glass. Surely she'd find both among all the trappings in the pantry. Then again, she wasn't sure she wanted to advertise the fact that she was engaging in her own nightly happy hour. Des would have something to say about that, and she wasn't sure she was up to dealing with her sister's self-righteous disapproval. The last time she'd had more than three drinks in Des's presence, she'd been treated to a fifteen-minute lecture about how she was going to turn into their mother if she didn't watch it.

Allie heard footsteps in the hall, and reached over to turn out the light on the table next to her chair, hoping whoever it was would think she was asleep and wouldn't bother her. As the voices drew nearer, she identified both Des and Cara, though she couldn't understand what was being said. Shifting in the chair, Allie held her breath until she heard the doors to their respective rooms closing. Once all was quiet again, she took one last drink before recapping the bottle. She wrapped it back in the brown paper bag, noting that it was now only two-thirds full. She hadn't realized she'd had that much to drink. She'd only intended a nightcap, a little something to help her through the uncertainty of the situation. Her heart hurt so much at being so far away from Nikki, especially since she had no idea when she would see her daughter again.

Allie stood and stumbled on her way to the bed to replace the bag in her suitcase. Clumsy fingers stashed the bag under a sweater. She moved things around until she found a nightshirt, then slowly and deliberately walked to the bathroom. Ten minutes later she crawled into bed, her head swimming.

As she began to lose herself to sleep, Barney's words came faintly back: *Allie, you've been here before*.

Something, not quite déjà vu, swept through her and pricked at the corners of her mind, but before she could examine it more closely, sleep took her under, and that tiny wisp of remembrance was lost.

CHAPTER FOUR

"So that's the Sugarhouse." Cara rolled down her driver's-side window to get a better look.

"That's this grand theater we're supposed to be restoring to its former glory, *or else*?" Allie scoffed. "Seriously? It's just a bunch of wood nailed together. And by the way, whoever did it did a crappy job."

"That's plywood, and I'm sure that whoever had it boarded up was trying to preserve the building." Cara studied the façade, which was, as Allie pointed out, totally covered with plywood nailed haphazardly across the front and the marquee. "And we can be thankful someone took the time to cover everything. Otherwise, we could be facing a mess from weather damage, vandalism. . . ."

"Must be the neighborhood," Allie muttered.

Cara shot her a dirty look but continued. "There's any number of things that could happen to a building left unprotected for many years."

"I'm sure it's a lot nicer inside." It was obvious Des was trying to sound optimistic. From the outside, the Sugarhouse possessed little charm.

"Why are we sitting here? Let's take a look." Cara hopped out, excited and eager to get to work, her bag heavy with tools she'd borrowed from Barney.

The three stood in front of the building, looking up at the marquee, and for one long moment, they were mesmerized.

"I have goose bumps," Des declared. "Anyone else?"

"Definitely." Cara held up her arms.

"Maybe a few," Allie admitted.

"Can't you just imagine people arriving, all dressed up and excited to see the movie or the play or the concert?" Des turned to Allie. "This is where it all started for Mom, Al. Can't you feel how thrilled she must have been the first time she saw her name up there on the marquee?"

Allie nodded but didn't comment, though Cara could've sworn the corners of Allie's eyes were wet.

"I didn't even notice this place last night when I stopped for gas across the street." Cara glanced at the gas station, wondering if the guy who'd set her straight about pumping gas was there again today, if he was still chuckling at her expense.

"And look, right next door to the gas station is a little bar." Des pointed out the sign with the giant green frog sitting on a lily pad. "The Bullfrog Inn. Cute name. I wonder if it's a nice place. Maybe we could all go one night."

"Sure." Cara nodded.

"What time is Barney's friend supposed to be here?" Allie walked to the corner of the building as if she hadn't heard, then walked back again, because there was nothing to see on the side of the theater except more boards covering who knew what.

Cara glanced at her watch. "Now, actually." From her bag she took a screwdriver and hammer and went directly to the board that covered what she suspected was the main door. "Let's see if I can get this off."

"Don't you think you should wait?" Des appeared nervous. "What if someone drives by and thinks we're breaking into the place? Or calls the police?"

"The cops won't have too far to go, since the police station is right across the street," Allie said.

"Well, that's certainly convenient. I'll bet that cuts down on the drunk driving around here." Cara eyed the board. It had been screwed into place. She put the hammer on the ground and went to work with the screwdriver on one of the corners. "I don't want to wait for the contractor. I want to see what's inside."

"You know how to use that thing?" Allie asked.

"It's a screwdriver, Allie, it has no working parts. I didn't have a lot of money to have my yoga studio renovated, so whatever I could do, I did. What I didn't know how to do, I learned. I wouldn't call myself an expert, but I can do simple things."

"If we had another screwdriver, you could teach me," Des told her.

"If I had another screwdriver, I'd be happy to do that." Cara smiled. She was really starting to like

Des. She still hadn't come around to Allie, but then again, Allie hadn't come around to her, either.

Des walked to the curb and glanced up and down the street. "There's a library on the other side of the parking lot."

"Maybe we could go there to wait for this guy." Allie sounded hopeful. "It's cold out here."

"It's just a little windy, that's all," Des told her. "Didn't you bring any warm clothes with you?"

"It's March, Des," Allie snapped. "It was eighty-five degrees when I left California. How was I supposed to know it was still winter here?"

Des held up her phone. "Easy enough to check the weather anywhere."

Blocking out their bickering, Cara turned one of the screws that held the right side of the board in place. After a brief struggle, she worked the screw free. Pleased with herself, she slipped it into her pocket and went on to the next. She'd managed to remove six more screws before she became aware of the voices behind her.

Des and Allie had argued from the sidewalk to the door, but once they reached Cara, they both fell silent.

"Wow, you've gotten almost all the screws out," Allie said.

"In another second or two, we'll be able to see what's underneath all this plywood." Cara removed the remaining screws, lifted the board, and placed it off to one side. "I was expecting something like solid wood for the main door, but not this."

The wide, thick wooden door was painted aqua,

the top half stained glass, depicting the drama and comedy masks.

"Beautiful. Tragedy and comedy." Des leaned over Cara's shoulder. "Mom had those little tattoos on her ankle, remember, Al?"

"That is so cool." Allie hung over Des. "I remember those."

Des ran a hand over the glass. "Nice. Not a chip, not a scratch. We should thank whoever boarded up this place for doing right by the old girl. The glass looks as perfect as it probably did on the day it was installed, and the paint hasn't even faded."

She pushed at the door, but it held firm.

"Oh. Barney gave me a key she thought might work." Cara dug in her pocket, then held up the key. "Allie, you're the oldest. Want to do the honors?"

"No thanks."

"I'd love to do it." Des took the key. "Geez, Allie. Our parents met here. They fell in love here. Doesn't that mean anything to you?"

"Right now the only thing that means anything to me is getting out of this wind," Allie replied.

Des rolled her eyes, slipped the key into the lock, and pushed. The door swung open onto a dark space.

"Oh my God, it's black as midnight in there." Allie stepped back from the door.

"I keep a flashlight in my car for emergencies," Cara told them. "It has a really bright beam. I'll be right back."

Moments later, Cara returned with the flashlight. "Ready to go in?" she asked.

"Don't you think we should wait for . . . whoever it is we're waiting for?" Allie frowned.

"We don't have to wait for anyone," Cara said. "We own this place. We're finally going to see what Dad left us."

"Agreed. Let's go." Des followed Cara inside, but Allie remained in the doorway.

A few seconds later, Cara heard Allie groan, "Oh, what the hell. Wait for me."

Cara shined the light on the floor. A rug with gold swirls on a dark background—blue? Burgundy? Brown?—lay under their feet.

"I wonder if the carpet is still any good," Des mused. "It'd sure save us a ton of money. I can't imagine what it would cost to replicate this design."

The flashlight flickered across the rest of the lobby. A series of three high and wide arches framed the left side. A large double door stood in the center of the wall on the right. Cara's light followed the lines of the arches and revealed a painted design around each.

"Wow," Des exclaimed. "Look at that."

"Gorgeous," Cara whispered. "This place is just . . ." She sought words.

"You nailed it," Allie said. "It's gorgeous."

Des sighed heavily. "How could we ever restore such a place, find someone who could match the paint and—"

"Maybe we won't have to." Allie sounded surprisingly optimistic. "Maybe it doesn't need to be restored. Like you said, it's been boarded up for a long time, so it hasn't been exposed to sunlight that would damage it." She added hopefully, "Maybe."

"I guess we'll know better when we can really see it. Maybe an electrician should be number one on our list," Cara said.

Des pulled a pen and a small notebook from her bag. "I'm taking notes. I don't trust us to remember everything." She wrote down "carpet," "decorative painting," and "electrician" in the notebook.

"I think we all concur the lobby's a wow." Cara turned her beam of light to the double doors. "I'm guessing the audience seats are through there."

"One way to find out." Allie followed the light to the doors and opened the one on the left.

Cara swept the wide beam of her heavy-duty flashlight across the room and noted, "Looks like the seats are still here. That should save us some money."

"If they're usable." Allie studied one of the seats. "They look kind of old." She ran a hand over it, releasing a cloud of dust, and coughed. "Dusty, too."

"You'd be dusty, too, if you sat in here for what, eighty or ninety years?" Des reminded her.

"Maybe they could be cleaned." Cara's flashlight moved toward the orchestra area. She stopped at the end of the aisle and turned the light upward to the ceiling.

"Seat cleaner," Des wrote on her pad.

"Hey, check this out," Cara called to them.

Allie and Des looked up to the area Cara had illuminated. Dazzling colors appeared overhead—red, gold, blue, green—in indistinguishable patterns. The ceiling itself was peacock blue, and a huge crystal chandelier hung from a center medallion.

"Oh my God, the chandelier." Allie gasped. "I've never seen anything like it."

"Spectacular. And the ceiling's painted with the same design as the lobby," Des pointed out.

"It's beautiful." Cara's flashlight swept the ceiling from side to side and back again. "It's domed and painted. Breathtaking. Pray it's stable and that the roof never leaked."

"Praying," Des said. She elbowed Allie in the ribs until her sister said, "Okay. Me too."

Cara's light danced across the entire ceiling and down one wall.

"Well, she's a true Art Deco lady." Allie marveled. "I don't know what shape the walls and ceiling are in, but she sure looks good from here. I guess the real test will be when the lights are all on. We're probably going to need a scaffold to inspect the ceiling closer, but from here, guys, I have to admit, I'm almost speechless."

"I'm excited." Her eyes shining, Cara turned to Des and Allie. "This is going to be an adventure. When it's finished, it's going to be fabulous. I can't wait."

"How long do you suppose all this is going to take?" Allie ignored Cara's enthusiasm.

"I guess we'll have to see what the contractor has to say when he gets here," Cara said.

"He's late." Allie pulled out her phone and checked the time.

"So what? It's given us time to scope all this out on our own," Des said. "I'm glad he's late."

Cara started carefully down the aisle, the light shining ahead of her.

"There's the stage." She paused to run the light from side to side, top to bottom. "No curtains, but maybe they're somewhere else."

Des and Allie followed.

"Dad and Mom both acted on that stage." Des shook her head. "I still can't believe we're actually standing here, in the place where they met."

"I have to admit, I never saw any of this coming," Allie said.

The beam from Cara's light settled on an area straight ahead. "There's an orchestra pit. How cool is that?"

"Shine the light up and back the way we came in," Des suggested.

Cara did, and Des exclaimed, "There! I knew there'd be a balcony!"

"We should find the steps and go up," Cara said. "Let's go back to the lobby and see if we can find them."

The three women headed back toward the front of the building.

"Maybe through the arches?" Des pointed off to one side.

"That's as good a place as any to begin," Cara agreed.

Following the light, they poked through the middle arch and stepped into a long, dark hallway. Cara flashed the light up and down.

"Maybe this way," she said. "There's something down here."

"Those steps go down." Allie pointed to the disappearing steps.

"Let's see where they go." Cara took the lead once again and they descended into the basement.

"Another hallway." Des sighed.

"And doors off on each side. I want to see what all is down here." Cara pushed open the first door to reveal a small room dominated by a large desk. Shelves lined the walls on two sides and there was a tall cabinet off to the side of the desk.

She stepped behind the desk and opened the top drawer. "Whoever used this room collected pens." She scooped up a handful and held them up.

Allie came closer. "Pens they lifted from other places—mostly local businesses, it seems." She read from the sides of several. "'First Bank of Hidden Falls.' 'Ford's Auto Service.' 'Flowers Bakery.' 'Crash Barton—Auto Insurance.' Are they kidding with these names?" She looked up at her sisters. "Would you buy car insurance from someone named Crash?"

"That has to be a joke," Des said.

"Please." Allie rolled her eyes. "This is the boonies. Anything goes. I wouldn't be surprised to find their dentist is Dr. Payne and their one and only doctor is named Blood."

"Why would you say that?" Des frowned.

"*Flowers* Bakery. Get it? *Flours*?" Allie stared at her sister. "*Ford's* auto? Everything about this entire town seems out of whack to me."

"I don't know," Des said. "I'm finding it more and

more charming. Those names are, well, kinda cute, in a hokey sort of way."

Allie rolled her eyes.

"Oh, guys! You have to see this!" Cara stood in front of the open cabinet holding something in both hands. "Look at these old movie posters! I bet these were in glass display cases in front of the theater."

"I didn't see any glass cases," Allie said.

"I'm sure they're behind some of those boards," Cara told her.

Des and Allie came around the desk to take a closer look.

"Al, it's the poster for one of Mom's movies." Des laid it flat on the desk. "Look how young she looks here."

"'Honora Hudson in *Walk of Fear*,'" Allie read aloud. "I remember when she did that film. We went with her that time, remember? They'd built the set outside of L.A. in the hills."

"I remember."

"I thought your mother's name was Nora," Cara said.

"She thought *Honora* Hudson sounded more like a star and would look better on the marquee, so she changed it, but everyone who knew her called her Nora." Des paused. "Actually, her given name was Eleanora, but she thought that sounded too old-fashioned."

"I wonder if there are more," Allie said.

"There are." Cara pulled a stack from the cabinet and quickly went through them. "None with your mom's name on them, though."

"How 'bout we take them with us." Des looked to Cara.

"Maybe just your mother's," Cara said. "This stuff is really dusty, and I'd rather get things cleaned off before we drag them into Barney's beautiful home."

"You have a point." Des stared at the poster on the desk. "Maybe we can clean this one up in the car before we get to the house."

"I'm sure we can find something to dust it off with," Cara told her.

Seeming to lose interest, Allie drifted back into the hall. When Cara joined her, she found Allie running her hands over the walls.

"What are you doing?" Cara asked.

"The walls are plaster, but I don't see or feel any areas where it's peeling. Which is a good thing, because that means the wall hasn't been damp. Which bodes well for the roof," Allie said. "At least in this section, it doesn't appear there's been any water damage."

"Which is almost a miracle, when you think about it." Cara, too, ran her hand over the wall. "That's just this section, though, and it's a big theater. Who knows what else we'll find?"

At that moment, something ran across Cara's foot. She screamed and took off for the steps.

"Cara!" Des called. "What happened?"

"Something . . . oh God, something big and furry! Right over my foot! Ugh!" She kept running, the light still in her hands.

"Oh, gross," Allie yelled, and ran up the steps behind Cara.

"Don't you dare leave me down here alone!" Des dropped the poster onto the desk and followed them.

The three women ran straight through the lobby and right into the hulking figure blocking the doorway to their escape. Visible in the daylight through the open door, the man wore a denim jacket over a dark green tee and well-faded jeans; a red Philadelphia Phillies baseball cap sat backward over his blond hair.

"Hey, Jersey." He stepped forward with an outstretched hand and, to Cara, a painfully familiar grin. "Good to see you again."

"Of course it would be you," Cara murmured, and turned off her flashlight.

He laughed out loud good-naturedly, his hand still aimed at hers. Reluctantly, she took it.

"You know each other?" Des joined them under the canopy of the marquee. "When did you have time to meet anyone?"

"We met last night." Cara added, "Briefly."

"But we didn't meet properly. Joe Domanski."

"Cara McCann." She tugged her hand from his grip. "So you're Barney's friend's grandson."

"Yup. Your aunt called this morning and asked me to stop by and take a look at the old place, see if we could figure out what it would take to fix it up. I have to admit I've always wanted to see what's inside. Sorry to be a little late," he added. "I had to pick up some supplies for a job I'm working on."

He turned to Des and Allie and asked, "So, are you all from Jersey, too?"

"You think I look like I'm from *New Jersey*?" Allie frowned.

"Montana, by way of Los Angeles," Des said. "Allie's from California."

"Why would you even ask if I'm from New Jersey?" Allie still appeared offended.

"Because he thinks he's funny, apparently," Cara said.

"So what was all the screaming about?" he asked.

"You heard that all the way out here?" Cara grimaced.

He nodded. "What happened in there?"

"A mouse—" Des began but Cara cut her off.

"A *rat* ran across my foot. It was huge," Cara told him.

He held his hand apart by about a foot. "'Bout this big?"

"Bigger." Cara moved his hands apart.

"I should have expected this." He shook his head slowly, a grim look on his face.

"What? You should have expected what?" Cara asked warily.

"You probably have a big ol' infestation of 'em." He looked at the building. "You're going to need an exterminator who has experience getting rid of them. Not too many have been successful in the past, but maybe you'll get lucky. I bet there are generations of 'em here."

"What?" Cara asked. "Generations of *what*?"

"Pocono Raceway rats." His expression was sober, but the twinkle in his eyes gave him away.

"I think the only rat here is you." Cara's eyes narrowed. She wanted to smack him. "You made that all up. I know about the Pocono Raceway. The Pocono Five Hundred, whatever they call that race."

Joe laughed.

"I thought maybe the Phantom of the Opera was chasing you, the way you were screaming and came running out."

"You're not funny, Joe."

"Hey, if you lose it like that over a little ol' rat, you might want to rethink what you're doing here."

"What did Barney tell you?" Cara still felt like punching the guy, but he'd had his little laugh. Now it was time to get to work. She could be professional even if he was determined to act like a juvenile.

"She said that her three nieces had inherited the theater from their father and they were here in Hidden Falls to restore it," he said. "And that since none of you have construction experience, you needed someone to oversee the operation, and she thought maybe that someone could be me."

"Why you?" Des asked.

"I guess because she's known me all my life and knows she can trust me and that I'm one hell of a contractor." Joe looked Cara in the eye and added, "I'm flattered she's willing to trust me with her family legacy."

"Perhaps she isn't aware that you have an eighth-grade sense of humor," Cara said.

"She probably assumes I've outgrown it."

"It's not like Barney to miss something so obvious," Cara replied.

They stared at each other for about ten seconds.

"So, there are a couple of issues that are immediately apparent." Cara went into business mode. "Obviously, we'll need an exterminator and an electrician."

"I imagine the electricity was cut a long time ago. But we can get that turned back on for you," he said.

"I can call the power company myself. I'm just going to need to know when it's safe to do that. What we need from you is the name of a good electrician to make sure the wiring is good, that sort of thing."

"Mack Williams," Joe replied. "I can give him a call if you like, see when he can take a look. He's the best around. I use him on all my jobs."

"Good. Please ask him if he could swing by." Cara had already decided to run the name past Barney, but if Joe used him, given all the faith Barney had in him, Mack Williams was probably the right choice.

"Do you have time to let me take a quick look inside?" Joe was gazing past the three women into the building.

"Sure." She hoisted her big flashlight.

"I have a bigger light in my truck. Give me a minute and I'll get it."

All three women watched him walk to the truck.

"He is *hot*," Des said under her breath. "Great rear view."

"He's a jerk," Cara said.

"Not my type, but yeah, great buns. All in all, I have to say he's put together quite nicely." Allie turned to Cara. "What makes him a jerk?"

"It's a long story," Cara replied.

"I can't wait to hear it." Des poked her between the shoulder blades.

Joe jogged back and Cara led them into the building. They gave him the tour they'd already taken.

"There's really a lot to do here. I mean, painting, carpets, lights, ceiling, seating, and that's just scratching the surface." Joe took off his baseball cap, smoothed the hair off his face, and put the cap back on. "You sure you want to take this on?"

"As if we have a choice," Allie said dryly.

Cara and Des ignored her. "Yes," they both replied.

"Well, you're right to get the electricity up and running first thing," Joe said. "Once we have light, we can evaluate the general condition of the building and see what it's going to take to not only repair it but bring it up to code. Then there are the mechanics— beside the electric, there's plumbing, HVAC—though I'm pretty sure the AC part is academic. The roof, the foundation, and the structural integrity of the building need to be assessed by an engineer."

"The sooner we get going on this the better," Cara said as they returned to the lobby.

Joe took a 360 look around and whistled softly. "This is going to be a major project, no doubt about that. But oh, mama, when it's done . . ." He shook his head, contemplating the end result. "It's gonna be something else."

"At least we agree on that," Cara said.

"I'll bet we'd agree on a lot of things."

"You'd probably lose that one. Back to business, sir."

"Right. Just so you know, this isn't going to happen overnight. No way right now to say how long, though. I won't be able to give you a ballpark number for the overall renovation until we can get the mechanics worked out. After we get the building secured, then we can look at the details—the painting, the carpet, the light fixtures, that sort of thing. Like I said, it's not going to happen overnight."

"Can you give us estimates as you go along?" Des paused in her note taking. "You know, after the electrician is finished, then maybe someone to look at the roof, then the foundation. Whatever order you think, but ask them to prepare their estimates and give them to us as you get them?"

"I'll ask each of the contractors to do that, sure."

"We'd appreciate it." Des turned to Cara and Allie. "We're going to have to budget the expenses. If we can keep a running tally, we'll be better able to do that."

"Agreed." Cara nodded.

"Can you call your electrician today and get back to me?" Cara headed toward the front door, following her beam of light. "And I guess we need to agree on what role you'll play. Barney thought maybe you could be the point person for the renovation. Help us find the subs, make sure they're all doing what they're supposed to be doing, not overcharging us."

"Like a project manager?" he asked.

"I guess that's what you call it." Cara thought for

a moment. Pete could probably work up a contract for them. "And there should be a contract between you and us. You should think about what you want—money-wise—for the job. Assuming you want to work on this with us."

"I wouldn't miss this opportunity. The Sugarhouse is legendary. Every contractor around is going to want to be part of this." Joe smiled. "And besides, if Barney wants me, I'm all in."

They walked back into the gray day, and Cara put her bag down on the ground and closed the door.

"Des, do you still have the key?" she asked.

"Right here." Des took the key from her pocket and relocked the door.

"Wouldn't there have been a ticket booth?" Allie was saying. "Every theater I've ever seen had a ticket booth outside, before you go into the lobby."

"I'm sure there would've been," Joe agreed. "It would've been somewhere right around here, I'm guessing."

"Maybe it was taken inside and put downstairs or somewhere in the back of the house," Allie suggested. "How 'bout we look for it next time? I've had enough darkness and dust for one morning, and I'm exhausted just thinking about everything that has to be done here."

"We didn't get to see the balcony," Des reminded her.

"So next time we'll find the stairway that leads up," Allie said. "I'm done for the day, and apparently Cara is, too, since she's putting the board back up."

Joe stood with his hands on his hips, watching Cara replace the sheet of plywood over the door.

"What are you doing?" he asked.

"I'm going to put this back so the stained glass doesn't get vandalized and so that no one gets into the theater," she said without turning around. She leaned down and took the screwdriver from her bag, then proceeded to retrieve the screws from her pocket. She could feel Joe's eyes on her as she replaced the first screw.

"Hold up there," he told her. "I have a better idea."

Joe went to his truck and opened the cab door. Moments later, he returned.

"Here you go." He held up the item he'd brought with him. "Battery screw gun."

He turned it on and went to work replacing the remaining screws as Cara passed them to him. In less than five minutes, the plywood was back in place.

"Bet you wish you had one of these babies." He held the screw gun up to Cara.

"It does seem pretty efficient."

"I'd be happy to teach you how to use it sometime." He put his head down and whispered, "If you promise not to call me a jerk again."

"I . . ." Cara grimaced. *Crap.*

"Most people get to know me before they call me a jerk." He smiled, then resumed his normal speaking voice so Des and Allie could hear. "I've left my crew alone long enough this morning, so I need to get moving."

"Thanks for stopping by." Cara started to turn to walk toward the curb, and her car.

"Cara, what's your number? So I can call you about the electrician." Joe held his phone in his hand.

"You already have Barney's number, right?"

"Just in case I can't get her." He stood with the phone in his hand, waiting.

She gave him her cell number and watched him tap it into his phone.

"Thanks." He put the phone back into his pocket and started toward his truck. "Des, Allie—nice meeting you both. I'm sure we'll be seeing a lot of each other. Cara, I'll be in touch."

"I bet he will be," Des teased after Joe had driven away.

Cara shrugged. "He wants the work, and I told him to get back to me."

"He could have asked for my number, or Allie's," Des persisted. "I bet you hear from him and it won't have anything to do with his fancy tools."

"Ah, there you are." Barney, dressed in dark jeans and a dark blue sweater under a tan corduroy jacket, came into the plant-filled conservatory where Des and Allie had been admiring the flowers, her handbag in one hand and a spray bottle filled with water in the other. "I'm so glad you're enjoying my little oasis."

"Barney, I've seen pictures of conservatories but I've never been in one." Des looked around the room at the many plants her aunt nurtured. "It's like a tropical paradise in here. I've never seen so many orchids in one place. They're spectacular. Which one is Lacy again?"

Barney had given her nieces the rest of the house tour earlier that morning, and Des had been totally captivated not only by the conservatory and its many plants, but by the fact that Barney had named many of her leafy friends.

"Lacy is that lovely cymbidium there on the end table. She's seven years old now, and still pumping out flowers, bless her. Which reminds me: Would one of you mist the ferns for me so I'm not late? I'm having lunch with some of the girls from bunco at the Good Bye. Anyone want to come along, meet some of the locals?"

"What's the Good Bye?" Des asked. "And I'll mist the plants for you."

"The Green Briar Café. Locals call it the Good Bye." Barney handed the spray bottle to Des, who placed it on a nearby table. "Story is that traditionally, that's where you'd go to break up with your significant other."

"So if your boyfriend said, 'I'll meet you at the café for dinner,' you knew you were being dumped?" Allie raised an eyebrow.

"So they say." Barney nodded.

"Then why would you go?" Allie made a face.

Barney laughed. "Some might not. Some might, just to see what the excuse is."

"Well, having been dumped myself, I think I'd

pass." A mug of coffee in hand, Cara came in and sat in one of the white wicker chairs. "You look nice, Barney."

"Thanks. I do clean up every now and then. After having had to dress up every day for twenty years, I like to be casual. Of course, some days I'm more casual than others, but I've earned that right."

"You certainly have," Des agreed.

"There's still chicken soup in the fridge, and salad fixings. Maybe even a few of Cara's brownies left for you girls for lunch. And while you're all sitting here, you might want to think about turning in those rental cars. I have a car that you can drive when I'm not using it, so keeping the rentals is a waste of money. Just my opinion, of course. I have my cell with me if you think of anything you need from downtown."

"Thanks, Barney," the three yelled in chorus after her.

"If you're worried about turning in your rentals and not having a way around, I have my car here. You're welcome to use it anytime," Cara offered.

"Thanks. I might do that. Barney's right—why waste money on a rental?" Des said thoughtfully.

"I'll leave my keys on the wall with Barney's. Just don't bring it back with the tank empty so that I don't have to deal with the gas-pumping thing again," Cara said.

"What's the big deal about pumping gas?" Allie asked.

"I don't know how to pump gas. In New Jersey, only the attendants can do that. It's the law. So I never learned."

"Seriously?" Allie snorted. "Even I know how to pump gas."

"Well, then, maybe you can teach me." Cara took a sip of coffee, then put the mug down and related the story of how she'd met Joe Domanski the night before.

The cushion on the chaise was thick and comfy and Des settled into it. "Either of us would be happy to teach you, Cara. It's really easy."

"Thanks. It doesn't look that hard, but I felt like the dumbest person on the planet last night."

"So we'll find a gas station out of town where you can practice. Just in case Joe is around."

"I appreciate it, Des. Of course, we can always walk into town and back. It isn't that far," Cara pointed out. "We can save some money and get exercise at the same time. Win-win."

"Not as good as a spin class," Allie grumbled. "And in case no one's noticed, it's cold outside."

"It'll get warmer. It's only March." Cara opened her notebook and shuffled things around in her bag, searching for a pen. "So I thought maybe we should start making some lists. Like what we need to do and who's going to do what."

"Well, basically, Joe's going to take care of who's doing what." Allie brushed aside the question.

"No, I mean, someone's got to be riding shotgun on that whole construction project. And someone needs to be in charge of the money, keep track of what we're spending, writing the checks." Cara sat back against the chair. "I think we need to start to focus our attention on the reason we're here."

"Cara, you're the obvious point person for the construction, since you at least know a hammer from a screwdriver." When Cara nodded her agreement, Des continued. "And I'm really good with money, so I can do that." She turned to Allie. "Unless you want that job . . ."

"Please. Do your thing." Allie waved a hand dismissively. "So Cara does the construction thing with Hottie Joe and Des has the checkbook. What does that leave for me? Because if I don't have a job, it means you don't need me here. And if you don't need me here"—Allie crossed her arms over her chest— "I'm going home."

"You can't leave, Allie. If you leave, no one inherits anything. I don't know about you, but I could use the money," Des said softly.

"Who are you kidding? You've invested every dime you've ever made. And if memory serves, you made one sweet bundle on that TV show of yours." Allie picked a dead leaf off a begonia.

"I worked really hard for everything I earned. And I hated every minute of it."

"Poor you." Allie rolled her eyes.

"What was that like, having your own TV show?" Cara asked, hoping to defuse the situation.

Des sighed. "The truth? I hated it. I never wanted it. I hated the attention and I hated that everywhere I went, people—"

"Yeah, we know. Heard it all a million times before. Poor Des. Had a smash TV show and made a fortune before she hit her teens. 'Everyone looks at me everywhere I go. People are always taking my picture.' Oh, boo-hoo." Resentment wafted off Allie in waves. "Why not just admit that you loved every minute of it? That 'I just wanted to be a regular kid' act grew old a very long time ago."

"Stop it, Allie." Des felt her heart speed up in her chest, the way it always did when she had to talk about that part of her life. "It wasn't an act. I *did* just want to be a regular kid."

"Hey, you don't have to pretend. I'm sure your new *sister* will be impressed when you tell her all about it."

"Allie, not every kid wants to be a TV star," Des said pointedly.

"And some kids do," Allie growled.

"I'm sorry you didn't get that chance. The show wasn't my idea. I did it because Mom made me. I wasn't given a choice." Des tried her best to contain her emotions. "So just stop it." She turned to Cara. "I'm really sorry, but Allie has never forgiven me because our mom pushed me into acting and not her, and she'd rather blame me than Mom."

"Mom pushed you because you were—"

"Drop it, Allie. It's gotten old." Des took a deep breath. "And Cara doesn't care who was or wasn't on TV. Could we talk about the present and what we're going to do about the situation we're in?"

When Allie didn't respond, Des added, "The will is very specific that we all need to be here, that we have to work together, that we have to stay."

"How would Uncle Pete know if I left early?"

Allie turned angry eyes on Des. "Would you rat me out?"

"No, but maybe Barney would."

"What do you think her role is in all this?" Cara wondered aloud.

"I don't know. Maybe it has something to do with the money," Des said, grateful to Cara for helping them to move past the drama.

"You still haven't come up with anything for me to do," Allie reminded them.

"We need someone to be in charge of the design and the décor, inside and out," Cara said. "The Sugarhouse is a historic theater, so we're going to want to restore it back to the way it was. Someone is going to have to do some research on theaters of this era. I looked online after we got back this morning, and I found a lot of information. There's even an organization you can go to for help in finding the right paint and ideas for refurbishing the seats and the curtains for the stage and, well, just about everything you need to restore a theater like this one. They also have guidelines on how to best use the theater once it's been renovated and—"

"Not our problem," Allie interrupted her. "Nowhere did the will say anything about what happens to the place after we restore it. It just said we had to do it. Since I have to be here and I can't leave without someone getting their panties in a twist, I'll be in charge of design. It doesn't sound very difficult."

"I'll email you the links for everything I found and you can decide if the information there is relevant."

"Thanks." Allie fell quiet.

"I'll bet the library here in town has some information. Maybe old newspapers that covered the theater opening," Allie said, breaking the silence a few minutes later. "And somewhere there have to be some photographs. Barney mentioned some old photo albums, and she also said that her grandmother and her mother never threw anything away, and that she put tons of stuff up in the attic. I'll ask her when she gets back from lunch."

"The Good Bye Café," Des mused. "So how do you set that date up? 'Honey, let's have dinner at the café tonight'? With a reputation like that, you'd have to know something was afoot."

Allie turned to Cara. "Did your husband really dump you?"

"Yes, he did." Cara nodded.

"Did he tell you over dinner?"

"Actually, yes. I think he figured if we were in a public place, I wouldn't make a scene."

"Did you?" Allie asked.

"No. He knew me well. We were in a restaurant in the town where I grew up and it was packed with people I've known all my life. He knew I'd never put them in a position to be embarrassed for me."

"You're way more considerate than I am," Allie said.

Cara shrugged.

"So what did he say?" Allie pulled one leg up under her.

"Allie, stop." Des cringed. She couldn't imagine asking someone that. "It's none of your business."

Allie feigned innocence. "Just trying to be sisterly. Isn't that the whole point of all this?"

"It's intrusive," continued Des. "Maybe Cara doesn't want to talk about it."

"I don't mind, Des, but thanks." Cara waved off Des's concern. "He said, 'I don't really know how to tell you this, but I've fallen in love with someone else and I want a divorce. I'm going to marry *her*.'"

Even Allie was shocked. "What a callous . . . How long were you married?"

"Four years."

"That's horrible, Cara," Des sympathized. "I'm so sorry."

"Oh, that's not the worst part." Cara's eyes narrowed. "The woman he was leaving me for?"

"Don't tell me you knew her." Allie was clearly caught up in the drama.

"Lifelong friend since grade school. She was one of my bridesmaids."

"No!"

"The bitch." Allie shook her head. "I always said, never trust your friends with your guy."

"Did he marry her?" Des asked.

"The wedding is in a couple of weeks, actually. They wanted to get married before the baby is born in May."

"Oh my God, he knocked her up?" Allie's eyes grew even wider. "That's just . . . God, I hate men. Where are the brownies?"

Des sat back and watched Allie and Cara bond over being divorcées. She'd figured Cara had been married, since her last name wasn't Hudson, and, since she hadn't mentioned a husband or child, had assumed she was DNC—divorced, no children. As far as she knew, Allie's husband hadn't left her for another woman, but still, she heard the depth of pain in both her sisters' voices. Besides the fact that she'd never been married, Des knew she'd never felt deeply enough about anyone to have married him. She'd come close to considering it once or twice, but never close enough. She wondered what it felt like to care that much about someone that they could inflict the kind of pain she saw on Cara's face. Just as well she'd never fallen that hard for anyone, Des reminded herself. She didn't need that kind of drama in her life. And look at Allie. She'd never been the nicest person, but since Clint divorced her she'd become bitter and bitchy. She looked from Cara to Allie and back again. Look what love had done to them.

And then there was the fine example of wedded bliss set by her parents.

Allie's phone buzzed and she looked at the screen. Her face lit up. "It's Nikki. I'm going to take this. . . ." On her way out of the room, Allie turned to Cara and said, "You didn't have children?"

When Cara shook her head no, Allie told her, "My daughter's the only good thing that came out of the last fifteen years of my life. I'd do it all again, just to have her."

Allie left the room, her "Hi, sweetheart. Yes, I'm here. Wait till I tell you about this fabulous house . . ." trailing after her.

"She's a royal pain sometimes, but she's a great mom. A much better mom than ours ever was. Nikki is Allie's whole world. She's a good kid. I haven't seen her since the divorce." Des picked up the mister that she had set on the table earlier and sprayed water on the ferns. "I understand Clint's put Nikki in a very posh private school. I don't know if that experience is good for her or not."

"If she's that good a kid, the school she goes to shouldn't change that," Cara said.

"I don't know, what with peer pressure . . ." Des shrugged. "Who knows what's influencing her now? I do know that Allie was very good with her."

"Maybe I'll get to meet her. We're going to be here a long time. If Allie and her daughter are that close, Allie isn't going to want to be apart from her until this project is done," Cara reasoned.

"I hadn't thought about it, but you're right. Nikki's my only niece and I adore her." Des paused. "You know, she's your niece, too."

Cara nodded. "The thought just occurred to me. My only, as well. I wonder what she'll think of me."

"Well, God knows what Allie might have said."

"True. I can tell she still isn't happy about me, but at least we're on speaking terms."

"I suspect she isn't happy about much in her life right now. I think the divorce was harder on her than she lets on."

"Maybe getting involved with the theater will be good for her, give her something else to focus on."

"Good idea you had, to have her in charge of the

design and the décor of the place. I could tell she liked it."

"Well, obviously I don't know much about her, but she looks like someone who has style and good taste and would know how to do what that place is going to need on the interior, and if she doesn't know, she'll learn. I think I'll go upstairs and put some of my things away. I was too tired last night and we got up so early this morning."

"Yeah, that's some bedside manner Barney has." Des dropped her voice to imitate their aunt. "'Girls! Girls! Your contractor will meet you at the theater in an hour. Better get up now if you want coffee and some breakfast before you go.'"

"Not bad for only knowing her for twenty-four hours," Cara said as she headed upstairs.

Des finished misting the plants that Barney had mentioned, all the while wondering what to do with herself for the rest of the afternoon.

If she were back in Montana, she might be working with a new rescue dog. It had been years since she'd been without a dog, and she missed the quiet companionship, that sense of knowing she wasn't alone. That something depended on her, that she mattered. She wondered if there was a shelter here in town where she could volunteer. Surely writing checks and keeping after the money wasn't going to be a full-time job, and she wasn't one to sit idly, waiting for something to do.

Des stood at the French doors and looked out into the woods that lay beyond the yard. Were they part of the Hudson property? She went outside and started down the steps, but the wind all but blew her off, and she wasn't wearing her coat. Giving up on the idea of a walk in the woods, Des went back into the house.

If she couldn't explore outside, she might as well become better acquainted with the inside. The library would be the perfect place to start. Somewhere on all those shelves she was sure to find the perfect book to curl up with in one of those big, cushy leather chairs.

Short logs and kindling had been stacked on the hearth in the library, and after checking to make certain the flue was open, Des arranged a few sticks and three logs in the firebox and searched for matches. She found a mechanical starter on the mantel and used it to light the logs. Once the fire was burning nicely, she searched the bookshelves, hoping something would strike her fancy. Apparently Barney's reading tastes leaned heavily toward suspense, since several shelves were packed with recent thrillers. Remembering that her father had liked them as well, she selected a Michael Connelly novel and, after giving the fire a poke, settled into the nearest chair.

The house was quiet, and it again occurred to her how much she missed having a dog around. She opened the book and began to read, but she'd barely gotten through the first several pages when she recalled something an old would-be suitor had said. Funny how she'd remembered his words, but not his name.

"I think the dogs are just substitutes for whatever it is you're missing in your life," he'd said. "Ever asked yourself who or what you're trying to replace?"

In a huff, she'd left the restaurant where they'd been having dinner and taken a cab home. He'd called several times after that night, twice leaving an apology on her voicemail, but she'd written him off the moment those words had left his mouth.

At the time, it hadn't occurred to her to wonder if maybe he hadn't been onto something.

She placed the book upside down on her lap and watched the flames flicker across the top log, knowing that if someone asked that same question of her now, she'd have an answer.

Not her mother, who'd neglected her except when she could use her to further her own interests.

Not her father, who, though he'd loved her, was always jetting here and there, and who had, as she'd so recently learned, led a double life.

It was Allie, the big sister, whose attention had always been so elusive. Allie, whose companionship she'd sorely craved for as long as she could remember. Allie, whose approval and love Des had never been able to earn.

And it was Allie who, even now, barely gave her a second thought. Allie who'd never been able to get past her jealousy to love her younger sister. Des would have given up everything if it would've made Allie happy, if it would have made Allie love her.

They should have been best friends, should have depended on each other when it became apparent

Nora wasn't dependable and their father was so rarely at home. They should have cared more for each other. They should have been more like sisters and less like adversaries.

Had there been times when Des might have fanned those flames when she could have put them out? If she were to be truthful, she'd have to admit maybe the blame for the ongoing tension wasn't all on Allie's shoulders.

Des wiped the wetness from her cheeks with the back of her hand.

Maybe now that we're living together under the same roof for the first time in years, and we're working on something toward a common goal, maybe now we'll get to know each other as adults. Maybe Allie can find her way past the old bitterness and put it aside, at least enough so that we can love each other the way sisters are supposed to.

Maybe . . .

Des stared into the flames for a moment more, then opened the book and tried to find her place, but her mind wasn't on reading. She closed the book, returned it to the shelf, and shut the fireplace doors. She turned out the light and made her way upstairs. Standing outside Allie's door, she raised her hand to knock, but heard her sister's laughter as she chatted with Nikki on her phone. Des dropped her hand, went to her room, and quietly closed the door behind her.

CHAPTER FIVE

The early-morning air was cool and crisp and held a whiff of the pines that stood sentinel at the very end of the backyard where the dense woods began. Cara had debated which way to go on her first early-morning run in Hidden Falls: along the sidewalks that led through the town, or down the path that led through the woods.

The sound of a door closing had awakened her at dawn, and it had taken Cara a moment to remember that she was in the house where her father had grown up, and not the little house she'd inherited from Susa in Devlin's Light. She'd gotten out of bed and looked out the window in time to see Barney stride across the street to join up with one of her walking buddies. Fully awake and never one to crawl back into bed once she was up, she bent at the waist hoping to relieve the stiffness in her back. She'd never gone this long without some sort of exercise, and she knew exactly how to work out the kinks.

She unrolled the yoga mat she'd tucked into her suitcase and went through her usual morning routine. Twenty minutes later, she felt better but still needed more. She changed into a pair of shorts and a sweatshirt and dug around in her gym bag for her running shoes. Sitting on the lone chair in her room, Cara tied the shoes and tucked her phone into the pocket of her shorts, then eased open the door leading to the hall. Descending the steps as quietly as possible, she hesitated for a moment before heading out the back door.

Once outside, Cara jogged toward the opening between the trees. A thick layer of pine needles, slick with dew, covered the ground, and she proceeded slowly, with a bit of caution, until the pines gave way to hardwoods that had yet to leaf out. The path snaked through the woods, and once she felt the ground hard beneath her feet, she increased her speed until she found her normal stride. It was a quiet, peaceful morning. Overhead birds called to each other and the temperature was perfect for a comfortable run. Before long, Cara felt her shoulders and neck begin to relax. Around another curve, the path began a steady incline, and what had been an easy slope became a slightly more challenging hill. Where once trees lined the path there were now large rock formations, and the bird chatter had been drowned out by something else. She stopped on the path, her breath coming in gasps that escaped her mouth in white puffs, and tilted her head to identify the sound. After a moment, she smiled. What she heard was falling water.

The last thousand feet were killers. Accustomed to running on the flat macadam of the streets of Devlin's Light, Cara had to work harder to maintain her pace on the unfamiliar incline of Hidden Falls, but she made it to the top of the hill. The noise of the water had grown louder with every step, and the vegetation that grew along the path was thicker, but through the dense branches she could see the mist that rose from the rocks over which water rolled down into a pond twenty feet below.

Cara knelt on a boulder the color of gunmetal and leaned forward to peer over the side. As waterfalls go, this was not one of the formidable affairs seen in movies—more of a spill than a rush—but it was breathtaking. The trees were still bare in mid-March, but she could envision how they might look once they leafed out and ferns grew along the water's edge and the mountain laurel bloomed. Were these the falls, hidden deep in the dense wood, that gave the town its name? She sat and watched until the dampness from the boulder seeped through her shorts and caused her bones to chill. Pleased to have made the discovery on her own, Cara eased herself up and took one last look before making her way back to the path.

The run downhill was easier than the run up. She slowed her pace when pine needles once again replaced bare dirt, and by the time she reached the back porch she was walking, her breath once again labored. She stretched for a moment while she cooled off, then went inside and poured a glass of water. Leaning against the sink while she drank, she let her eyes settle on the opposite wall, where a faded green teapot-shaped clock marked the passing of time with loud clicks as the second hand swept past numerals painted in a fancy script. Her eyes still on the clock, Cara finished the water in fourteen seconds, then rinsed the glass and placed it on the counter before heading upstairs for a hot shower.

By the time she came back down in comfy sweats, her damp hair in a high ponytail, Des was working on a bowl of Cheerios, Allie was pouring the last of the one percent milk into a coffee mug, and Barney was at the stove, working over something in the frying pan.

"I guess you had some sleep to catch up on today. You're the last one down," Barney greeted Cara. "Coffee?"

"I'd love some." Cara helped herself. "And actually, I was up early enough to hear you leave, Barney."

"Oh, did I wake you? I'm so—"

"No, no. It was a good thing. I'm used to a lot of physical activity and I've been feeling restless since I left home. I did a little yoga, then went for a run." Cara fixed her coffee and headed to the table. "I followed the path out back that goes through the woods." She took a sip, then sat at the table. "You'll never guess what I found."

"Bigfoot." Allie yawned and began to scroll through her email.

Cara laughed. "I think I found the hidden falls. Am I right?" She looked at Barney for confirmation. Barney nodded.

Allie turned back, her face blank, and Cara said, "You know, like the name of the town? Hidden Falls? Is that still your property, all the way to the top of the hill, Barney?"

"To the top of the hill and down the other side as far as Jackson Street, so yes, the falls are on our property. If you found them, you went quite a ways." Barney took her seat at the table, a plate of scrambled eggs and toast in her hands. "That's quite a climb. Eggs, Cara?"

"No thank you," Cara declined. "I had no idea where I was going, but the trail kept going up, so I had to see where it ended. I got almost to the top and I heard water splashing. When I got to the clearing and looked out over the rocks . . . there it was." She sighed. "Beautiful. You two have to see for yourselves."

"Ahhhh . . . that'd be a no for me, thank you, but feel free to take a picture." Allie never raised her eyes from her cell. "I didn't come equipped for mountain climbing."

"Well, it's technically a hill," Barney told them. "A steep one, though, to be sure. Cara, I'm tickled that you made it all the way up. My brother and I used to love that place." She stared out the back window, and Cara wondered if Barney might be watching for the children she and Fritz had once been.

"When your dad and I were kids, it was the big thing to go up there and dive off the rocks into the pool. I guess kids still think that's pretty cool, 'cause every summer I have to chase a bunch of them out. The fall is only about nineteen, twenty feet or so from top to bottom, and the pool is deep enough to dive into from that height, but you can get hurt real bad. Especially if you don't know the layout of the pool, where the hidden rocks are and so on."

Something in Barney's expression prompted Cara to ask, "Was anyone ever hurt, falling from the top?"

"Just once. And that was an accident. A slip off the rocks." Barney pushed her plate aside as if she'd suddenly lost her appetite.

"How long ago was that?" Des asked.

"Long enough that people don't even talk about it anymore." Barney picked up her pen and a small notepad that had been off to the right of her plate. Changing the subject, she asked, "Who wants what from the market?"

"I'm fine with whatever you like, Barney," Cara told her.

"No, you're not. You've barely eaten a thing since you arrived." She slid the paper and pen over to Allie and said, "Write down something you like for breakfast. Brand, flavor, whatever. Then pass it along to the other two."

Allie put down her phone, picked up the pen, and wrote something, then held up the paper for Barney to read.

"Yogurt? Could you be more specific?" Barney

frowned. "Know how many kinds of yogurt are in the market these days? There's low-fat. No-fat. Organic. Greek. Fruit. Plain. Chocolate, vanilla, and strawberry."

"Good point." Allie lowered her head and wrote a few words before passing the paper to Cara.

Cara glanced at what Allie had written. "Low-fat Greek yogurt. Plain or blueberry." She looked up at Allie and said, "You know they add a lot of sugar and some other questionable artificial things to make up for the lack of flavor when they take out the fat, right? And that the latest research says that fat is actually good for you?"

Ignoring Cara, Allie reached for the paper and added artificial sweetener and one percent milk to the list before giving it back to her.

Cara shook her head and wrote down half-and-half and raw sugar, then paused to raise her eyes to look at the others. "I can make granola if anyone else would eat it besides me. The recipe makes a truckload." She glanced from face to face. Only Allie didn't nod.

"I'd love to try it," Des told her.

"Me too." Barney nodded. "Write down what you need."

Cara started to write down the ingredients. "My mom used to make it all the time."

"Why does that not surprise me?" Allie muttered.

"What's that supposed to mean?" Cara put down the pen.

"It means I'd expect nothing less than homemade granola from someone who grew up in a commune."

"I can't tell for sure if you're being deliberately snotty or if you're just plain rude." Des glared at Allie.

"Hey, it's okay. My mom *was* born in a commune." Cara smiled wryly. "The granola is great on yogurt, by the way."

"Did she make that, too?" Allie asked dryly.

"She did when she could get raw milk." Cara bent her head and went back to writing her list.

"Cara, I didn't know that about your mother. Fritz never said," Barney told her. "Are your grandparents still there? Did your mother have siblings?"

"My grandparents moved on a long time ago. My mom didn't really keep in touch with them, nor they with her. The last we heard, they were out west. New Mexico, Arizona, California—who knows where they are or even if they are still alive? As for my mom having siblings—she said all the kids in the commune were raised as brothers and sisters. So if any of them were her actual blood siblings, she never really knew." Cara couldn't help but feel a touch of regret. Those gathered around the table at that moment represented her only known living relatives. "So maybe I have cousins somewhere." She shrugged. "I doubt I'll ever know."

Cara's phone began to ring in her pocket. She took it out and looked at the unfamiliar number.

"This is Cara McCann."

"Cara, good morning. It's Joe Domanski. I hope it's not too early to call."

"What's up?"

"I'm here at the theater, waiting for the electrician, and just realized I don't have a key."

"If you'd let me know, I could have met you there."

"I just got the call from the electrician that he was free about fifteen minutes ago. If I'd known earlier, I would have told you."

"I'll be down in five minutes, ten at the most."

"Great. See you then."

"Joe's at the theater. He's going to be showing the electrician through the building this morning, but he doesn't have a key." She stood and asked, "Anyone want to come with me while I run the key down there?"

"I'm sure he'd rather see you than either of us," Des told her. "Besides, I have a meeting with the bank this morning to sign the signature card for the checking account."

"Allie?"

"Don't look at me. I'm going to try to find a nail salon to fix this broken nail." Allie held up her left index finger.

Cara rolled her eyes and rinsed out her mug.

"Barney, is there a spare key that we could give Joe?" she asked.

"No, but you could have one made down at the hardware store. It's in the middle of the block across from the Good Bye," Barney told her.

"I'll do that. That way, he won't have to call me whenever he wants to show someone something." Cara started for the door.

"He'll just find another excuse," Des teased. When Cara made a face, Des laughed. "You just remember where you heard it first."

When Cara arrived at the theater, Joe and a man who looked to be in his fifties were standing out near the curb, talking.

"Here she is," she heard Joe say. To her, he said, "Thanks for coming out so early."

"No problem. I'm an early riser." Cara gestured to the door. "Glad you got the boards down."

"Thought it'd save some time." Joe pointed to the man standing next to him. "Say hello to Mack Williams. Best electrical man in three counties. Mack, meet Cara."

"It's five counties, not that I'm keeping track." Mack smiled and extended a beefy hand in Cara's direction. His hair was silvery gray and long enough to pull back into a ponytail. He wore jeans and a navy tee and carried a clipboard. "So you're Fritz's girl."

"One of them, yes." She shook the proffered hand and then let it drop.

"How many are there?"

"There are three of us." Cara smiled. "That I know of."

"You're one of Nora's girls, then."

"No, that would be my half sisters."

Mack looked confused, so Cara went for the short answer. "My dad was married after Nora passed away."

"I remember when she passed. Hadn't heard he remarried. But nice to meet you, all the same."

Joe gestured for Cara to unlock the door.

"Barney said they make keys at the hardware store." Cara unlocked the door. "I'll stop there and have one made for you. That way you . . ."

". . . don't have to bother you every time I want to show someone around." He finished the sentence for her as he turned the red Philadelphia Phillies cap backward on his head. His hair spilled across his forehead and there was no looking away from those crystal-blue eyes. The man even had dimples.

Allie and Des were right. The guy was hot. As much as she tried to forget, when she'd walked into the gas station that first night, for a moment, all she saw was Joe. Of course, that was right before he made her feel like an idiot, and his personal stock had fallen big-time. Now, though, with those blue eyes focused on her, his appeal was hard to ignore.

"I was going to say, you wouldn't have to depend on me to open it for you. You're doing us a favor."

"Anything for Barney." Joe moved the board to one side so that they could enter the building. "I think you might want to replace the locks for now. In the future, a good security system will be necessary, but for now, the locks and the board-up will do."

"Good point," she agreed.

"Mind if I go on in?" Mack stood behind them, a large flashlight in his hand.

"Right behind you, buddy." Joe stepped out of the

way to let Mack pass. He, too, carried a large light. "You coming, Cara?"

"Sure."

"Where's the electrical panel?" she heard Mack ask.

"I'm guessing in the basement," Joe told him.

The two men walked quickly, and Cara hustled to keep up, following the streams of light. The last thing she wanted was to be left behind in the cold, dark building.

"Which way to the basement?" Mack asked.

"There's a hallway off to the left behind those arches," Cara said. "The steps are at the end of the hall."

"Makes sense," Mack replied.

"Cara, you still with us?" Joe stopped and turned, and Cara, close behind, walked into his back.

"Sorry. I couldn't see you, just the light."

She was close enough to smell whatever soap he'd used that morning, and it occurred to her that it was a good thing she'd showered after her morning run. Not that it mattered, but still . . .

"Here. Go ahead of me." Joe took her arm and, with one hand on the small of her back, guided her so that she was between the two men. "Just keep your eyes on the light and you should be fine."

The light from Joe's flashlight began to flicker.

"Let me guess. When you were a kid, your idea of a good time at parties was freaking out the girls by turning off the lights and making scary sounds, like in one of those creepy movies."

Joe laughed. "Sorry. I hit the switch by accident.

Mack, you find anything yet?" he called to the electrician, who'd gone on ahead by several steps and was shining his light against the wall.

"Yup. Got the panel right here. Give me a minute. . . ." Mack's light was now trained brightly on the electrical panel. "Huh. What do you know about that? Huh."

"That was two 'huhs,'" Joe said. "Which means . . . what?"

"Means it looks like this thing has been updated a lot more recently than I would've expected. No more than fifteen, twenty years."

"You mean the wiring isn't that old?" Cara went to take a closer look.

"Well, some of it, at least. Much as I can see," Mack told her. "Look here. You got circuit breakers."

"How could that be?" Joe leaned closer to take a look. In doing so, he was so close to Cara's back he was almost leaning on her.

"Beats me." Mack scratched the back of his head. "I expected to find all knob and tube. You know"—he turned to Cara—"the stuff you find in old houses. But this has been updated."

"All? You mean the entire building?" Cara couldn't believe they'd be that lucky.

"Can't say for sure about that. I'll still have to go through the place. Could have more than one box. Nothing would surprise me now, not after seeing this."

"Uncle Pete did say something about someone having bought the building about twenty years ago who was going to renovate it. But he ran out of money and didn't finish what he started. Eventually, my dad bought it back."

"I can give Tommy Mercer a call." Mack closed the panel door. "He was the main man when it came to electrical work around here, up till he retired about seven years ago. I can't imagine anyone else would've been called in to do the work. He'll know the story."

Mack started back toward the steps, Cara and Joe following close behind.

Cara walked between the two lights, following the path they made ahead of her. Once outside, she turned to Joe.

"As soon as Mack gets the electricity up and running, I'll want the exterminator to come in."

"We only have one guy locally, Eddie Waldon. Barney knows him real well. He's really good at what he does." Joe walked with her to her car. "I'll give you a call after I hear what Tommy Mercer has to say. Then maybe Mack can go back through and write up an estimate. I have to warn you, though: Even if most of the knob and tube has been replaced, it's still going to be a big number. You have all the lighting in there that might need to be updated. Spotlights. Floodlights. Footlights. The overhead lights. That chandelier in the lobby is something else."

"I get it," Cara said. "We're not expecting a quick fix."

"Good. I'd hate for you to be disappointed." He took off the baseball cap and ran his hand through his hair. A section flopped onto his forehead, and he tried unsuccessfully to push it back where it belonged. It made him look almost boyish, which she had to admit some might consider adorable.

She took the car keys from her bag. "I'll stop at the hardware store and get that key made for you."

"I'm going there anyway to pick up something for a job. Why don't I have the new one made and I'll drop off yours at the house later?"

"Okay. If you're sure you don't mind." She handed him the key.

"Like I said, I'm headed there anyway." He paused. "Want me to look at a new lock set for that door while I'm there?"

"That'd be great, but Joe—don't you have work to do of your own?"

"Yes." He crossed his arms over his chest. "Why?"

"I feel guilty that we're keeping you from it."

"I've got good crews. I don't need to hang over them every minute to tell them what to do, which is a good thing, since I have two jobs going concurrently right now."

"You're lucky."

"You're telling me." He nodded. "Lucky in many ways. I'm happy to help Barney out in any way I can. There wouldn't be a Domanski Construction if it weren't for her."

Before Cara could ask what he meant, his phone rang. He pulled it from his pocket, looked at the screen, and told her, "One of my guys. I'll get that key made and drop one off to you."

"Thanks, Joe. For everything."

"Sure." He turned away as he answered the call.

As Cara drove back to the house, she made a mental note to call Pete to talk about drawing up a contract for Joe. Joe had already put in several hours of his time, and there'd be a lot more in the future. That comment about owing Barney aside, he should be paid like any professional.

Cara sighed. She hated to be dependent on Joe, but she needed his expertise. Cara was ready and willing to learn all she could, but she wasn't foolish enough to think she could run this job on her own. She needed him, pure and simple.

Allie, Des, and Barney were still seated at the kitchen table when Cara arrived back at the house. She noticed that Barney had changed into a black pencil skirt, tights, and a nice sweater.

"Was the electrician there?" Des asked. "Did you talk to him?"

"I did. It might not be quite as bad as we originally thought." Cara related what Mack had told her and Joe.

"Oh yes." Barney nodded. "Tommy Mercer would know for sure. Douglas Freeman—he was the one who bought the theater from Fritz some years back—had big plans for that place. He did some renovations, as I recall, but his money ran out before he could finish it. Fritz bought it back 'as is'—though unfortunately I don't know how far along Freeman got before his interest waned along with his bank account."

"Speaking of which"—Cara headed for the coffee-pot and poured a mug—"how'd you make out at the bank this morning, Des?"

"Fine. Barney went with me and introduced me to the new bank president. They had the account all set up, so all I had to do was sign the signature cards." Des glanced from Allie to Cara. "You two should stop down and add your names as authorized signees. I realize we decided I'd be in charge of the money, but I think more than one of us should be able to sign."

"Speaking of money, how much is in the account?" Cara asked.

"Sit down. I was just about to tell Allie." Des took a deep breath. "There's a million dollars."

Cara choked on her coffee. Allie stared as if she hadn't heard correctly.

"A million . . ." Cara said.

"U.S. dollars?" Allie asked.

"Yes. One million U.S. dollars." Des's eyes sparkled. "Can you imagine what we can do with all that money?"

"Hold up there, kiddo." Barney made the time-out sign. "Yes, it's a lot of money, but trust me, it's going to go faster than you think. If I were to guess, I'd say the electrical work alone is going to be at least a hundred thousand or better. Think of all the contractors you're going to be bringing in. A million dollars sounds like a heap of money, but believe me when I tell you, it's not an endless stream." She turned to Des. "You're going to have to keep track of every dime, and you're going to have to make very good decisions about where to spend it. If you're careful, and you don't run amok, you should be fine." She took her car keys from the hook near the back door. "A lot of construction loans came across my desk when I was at the bank, and a lot of those projects went south because the owners were careless and ran out of money."

"What if we're really careful and we run out anyway?" Cara asked quietly.

"Well, then I guess you'll have to figure out a way to come up with the additional funding. Maybe you'll need to apply for grants." Barney shrugged. "My best advice is to treat every dollar as if it's your last."

Allie leaned her forearms on the table. "I'm starting to wonder if the three of us shouldn't have just challenged the will and said the hell with the theater."

"Are you crazy? And miss out on all the fun?" Des kicked her under the table.

"I can't tell if you're being serious or not." Allie stared at Des.

"I *am* being serious," Des said. "I think this is going to be a life-changing experience for all of us. Might be the hardest thing any of us ever have to do, but we're going to kick butt, and that building is going to look like new when we're finished with it."

"Des is right," Cara agreed. "We're all going to have to step up: Des with the accounting, me with the construction, and you with the décor."

"At least I got the pretty stuff," Allie said.

"Pretty, but you're going to have to do a lot of research so the renovation is historically accurate," Des reminded her.

"Okay, so Des is going to keep an eye on the money." Allie looked across the table at Des, then glanced at Cara. "So how are we supposed to know if the estimates are accurate, if the prices are in line with what they should be? That's what you're saying, right? That we have to be careful not to overpay for the work we contract for and that we have to make sure we don't hire crooks or incompetents?"

"That's what Joe's going to be doing. He's bringing in the contractors he thinks are right. Contractors he knows personally, people he's worked with in the past and trusts." Cara looked to Barney. "We can trust him, right?"

Barney nodded. "Absolutely. Everyone in town knows him and knows he doesn't put up with any nonsense on his jobs. If he's running the job, none of the subs will try to overcharge. They know if they do, he'll never put them on another of his jobs, and word will get around why."

"I told him I'd call Uncle Pete and have him draw up a contract between the three of us and him."

"Get that done ASAP. Joe will be more than fair when it comes to his compensation." Barney put on her jacket. "Garden club luncheon today, girls. I'll be back around three."

"Barney, Joe said something about not having a business if it weren't for you," Cara said, just as Barney opened the door. "What did he mean by that?"

"Seems if he'd wanted you to know, he'd have elaborated. And apparently he did not, otherwise you wouldn't be asking." Barney stepped outside and closed the door behind her.

"Guess she told you." Allie barely glanced up from checking her email.

"Guess she did." Cara sighed.

Barney was right. It was none of her business. Still, Cara couldn't help but wonder what the relationship was between the young contractor and her aunt. Maybe by the time the project was completed, she'd have figured it out. In the meantime, she needed to talk to Pete Wheeler and get the contract in the works.

Cara made the call, but Pete was in court and she had to leave a message. When she came back downstairs, she found Des and Allie in the small sitting room. Des was holding up a pillow on which an elaborate flower garden had been needlepointed.

"Our grandmother made this," Des was saying.

"Our grandmother who we never got to meet because our aunt wouldn't let our father come home," Allie said.

"She told him not to come back till he fessed up. I'm not so sure she was wrong," Des told her. "What he was doing was wrong."

"She'd have been right, if it had worked," Allie said.

"She was right whether it worked or not," Des pointed out.

"It's hard to imagine that Barney actually thought

that giving him an ultimatum would work." Cara sat on a chair with red velvet cushions. "I'd have thought she would've known him better than that."

"Yeah, well, we all thought we knew him," Allie reminded them. "Look how wrong we all were."

"I don't think we were wrong so much as he just didn't give any of us the whole story," Cara said.

"One thing I don't understand." Allie turned to Cara. "Why did you have to do all the work on your studio yourself? Why didn't you just hire people to come in and do it for you? I'm sure Dad would have picked up the tab."

"I wasn't raised like that. I guess you'd have had to know my mom," Cara said. "Money never meant very much to her. We had a very modest home in our little town, and she never would have moved out of that house or out of Devlin's Light. It was more important to her that I learn to do things for myself and stand on my own two feet. She had very strong feelings about being where you were meant to be and doing what you were meant to do. She was very happy living her life on her terms, which meant for the most part that she liked to live on what she made in her shop. I guess Dad learned that early on in their relationship, and if he wanted to be with her, he had to respect that. She once told me that in the beginning, he'd wanted to buy up some properties right on the beach, knock them down and build something grand for her, and she was horrified at the very thought."

"Our mom would have been all in," Des said.

"She would have offered to drive the pile driver and knock 'em all down if it meant she had a palace on the beach."

"She wasn't that bad, Des." Allie frowned.

"Sure she was." Des turned to Allie. "Her being our mother, and being dead, can't change the facts. And why would you want to?"

"It's disrespectful to talk about her like that." Allie's phone pinged. She picked it up and appeared to read an incoming text.

"I think it's more disrespectful to try to make her something other than what she was. Mom never backed down from who she was, Allie. She accepted herself with all her faults, and I think we should, too. She was a bitch at times, but there was always a sort of defiance and pride to her bitchiness, like she could take on the world and the hell with what anyone thought."

"She did get that way with Dad," Allie admitted. "Like, if he didn't like the way she was, he could leave."

"And eventually, he did," Des reminded her.

"I always thought she drank to spite him."

"I think she drank because she really, really enjoyed the buzz. The way some people enjoy smoking cigarettes. They know in the long run that it isn't good for them, but they like it so much, they keep doing it anyway," Des said. "I think alcohol was like that for Mom. She just flat-out liked being drunk."

An uncomfortable silence followed. Finally, Des said, "Dad, on the other hand, was so much fun."

"He *was* fun." Allie finished her text and put the phone on the table next to her. "God, the things he used to do, always over-the-top things. You never knew what he was going to do. Birthdays, Christmases—it seemed he tried to top himself every year."

"He'd go for months without calling, then there he'd be with plans for something wonderful," Des said.

"Like plane tickets for the two of you to go somewhere you'd really wanted to go." Allie sighed. "For my sixteenth birthday, we flew to New York and stayed for an entire week in a big suite at the Plaza because I loved *Eloise* when I was younger. You know, the book about the little girl who lived on the top floor of the Plaza Hotel?" She smiled at the memory. "Dad arranged for us to do all the things I loved. We had a private tour of the Met, and I loved it so much that I made him take me back two more times before we came home. We went to the Cloisters and the Museum of Arts and Design. Back then it was called the American Craft Museum. Because I loved clothes, we hit the museum at the Fashion Institute of Technology. I went shopping every day and ordered whatever I wanted for breakfast every morning from room service, and I picked all the restaurants where we ate. We went to the opening of *The Lion King* and went backstage and I met the entire cast. It was fabulous, but the best part was having Dad all to myself for seven whole days." She paused. "Well, that and the fact that he knew how interested I'd become in art, and how badly I wanted to go to the Met, how much it meant to me. I was just starting to play around with watercolors, and for me to see all those incredible paintings? Total inspiration."

"I remember that." Des smiled. "I was so jealous that he took you out of school for the whole week and you came home with all those gorgeous clothes and bags and shoes."

"I hope you're not complaining, because I distinctly remember your sixteenth birthday and the surprise musical guests that showed up." Allie turned to Cara. "Dad had hired a band to play at Des's party, and right in the middle of a set, the band stopped playing and the place went dark, and when the lights went back on . . ."

"NSYNC just picked up where the band had let off. I thought I was gonna die, Cara. Can you imagine? The top boy band maybe of all time, and they were all mine for the night." Des laughed. "I was the envy of all my friends."

"Not to mention your sister," Allie told her. "I had such a crush on Justin Timberlake, and there he was, singing 'Happy Birthday' to you."

"Held my hand while I blew out the candles," Des reminded her.

"There are some things one never quite forgives or forgets," Allie told her.

Her tone was light, but Cara couldn't tell for certain if she was kidding.

"I guess since you lived on the East Coast, Cara, a trip to New York wouldn't have been as special as it was for me." Allie's voice held just a hint of *top that*.

"Did Dad do anything to make your sixteenth birthday special?"

"He took me to the premiere of *Die Another Day*. I was—still am—a huge James Bond fan. And Pierce Brosnan? Yes, please." Cara grinned.

"Oh, we got to go to premieres all the time since we lived in L.A. and Dad represented so many stars." Allie's expression implied that movie premieres were no big deal. "Where did you stay when you were out there?"

"Oh, the premiere wasn't in L.A. It was at the Royal Albert Hall in London. It's one of my favorite memories ever. We walked the red carpet and I got to meet the entire cast." Just thinking about that night made Cara happy. "Halle Berry was there, and Madonna. Oh, and I got to meet the queen."

"The queen." Allie blinked. "You mean the queen of England?"

"Yes. She was very gracious, though I know she had no idea who I was and couldn't have cared less. Still, it was fun."

"What did you wear?" Des wanted to know.

"A long white Stella McCartney gown. Dad had sent her my measurements so that all I needed to do was to show up at her studio and have a few alterations done. She pinned it on me herself. I was black and blue from pinching myself. It was one of the few times Mom gave in to Dad's wanting to spoil me."

"Well, that tops my week in New York," Allie grumbled.

"Hey, this isn't a competition, Allie," Cara protested. "Dad obviously put a lot of thought into giving each of us something special. He tried really hard to give us what we most wanted, and he succeeded. I'd love to have spent a week doing New York with him, but I never did." She turned to Des. "And to have NSYNC serenade me on my birthday? Are you kidding? He knew it was your heart's desire, and he made it happen for you."

Des nodded. "You're right."

Allie stared at Cara. "Still. You got to meet *the queen of England,* wearing Stella McCartney." She stood abruptly. "I'm starving. I'm going to heat up some of Barney's soup."

She picked up her phone and swept out of the room.

Des looked at Cara. "I guess we've been dismissed."

"Looks that way."

"How 'bout we have soup, too?" Des suggested.

"It'll piss her off even more," Cara said.

"Of course it will." Des's grin was pure mischief. "Coming?"

CHAPTER SIX

"Cara, we picked up almost everything on the list for the granola." Des stuck her head into Cara's room, her cheeks red from the chilly March wind. "Barney told me to tell you she's really psyched to try it, so maybe you could make it today and we'll have it for breakfast in the morning. Assuming that the things we couldn't find aren't critical."

"I'll be right down." Cara finished the text she was writing to Darla, which promised photos of the theater as soon as the front had been uncovered. She hit send and then headed for the kitchen.

"We were able to get everything except the brown rice flour, and sorry, but the only rolled oats the store had weren't organic." Barney was just placing the ingredients on the kitchen table.

"That's fine, as long as they're not instant, but I don't know what we can substitute for the rice flour."

"They're the old-fashioned kind. And I picked up

some plain yogurt, too, and some strawberries. I saw a picture of a yogurt parfait that had granola and fruit in it and I thought it looked delicious. Healthy, too, I'm sure."

"Mom used to do that sometimes. She had the prettiest light blue glass dishes." Cara went to the table and looked over the ingredients. "Thank you for getting all this stuff. After you left, I remembered that Mom sometimes used dry powdered milk in her recipe. We'll see how it goes without it. I doubt it'll make that much of a difference."

"There's a new natural foods store right outside of town but they close at two on Fridays. Damn." Barney was visibly aggravated with herself for not thinking of it sooner. "I'll bet they have powdered milk and maybe even the rice flour. Or I can run back to the market to get the powdered milk."

"Thanks, Barney, but it's not necessary. We'll wing it with what we have right here." Cara turned on the oven to preheat it. "Now, I'll need the largest mixing bowl you have."

"Let's see what we have in the butler's pantry." Barney disappeared for a moment and returned with a large bowl. "Will this do?"

"Got anything larger? Even a pot you make soup in. I just need to mix it. Then I'll need cookie sheets to spread it out and bake it on, then something airtight to store it in."

"I have several sizes of soup pots. Come take a look."

Cara followed Barney and glanced at the displays

of silver serving pieces and candleholders behind the glass doors. "I can't imagine what it would be like to live in a time when all of this"—she waved her hand in front of the built-in cabinets—"was used all the time."

"It wasn't so very long ago," Barney told her. "My parents entertained frequently. All the silver you see there was brought out every weekend." She smiled. "It was a very different time, a different way of life." She opened a lower cabinet door and brought out a large pot. "How 'bout this?"

"Perfect," Cara told her.

"And there are baking sheets in the lower cabinet on your left."

Cara sorted through the baking sheets until she found two that she thought would suffice. "These will do nicely."

"Now I'll just have to poke around and see what we can come up with that might be airtight. Why don't you go on and get started? This might take me a few minutes."

"Good idea." Cara gathered her findings and went back into the kitchen.

When Barney emerged from the pantry, she had several large cookie tins in her hands. "Will these do? I use them to store homemade cookies around the holidays. Best I can come up with."

"They'll be great." Cara measured the dry ingredients into the pot, then stirred the mix with a long-handled spoon. "Barney, would it be okay if I poked around in my dad's old room?"

"Sure." Barney opened a drawer for a towel and began to dry the tins. "Any particular reason?"

"I guess I'm hoping to find something that might give me a clue as to who he was." Cara put the pot aside and began to chop the almonds.

"You don't think you know?" Barney appeared mildly confused.

"Not really. I know who he was when he was with Susa and me. At least, I know the man he wanted us to know. The rest of it . . ." Cara shrugged. "I don't think I have a clue."

"What is it you want to know?" Barney asked.

"Who he was when he was younger. When he was a kid. A teenager. I guess I want to see if I can figure out what made him do what he did." Cara mentally checked the recipe and continued to add what she needed.

"Cara, no one can answer that but Fritz, and he had his chance and chose not to take it. You're welcome to go through his room, though there's not much left. He took his clothes and anything that meant something to him a long time ago. Everything else—books, records, that sort of thing—got packed up and sent to the attic years ago."

"What did Dad read when he was a kid?" Des stood in the doorway, apparently having heard the conversation.

Barney put the towel down and pulled a chair from the table to take a seat. "As I recall, mostly adventure-type books. *Treasure Island* and *The Call of the Wild. Around the World in Eighty Days.*"

"He read those to me when I was a child," Cara recalled.

"Me too." Des leaned over the pot of granola and sniffed. "You put cinnamon in. I love the smell of cinnamon. It reminds me of Christmas."

"It doesn't surprise me that he was into adventure books. He always made up stories about finding buried treasures and solving mysteries." Cara smiled at the memory. "Of course, they all starred me as the heroine."

"Funny, he always did the same with us, too. Allie and I were the sisters who traveled the world in a hot-air balloon with our monkey sidekick and a cooler filled with lemonade."

"You had a pet monkey when you were a kid?" Cara asked.

Des made a face. "Please. Our mother never even let us have a goldfish. The monkey was made up."

"God, we had such a menagerie." Cara laughed. "At one point we had two dogs, three cats, a parrot, a goat, and a llama that someone had given my mother in exchange for yoga lessons."

"No wonder Dad fell for her. She sounds like she was so fun," Des said. "He always wanted pets for us. My mother was just too finicky."

"Mine was just the opposite." Cara gave the granola one last stir, then proceeded to spread the mixture onto the sheets. "Barney, you said Dad had some records that got packed up? What kind of music did he listen to?"

"Oh, he had a whole box of old forty-fives. Mostly

early rock and roll. Lots of fifties stuff. Elvis and Chuck Berry and some of those old slow songs they used to play at the school dances." Barney grinned. "Somewhere upstairs there's a red leather case with a whole lot of vintage rock on vinyl and an old record player that we used to keep in the upstairs sitting room because my mother would not have that stuff playing down here on the first floor where someone stopping by might hear it." She paused, the smile still on her face. "We had a cook named Wanda who brought a small radio with her, and on days when my mother wasn't home, she'd plug it in here in the kitchen and turn it up. She taught Fritz and me both to dance right here on this floor."

"I'd love to hear those records," Des said.

"Me too." Cara slid a cookie sheet onto the oven's top rack. The second sheet followed and she closed the door. "I wish we could play them."

"You'll need to find that record player." Barney paused. "I'd start with the attic. That's the most likely place."

"Do you think it still works?" Cara set the timer for twenty minutes.

"Worked fine last time we played it. Of course, that was some years ago, but I can't see any reason why it wouldn't work. Assuming you could find it."

"Okay, so Dad liked to dance and he liked rock and roll. What else?" Cara asked.

"Well, he collected baseball cards, but back in the fifties, who didn't?" Barney thought for a moment before adding, "Oh, and he was athletic. He ran track in high school. He was on a relay team, I seem to recall."

"Any chance his old yearbooks are still around?" Des sat on the window seat, her left foot tucked under her.

"Of course. In the library," Barney told her. "Used to be on the bottom shelf behind that brown leather chair."

"I'll see if they're still there." Des went to search, but she'd barely reached the front hall when the doorbell rang.

"Get that please, Des, since you're right there," Barney called to her.

"Sure."

Cara heard voices, then footsteps in the hall that drew closer.

"Look who stopped by," Des said as she and Joe Domanski came into the kitchen.

"Hey, Joe." Barney beamed as she greeted him. "Come on in. Can we get you a cup of coffee or something? You look chilled."

"Yeah, the winds have picked up and the temperature is dropping. I heard maybe some flurries later tonight." Joe turned to Cara. "Hey, hi."

"Hi." Cara smiled and went to check the granola.

"Was that a yes or a no on the coffee?" Barney asked.

"It was a no, thank you. I can't stay. I told Cara I'd drop off the key to the theater that she gave me this morning after I had a duplicate made." He turned to Cara. "But I bought that new lock set we talked about, so I didn't bother having the dupe made. I'll install the new lock first thing tomorrow but if it's okay with you, I'll hang on to your key to open up in the morning."

"Of course. Thanks, Joe." Cara closed the oven door. "What do we owe you?"

"I left the invoice in the truck but I can—" He stopped and sniffed. "Wow, whatever you're making smells really good."

"Cara's making granola," Des told him.

"That's granola? Really?" When Cara nodded, he said, "Nice."

"Tell you what," Barney continued. "You come back in the morning and we'll feed you breakfast, and you can sample Cara's granola before you install the new lock."

"That'd be great. Thanks." Joe looked at Cara as if for confirmation.

"Sure. There's a ton of it. You're welcome to join us." Her cheeks began to burn just a little, so she turned away. "And you can bring us the invoice for the new lock so we can pay you back."

"Fair enough." Joe kissed the top of Barney's head and half backed out of the kitchen. "I guess I'll see you all in the morning."

"I'll walk you out, son." Barney rose, and she and Joe left the room.

"Deny it all you want, girl, but he has his eye on you." Des grinned. "For a moment, it looked like he didn't see either Barney or me."

"Don't be silly, Des. Barney was the one who got the kiss on the head. They seem pretty close."

"Yeah, what do you suppose that's all about?" Des wondered aloud. "All we know is that his grandmother and Barney are good friends."

"She's probably known him since he was a kid. Sometimes families get really close. . . ."

Barney's footsteps heading back to the kitchen echoed in the hall.

"Nicest boy in town, I swear," Barney announced as she came back into the room.

"He seems to be," Des said, her eyes on Cara.

"Oh, he's had a time of it, that one." Barney nodded. "Turned out better than anyone gave him credit for, that's for sure."

"What does that mean?" Cara turned to her aunt.

"No one had very high expectations for him, that's all. No one but me and his mom and his grandmom, anyway." Barney verbally patted herself on the back. "I never doubted the boy for a minute."

"What's the story?" Cara asked, intrigued.

"Well, I'm not one to gossip, but his father . . ." Barney confided. "He was a piece of work. Inherited a very lucrative business from *his* father. That man, Joe Junior—our Joe is Joe the third; we used to call him J3—drove that company right into the ground."

"Didn't he do a good job?" The timer went off and Cara took the cookie sheets from the oven and placed them on top of the stove.

"He did when he wasn't drinking, which unfortunately wasn't often enough to keep the business afloat," Barney told them. "A wife and three kids, and

Joe Junior couldn't keep himself sober long enough to complete a job. After a time, no one wanted to hire him, and the business tanked."

"It seems to be doing well now. Joe said he had men on a couple of jobs." Cara recalled their conversation at the theater. "He said he didn't mind being late to his jobsites because he had good crews working for him."

"Oh, young Joe brought the business back better than ever, worked his tail off to make it happen. Hardest-working man I know."

"Where's his father now?" Des asked.

"Over in Rose Tree," Barney said dryly.

"What's that?"

"Cemetery." Barney's face darkened. "Drove home from the Bullfrog one night, drunk as a skunk, hit a car in the opposite lane. Just like that, wiped out three lives. His was one of them."

"How long ago?" Cara searched the drawers for a wide spatula.

"About four years ago, I guess. Maybe a little more since Joe took over the business and started building it back up. He was in the army for a while, right out of college." Barney lowered herself into the nearest chair as if suddenly too tired to stand. "I think he'd have liked to have moved on from here, but he had obligations."

Cara was about to ask what obligations kept him in Hidden Falls—did he have a wife, a child?—but Allie had followed her nose into the kitchen, her phone, as always, in her hand.

"Oh, yum! Someone made cookies. They smell awesome."

"Cara made granola," Des told her.

"Doesn't smell like granola to me." Allie went to the stove to check out the cookie sheets. "It smells like"—she sniffed the air—"oatmeal cookies."

"Close enough." Cara scraped the granola with the spatula to form chunks. "If you wait a few minutes you can try it out. It's too hot right now."

"Did I hear the doorbell?" Disregarding Cara's warning, Allie reached for a chunk, then blew on it to cool it before popping it into her mouth. "Tastes like a crunchy cookie. Yum." She nabbed another chunk before heading to the table.

"Joe Domanski stopped to let us know he picked up a new lock for the theater," Barney explained.

"This is really good, Cara." Allie ate the second piece. "I apologize for my skepticism."

"I can't resist." Des took a few chunks off one of the trays. "The smell is so tantalizing."

"Joe thought so, too. He's joining us for breakfast in the morning before he installs the new lock." Barney drifted toward the tray and helped herself to a bit of the granola.

"So Joe the hot contractor is coming for breakfast." Allie sat at the table, cradling her snack in the palm of her hand, and grinned at Cara.

"It's the granola he's coming for, Allie. Just granola." Cara hoped she hadn't sounded as defensive as she felt.

"You keep telling yourself that." Allie smirked.

"God, this stuff is addictive." She went back to the trays, where Des stood picking at the smaller pieces.

"Keep it up, you two, and there won't be anything left for the morning." Cara began to scoop the granola into the tins Barney had set out for her.

"You know who he reminds me of? That super-hot guy on *Game of Thrones*."

"Could you be more specific?" Des tried to shoo Cara away from her hand and Allie looked like she wanted to sneak more granola. "There are only about a thousand guys on that show, several of whom would qualify as super-hot."

"You know who I mean. The hot blond guy who sleeps with his twin sister."

"Who sleeps with his sister?" Barney's head shot up from a note she was writing to herself.

"Jaime Lannister on *Game of Thrones*," Allie told her.

"Oh, that's disgusting. Don't tell me things like that." Barney made a face. "I'm glad I never watched it. And don't compare Joe to someone who does something like that."

"I can see the resemblance," Des broke in. "It's the eyes and the hair. Definitely."

"I don't see it at all," Cara grumbled.

"You watch, too?" Allie raised an eyebrow.

"Religiously," Cara admitted.

"Oh my God, I've got a bunch of heathens under my roof." Barney raised her eyes to the heavens.

"This guy is so hot, even his sister can't resist him," Allie went on with a wicked glint in her eye, intended, no doubt, to bedevil Barney just a little more. "They have three kids together, but everyone thinks the kids are—"

"Enough." Barney covered her ears with her hands. "I don't want to know about it. And you're not watching that sort of thing on my TV."

"Barney, you have cable, right?"

"Yes, but not for the likes of that."

"The new season doesn't start for months yet, but we can watch the old episodes," Des said. "We can watch in my room."

"Count me in." Allie turned to Cara. "You in?"

"Of course. I have my laptop with me. We can watch on that." Cara took a cereal bowl from the cupboard and filled it with granola. She placed it on the table where everyone could reach it while Barney muttered, "Where's Mary Tyler Moore when you need her?"

"Can you make more?" Allie helped herself.

"I don't think there's enough honey."

"Put it on next week's grocery list," Barney told her.

"Oh, I was on my way into the library for those yearbooks when the doorbell rang." Des snapped her fingers as she remembered. "I'll be right back."

"What yearbooks?" Allie asked.

"Dad's old high school yearbooks," Cara told her.

"Oh, cool. Is Mom in there, too?"

"Nora was four or five years younger than Fritz, if memory serves me," Barney reminded her. "She wouldn't be in the same yearbook."

"No, but there are some great shots of Dad." Des

returned with a small stack of yearbooks and placed them on the kitchen table. She opened the top book. "Look here, Dad's senior picture."

She held up the page where a young Fritz, dressed in a dark suit and tie, smiled for the camera.

"Damn, he was good-looking back then. No wonder Mom fell for him." Allie's eyes lingered on the page.

"And check this out," Des said. "Dad ran track. Look at those legs."

Allie and Cara both leaned in to take a look.

"I don't remember him talking about what an athlete he was in school," Cara said.

Allie shook her head. "Me either. He looked really good back then."

"He stopped running about ten years ago. Said his knees bothered him," Des reminded them.

"But he still played golf," Allie said. "I don't think he was very good at it, but he did it because he thought it'd be good for his business. So many actors and other agents played. It made Mom crazy, because the clubs he bought were really expensive and he donated them to Goodwill when he got tired of it."

"Fritz always did tire of things easily. Even as a kid, he'd go all in on something, get bored, then move on to something else." Barney shook her head. "He had a very short attention span."

Allie reached for one of the other books. "This would've been his sophomore year." She opened it and thumbed through the pages.

"Let's see. I think that was the year he joined the drama club. Made the varsity baseball team. See if you can find the sports section, Allie." Barney waited while Allie searched the book.

"Yes, here. The varsity baseball team. Oh, and look. I think this is Uncle Pete." Allie tapped on a photo, and everyone gathered around to take a look.

"Oh yes, that's Pete." Barney stared, then smiled slowly. "Of course, Pete had a lot more hair back then." She continued to study the picture. "Damn if he doesn't look like Gil in that picture. I'd forgotten how much alike they were."

"Who's Gil?" Des and Cara asked at the same time.

"Pete's older brother. He was in my class."

Her voice held a touch of softness, and her three nieces exchanged curious glances. Cara said, "You and Pete's brother were friends?"

Barney smiled. "Of course. Everyone grew up knowing everyone else. The Wheelers lived across the street in that big brick house." A shadow fell across Barney's face, but as if she refused to let it linger, she brightened. "When you're a kid and the town is very small, the pool of potential playmates is limited. You tend to make friends everywhere."

"Is Gil a lawyer, too?" Des asked.

"He would have been," Barney said simply.

"He would have been . . . ?" Des repeated.

"If he'd lived," Barney replied.

"What happened to him?" Cara, who'd been leaning over Des's shoulder, took the seat next to her.

"He was in an accident a week after he graduated law school. He never did get to practice." Barney swallowed hard. "It was a long time ago, girls." She reached over and took another book from the stack. "Let's see what your father was up to in his junior year."

And with that, she changed the subject.

"You said Dad was in the drama group. All four years or any particular one?" Allie asked.

"The book in front of you, sophomore year. Fritz tried out for a role in the school play on a dare, and ended up playing the lead in *Our Town*. I don't think anyone was more surprised than him that he liked it so much. After that, he tried out for every play, and he got very much involved with the Sugarhouse. He did summer stage there every year for years."

"That's where he met our mother," Des said.

Barney nodded. "She was very good on the stage. The acting bug bit her real hard. Once she got a taste of the stage . . . Some say it was the applause she liked, but I don't judge. After that, nothing would do but for her to go to Hollywood. She was convinced she was born to be a star, got Fritz to take off with her, abandon everything here. She did well, too, for a time, as you both know. No need to rehash ancient history."

"What else did Dad abandon besides the theater?" Cara had watched Barney's face closely, and knew there was something her aunt wasn't saying.

"Responsibilities he had here," Barney replied.

"What other responsibilities?" Cara couldn't resist pressing.

Barney sighed. "The Hudsons have been in this town since its earliest days. My ancestors—your ancestors—have played an important role in the town's development. In its prosperity."

"Uncle Pete told us about all that." Allie waved a hand as if they knew it all. "About the hospital and the land for the school and money for a college and everything that our great-grandfather—I think that's the right guy—everything he did for his miners, and for their families. The mines must've been pretty much done by the time Dad was in his twenties. But what was Dad supposed to be responsible for?"

"The bank," Barney said simply, as if that said it all.

"The bank you ran?" Des asked.

"Yes. Your father was supposed to take over from our dad. Fritz majored in finance in college, and he worked summers in the bank from the time he was fifteen. We both did."

"I thought he did summer stage," Des said.

"That was after work, on weekends, and whatever vacation days he could talk Dad out of. The theater was supposed to be his recreation. The bank was supposed to be his future." Barney leaned back against the counter. "Then he met Nora, and we all know where that led."

"So you pitched in when he stepped out," Cara noted.

Barney nodded. "I'd always sort of resented the fact that it had been taken for granted that Fritz would take over the bank, instead of me. After all, I was the older Hudson child. But back then, men ruled. I worked for years in that bank and I knew everything about running it by the time my dad passed away. There were some who thought a woman wasn't up to the job. And it was a lot of responsibility, taking care of the money and the investments of so many people. You have their lives, their futures in your hands. It weighs heavily when you stop to think about it." Barney forced a smile. "And when you're in that position, you think about it most of the time, especially when the world was changing as it had, the financial world so uncertain. It's quite daunting, having that many people looking to you to always make the right decisions. Especially when you personally know everyone who has accounts with your bank."

"Sounds like you didn't like it very much," Allie observed.

"Actually, I loved it. I'd give anything to . . ." Barney shook her head as if to shake off the unfinished thought, then straightened her back. "Now, do we want to look for photo albums before dinner?"

"I'd rather look for the record player and that box of old records you told us about, Barney. You think they're in the attic?" Des went to the sink and rinsed her fingers of the stickiness from the honey in the granola.

"That's as good a place to start as any." Barney nodded. "Anytime I can't find something, I look there first."

The four women trudged up to the third floor,

stopping at the landing at the very top. There were two doors on the right and one on the left.

"Where to, Barney?" Cara asked.

"The two rooms on the right were the maids' rooms, back when the house was first built. They're small, and these days there's nothing except furniture and some things in the closets. The door on the left leads into the attic, and the records and the player would be somewhere in there." Barney headed for the left and opened the door. "Take care walking around in here. I wasn't kidding when I said neither Mother nor my grandmother ever tossed out a thing."

The girls followed Barney.

"There's a light switch here somewhere. . . . Ah, here it is." Barney turned on the light.

"Wow," Cara exclaimed.

"I never saw so much . . . stuff." Des looked around as if in awe.

"Who knew I came from a long line of hoarders?" Allie murmured. She touched the lid of a nearby trunk. "What's in here?"

Barney turned to look. "Could be anything. There must be twenty trunks like that up here, maybe more. Some hold clothes, some old letters and personal items. There's one that's packed with old dishes that belonged to my great-grandmother. My grandmother hated them and never used them, but because they belonged to her mother-in-law, she couldn't part with them. I'll let the three of you fight over them someday. God knows I have no use for them." Barney made her way through a maze of boxes. "All the newer stuff is over here. The records might be in one of these boxes, so let's start here."

For the next fifteen minutes, boxes were open, the contents briefly scrutinized, then closed up again while the search for the records went on, punctuated by the occasional sneeze as dusty containers were handled.

"You know, it'd be a good idea to start marking these boxes as we go through them. There are things we're not looking for right now that we might be interested in later." Des stood and brushed her dusty hands on her pants. "I'll run downstairs and grab a pen."

Ten minutes later, they were still looking.

"Any chance Dad took the records with him?" Allie asked.

"No. They were still here when I . . . Oh, here. Here's the record player." Barney lifted a light-blue and white case from one of the eaves. She set it on a trunk and unlatched the lid. "Ever see one of these?" She held up a small plastic disklike thing.

Cara and Allie both shook their heads.

"This is an insert that you'd put inside one of the forty-five singles so they'd play."

Both women stared at her blankly.

"The center piece here on the record player is tall and thin so you could stack more than one record on at a time. The albums had a small hole in the center and they'd fit right over this center piece. But the single recordings had a larger hole, so you'd slip one of these into the hole so it'd fit over the center thing there and you could play the record." Barney looked from Allie to Cara, then to Des, who had joined them, pen in hand. "I guess I'll have to show you once we find the box with the records. Remember, they're in a red leather case, not a cardboard box."

"I just saw a flash of something red." Allie looked around. "There, Des, right behind you. Under that coat box."

Des moved the box and found the red leather case. She opened it and looked inside. "This is it. The mother lode." She grinned. "Let's go downstairs and play some of them."

Barney snapped off the light and closed the door behind them as they all made their way downstairs.

"I can't wait to see what's in here," Des was saying as she went down the steps.

"I can't wait to see what else is in the attic," Cara said. "Did you notice the old lamps? And all those picture frames leaning against the back wall? I really want to get a look at those."

"Photographs or paintings?" Des asked.

"I couldn't tell," Cara replied. "I'll check them out later."

"I wanted to look in the old armoires. I'll bet there are some funky old clothes up there." Allie reached the first floor ahead of the others. "Nikki would have a ball up there. She always loved playing dress-up."

"Well, I don't know how many of the clothes qualify as funky, but there are definitely a lot of them. You're welcome to go up and look around whenever you like, and when Nikki is here, she's welcome to dress up in anything that strikes her fancy. Like I said, this is your family home as much as it is mine," Barney told them. "In the meantime, let's go into the kitchen and we'll see how these old records sound while we fix dinner."

They opened the red case on the table and each took a handful of the black vinyl disks.

"Barney, you were right. Dad really was an Elvis fan." Cara held up a half dozen records.

"Well, actually, the Elvis records were mine," Barney admitted. "I was a huge fan." She chuckled. "Mother was appalled, so we told her the records were Fritz's. Somehow it didn't offend her quite as much if her son bought them. Totally unacceptable for her daughter."

"Why? What was the big deal?" Des asked.

"Oh, you know, in the early days, rock and roll was considered the devil's music." When the girls laughed, Barney told them, "Seriously. There were admonitions from church pulpits all across the country warning parents not to let their kids listen to it. My mother took that all to heart—the pastor of our church here was certain the apocalypse was near—but my father thought it was all rubbish." Barney ran her finger under the arm of the record player. "Good. The needle is still there. Let's hope it still works." She reached for one of the records. "I can still hear my dad. 'For God's sake, Evelyn, it's just *music*.' She never agreed with him, but she let Fritz buy whatever he, or whatever I, wanted." She glanced at the record she'd picked without reading the label. "Not Elvis, but still, an oldie and a goodie."

She put the record on the machine and they all watched as the handle automatically lowered. A few seconds later, the room was filled with the sound of guitars strumming. Barney reached over and lowered the volume and looked up at her nieces.

"The Everly Brothers. 'Bye Bye Love.'" She moved slightly to the music. "Oh my, but those boys could sing."

The girls sat at the table going through the records and making stacks of the ones they wanted to hear. Barney started dinner, singing along with every one of the songs.

Ritchie Valens, Buddy Holly and the Crickets, Chuck Berry, the Platters, Ray Charles, and lots and lots of Elvis. Some of the records were badly scratched from having been played so many times, but Fritz Hudson's daughters sat and listened to the songs their father and their aunt had loved once upon a time.

"Dad always loved music," Cara recalled. "We had a little of everything in our house—show tunes, opera, classical, rock, but I don't remember any of these. Which were his favorites?"

"He liked the ballads best," Barney told them. "The more romantic, the better. Your father was a big hit with the girls back then. Girls were always calling the house, and my mother, of course, disapproved of any girl forward enough to call a boy on the phone. So she made it a point to answer the phone in the evening, and anytime a girl called Fritz, Mother wrote down the girl's name."

"Why?" Allie asked.

"So that she could tell my brother that he wasn't to go out with *that* girl." Barney laughed and shook her head. "Oh, how times have changed."

"So did he ever go out with any of the girls who were blacklisted?" Cara began to set the table.

"Of course he did. I imagine that by the time he graduated high school, he'd been out with all of them at least once. Like I said, Hidden Falls is a small town: There were only so many girls to go around." Barney took fresh vegetables and a head of lettuce from the refrigerator and placed them on the counter.

"I'll do the salad," Des said.

"You know, the yearbook photos don't do him justice, but your father was quite the stud in those days." When Allie snickered, Barney turned to her with twinkling eyes. "Yes, I said 'stud.' He and Pete always had pretty girls on their arms."

"What about Pete's older brother?" Des asked. "Gil."

"What about him?" Barney opened the oven and slid in the marinated chicken she'd prepared earlier in the day.

"Did he always have a pretty girl on his arm, too?"

A slow smile on her lips, Barney replied softly, "Every day."

By the time dinner had ended and the cleanup was completed, they'd played all the records, some familiar, as they'd heard them on classic rock radio

stations, other songs and artists completely new to
the girls. One at a time, Barney taught them each
how to jitterbug, and before long, they were paired
off, Barney and Des, Allie and Cara, dancing to fifties
rock and laughing so hard their faces hurt. By the
time they called it a night, they knew all the words
to "Blue Suede Shoes" and sang the chorus as they
danced up the stairs to bed.

Alone in her room, Cara tried to put together
what she'd actually learned about her father. There
were the little things: that as a young man, he'd
liked girls and girls had liked him, too. He loved the
popular music of the day, romantic ballads at the top
of that list. He was good at sports—baseball, track—
and had developed his love of the stage apparently by
accident as a high school sophomore.

Cara dressed for bed, and over the next few minutes heard the rest of the house settle as well. She
opened her bedroom door and peered down the hall.
There were no lights coming from under the doors
of either of her sisters' rooms. Barney had stayed
downstairs to read in the library, and the house was
very still. Cara tiptoed down the hall and around the
corner, then paused at the door to her father's old
bedroom. As quietly as she could, she turned the
knob, pushed the door open, and stepped inside, her
fingers searching the wall until she found the light
switch. There was the heavy mahogany bed covered
with a blue chenille spread, a tall chest, a dresser,
two side tables, an old pine desk with a scratch-
covered top, and an overstuffed blue and white plaid

chair. There was nothing in the closet other than a few wooden hangers and a long-forgotten blue tie that had fallen to the floor. The built-in bookshelves held nothing but dust.

She moved the chair a little closer to the window and stared out at the dark night. The promise of financial reward aside, Cara had made this trip hoping to regain that feeling of closeness she and her father had shared, that feeling that had been shattered when she learned the truth about his life. She'd hoped to find him there, in that house, through things he'd been surrounded by, things he'd loved, and in finding him, she hoped to understand some of the choices he'd made, and so far, she wasn't sure she'd done that.

Not that the past week hadn't been without its jaw-dropping surprises: mainly that Fritz had an older sister that he'd never thought to mention, and that his story about having had a terrible childhood that kept him from talking about his family was, as Barney had stated, bull. Barney's version—that she wouldn't welcome him back until he did the right thing as far as his two wives were concerned—was clearly more believable. If his life in Hidden Falls had been so horrible, why would he have insisted that his three beloved daughters go there, stay there for an indefinite period of time? Learning that he'd walked away from his position at the bank had raised more questions than answers.

Walking the floors of this house, climbing the steps he'd climbed so many times, running down the path through the woods that he'd surely taken to get to the falls, sitting here in the quiet of a cold night, in his chair, looking out his window at the view he saw every day—those things brought her closer to the man she was still discovering. But there were still so many questions to be answered before she'd understand how and why he'd become the man who'd tell so many lies to people he so clearly loved.

Cara returned to her room and crawled into bed. Earlier she'd borrowed an old worn copy of *Gulliver's Travels* from the downstairs library, a story her father had read to her many times. Bunching up the pillows against the headboard, she began to read, but she lost interest after the first ten pages. What she'd loved about it as a child wasn't so much the story, but the time she had shared with her father as he read to her, the sense of adventure he infused in every page. She turned off the light and settled into the warmth of the quilt, wondering where else she might look to find the real Fritz Hudson.

CHAPTER SEVEN

Cara had barely gotten out of the shower when she heard the doorbell ring. It was eight twenty-five on a Saturday morning and she'd finished an early run, stretched before and after, and she still hadn't been able to get downstairs before Joe Domanski arrived for breakfast. She'd hoped he'd find her cool, calm, and relaxed when he got there, but no. Now she'd have to rush to dry her hair, and unless she wanted to make it to the kitchen before he finished and left, she'd have to forgo makeup.

She had time for a swipe of mascara—not that it mattered. Joe wouldn't notice—not that she wanted him to. She really hoped she wouldn't turn into one of those women who painted all men with the same brush of suspicion. But right now, she was still bruised by Drew's betrayal, and besides, her current agenda didn't include anyone whose last name wasn't Hudson.

She ran downstairs, pausing at the bottom step to catch her breath so she could walk into the kitchen with some semblance of cool.

Not that it mattered.

From the hall, Cara could hear the chatter, Des's voice above Barney's debating the merits of print books versus reading electronically. Everyone was seated, their plates already filled with the pancakes and bacon Barney had made.

"Good morning," Cara called to no one in particular as she made her way to the coffeepot. She poured a cup and headed for the only empty chair, which was between Allie and Joe.

"Morning to you, too," Barney replied.

Des smiled at Cara as she started to pull the chair out from the table, but Joe reached over, held the chair for her, then helped push it in once she was seated.

"Thanks," Cara told him.

His nod was a silent "You're welcome."

"So what's your pleasure this morning?" Barney stood to act as hostess. "We've got blueberry pancakes, bacon, eggs if you want them, and your delicious granola. Also strawberries, blueberries, and some yogurt."

"Wow. So many choices," Cara said.

"Now that I'm retired, I enjoy cooking a big breakfast now and then."

"I'll grab a pancake—sit, Barney, I'll serve myself." Cara speared a pancake from the plate Des passed to her and decided to add granola and fruit for a chaser.

"The granola was great," Joe told her.

"Thanks. Old family recipe," Cara told him. "Barney, the pancakes are perfect. I could eat these every morning."

"Imagine what you'd look like then." Allie looked up from the phone, her eyes dark and unreadable.

"I shudder to think." Cara cheerfully poured a small amount of syrup onto her pancakes from the blue and white pitcher Joe passed to her. She deliberated momentarily before pouring on a little more. "In for a dime, in for a dollar, as my dad used to say."

The silence that followed was deafening.

"As *our* dad used to say," she corrected herself.

"I never heard him say that," Allie noted coolly. "You, Des?"

Des shrugged. "Doesn't matter, Allie."

Allie dipped her head and went back to her phone, mumbling, "Whatever."

"What's so engrossing that it's worth being rude for?" Des asked Allie.

"Nikki sent me a text with some pictures from yesterday's lacrosse scrimmage." Allie held up the phone and Des took it from her.

"Nikki is Allie's daughter who lives in California with Allie's ex," Barney explained to Joe. "Sorry that some of us can't keep our eyes from our personal devices at the breakfast table."

"I miss my daughter," Allie shot back. "I miss being part of her everyday life, all right? I'm sorry if that makes me rude." She looked at Joe as if expecting a response.

"I don't mind," he told her. He even sounded sincere. "Really. If I had a daughter who was so far away, I'd be glued to my phone, too. It must be tough on both of you."

"Thank you." Allie lifted her head. "It is tough."

"I can't believe how tall Nikki has gotten," Des remarked as she scrolled through the photos. "Who's the blond woman in the last one here? Standing next to Nik?"

"Oh, that's Courtney's mother. Court is Nikki's best friend. They live in the same neighborhood and they give Nik a ride home after games when Clint's not available. Which seems to be every day now," Allie said blithely, though Cara detected an undercurrent of something she couldn't put her finger on.

"I guess you might like to see what your niece looks like." Allie passed the phone to Cara. "The tall girl in the back is Nikki."

Cara studied the screen. "She's beautiful. She looks a lot like you, Allie." She smiled as she passed the phone to Barney via Joe. "I hope I get to meet her one of these days."

"She'll come out here sooner or later," Allie noted. "Clint mentioned some business trip he had coming up that coincided with her spring break, so maybe sooner rather than later. We'll see."

"She's very pretty, Allie. And Cara's right—she does look like you." Joe handed the phone to Barney. "Maybe once you get the theater up and running, she might like to get involved with some of the productions."

Allie's eyes widened in near horror. "No, no, no.

I'll be long gone by the time that place is ready to open. I'm not spending any more time here than I have to."

Joe laughed. "Well, granted, we're not L.A., but Hidden Falls isn't exactly Mayberry, RFD, either."

Allie rolled her eyes. "Please. You're the very definition of 'the boonies.' Complete with the Poconos version of Sheriff Taylor."

"Are you referring to Ben?" Barney's eyes narrowed. "He's not the sheriff. He's chief of police."

"Sheriff Taylor's the role Andy Griffith played on that Mayberry show, right?" Joe grinned. "I can't wait to tell Ben that."

"I loved that show," Barney said. "Such good, wholesome entertainment." She looked at Allie and said pointedly, "Best I can recall, nobody slept with his sister in Mayberry."

"Who knows what goes on behind closed doors?" Allie smiled sweetly. "But it's hard to deny the truth. This place is strictly Small Town USA."

"Hey, we've got just about everything here you could want." Barney went into defense mode. "So we're not much for fancy restaurants . . ."

"But you've got that Good Bye place, which I'm sure is a bundle of laughs on any given night," Allie deadpanned.

". . . and there are no nightclubs between here and Scranton . . ." Barney continued.

"But there is the Bullfrog Inn," Allie pointed out. "I'm sure that place swings on the weekends."

"Actually, it does, especially on Saturday nights,"

Joe told her. He glanced around the table. "Why don't you all come down to the Frog tonight? Meet some of the locals, see what passes for a good time in Hidden Falls."

"I'm in," Des said before anyone else could pipe up. "I'd love to go."

"Me too." Cara finished her breakfast and carried her dishes to the sink before pouring a second cup of coffee. "It sounds like fun."

"Maybe to you two." Allie had returned to her phone and was typing a text, presumably to Nikki. "You're both from small towns, so you wouldn't know the difference."

"Between what and what?" Des frowned.

"Between a hole-in-the-wall bar and a really nice club." Allie seemed to dismiss her sister.

"How would you know if it's a hole-in-the-wall if you've never been there?" Des asked.

"It looks like one," Allie replied.

"Let's not pass judgment until we've seen for ourselves." Des took her plate to the counter. "I say the three of us head out to the Bullfrog tonight around . . ." She glanced at Joe.

"Nine is a good time," he told her. "Too much earlier and you'll be ready to leave by eleven. Too much later, no place to park."

"Nine it is. We'll be there," Cara said. "Barney?"

"Oh, I rarely miss a Saturday at the Frog," she replied. "All my single friends go." She paused for a moment before adding, "Of course, they're all widows, divorcées, and old maids like me."

"Well, you all go and have yourselves a swell time," Allie told them.

"Uh-uh. You're going, too." Des snatched the phone from her sister's hands. "You're not going to stay here and text your daughter all night and then get upset when she stops answering 'cause she's somewhere with her friends and doesn't want anyone to know that her mother texts her twenty-four seven."

"I don't . . ." Allie protested, and reached for her phone.

"Allie, you do." Des plunked the phone in her sister's outreached hand. "We're all going, and maybe for a few hours you'll forget that you're someplace you don't want to be."

"Well, then. That settles it. The Hudson girls will be out in force tonight." Barney beamed and turned to Joe. "You make sure you save us a good table if you get there before we do."

"I'll do that."

"Before I forget, what do we owe you for the new lock?" Des asked.

Joe dug in his pocket for the receipt and handed it over.

"I'll write you a check." Des got up from the table. "Be right back."

Des was back in minutes with a check in her hand. "I set up a little workplace for myself in Barney's office," she told the others. "Barney offered to clear out some space in one of the file cabinets so we can keep all the theater bills together." She handed the check to Joe.

"Thanks, Des. I'll go on over to the theater and install that lock now." Joe stood. "Thanks for breakfast. Everything was great. I'll see you all tonight." His eyes lingered for a second on Cara, and she had the feeling she was being asked to respond somehow.

"I'll walk out with you." Barney rose from her chair. "I need to bring in the mail. It's always here early on Saturday."

Des proceeded to wash the dishes while Allie continued to send texts to her daughter and Cara cleared the table.

Barney came in with an armful of mail she skimmed through before tossing the junk into the paper recycling bin near the back door.

"So what does one wear for a night out in Hidden Falls?" Allie asked.

"Something nice but casual." Barney took two white envelopes from the stack of mail and placed them in a basket on the counter.

"I'm looking forward to it. I could use a night out," Des announced. "But right now, I want to walk over to the library, maybe see about some old photos, old newspaper articles, whatever I can find, about the theater. I also want to check into how to apply for grants that might be available for projects like ours just in case we need to go that route in the future."

"Maybe they have something about the local government," Cara said. "We should know what permits we're going to need."

"I thought we'd need to go to the town hall for

permits." Des finished washing the last of the breakfast dishes and dried her hands.

"Girls, from my experience, the contractors apply for the permits, and 'town hall' is a relative term here. The mayor has a small office in the back of the police station and there's a conference room where the council meets once a month to discuss the borough's business. But that's about it."

Des handed a towel to Cara, who began to dry the dishes Des had placed in the rack.

Barney took her bag from the back of the chair in which she'd been sitting and swung it over her shoulder. "Thanks for taking care of the dishes, girls. I'm off to pick up some plants I ordered from the garden club's sale. If it stays as warm as it is today, I might get some early planting done." She smiled at the thought as she went out the door.

"I guess I'll run up and grab my bag and my notebook." Des stretched her arms over her head. "The walk will do me good. I'm feeling like a slug from sitting around so much."

Cara stood in front of the small closet. She hadn't packed with nights out in mind. Jeans might be okay, but she wore them or sweatpants every day. Finally she decided on her denim skirt—the only skirt she'd brought with her—and a black turtleneck sweater, black tights, and flats. When she went downstairs, she was amused to find that Des was dressed almost identically, the big difference being that Des wore fancy cowboy boots that somehow didn't look out of place in the grandeur that was their family home.

Of course, Des's sweater probably cost five times as much as mine, Cara mused as they waited for Allie to join them, *and those boots must be worth about six car payments.*

"Honestly, she's always been late for everything," Des grumbled. "My mother was the same way."

"And Dad was just the opposite," Cara recalled. "Always five minutes early for everything."

Des nodded. "He always said that being late was one of the rudest things you could do. That it showed a complete disrespect for the people who were waiting for you, like you thought your time was more important than theirs."

"Pounded into his head at an early age. Our father was a demon about punctuality." Barney came into the room, strapping on her watch as she walked. She also had on denim, hers an A-line skirt worn with a crisp white button-down shirt. The long sleeves ended in tidy cuffs that were secured with gold cuff links that had blue stones in the center. A necklace of gold beads and what looked like the same blue stones lay against her collarbone. "Well, it looks like denim is the uniform for tonight." She seemed pleased. "Totally appropriate for where we're going. No one dresses up very much for the Frog, though some concessions are made, since it is the weekend."

"I love your cuff links," Cara said. "Such a pretty shade of blue."

Barney held up her wrists to better show them off. "Lapis," she told them. "They belonged to my dad. The necklace came from an arts show we had here last fall. A woman in Scranton makes all sorts of lovely jewelry using semiprecious stones."

"I have a friend in Montana who makes jewelry." Des held up her arm. "He made this bracelet. Montana silver, Montana sapphires."

Barney took Des's hand to inspect the bracelet. "That's lovely. The silver has a sort of rustic look to it. Unexpected with sapphires, though they are rough-cut." She smiled at Des. "Your friend has talent."

"Thank you. I'll let him know that his work is appreciated as far east as Pennsylvania."

"Now, where is that girl?" Barney frowned and went into the hall and looked up the stairwell as if she could will Allie to come down.

"I'll go up and see if I can move her along." Des took the steps two at a time. "Not that anything I have ever said or done has made a difference."

A moment later, Cara heard muffled voices and the slamming of a door. Des returned to the living room, a scowl on her face.

"I see that went well," Cara said.

"I received the usual chewing out. She always gets in such a funk when she's made to do something she doesn't want to do." Des laughed in spite of her sister's bad mood.

"Pity." Barney's tone made it clear she had no sympathy for Allie.

Five minutes later, Allie made her appearance in

jade-green sky-high heels, tight black pants, a long-sleeved shirt of camel silk unbuttoned to one step above cleavage, and perfect makeup. She glanced at the others, who had gathered in the hall when they heard her footsteps in the upstairs hall.

"Oh. Apparently I didn't get the memo," Allie said.

Des raised a questioning eyebrow, and Allie replied, "Denim night. Should I change?"

Des rolled her eyes and shook her head.

"I'll drive," Barney announced as they filed out the back door. "I like to take Mother's car out every now and then. Keeps the battery charged."

Barney disappeared into the garage, and a minute later, an engine's roar caused everyone to jump just before long white fins emerged. Backing out slowly, Barney maneuvered the car from the garage into the driveway. The others stood drop-jawed at the sight.

Allie found her voice first. "What the hell is that?"

Barney smiled from behind the wheel. "Behold the 1968 Cadillac Deville, girls. Convertible, of course, but it's too cool an evening to put the top down. Too much of a pain in the butt, to tell you the truth. But I put it down when the weather suits just to keep all the working parts working. Hop in."

"This thing is almost fifty years old," Cara exclaimed. "And it's still running?"

"She's been well cared for over the years." Barney waited patiently while Allie and Des climbed into the backseat. Cara slid into the front passenger bucket seat.

"I'll say." Cara ran her hand over smooth leather the color of ripe tomatoes. "There's not a mark on it."

"Her. Mother called her Lucille—as in Ball—because of her hot red leather." Glancing over her shoulder, Barney confirmed, "Everyone in? Good."

She stepped on the gas and Lucille shot to the end of the driveway.

"Dear God, what does this thing have under the hood?" Des asked.

"A 472 V-8. Largest V-8 available at the time for a passenger car." Barney grinned and took off to the stop sign at Hudson and Main.

"This was your mother's car?" Cara held on to the door handle.

"It was a birthday present to her from my father the year she got her driver's license. Mother always liked a fast car. She had a bit of a lead foot." Barney's mouth turned up at one corner and she glanced over at Cara. "It was somewhat of a scandal. Back then there were still people who thought it unseemly for a woman to drive. My mother was a very proper soul and often caved to tradition, but when it came to this car, she threw propriety to the wind. She just flat-out loved Lucille. It was a sad day when we had to take the keys from her."

Barney's smile faded. "Dementia is a terrible thing, girls. It takes the best that you are and leaves the rest. Mother remembered how much she loved this car and how much she loved driving it, but she forgot how. Whenever she said she wanted to drive into town, we had to tell her Lucille had a flat. She had a hissy every time, but I figured we saved countless lives with that one white lie."

Barney fell silent for a moment, then said, "I'm telling you all right now, if the day ever comes that I forget where the brakes are, you can fit me for a pair of cement shoes and drop right off the bridge into the Susquehanna."

No one said a word. Cara couldn't tell for sure, but it sounded like Barney was serious.

They arrived at the Bullfrog and Barney stopped out front to assess the parking situation. Without warning, she made a U-turn in the middle of the street, then turned again to park in the gas station.

"Is this the same gas station where—" Des asked Cara.

"This would be the place," Cara admitted, "and I still have to learn how to pump gas."

"Take you three minutes to learn," Barney said as she got out of the car. "Sit tight. I'll be right back."

Barney went into the gas station and chatted for a moment with the woman at the cash register. Smiling, Barney returned to the car.

"All right, girls. Sally's open till eleven, so Lucille will be in good company. Let's go," Barney told them.

"You're leaving the car here?" Cara asked as she got out.

"Well, I'm sure as hell not parking it out back of the bar where any Tom, Dick, or Harriet can scratch Lucille's pretty finish."

Barney waited while Des and Allie climbed out, then locked the car.

"Now, if for any reason it appears that I might've had one or two beers too many," Barney told them as they walked toward the side door of the bar, "feel free to take my keys. I'm not one to argue where safety is concerned, and frankly, it wouldn't be the first time someone else drove my car home with me in it."

She opened the door, and music and chatter spilled out. The four women made their way into the main room. Several tables were scattered around and the lights were low, but not to the extent that Cara couldn't see where they were headed. Two tables from the bar, Joe Domanski stood next to a pretty blond woman who seemed to have his complete attention.

There, see? Cara told herself. So much for the hot contractor wanting me.

"Looks like Joe got us a good table. This way, girls," Barney said over the music.

Cara had no choice but to follow Barney, Des, and Allie as they plowed a path through the crowd, which deepened the closer they got to the bar, stopping every few feet while Barney greeted seemingly everyone and introduced the girls each time.

By the time they reached the table where Joe stood, still talking to the young woman, Cara figured she'd said, "Nice to meet you," following an introduction, or, "Excuse me," as she elbowed her way forward, somewhere in the area of thirty or forty times.

"Hey, guys. Glad you made it." Joe had turned with a welcoming smile.

"Quite a crowd," Barney said. "Is your grandmother here yet?"

"She's three tables over talking to my mom." Joe gestured with the beer bottle in his right hand.

"I need to talk to Gloria," Barney told them. "Give Joe here your bar order. Joe, start running a tab for us."

And with that, Barney was once again off through the crowd.

"So, what can I get you?" Joe asked as Allie and Des took seats at the table, which could easily accommodate six people.

"I'll have a vodka, straight up. Light on the ice." Allie hung her bag over the back of her chair.

"Seriously, Al? Straight vodka?" Des said disapprovingly.

Allie sighed. "All right, make it a gimlet." She turned to her sister. "There. Better? As if a little lime juice makes a difference."

"Suit yourself. I'll have a beer," Des told Joe.

"Me too." Cara nodded and took a seat, wondering where the blonde had disappeared to.

"What kind?" Joe asked.

"Whatever you're drinking." Cara pointed to the bottle in Joe's hand.

"Two Yuengling lagers, coming up." Joe headed for the bar.

"What's Yuengling?" Des wondered aloud.

"I actually know this." Cara turned to her. "It's a Pennsylvania beer. I think it might even be from somewhere in this general area. A bar in Devlin's Light sells it. I think it's something like one of the oldest breweries in the U.S."

"Actually, I think it is the oldest." Joe returned

with their beers and handed them out. "Established 1829 in Pottsville, which is about ninety minutes from here." He turned to Allie. "And here's your gimlet. You're in luck. PJ remembered to pick up limes today."

"Who's PJ?" Allie asked.

"The bartender's wife," Joe replied.

"Well, thank you, and thank her." Allie tipped the glass in Joe's direction and took a long sip.

"Thanks for the beer." Cara raised the bottle to her lips and tasted the unfamiliar brew. It was better than most she'd tried, though she definitely preferred wine. She'd gone with beer because the Bullfrog just didn't give "good wine" vibes. She wanted to appear as if she belonged there. She tried to act natural, as if she felt right at home, but she felt out of place and awkward. Did Joe feel obligated to keep them company because of Barney? What had happened to the girl he'd been talking to earlier?

Country music flowed from the speakers and several couples headed for the small dance floor. Cara sighed. Even the music was unfamiliar.

Joe sat in the empty chair to her right, his eyes on the dance floor. Cara followed his gaze to see the blonde dancing, close and slow, with a guy dressed all in black. Joe never took his eyes off her.

Well, I guess that lets me off the hook, Cara told herself. *No reason to feel obligated to make small talk with someone who is obviously obsessed with someone else.*

The song ended and the couple Joe had been

watching broke apart. The blonde went to the bar and the guy in the black tee and pants disappeared into a side room, where there appeared to be a crowd.

Curious, Cara asked, "What's in there?"

"Darts and pool." He turned to look at her, his eyes meeting hers. She tried to look away but couldn't. There was something about his blue eyes that got her every time. "Do you play?" he asked.

"Darts, yes. Pool, no," she said.

"Maybe we can play later." His eyes drifted from Cara's face to the bar, where the blonde was now cozying up to a guy with a lot of facial hair and a man-bun. Joe's eyes narrowed, and he stood. "Excuse me for a minute." Leaving his beer on the table, he headed for the bar. Cara watched as he took the blonde by the arm and whispered something in her ear. The young woman rolled her eyes and half nodded. Joe walked back to the table, shaking his head.

"Everything all right?" Cara heard herself ask. She knew that whatever was going on in Joe's life wasn't any of her business, but she couldn't seem to help herself.

"Just peachy," he muttered.

"I called our lawyer and left a message for him to draw up a contract," Cara said. "You're going to have to let me know how you want to be compensated for your time."

"I haven't decided yet whether I'm going hourly or flat fee," he said, "but I'll have a number for you soon."

"If we think it's too high, we'll have to negotiate," she warned him.

"I'd expect you to, if my number's too high. However, since I'm known for being fair and reasonable, there shouldn't be much discussion."

"I guess I'll be the judge of that."

"That's your right, of course. But I guarantee you won't find anyone who'll say I overcharged them." His eyes swept the bar area and settled on the far end. "Excuse me for a minute."

Joe took a long sip of beer and set the bottle on the table with a bang. He got up and walked back to the bar, where he cornered the blonde and appeared to have what looked like some pretty stern words for her. The girl made a face at him and walked to the opposite side of the bar, where she hopped onto a stool and signaled the bartender.

When Joe returned to the table, his eyes—and most likely his mind—were still on the blonde, so Cara said, "Look, you don't have to hang out with us. We're fine. I know you feel like you have to sit here because of Barney, but really, it's okay if you'd rather be talking to someone else."

Joe rested an elbow on the table and leaned a little closer to her. "There isn't anyone else I'd rather be talking to."

"Really, Joe. It's okay." She tried to sound perky but wasn't sure she'd hit the mark. "We'll be fine."

He leaned a little closer. "Is this your way of telling me to get lost?"

When words stuck in her throat, he said, "'Cause

I really like the view from right here. You can tell me if you aren't interested. It won't kill me. Won't make me happy, but I've been rejected before and I survived. But for the record, in case you haven't figured it out, I am definitely interested in you." He leaned even closer, close enough that she could feel his breath on her cheek. "But if you tell me to take a hike, I am out of here. I've never forced my attention on any woman and I'm not about to start now."

He seemed to look past her for a moment. "Oh, for the love of . . . That girl is going to be the death of me yet." He looked down at Cara and said, "Don't go anywhere. I'll be right back."

She didn't need to turn around to know he was after the blonde again. Moments later, he returned to the table, the young woman in tow.

"If you want another beer, I'll get you one. If you want to dance, dance with someone your own age," he said as he plunked her into a chair. "We both know what you're doing, Jules. Everyone in the bar knows what you're doing, so don't think you're being cool."

"I hate you." The girl looked up at him. "I wish anyone was my brother except you."

"Well, that would certainly save me from a lot of aggravation. Make my life a lot simpler." Joe sat down between Cara and the girl. "Now say hello to my friend Cara."

"Hello, Cara." The girl muttered the words flatly.

"Cara, say hello to my sister Julie."

"Hello, Julie."

"Julie's boyfriend broke up with her this morning, so she's trying to show everyone in town that she doesn't give a damn by making every man here under forty think he has a chance with her." He patted his sister on the back. "Swell idea, kiddo."

"Shut up, Joe." Julie stuck her tongue out at him, and he laughed.

"And now your true level of maturity is making its way to the surface." He turned back to Cara. "Julie is twenty-two, but sometimes she acts like she's in third grade. She's my cross to bear."

"You love me." Julie poked him.

"If I didn't, I'd let you go ahead and continue to make a fool out of yourself." His voice softened. "Okay, so Brad broke your heart. I get it. We've all been there."

"He sent me a text." Julie's eyes welled with tears. "After three years, he broke up with me in a *text*."

"What a coward." It was none of her business, but Cara couldn't help herself. What kind of man did something like that?

"That's what I told her." Joe nodded. "He's a coward and an idiot."

"I wish you'd go beat the crap out of him." Julie sniffed. "He's over at Ellie Jenkins's house right now."

"How do you know where he is?" Joe asked.

"I drove past her house on my way here and his car was outside."

"Why? That's out of your way."

"Because I just felt like that's where he'd be, okay? Lately I've felt this vibe between them. . . ."

"Better to know now," Cara told Julie. Joe rested his hand lightly on Cara's back as she leaned past him in order for Julie to hear her over the music. "Believe me, it could be a lot worse."

"I guess." Julie looked up at Joe. "I'll take that beer now, thank you."

"Cara? Another?" Joe stood.

"No, I'm good, thanks."

"Allie? Des? Can I bring you something from the bar?"

"Yes, thank you. Another of these." Allie raised her empty glass.

Des passed.

"So you had someone cheat on you, too?" Julie asked Cara after Joe walked away.

"My husband. With one of my best friends."

"Ouch, that stinks. Ellie and I have been best friends since ninth grade." Julie looked about to cry again. "I hope he's your ex-husband."

Cara simply nodded.

"I hate cheaters. I would never cheat."

"Me either," Cara agreed. "But Joe is right. It's no consolation, but I don't know anyone who hasn't had their heart broken at least once. Or twice."

"Other than your ex . . . ?"

"When I was in school, a few times. You know how everything feels so final when you're fifteen." Cara smiled. "And sixteen and seventeen. The boy you wanted to go to the prom with asked someone else. You thought someone liked you; then you found out he was using you to get close to your best friend.

You could write it a thousand different ways, but it all comes back to the fact that no one is immune from heartache. This guy . . ."

"Brad."

"Brad is way too immature and thoughtless for a girl like you. You deserve so much better. Certainly someone who isn't a coward."

"What would you do if you were me?" Julie asked.

"For one thing, I'd cut the drama. Don't give anyone anything to talk about. If you want to sit at the bar and talk to someone, go ahead. But I'd be a little less . . . visible."

"What did you do? I mean, when you found out your husband was cheating?"

"I did the only thing I could do. I went about my business and tried to keep a low profile for a while and hoped the gossip would die down. Which it won't for a while yet—they're getting married—but I had a good reason to leave town."

"What was the reason?"

"My father died and I had to come here to fulfill the terms of his will."

"I'm sorry about your father. Were you close?"

"Not as close as I thought we were."

"I hear you. When my dad died, I found out he wasn't the man I thought he was. It hurts."

"It does," Cara agreed.

"But it's kind of cool about having to do something because of a will, right? That's the sort of thing you see on TV. A man dies and his heirs have to come to this big old haunted house. . . ."

Cara laughed. "We did come to stay with our aunt, but the house isn't haunted—at least not as far as I know."

"Who's your aunt? Do I know her?"

"Barney Hudson."

"Oh, Barney. Of course I know her. She's a friend of my grandma's. She's the best lady. She helped Joe so much."

"He said something about that the other day."

"Yeah, she stepped up for him big-time." Julie eyed Cara. "Are you and my brother, like, a thing?"

"No, no. He's helping me and my sisters with a big construction project."

"The theater." Cara could see Julie putting it all together in her head. "The old Sugarhouse. He's been talking about it all week. So you're *that* Cara."

Before Cara could ask what that meant, Joe was back and distributing drinks.

"I see a couple of girls from my high school down at the end of the bar." Julie stood. "I think I'll go say hi. Thanks for the beer, Joe. And Cara, thanks for the talk and the advice." She leaned close to Cara and whispered, "I think my brother likes you. He's a ginormous pain in my ass but he's the best guy who ever lived. If he's wasting his time, tell him flat-out." Julie smiled and went off in search of her friends.

"What was that all about?" Joe moved his chair a little closer to Cara's and sat.

"Oh, just some friendly advice from one cheatee to another."

"*Cheatee?*"

"One who has been cheated on, as opposed to one who cheats, he—or she—being the cheater," Cara explained.

"Some guy cheated on you?"

Cara nodded. "Big-time."

"Oh, come on. No man is that stupid."

"Oh, but he was."

"Seriously?"

"Yep."

He muttered something under his breath that sounded like "Fool." Aloud, he asked, "You moved on yet?"

"Let's say I'm moving on." She picked at the label on the beer bottle. "I think by the wedding I'll be fine."

"What wedding?"

"His."

"Ouch. I hope that's soon."

"A few weeks. Have you ever been in a situation like that? Had your heart broken?"

"Are you kidding? I'm thirty-five. A man would have to be a monk to live that long and not have had his heart broken a couple of times."

"That's pretty much what I told your sister. It happens to everyone."

"Well, I'm sorry it happened to you. I hope you hadn't been in too deep."

"I was married to him. My divorce was final two months ago."

Joe's jaw dropped slightly.

"Hey, it happens." She shrugged and smiled as if to make light of it.

"He must've been one supreme asshole. I can't imagine any man walking away from you."

"He told me she was his 'soul mate.'"

"You know, I hear that expression a lot but I have no idea what it means," Joe said.

"To tell you the truth, I don't think I do, either." Cara thought for a moment. "Barney said that my father told her that he and my mom were soul mates. It does sound romantic."

"Nice for your folks, I guess, but again, I don't have a clue."

Cara laughed and Joe held out his hand. "How 'bout we take our unromantic selves out onto the dance floor? Nothing like slow-dancing to a country song in your favorite bar to put a smile on your face."

"I don't think so. You're my contractor. I'm pretty sure there's a no-fraternization clause in the contract we're having drawn up."

"Yeah, well, it hasn't been signed yet." He stood. "Come on. It's just a dance. What could it hurt?"

"I heard you have two left feet."

"Not from anyone around here." Joe pulled Cara from her chair. "How can you resist a good country tune?"

"Yeah, the lyrics are always so heartfelt. 'I crashed my truck. My dog died. My man ran off with a girl from the car wash and I got the blues,'" Cara sang as they walked to the small dance floor.

"Not this song. That's the great Johnny Rivers. 'Swayin' to the Music.'" Joe hummed along, singing a word here and there.

"I don't know it," Cara told him.

"It's the best song. See, this guy's just happy to be home with his girl, slow-dancing to a song on the radio. It's late at night and they're just two people in love dancing together 'cause it makes them feel good. That, to me, is romantic."

"I'd listen more closely to it if I could hear it over the noise in here."

"That's what you get in your basic neighborhood bar on a Saturday night."

She felt the pressure of his hand on the small of her back as they moved to the music, their bodies touching. Her left hand rested lightly on the back of his neck, and he smelled like plain, basic soap. Drew always smelled of some cologne he thought was manly but Cara found overpowering and unpleasant. The contrast between the two men couldn't have been sharper. She was pretty sure Joe's sense of his own masculinity didn't need a boost from anything that came in a bottle.

The song ended and they stepped apart.

They walked back to the table, where Des and Allie appeared to be arguing.

"Can it, Des," Allie all but growled.

"Hey, I have an idea. Let's get a picture of this happy family gathering," Joe deadpanned and took out his phone. "Go ahead, Cara. Stand behind your sisters."

The look Allie gave him was pure evil but when it came time to smile, she dazzled.

"Let's get one with you, Joe," Des said. "The Hudson sisters out on the town with their trusty contractor."

"We need someone to take it," Allie reminded her.

"I have long arms. I can take it," Cara volunteered.

"Selfies are so last year." Allie sighed.

"I'll take it." A man who'd been standing behind Cara and off to the left reached for the phone.

"Thanks, Ben." Joe handed over the phone and joined the group.

"Oh God, not you," Allie groaned.

"Nice to see you again, too, Ms. Monroe." Ben took the picture and held the camera up to take a look. "Great shot of everyone except you, Ms. Monroe. You're making a face that looks like . . . well, here, see what you think."

Ben passed the phone to Allie. She didn't bother to look at the screen before she deleted the picture. "Oops. Sorry. Guess you'll have to take another."

"I'd be happy to." Ben raised the camera and shot just as Allie flashed a million-dollar smile. He took one look at the screen and said, "Wow. You really can turn it on when you want to."

Allie fixed the smile on her face and went back to her drink. Ben leaned over the back of the chair next to her and started to say something, but before he could get a word out, she turned to him and said loudly, "I'm not driving so it's none of your business.

Go find someone else to harass." She turned her back, apparently hoping he'd walk away. Instead, he leaned over her shoulder. Cara couldn't hear what he was saying, but whatever it was, Allie all but flipped out.

"Wow, I don't know what that's all about," Cara muttered. "But neither of them look very happy."

"Ben's a big boy, he can take care of himself." Joe watched the heated exchange with interest. "Maybe it's Ben who's chewing Allie out. Funny, I didn't even see them talking to each other tonight."

"I don't think they really even know each other." Cara recalled the scene in the driveway the night they arrived.

Just then, Des took off alone for the bar, and Barney and her group of friends headed for the dance floor, where they took part in a lively line dance to yet another song Cara had never heard. When one of the ladies slipped and fell, Barney and two others helped her up, the three of them laughing good-naturedly. Cara glanced over at the bar, where Des was now in conversation with a tall bald man whose arms were covered with tattoos and who appeared to be hanging on every word Des said. Allie was still having words with Ben Haldeman.

Cara smiled. *Our first night out as a family in Hidden Falls, and it's all going pretty much the way I could have predicted: Barney's having a rousing good time, Des is making new friends, and Allie is pissing someone off, specifically, the local chief of police.*

Yes, she thought as she looked around, *just about the way I would have pictured it.*

She glanced at Joe, whose head was tilted as he listened to something his sister was telling him. There was no point in trying to convince herself that she wasn't tempted. Joe was hot and fun and definitely qualified as a good guy, but then again, there'd been a time when she'd thought Drew was hot and funny and a good guy, too, and look how that had turned out.

Besides, she wasn't ready to completely let her guard down. There was time enough to see where their mutual attraction might lead. She was pretty sure she'd know when the time was right.

CHAPTER EIGHT

The bright light pierced a gap in the curtains and stabbed Allie in the eye as if it were hell-bent on waking her in a way that would annoy her for the rest of the day. She pulled the blanket over her face and groaned. As she turned over, she grabbed her phone to check the time. Surely it couldn't be later than six.

Eleven? How could that be?

She ran her hand over her face and sat up, only to be greeted with a pounding head, eyes struggling to stay open, and a mouth that was dust dry. There were few things Allie hated more than hangovers, and yet here she was, her head in her hands and her stomach churning.

"Damn." She went into the bathroom and splashed cold water on her face. It helped a little, if only to assure her that she was in fact awake.

Ten minutes later, craving coffee, she stumbled

downstairs and into the kitchen after having made herself as presentable as possible, adhering to one of her own personal rules: When you are deathly hung-over, it is important to appear anything but.

Why had she had those last few shots? She knew the real answer: to spite that damned nosy cop—but she wasn't ready to admit it yet.

The house was quiet—so quiet that she knew no one else was about. Where would Cara and Des have gone on a Sunday morning? Des wasn't a churchgoer, she knew that much about her sister. And where was Barney?

Allie sat at the table and pulled up the photos on her phone that had sent her reaching for the clandestine bottle in her suitcase when they returned from the bar around midnight. The first picture and text from Nikki had been innocent enough: *Me and Courtney before the big sophomore dance last night*, she'd written under a photo of her and her BFF, both adorable in pretty dresses, their hair and makeup perfect. Allie had been thinking how the tenth-grade boys must have fallen all over themselves when these two walked in, when it occurred to her that Nik was wearing a dress she'd never seen before. Without stopping to think, she typed: *I don't recognize the dress?*

A moment later came the reply: *Courtney's mom took us shopping this morning. Isn't it the best dress evah?*

Allie had to take several deep breaths before responding: *It's lovely. It's perfect on you.*

Nik's last text of the night—*Thanks, Mom! Night! Love you!*—was attached to a series of pictures taken before, after, and during the dance. Nikki and Courtney. Nikki and Clint, who was, surprisingly, wearing a sport jacket, button-down shirt, and khakis. Odd attire for dropping Nik off at school or at Courtney's. Clint's at-home wardrobe had always been pretty much old jeans and an even older T-shirt. Then there were Nik and Clint standing next to Courtney and her mother. Clint was on one side and Courtney's mother on the other, like bookends, their offspring between them. The last photo, taken apparently at the dance, was of Clint and Courtney's mother standing with another couple. *That's what they look like,* Allie thought. *A couple.* She enlarged the photo to study the look on the woman's face. *Oh yes, indeed. That's the look of a woman in love—or at least in lust.* Either way, it hit Allie like a thunderbolt.

Allie sat stock-still on the window seat, her stomach suddenly feeling as if hot molten lead had been poured inside her.

She had to fight the urge to call him. He'd never admit it. Never. Hadn't he vehemently denied that there was another woman in his life?

"Damn him." Allie pushed her coffee away along with the hot angry tears she felt welling up. He'd played her. Pure and simple. He'd played her to get close to another woman. Taken her daughter from her under the guise of what was best for Nikki, when he was actually using Nikki to get to know this woman.

Would he really do that, use his daughter to give him an excuse to get close to a woman?

Of course he would. And apparently, he had.

Allie had run through her savings to pay her half of the tuition to a school she couldn't afford because Clint had shamed her into it with his snotty little jab, *Give her the best, or be content with the rest?* And most painful of all, Allie had had to trade her weekdays and nights with Nik for just the weekends in order for her daughter to attend this incredible school.

And this realization had come directly on the heels of her having to deal with a holier-than-thou Ben Haldeman at the Bullfrog last night.

He'd sat next to her in the seat Des had occupied, even after she'd made it pretty clear she had no intention of speaking with him beyond her initial "I'm not driving, so go find someone else to harass" declaration.

She'd tried to ignore him, but he didn't move. Finally, his very presence irritated her so much she couldn't keep her mouth shut any longer. "That's my sister's seat," she'd told him.

"When she lets me know she wants it, I'll vacate," he'd replied.

Allie had turned in her chair and done her best to ignore him. She'd been doing a pretty respectable job, too, until he leaned over and whispered in her ear, "That's your, what, fourth drink in"—he'd glanced at his watch—"oh, roughly fifty minutes? Which averages out to about one drink every twelve and a half minutes."

"You just did all that advanced math in your head? Who says we don't use it once we leave school?" She didn't bother to turn around.

"Well, we law enforcement types use math for all sorts of things. It wouldn't even be a challenge for me to make a quick calculation of what your blood alcohol level might be right now."

"Doesn't matter, does it, since, as I've told you, I'm not driving. I have to assume I'm not breaking any laws since you're not snapping your handcuffs on me." She looked at him over her shoulder and lowered her voice. "You ever use them for something other than restraining bad guys—or bad girls, Sheriff?"

"It's Chief." His eyes darkened and narrowed.

"Chief. Sheriff. All the same. Means head lawman in his respective jurisdiction, right?"

"Close enough."

"So why aren't you out following unsuspecting drivers home so you can scare the living crap out of them?"

"I'm off duty."

"I see." She turned and deliberately took a long, slow sip of her drink.

He'd fallen quiet for a moment, then asked softly, "Bad day?"

"Why does it matter to you? You don't know me. What difference could it possibly make to you?"

He'd nodded in Barney's direction. "It'd matter a great deal to her if something happened to you. And if it matters to her, it matters to me, because she matters. Barney matters a great deal to a lot of people around here." He stood and took a card from his wallet and handed it to her. "You ever want to talk about it, you ever need a friend or you want someone to just listen and not judge, give me a call."

He'd walked away and left Allie sitting there with her mouth open.

She'd told herself he was the nerviest person she'd ever met, that he must be one of those people who just couldn't help sticking his nose everywhere it didn't belong. Maybe that was why he became a cop—so he could get in other people's business. She'd started to drop the card on the floor, but something stopped her. She'd put it into her bag and tried to forget that the conversation ever happened.

A noise from the backyard drew her attention. She peered out the window and saw Barney emerging from a shed with a shovel in one hand and a rake in the other. A cardboard box holding what looked like a dozen or so plants stood open on the grass. Coffee in hand, Allie stepped onto the porch.

"Good morning, sunshine." Barney turned to her with a smile. "Sorry you missed breakfast. There's some fruit salad left in the fridge, though."

"I'm good, thanks." Allie walked down the steps and onto the patio. The bricks were raised here and there, and she carefully made her way to where Barney stood looking like the wife of Old MacDonald, her appearance so different from her usual put-together look. Old worn jeans, old sweater with moth holes on the front, sneakers that had clearly seen many other springs. Soft leather gloves, the color of ripe bananas, hung from her pants pockets, and sunglasses perched atop her head.

"Picked up my plants from the garden club the other day," Barney said. "Good day to get them in the ground while the earth is soft from last night's rain and the temperature is nice and warm. The sun's getting a little higher every day." She raked dead leaves from what had apparently been last year's garden, exposing the raw earth beneath the composted matter. Here and there, small stubby fingers of green pushed through the soil.

"What are they?" Allie pointed to the stubs.

"Daylilies. Those fat little stems pushing up—the ones with that dark purple color mixed with the green—those are peonies. I'm pretty sure my grandmother planted those. Live forever, those things."

Allie bent down to see what was in the box. "Isn't it a little cold to plant flowers? Those are flowers, right?"

"A few perennials—good to get them going early and they can take a frost, most of 'em—and of course peas and some lettuce. Peas like the cold, but I might be a little optimistic where the lettuce is concerned. But it looked so pretty, I couldn't resist."

The name of each plant was written on a little white plastic stick wedged into the dirt in the pots. Hollyhocks. Echinacea. Veronica. Astilbe. A few daylilies.

"Is all this your garden?" Allie pointed to the carpet of dead leaves that surrounded the large patio and extended into the wide beds on three sides. Barney's outdoor furniture was lined up on one side, each piece still wrapped in its protective cover against the weather.

Barney nodded. "It seems to grow a little every year. Guess I have no willpower when it comes to flowers."

"I had roses at my house in California." Allie recognized the wistful undertone in her voice. She tried not to think about it, but damn, she did miss that house. "I planted them myself. They bloomed so beautifully last year."

"My mother and grandmother both had roses. They never did much for me. Maybe you'd do better with them. They're all on the other side of the house. Take a look, why don't you?" Barney gestured toward the left side of the house. "Of course, they're just sticks right now, haven't started to leaf up yet, but maybe when they do, you could see what you can do with them."

"I really don't know anything about roses. I just got lucky."

"Gardening is part luck, part experience, part knowledge. You've apparently had some experience with them and you've had luck. So I'd say you probably have more knowledge on the subject than you realize. Certainly more than me."

Allie shrugged and stood watching Barney rake for several more minutes before asking, "Any idea where Des and Cara might have gone?"

"They hiked up to the top of the falls. They took

a thermos of coffee and a couple of the muffins Cara made, so I guess they planned on staying for a little while. You could probably join them."

"Not likely," Allie muttered.

"Not up to the challenge this morning?"

Allie shook her head. Just forcing herself not to text Nikki to interrogate her about Clint and Courtney's mother was enough of a challenge this morning.

"What's everyone doing today, do you know?" Allie checked the screen on her phone for updates. There were none.

"Cara is meeting Joe and the exterminator at the theater around one to see what they can do about whatever has moved in. Des said she wanted to spend some time in the attic to look for a box of old photos of the theater that my mother stashed up there." Having cleared all the beds, Barney traded the rake for the shovel and leaned upon its handle. "What about you?"

Allie shrugged.

"Grab a shovel from the shed, then, and help me get this bed ready." Barney gestured toward the area she'd just finished raking.

"Oh, I don't really—"

"Do you good, Allie." Barney turned her back and began to turn over the soil.

Allie sighed and went to the shed. She tested the array of shovels, searching for the lightest in weight, and carried it back to the bed where Barney was working.

"Barney, what would you like me to do?"

"We need to just turn the dirt, like this." Barney demonstrated, digging up a shovelful of soil and dumping it back onto the spot where she'd dug it.

Allie mimicked the motion and began the task of helping Barney. The work was mindless, and for the first five minutes it wasn't too bad. Before long, Allie's hands and wrists began to ache, and her head was pounding even louder than it had been. She rested against the shovel handle and closed her eyes. It didn't help.

"Looks like you could use an aspirin or something," Barney observed without breaking the rhythm of her digging. "There's a bottle in the cabinet next to the sink in the kitchen. Go on in and take a couple. I can finish up here."

Allie stabbed the point of the shovel into the dirt and left it standing there. She hurried toward the steps, her stomach roiling.

"You also might want to try a glass of milk with a raw egg in it," she heard Barney say as she reached the porch. "I hear it's good for hangovers."

One hand over her stomach and the other over her gagging mouth, Allie beat a quick path to the powder room.

"It's really peaceful here." Cara sat on a large rock next to Des, her feet dangling over the edge, a plastic travel mug in her hand. She'd drunk most of the coffee, so all that remained was a cool puddle in the bottom of the mug.

"Agreed," Des said. "The falls are like white noise, you know? I like it. It's soothing."

"It is. There's something sort of, I don't know, mystical or unearthly about the place. I could totally see this as somewhere forbidden lovers met, or where something tragic had occurred."

"You should write a novel," Des told her. "One of those Gothics. You've got a dramatic flair, you know?"

"I'd expect you or Allie to have more of a sense of drama, since your mother was an actress. My mother? Not a dramatic bone in her body. As far as she was concerned, the less drama in her life, the better."

"My family was just the opposite. We were all drama queens. Especially Allie, but don't tell her I said so."

"Cross my heart. But at least you had an outlet for it. Your TV show, I mean."

"I'd have been happier finding a different outlet. Allie was so much more suited to that whole scene than I was. She loves attention and she has a real flair for the dramatic in everything she does."

"So why you and not her?" Cara had been wanting to ask.

"Allie has the desire and the will, but the truth is, she didn't have the talent gene. Not one iota. I'd never say it to her face, but my mother never missed an opportunity to remind her. If I'd known then what I know now . . ." Des blew out a long breath. "I wish the show had never happened. It totally ruined my relationship with Allie."

"Because she was jealous . . ."

"She still is. She just can't let it go. Honestly, if I'd had any idea what it would have cost me, I'd have fought a lot harder against it than I did."

"Were you ever close?" Cara asked.

Des nodded. "Until I was signed for that show, we were best friends. We were homeschooled some years because Mom shuttled us around with her a lot, so we were together almost all the time. I've tried so hard over the years to find a way to get her to move past it, but it's like she's stuck at twelve years old and she can't forget that I had something she wanted."

"Maybe being here together and working toward a common goal will help you get close again," Cara said.

"That's what I'm hoping." Des appeared close to tears, so Cara rubbed her back to comfort her. "That's why I'm here."

"How'd you end up on TV in the first place?"

"When we were little, my mom would take us onto sets with her. She thought it made her look like a devoted mother. Then sometimes the script would call for a child, and one or both of us would be in the film. When I was nine, a TV producer friend of hers saw me in some film and thought I'd be good in a kid's show he wanted to do. I was the right age and had the look he was going for. I was small, perky, and cute. Allie was tall and skinny and, at twelve, was just going into an awkward stage."

"So you got the part."

Des nodded. "At first it was fun. It wasn't the acting I disliked. I kind of liked being someone else for a while. Our home life was totally screwed up. My mother drank and my father was never home."

"I guess we now know why." Cara couldn't help but feel a twinge of guilt knowing that the reason their father was absent in Des and Allie's life was because he was so involved with hers.

"For whatever reason." Des paused. "You don't think I hold that against you, do you? Because I don't. None of us had anything to do with what happened back then. Those were choices our father made."

"I understand that, but still . . ."

"There's no 'still.' My mother was impossible to live with by that time, and Dad fell in love with someone else. Period." Des sighed. "Anyway, the show was a huge hit and it got bigger every year. Allie hated me so much back then. She'd wanted her own show so badly, which only made our home life even suckier than it had been. The older I got, the more I disliked it. You know how when you're a teenager, you go through stages of insecurity and self-doubt, not to mention your body is changing and there are times when you don't want anyone to look at you?"

"Do I ever," Cara said.

"Well, imagine going through that with the whole world watching. I couldn't go anywhere or do anything, and my only friends were the other kids on the show. Which wasn't too bad until I found out that one of them was sleeping with our TV dad and two of the others were doing cocaine between takes."

"Yow."

"Yeah. The show finally ended when TV Dad was arrested for having sex with a minor. I was so relieved when we were canceled."

"Why'd you do it if you hated it so much?"

"My mother's career was starting to go down the tubes. She drew a nice salary for 'managing' my career."

"Dad let her do that?"

"She had those contracts signed before he even knew about it. Even when he realized how unhappy I was, he couldn't do much about it." A small smile spread across Des's lips. "Though I always wondered if he was the anonymous source that blew the whistle on TV Dad and his underage honey."

"I guess if he couldn't get it done one way, he'd find another."

"True. But enough about me. What time is your meeting with Joe today?" Des asked.

"I told him I'd stop by the theater around one. The exterminator will be there. Thank God. I want whatever is living in there to leave and find another home."

"Do you want to go out with him?"

"I do." Cara pulled some leaves off a nearby bush and tore them into strips, sending the pieces over the side of the rock to the pond below. "And then I don't."

"Why would you not want to go out with him?

He's nice, he's smart and capable, he has his own business, and, oh yes, did I mention he's adorable? In a very hot way?"

"Why don't *you* go out with him?"

"He's not the least bit interested in me. It's you he's had his eye on since day one." Des thought for a moment. "Seriously, Cara—why would you not want to go out with him?"

"I've only been divorced two months. Yes, Joe is all those things, I agree. But when I first met Drew, he was all those things, too. For almost the entire time we were married, he was all those things."

"That didn't work out in the end. I get it. But it doesn't mean that every nice, smart, adorably hot guy is going to be a jerk."

"It doesn't mean that he won't be, either." Cara straightened her legs out in front of her. "How can you tell the guys who at some point will turn into assholes from the ones who won't?"

"You're asking the wrong person. I've never gotten that far with anyone. I've had 'relationships' but never anything I felt was deep enough to last a lifetime." Des's voice softened. "And I want that, something deep enough to last a lifetime. My parents' marriage was terrible. I'd never admit it to Allie, but I don't blame Dad one bit for falling in love with your mother. Our mother was an alcoholic who verbally abused all of us. We were never able to depend on her, the way you should be able to depend on your mom." She turned to look at Cara. "The way I bet *you* could depend on your mom."

"Yes. Susa was always there for me. She was always there for everyone she cared about."

"And she and our dad probably had a pretty good relationship, right?"

"They sure seemed to. Except for, you know, that one little omission on Dad's part."

"My parents argued all the time. About everything."

"Mine never did. At least, I never heard them or saw a sign that they were less than happy just to be in each other's company."

"That's what I'm talking about. That's what I want. I've never felt that kind of . . . comfort, security, with anyone I've ever dated. A couple of times I came close to seeing if that would happen, but in my heart I knew it wouldn't, so I walked away. I mean, it always felt like more trouble than it was worth." She grinned. "'Why bother?' should probably be written on my tombstone."

"I thought I had all that with Drew. The closeness, the comfort, the trust—everything I ever wanted. I believed it. I totally committed myself to him, to our marriage." Cara shook her head. "And I was wrong."

"So you wouldn't go out with Joe because Drew turned out to be an asshole?"

"Why would I want to make that mistake again?"

"Because next time might not be a mistake."

"I still feel raw. I still can't think about Drew with Amber without wanting to cry."

"Do you still love him? Drew?"

"I hardly feel anything for him."

"Then why do you still feel burned?"

"I don't know. Maybe because I can't trust myself anymore to know when something is real and when it isn't. I feel stupid for trusting him even when I started to see signs that maybe I shouldn't."

"Like what?"

"Just arguing over stupid things. It seemed like he was looking for ways to start an argument so he could storm out. I thought it was because I was spending so much more time at the studio, but in retrospect, I think it was just an excuse for him to see Amber and play the wronged husband."

"That burning you feel? I think it's your bruised ego. I think you feel raw because from what you've said, it seems it was all very public and everyone in your little town knew about it and on top of that, the woman he left you for is—was—a friend."

"All that's true." Cara shrugged. "Maybe it's just that having been publicly humiliated still hurts when I think about it. God knows I don't want him back. But it doesn't mean I can tell the difference between a guy who is sincere and a guy who *seems* sincere."

"I don't know a whole lot about men, but I do know that none of them come with guarantees."

"Well, they should. They should come with grades or little caution cards. 'Lies without conscience.' 'Will cheat every chance he gets.' 'Really does think that dress makes your ass look fat.' 'Only pretends to like puppies.'" Cara stood and brushed off her shorts.

"Yeah. Then we'll all be fighting over the ones

that say, 'Will never look at someone else when he's out with you.' 'Totally trustworthy.' 'A forever kind of guy.'"

"'Great kisser.' 'Sweet and cuddly after sex.'"

Des laughed. "Maybe someone will come up with an app for that."

"I'd definitely download it. Right now, I need to get moving. I want to call my friend Darla and have some time to chat before I leave to meet Joe." Cara picked up her coffee mug and the thermos. "Are you going to stay up here for a while?"

"No, I think I should get going, too. I'm determined to find that box of old theater photos in the attic. They might come in handy if we run out of money and have to apply for grants."

Des followed Cara down the trail, running behind her and matching her stride for stride until they reached the edge of the woods.

"Okay, I'm done." Des appeared to be trying to laugh, but she was too winded. "I don't know what made me think I could keep up with you."

Cara stopped so Des could catch up. "I'm sorry, I didn't know that you were trying to. I would have slowed my pace."

Des bent at the waist and sucked in air. "I will start running. Tomorrow."

"Just pace yourself, start out on a slow and short run, then build up the distance. Don't torture yourself by going too far too soon."

They followed the path toward the house. Off to the left stood the outbuildings—the garage, the carriage house that connected to the main house via a stone porte cochere, and another building that could have been a stable at one time.

"Can you imagine what this place was like back in the day? I'll bet it was the coolest place in Hidden Falls," Des said.

"No doubt it was," Cara agreed. "I can just see a carriage coming up that long drive." She paused and glanced at the carriage house. "I wonder if they're still in there."

"What, the carriages? It wouldn't surprise me, since we're apparently descended from a long line of hoarders. Let's check it out."

They crossed the driveway and walked under the porte cochere. The carriage house had tall double doors set with high windows in the front, well over the heads of Cara and Des, and the doors were solidly locked.

"I saw a door on the other side," Cara said. "Maybe it's unlocked. I'd love to see what's in there."

But the side door was locked as securely as the front. However, the windows, though dirty, were low enough to peer through.

Des tried wiping away the dirt from the glass panes with her hand.

"Let me try." Cara pulled up the bottom of her old sweatshirt and rubbed the glass. "That's a little better."

She held her hands around the sides of her face to block out the glare from the sun. "Oh, it's empty."

She stepped back for Des to look.

"I'm disappointed," Des admitted. "With everything they held on to over the years, they apparently got rid of the carriages. Bummer. I'd have loved to see them."

"I'll bet there are photos somewhere. Maybe when you're looking for pictures of the theater, you'll come across some of the carriages. I'm betting that whoever put the photos in the attic didn't bother to organize them."

"Just think what fun you'll have when you finally find the stash."

"If I find it. You saw the amount of stuff in the attic. Finding anything is going to be like, well, needle, haystack." Des stepped away from the window and, drawn to the area, Cara took one last look.

The carriage house was dark inside, but even in the dim light, Cara could see what looked like concrete floors and a high ceiling. A row of windows across the back would have let in tons of light had they not been filthy and had the trees behind the building not grown smack against the wall.

It could be a glorious space, Cara thought. There were so many things it could be used for. A guesthouse, maybe. Or a yoga studio. Not that she was planning on sticking around after the challenge had been met—and she was certain they would complete the challenge—but there was no denying the space spoke to her. Maybe sometime she'd ask Barney for the key so she could go inside and take a look around. But it wouldn't be today. She had just enough time to clean up and get over to the theater. Ridding the old place of its unwanted inhabitants was the priority, and it couldn't happen soon enough.

Living alone these past years hadn't prepared Des to live with three other women, and she was savoring the peace and quiet of the attic. Not that she hadn't enjoyed spending some time with Cara—she had. It was an interesting experience, meeting and getting to know your own sibling for the first time as an adult. She liked Cara. She was straightforward and open and thoughtful. In some ways, she felt closer to this woman she'd just met than to the sister she'd grown up with.

It was too bad Cara and Allie had married such jerks. They both deserved better. Every woman did.

She thought back to her last few relationships and acknowledged that none of them had lasted because they shouldn't have. Kent was destined to join that long list of guys who couldn't cut it with Des, she knew. It hadn't even occurred to her to give him a call since she got here. She couldn't remember the last time she'd met a guy who gave her that little jolt that you get when you're with someone who does it for you.

Okay, there was that guy at the bar last night, but he was so totally not her type, interesting though he had been. Tall, bald, sculpted arms covered with tattoos, he'd come up behind her at the bar and said hello. She wasn't even sure he'd been talking to her until she realized he was staring at her. Finally, she smiled and looked away, busying herself trying to catch the attention of the bartender.

"You're one of the Hudson sisters," she'd heard him say.

Des had turned and looked up at him. Deep brown eyes had gazed down on her from a rugged face that, while not handsome, was arresting.

"That's right." Curious, she asked, "How would you know that?"

"You look like a Hudson. What are you drinking?"

"Yuengling."

"Two Yuenglings," he'd called to the bartender, who acknowledged with a nod.

"So which of the sisters are you?" He'd turned his attention back to Des.

"I'm Des," she told him.

"I meant, one of Nora's or one of the second wife's?"

"I'm Nora's younger. My father's second wife only had one daughter." She'd nodded at the table where her sisters sat. "Cara, in the black sweater."

"Sitting with Joe?"

"You know him?"

"Went to kindergarten all the way through college with him."

"You went to college?"

He'd laughed out loud good-naturedly. "I can't tell if you're trying to make conversation or if you're trying to insult me so that I'll leave you alone."

"Conversation." Des had felt color rising from

her chest to her cheeks. "I didn't mean it the way it sounded."

"Uh-huh." He was still smiling when the bartender set their beers up on the counter and Des handed the man a ten-dollar bill.

"On the house." The bartender turned to the bald man and said, "See you at the meeting this week, Seth?"

"I'll be there." The bald man had glanced down at Des. "I'm Seth, by the way. I'm a friend of your aunt's."

"It seems like everyone in Hidden Falls is a good friend of Barney's."

"Everyone is." He took a long drink from the bottle, then set it on the bar. "How are you liking Hidden Falls so far?"

"I like it pretty well. Aside from its obvious shortcoming, that is."

"What shortcoming?"

"There's no animal shelter."

"What?"

"There's no rescue shelter for animals in Hidden Falls. I asked Barney about it the other day and she said there wasn't a shelter of any kind for lost, abandoned, or abused animals."

Seth appeared to reflect on what she'd said. "The police pick up lost dogs and take them to the station until they can track down the owner."

"What if they can't?"

"I'm not sure."

"And animals that have been abused?"

"Anytime anyone sees anything going on that

shouldn't, they call Ben—that's the chief of police—and he personally looks into it."

"And does what?"

"Whatever needs to be done."

"He'll take a dog away from someone who's abused it?"

"I guess so."

"And where would he take it?"

"You'd have to ask him that."

"Dogfights?"

"Not that I know of."

"Cockfights?"

A smile had played on his lips, but he just shook his head no.

"No strays?"

"Well, sure. From time to time we've had some strays. People sometimes do stupid things, like bring their dogs up into the mountains and let them go."

"What do you do in cases like that?"

He'd rubbed his stubbled chin. "I think the last time, someone took the dog in. Or maybe took it to the SPCA over in Harlow Park. Not sure, now that you ask." He stared at her with dark eyes. "Where are you headed with all this?"

"I'm trying to figure out what Hidden Falls does with animals that need help."

"What would you like to see done?"

"I think this town should have a rescue shelter. What would someone do if they wanted to start one?"

"I guess they'd look into the ordinances regarding kennels or keeping animals."

"Maybe the library has that information," she'd said mostly to herself.

"And if there are no ordinances, I guess the next step might be to bring it up to the town council."

"Right. That makes sense. Thanks for the tip. I'll keep that in mind. I'm sure Barney knows when and where the town council meets."

"There's a meeting on Wednesday. Seven p.m. The conference room in the back of the police station." He'd smiled again. "If you're thinking about going, go early if you want in. The place fills up fast."

"There are that many people in Hidden Falls who show up for these meetings?"

"Not much else to do on a Wednesday night around here."

Right then, an older man had come up behind them and slapped Seth on the back and begun to rail about something. Des turned away so as not to appear to be eavesdropping. She tried to ignore a ping of disappointment because she'd been enjoying the conversation with Seth. He'd seemed genuinely interested in her thoughts about a shelter and had given her what sounded like good advice. Despite his tough appearance, he was soft-spoken and thoughtful and cute in his own way. That is, if a bald giant covered with tattoos could be considered cute.

Once the idea of setting up a shelter took hold, Des had had a hard time thinking about anything else. She sat up half the night making lists of the steps she might take. She had the time, the resources, and the experience to run a shelter. All she needed was the place.

Don't get ahead of yourself, she warned herself. She already had one big project on her plate. She wasn't sure how much of her time it'd take to keep the theater's records and paying the contractors' bills once they started on the actual renovations.

She'd check the internet to find the closest rescue group and see if they could use her services. She missed having a furry friend by her side. Maybe at some point she'd talk to Barney, find out how she'd feel about Des possibly bringing a dog into the house. Hypothetically, of course.

But right now, there was the job of locating the photos. She'd love to find pictures of the opening night to share with the local newspapers, maybe even the TV stations in Wilkes-Barre and Scranton. It would be great publicity to drum up interest for the theater in Hidden Falls, and publicity could increase their chances of getting those grants if need be.

And wouldn't it be great if they took photos all throughout the renovation process, maybe put them together in a book with some of the older ones? Des could see pictures of the boarded-up front door side by side with a shot from the 1920s showing the door partially open for a handsomely dressed patron going in. The more she thought about it, the more the idea appealed to her. The book could be an effective fund-raiser, and they needn't wait till they were running out of money to put the book on sale.

She'd have to discuss it with the others, of

course, but she was pretty sure they'd agree it was a great idea. And she'd probably have to turn the actual design process over to Allie, who had a much better sense of such things. But as long as it brought in funds they might need and generated interest in the theater within the community, Des didn't care if her sister got all the credit. The important thing was that it was done, and done right.

But first, she had to find those photos.

CHAPTER NINE

Cara was five minutes early for her meeting with Joe and the exterminator, so she sat in her car rehashing her phone conversation with Darla. There really wasn't anything new in Devlin's Light, Darla had assured her.

"Is the wedding still the big topic of conversation?" Cara had asked.

"In my shop, it is," Darla grumbled. "Honestly, ever since I sent in my regrets to the wedding, Angie has been impossible. I mean, seriously. Why would they even invite mc? I was your matron of honor, for crying out loud, and I'm still your best friend."

"Amber was one of my bridesmaids," Cara reminded her, "but it didn't stop her from stealing my husband. I'd say that ranks way above accepting their invitation."

"You don't really think I'd go, do you? I'm much too loyal. And then there's the cake. Angie promised

Amber that we'd do the cake. Which I've already told her I won't do." Darla paused. "Not only do I not want to be a part of their festivities, but the temptation to put something nasty into it would probably be more than I could resist."

Cara laughed. "I'm not even going to ask what nasty ingredients you had in mind. But really, I wouldn't think less of you if you went, or if you made the cake."

"Yes, you would."

"Well, yeah, I probably would. Though I have to admit it's getting easier, being away and out of the loop. I don't want to know what color the bridesmaids' dresses are and I don't care what's on the menu."

"Well, that's another thing. When Carol Cramer found out that her assistant had booked Carol's inn for the reception, she made the woman call back and tell Amber, 'So sorry, I made a mistake. We're already booked for that day.'"

"You're kidding."

"Nope. No reception for you." Darla mimicked the Soup Nazi from the old *Seinfeld* show. "So they're scrambling to find another place, which has Angie crazy, since the wedding is so soon. Everyone knows *the* place in Devlin's Light is Carol's on the Bay."

"Just like everyone who's anyone has their special-occasion cakes made by Darla's Delectables." Cara smiled.

"Right. Shut out all around. Carol said she didn't feel right since you'd had your reception there, and besides, she was too close to your mother."

"It's so weird that Drew would even want to have the reception in the same place we did."

"I know, right? It seems just a little creepy to me." Darla seemed to hesitate for a moment. "But you're really okay?"

"I'm even a little more okay after this phone conversation. It's nice to know that my friends have my back."

"Totally."

Cara hadn't been lying when she told Darla she was feeling a lot better about her life. Just hearing about the loyalty of her friends had boosted her mood, and having other things to do had shifted her focus from her broken heart and all the gossip to getting to know her newly found family. Every day drew her more deeply into Hidden Falls, and farther from Devlin's Light. Though Drew and Amber's wedding hung over her like a storm cloud, she was hoping that once the day came and went, the storm would pass and the clouds would clear from her head.

A door slamming brought her back to the here and now. She looked up as Joe emerged from his truck and headed directly toward her car. He was smiling and looked happy to see her.

Joe always looked happy to see her, and that was a fact. One she didn't really want to deal with.

Cara turned off the ignition, grabbed her bag, and swung the car door open.

"Good afternoon," Joe said as she slid from behind the wheel. "Sorry I'm a little late."

"Not all that late." She looked around. "I don't see the exterminator."

"He's just pulling up." Joe gestured to the old station wagon that was parking in front of his truck. "Let's go open up the theater and we'll let him do his thing."

Cara followed Joe to the sidewalk, where he made introductions.

"Cara McCann, meet Eddie Waldon. Ed, Cara McCann."

"Joe tells me you're one of Fritz's girls. Good to meetcha. Me and Fritz went back a ways. I was sorry to hear he'd passed." The man looked to be in his late sixties, with thinning brown hair gone to gray. His deep frown lines made his face appear droopy, but his eyes were alert and sparkling.

"Thank you. It seems everyone in town knew him and my aunt."

"True enough. Fritz was quite the guy. I remember seeing him in a couple of plays at school and right here at this theater."

"Barney mentioned that he'd started acting in high school," Cara said.

"He was real good, too. I always thought we'd be watching him on the big screen one day. Big surprise when he married Nora and she went on to be the star."

"I didn't realize he'd been that serious about it."

"Oh hell yeah. He was as good as anyone I'd ever seen, and back in the day, there were lots of good actors coming through Hidden Falls to do summer stage." Ed gestured to the theater. "I really thought Fritz would hit the big time."

"Well, he did that, but as an agent instead of a performer," Cara said.

"Guess he wanted Nora more than he wanted a career as an actor. Yep, they were a pair. He had the talent and she had the ambition. Nothing would do for her except to go to Hollywood. He figured the only way to get her was to take her there, so he became her manager and off they went to the West Coast."

"But she must've been good or she wouldn't have been cast in all those films."

"She was good. He was better." Eddie turned to Joe. "You didn't call me down here for a lesson in local history. Let's go inside and take a look around."

"I have some big flashlights in my truck," Joe said as he unlocked the door. "Let me get them."

"No need," Eddie told him and took off into the building. "I always come prepared." His voice trailed away as he went into the lobby.

"Looks like Eddie's off and running," Cara said.

"Let's catch up."

In the dark, they could see Eddie's flashlight beam disappearing into the lobby.

"Actually, I think I'll skip the part where I trail behind the guy who's looking for things that live in there." Cara hesitated in the doorway, then backed out.

"Well, he'll let us know what he finds." Joe closed the door behind them.

"I didn't mean that you shouldn't—"

"I wouldn't be of any use to him," Joe said. "But

hey, I have some good news for you. Mack called while I was on my way over here. He only needs one more day to get the main electrical up to snuff. Then we can get the power back on."

"That's *great* news. We want to explore more of the building, but it's tough when you can't see. I'll call the electric company today."

They stepped out onto the tiled area where the ticket booth once stood. "So, boss. What's next on the agenda?" Joe said.

"Once we establish the structural integrity of the building, we can get the other trades in here. I'm assuming you have everyone lined up?"

"I do."

"Then as soon as we get a green light from the engineer, everyone can start to do their thing." Cara paused. "Barney said the contractors would get the permits?"

Joe nodded. "That's how it's done. Saves you time, and besides, the guys we have lined up to work on this are all very experienced and know how to cut through red tape."

"Good," Cara said. "I can't wait until the lights are on and we can go through the entire building and check out everything we've missed."

"I'll call you as soon as I hear from Mack."

Cara smiled and nodded, not wanting for even Joe to know how antsy she was to get to work. It'd been frustrating not to see the overall picture inside the building.

Eddie appeared in the doorway. "You're going to

need some traps set in that basement. There are definitely mice, rats, maybe some squirrels."

"Swell." She grimaced. "What do you suggest?"

"I like these new electronic traps," he told her. "Like a tube with an electrical charge. You put your bait in at the far end; the animal follows its nose to the bait, trips the charge, and bam! No fuss, no muss. One less little bugger."

"What do you do with the, you know . . ."

"You take the trap to the trash, turn it upside down, and the animal falls out. Easy peasy." Eddie headed for his station wagon. "I've a bunch of them at home. I'll swing by later and set them up."

"Sounds good," Cara said.

"Want to work up a number for the job in its entirety?" Joe asked Eddie.

"I'll try to have something for you by Tuesday, but keep in mind I can't tell how long it's going to take to clear out that building. You've probably got generations of mice and rats in there."

A shiver raced up Cara's spine and she shuddered. "I dislike mice, but I really hate the thought of rats. Especially generations of rats."

"These aren't those big city rats—these are field rats, smaller, not aggressive. But a nuisance all the same. Hard to tell how much damage they may have caused, but you can assess that once you get the electricity working." Eddie started toward his truck. "Oh, and there's a piece of clapboard around the back that's been pushed to one side. Something's been coming and going would be my guess."

"Define 'something.'" Cara resisted the urge to outwardly cringe. It had been bad enough that once Joe had seen her run screaming from the building.

"Could be a raccoon, maybe even a family of them. They're not in there right now, best as I can tell, so maybe board up that spot, set out some Hava-hart traps."

"I'll take care of the board-up. Now, what about insects? Termites?" Joe asked as he and Cara walked the older man to his car.

"I can do a test on the exterior, but inside looks pretty clean. You got lucky there." Eddie opened the back of the station wagon and put his equipment inside, then slammed the hatch. "You give me a call when the electric is up and running, and meanwhile I'll get working on that estimate."

"Thanks, Eddie." Joe watched the car pull away; then he turned to Cara. "Have you had lunch? I got a late start this morning, so I didn't get much of a breakfast. At least, nothing like what I had yesterday. We can head down the street to the Green Briar and grab a sandwich."

When she hesitated, he said, "Oh, come on. I hate to eat alone. Besides, we can talk about what's going on with the theater."

"Okay." Cara shook off the thought of the "some-things" that might be living in the theater and told herself, *This is not a date. It's a business meeting.*

He locked up the building, then said, "Feel like a walk? It's not far."

"Sure." They crossed the street in front of the gas

station. The woman who'd been inside at the counter the night Cara stopped for gas was outside, and she waved to Joe.

"How's it going, Sally?"

"You know, Joe, it'd be nice if just one Sunday morning I didn't have to pick up litter from Saturday night," the woman grumbled. "'Course that's pretty much what you get when your business is next to the only bar in town."

"If you leave it, I'll take care of it later."

"Thanks, but I can't stand looking at the mess."

"Nice of you to offer to help her," Cara noted as they kept walking.

"We all try to give her a hand keeping up the place. Herbie, her husband, built the station back in the late fifties, the first gas station in Hidden Falls proper. Before that, you had to drive out onto the highway toward Powell to put gas in your car, so they say. Herbie passed away a few years ago and Sally's tried her best to keep the business going, but she's in her late seventies now and it's getting harder for her. Their son would've taken over eventually, but he went to Iraq and came back in a box." Joe's jaw set tightly.

"Was he a friend of yours?" Cara asked.

"Everyone in Hidden Falls is a friend. It's a small town, I'm sure you noticed. Not many moving in, a lot of the younger people moving out."

"You stayed."

"I have family here. My mom, my sister. Friends." He didn't elaborate on why he needed to stay—after all, Julie was an adult, too—and Cara didn't ask.

"And you have a business," she added.

"There is that."

They walked past an ancient drugstore, the front windows of which displayed every piece of equipment that ensured the good health and safety of the town's senior citizens. Next to the drugstore was a bookstore, a sporting goods store, a beauty parlor, and the Hudson Diner. A parking lot separated the diner from the rest of the stores on the block. The Green Briar was on the corner.

Joe held the door for her, and she stepped inside the charming café. Pots of pachysandra and ivy hung in the windows, and photos depicting the town's earlier days lined the walls. Cara noticed several large prints of the theater, crowds of people milling about outside. When the hostess greeted them and led them to a window table, Cara asked for one of the wall tables instead.

"Do you mind?" she asked Joe. "I wanted to get a closer look at the photos without having to lurk over someone trying to enjoy their meal."

"Not at all." He held her chair for her, then sat himself.

Manners, she could almost hear her mother say. *I love a thoughtful man with good manners.* Her father always held chairs and doors for her mother—for just about everyone, come to think of it. She couldn't recall him ever cutting someone else off in order for him to pass in front of them. Being first never seemed important to Fritz. That small memory made her smile.

"I've eaten here so many times I guess I don't see the décor anymore. I should've remembered all the old photos, especially those of the theater." Joe opened the menu, gave it a quick glance, then closed it again.

"I'd like to get a closer look at the one behind the table that's two away from us, but I don't think the couple sitting there would appreciate a stranger hanging over their table while they eat."

Joe turned and looked over his shoulder, then turned back to Cara. "Let me know when they leave and we'll try to sneak a look before someone else is seated."

"They look very intense," Cara noted, nodding in the direction of the couple. "Do you think one of them is dumping the other?"

Joe looked at her blankly for a moment, then laughed. "You mean the whole goodbye thing?"

Cara nodded.

"Barney told you that."

She nodded again.

"I personally don't know of anyone who was ever dumped here, but that's not to say it never happened. Seems to be more of a perception among the older folks in town, so maybe the reputation was earned before my time. You might ask Barney for more clarification."

"I think my sisters will be jealous that I got to see the place first. It sounded almost mystical the way Barney described it." She scanned the menu.

"Everything's pretty good here."

Cara felt his eyes on her, but she wouldn't let herself look up to meet his gaze. *Business lunch*, she reminded herself.

"By the way, Cara, before I forget, thanks for giving my sister a pep talk last night. I'm not sure exactly what you said to her, but it seemed to have straightened her out real fast."

"I'm not sure anything I said made any difference. But I was sorry she was having such a rough time. The ex-boyfriend doesn't deserve her."

"He never did. He was a jerk when he was in high school and he still is."

"Some guys never grow up."

"True enough." He smiled at the approaching waitress. "Some women don't, either."

"Hi, Joe." The waitress flashed a fancy smile that went all the way to her eyes as she edged closer to him.

"Jessica. This is my friend Cara." Joe tipped his water glass in Cara's direction before taking a sip.

"Hello." Jessica gave Cara the once-over.

"Cara is Barney Hudson's niece," Joe told her.

"Oh. We all know Barney." Her attitude softened a little, but she still stood closer to Joe than might've been necessary to take his order.

"Cara, have you decided?" Joe asked.

"The roasted veggie wrap looks good. I'll have that and an iced tea." Cara folded her menu and handed it to Jessica.

"You having the usual, Joe?" Jessica posed, her pencil held just so over the order pad.

"No, I'll have a cheeseburger. Medium rare."

After the waitress took the menus and walked away, Joe said, "Roasted veggies in a wrap?"

Cara smiled and nodded.

"I don't believe I've ever met anyone who actually ate one of those things. I thought they only put it on the menu because they thought it made them look cool."

"Don't knock it till you've tried it."

"Fat chance of that happening."

"Fat is exactly what you're going to get with that big old burger."

"You may have noticed I'm lean and mean. No fat on this boy."

"Maybe not on the outside." She raised her eyebrows. "What are your cholesterol levels?"

"I have no idea." Joe stared at her. "So I'm guessing you're a vegetarian?"

Cara nodded.

"Because you have high cholesterol?"

"My cholesterol is fine. I just can't bring myself to eat anything that could've been someone's pet at one time."

"They don't make burgers out of pet cows."

"How do you know?" she asked. "Do you know where that meat came from?"

"Yes, as a matter of fact, I do. Didn't you notice that the menu stated that all beef came from the Thompson farm right here in Hidden Falls?"

"A local farm?"

"About as local as you can get. It's less than a mile from here."

They debated the merits of a plant-based diet versus that of an omnivore until the waitress appeared with their meals. "Anything else?"

"Just our iced teas," Cara said. After the waitress walked away, she looked pointedly at Joe's burger. "Are you sure the Thompson kids didn't used to play with—"

"Uncle," he conceded. "This conversation is over."

They ate in silence for a moment before Cara asked about the waitress. "An old friend?"

"Sort of." Joe looked slightly uncomfortable, then admitted, "She dumped me for Ben once."

"Ben the police chief?"

"Right."

"He's dating her?"

"No, no. That was a long time ago. By the way, what was all that about last night, between Ben and Allie? She say anything to you?"

Cara shook her head. "She didn't say one word in the car on the way home. Of course, with Barney singing the entire way, no one was saying much of anything."

"What was she singing?"

"Some song about a girl who caught her guy cheating and slashed his tires and knocked out his headlights with a baseball bat." Cara paused. "At least, that's what I think she said."

"'Before He Cheats,'" Joe told her.

"What?"

"The song. Carrie Underwood. You'd like it if you heard it. Especially after what you told me about your ex." He leaned slightly toward her. "Does he have a car he's particular about?"

Cara thought about the old MG convertible that Drew kept locked up.

"He does."

"Are you going to tell me it wouldn't give you just a little bit of satisfaction to work it over?"

"It would." No need to think twice.

"There you go, then. Another universal message brought to you by country music."

"It seems that's all the radio stations play around here."

"This *is* country, Cara. Bluegrass, blues, some classic rock. I do realize that by some standards, this isn't a very sophisticated part of the country. We fish, we hunt, we boat, we farm. I can't remember anyone ever having a cocktail party. There are no wine bars but there is a vineyard. A couple of new farm-to-table restaurants opened up between here and Wilkes-Barre, but the locals are the farm and the table in that equation. Might be different where you're from."

"Not really. I'm from a small bay town. We fish but not the way you do around here. We have farms and vineyards. Our one farm-to-table restaurant is owned by the sister of the guy who does the farming. The vineyard is owned and run by a couple who grew up in town."

"What did you do there?"

"I own a yoga studio." She could tell by his face that he hadn't seen that coming. "What's that look for? What were you expecting?"

"I don't know. Teacher, maybe, something more . . . traditional."

"My mother was far from traditional and she raised me that way." Cara told him about growing up with Susa.

"A real free-spirited flower child, eh?"

Cara could've said so much more but she let the moment pass. Suddenly, thinking about Susa brought a lump to her throat, so she simply said, "She was that."

Cara watched Joe take a bite of his burger and was tempted to whisper, "Moo," but thought maybe she'd pulled that chain enough for one day.

"Is Barney excited about the theater renovation?" Joe asked.

"Oh yes. And I know she's happy you're going to be our project manager."

"I can't think of anything I wouldn't do for her."

"You've said something like that before. I understand she and your grandmother are good friends, and that you're close to her."

"It goes beyond friendship," he said simply.

When he didn't elaborate, she didn't push, even though she really wanted to.

Joe must've read her mind. "You want to ask but you're too polite."

"I'm curious. It's not just you, though. Everyone seems to sort of revere her. I'm just getting to know her, and I really like her. But I just met her, so I don't know her. Which is odd, since she's my aunt." Cara thought for a moment. "Of course, that's probably not as odd as just meeting my sisters for the first time."

"So you want to know why everyone in Hidden Falls has Bonnie Hudson on a pedestal."

"Yes. I'd like to see her through your eyes."

He munched on a potato chip, then ate a few more before asking, "How much do you know about your family?"

"Only what I've learned since my dad died. I know they've been in these parts for a long time. I know that my great- or great-great-grandfather owned a coal mine and gave land for a hospital and a school."

"He owned more than one mine, and at one time, almost everyone who lived around here worked for him." Joe reiterated almost verbatim the same story Pete had told them when they'd met at Pete's office to discuss Fritz's will. He ended by saying, "The college over in the next county, Althea College, was funded with profits from the Hudson mines. It was named after your great-great-grandmother."

"I've never heard of her. How do you know so much about the Hudsons?"

"Cub Scouts. I earned my badge for local history by writing a little book about them."

"I'd love to see it. You know so much more than I do."

"I have no idea where it is now, but I do know the library has several books about the area that are heavy on Hudson lore. I referred to them when I was working on that badge. I also interviewed some of the older folks around here. People who remembered old Reynolds Hudson. He was well liked, respected."

"So he named this college after his wife?"

"His wife or his mother, I don't recall which. Barney would know. And I only remember her name because there's a portrait of her in the bank lobby with her name on a plaque beneath it."

"Barney said she worked in the bank." Cara corrected herself. "*Ran* the bank."

"She did. Barney had worked in the bank for several years before their father died suddenly of a heart attack. The board of directors went into a panic at first, but they were sure it was only a matter of time before Fritz would come to his senses and return and take over. Barney went to the board and convinced them to let her run the bank until Fritz came back. Of course, she was pretty sure he was gone for good, but none of them even guessed."

"Foxy Barney." Cara smiled. She could see Barney pulling it off.

Joe nodded. "Masterfully outfoxed them all. And you talk to anyone in Hidden Falls, and they'll tell you the bank was never in better hands."

"So all this would've been before your time. How do you know all that? It wouldn't have been common knowledge."

"I heard it all from my grandma. She was Reynolds's secretary for years; then, when he passed away, she became the first female teller the bank had."

"Women have been bank tellers for years," Cara noted.

"Not in Hidden Falls. The bank had two tellers, and they'd always been men. The guy my grandmother replaced was in his mid-seventies and had gone to grade school with old Reynolds."

"So I guess over time, people got past the fact that Barney was a woman and began to accept her and respect her because of her position with the bank. Interesting."

"No, it was the way she used her position that people came to respect. She started the student loan program, offered really low interest rates, reduced the rates if you came back to Hidden Falls and taught here or joined the police force. She gave low-rate mortgages, business loans, car loans, personal loans, you name it. She was very generous and always fought for the little guy. If it was at all innovative for the time—or for the area—and it benefited people in Hidden Falls, Barney made it happen." Joe crunched another chip. "There'd be no Domanski Construction without Barney."

"She gave your dad a loan?"

He smiled wryly. "I said she was generous, I didn't say she was stupid. She gave *me* the loan. When she couldn't get the board to okay it—because of the circumstances under which I took over the business—Barney gave me the money from her personal funds. She saved my business, a business that my grandfather started over fifty years ago. She saved my family. And mine wasn't the only ass she's saved in this town."

"I had no idea," Cara said softly. That certainly explained his devotion to her.

"So when someone in Hidden Falls says they'd do anything for Barney, they mean it."

"Wow. That's some legacy. I guess that's why she never married."

"What? You mean because of her position with the bank?"

She nodded and he shook his head no.

"Barney never married because the man she was in love with died."

"Wait—you mean Pete Wheeler's brother?"

Joe nodded. "Right. Gil Wheeler."

"Barney was in love with . . ." Cara paused. "How did he die?"

"He fell from the rocks above the falls."

"The Hidden Falls? The ones way up the hill behind the house?" The ones she and Des had visited that very morning?

"Yeah."

"That's why she hates the mural," Cara murmured.

"What mural?"

"There's a mural depicting the falls in the dining room. Barney obviously hates the thing, but she won't have it painted over because it was done by a famous artist who has a connection to the family. I guess the banker in her can't bring herself to destroy something that adds so much value to the house, but at the same time, she never uses the dining room because that mural reminds her of what happened to Gil."

"As many times as I've been in that house, I've never been in the dining room. I guess that's why."

"Do you know how the accident happened? Des

and I were up there just this morning. You can go right up to the edge of the rocks, but the drop-off is obvious. Gil would've known that, right?" A horrible thought occurred to her. "Please tell me Barney wasn't with him."

"No. But his brother was, and so was Fritz."

"My dad and Uncle Pete . . ." It was almost too much information for Cara to absorb so quickly. "Uncle Pete's brother was in love with Barney?"

"Uncle Pete?" Joe questioned.

"He was my dad's best friend. I've known him all my life. I had no idea he'd had a brother who died."

"Maybe it's something he doesn't like to talk about."

"What did they say happened?"

"Nothing."

"But you said they were there."

"They were. They both said they didn't see the actual fall, that the last they saw, he was standing on the edge of the rock. They figured he got too close to the edge and lost his balance."

"If he knew the family that well, he must've been up there before. He'd have known . . ." Something wasn't adding up. "There must have been more to it than that."

"If there was, we'll never know. Two of the three are gone and Pete doesn't come back all that often, and when he does, it's mostly just to check in with Barney. Right after Gil's funeral, Pete left for law school and Fritz took off with Nora for Hollywood."

"He didn't even stick around to be there for his

sister?" Cara was horrified. "She must have been devastated after Gil died."

"I'm sure she was. A few years later, when their dad passed away, Fritz came back for the funeral. He and Nora stayed a few days at the house with Barney before heading back to L.A."

"Poor Barney. Lost her love, lost her father, left alone in that big house all these years."

"Well, her mother was alive up until about fifteen years ago. She was in the early stages of dementia when your grandfather passed away, and that progressed as the years went on. Barney had live-in help for her, though."

"No wonder Barney was happy to see us. Even three strangers must be a welcome change after living alone for so many years."

"Don't feel too sorry for her. She has a full life. She has a finger in every pie in town."

"I can tell. Barney has something to do almost every day."

Cara ate slowly, barely tasting her food. Finally, Joe asked, "Cara, are you all right?"

"Sorry. I'm having a hard time reconciling the loving, caring man who was my father, with a man who would leave his grieving sister to elope with his girlfriend and who didn't look back."

"Maybe Barney can shed some light on the situation."

So Barney, tell me about the time the love of your life fell off the rocks up at the falls and died and your brother took off with Nora.

"She did say that something had happened up there once but that no one talked about it anymore." She tapped the side of her glass with her fingertips, trying to remember exactly what Barney had said. Maybe Des or Allie would remember.

"Can I get you anything else?" Jessica asked, having noticed they'd both finished eating.

"Nothing more for me, thanks." Cara sipped the last of her drink.

"Just the check, please."

Jessica handed it to Joe and looked about to say something to him when she was beckoned to another table.

"See you at the Frog on Wednesday night?" she asked before she tended to her other customers.

"Don't know. I'll be at the meeting but not sure how long it's going to go this week." He stood and held the back of Cara's chair.

"Joe, the people at the front table are gone. Can we take a close-up look at the photo of the theater?"

"Sure thing." He walked her over to the photo.

Cara craned her neck to get a better view. There was glare on the glass, but even so, she could see the building as it had looked many years ago.

"It was so handsome," she said almost to herself. "The marquee is so fancy and all the lights around the door make it look like a big fairy house."

"I hadn't looked at it in quite that way, but okay." Joe looked down at her and grinned. "I think if you look closely you can see people coming out. Or maybe they're going in. My gran said that going to see a play or a movie at the Sugarhouse was the thing to do back then. Everyone dressed up for the occasion."

"I can't see how anyone's dressed from here, but there must be pictures in the house. I wonder if the owner would let me borrow this one."

Joe looked around. "I don't see Madeline—the owner—but I'll see if I can get ahold of her. She might let you take it long enough to have a copy made."

Joe paid the cashier, after stopping at two tables to greet acquaintances, and he and Cara finally walked out into the warm afternoon.

"This is such a nice change from the weather earlier in the week," Cara noted.

"It's really unpredictable this time of the year. We don't count on it staying warm until May."

"It'd be great if it stayed warm, though. The theater's cold as a tomb in the basement."

"I don't even know how long it's been since there was heat in that building."

"What kind of heat did it have, do you know?" she asked.

"There's a big furnace in the utility room downstairs. I'm sure it was coal originally, then changed to oil."

"The furnace should be checked for efficiency and to make sure it's running."

"There's one oil company in town," he told her. "They can bring someone in after the electricity is turned on."

"I'm assuming the water was turned off a long time ago."

Joe nodded. "After the bills weren't paid."

"So is there a lien?"

"Your dad paid it after he bought the place back."

Cara nodded. Her dad was responsible about money, and would have made sure there weren't any legal issues for the girls to deal with.

"So how does it feel to be the owner of a theater?" he asked as they crossed Main Street in front of the theater. Eddie's station wagon was back, parked exactly where it had been parked earlier.

"Actually, it feels pretty good." She looked up at the structure and saw it as it was in the photo in the Good Bye.

"Intimidated?" he asked.

"Are you kidding?" Cara laughed. "I'm absolutely up for the challenge."

"Oh, it's going to be a challenge, all right."

"We will totally rock it. We'll have this place looking as good as new by the time we're done."

"I like a woman with confidence."

"I'm confident that with the right people, we'll do just fine."

"I promise you, we'll only have the best working for you."

"Barney trusts you; I trust you, too." Cara stopped in front of her car. "Thanks for lunch."

"Anytime." He said it as if he meant it. "I'll get those estimates to you as soon as they come in so you can look them over. If you have any questions about anything—the cost of materials, labor, whatever—ask me. That's what I'm here for."

"That would be great, thanks." She walked to the driver's side and unlocked the door. "See you."

"I sure hope so."

Cara was aware that Joe was standing on the sidewalk, aware that his eyes were on her car as she pulled away from the curb. It wasn't until she began to round the corner that she saw him turn away and disappear into the theater.

CHAPTER TEN

It seemed that all hell had broken loose by the time Cara returned to the house. Allie was pacing the kitchen like a caged animal and muttering to herself.

"What happened?" Cara asked.

"My daughter . . ." Phone in hand, Allie continued to pace.

"Oh my God, Allie. Something happened to Nikki?" Cara tossed her bag onto a nearby chair.

"She's been dumped at the airport by her idiot father. I'm supposed to pick her up at six and I have no car. . . ."

"Slow down and start from the beginning. Obviously she called. . . ."

Allie nodded. "She said she's on spring break as of Friday, and Clint had to go to London on business, so he made arrangements for her to stay with her friend Courtney. But at the last minute, Courtney's mother wasn't available, so Court went out of town, which of course left Nikki with nowhere to go. So he put her on a plane to fly out here for the week."

"But that's fabulous. You've been missing her, right? So okay, you got short notice, but the important thing is that she's going to be with you for a whole week." Cara sat on the window-seat cushion. "Why are you angry?"

"Because . . . because . . . he always does stuff like this. He makes plans for himself, and then it's like, 'Oh, yeah. Nikki.' Then he scrambles to find something for her to do." Allie's eyes crackled with raw anger. "And this business trip? I think it's a sham. I think he's off with his girlfriend."

"Clint has a girlfriend?" Des came into the room from the front hall. "Since when?"

"That's a very good question." Allie told them about her suspicions regarding Courtney's mother and Clint. "I think at the last minute, she decided to go with him."

Des put her feet up on the rungs of the chair next to her. "So what brought all this on, anyway?"

"He put Nikki on a plane early this morning. After several stops, she'll be landing in Scranton in about two hours."

"Nikki's coming here?" Des all but clapped her hands with glee. "I can't wait to see her!"

"Neither can I, but I have to pick her up and I have no car. . . ."

"You'll take mine," Cara told Allie.

"Thanks, Cara." Allie grabbed a handful of tissues before dropping into the nearest chair. "What am I going to do with her for a week? I haven't planned anything."

"What do you usually do when you're together?" Des asked.

"We go shopping, have lunch, watch movies."

"That's it? That's all you do?" Cara looked confused.

"What else is there? What did you do with your mother when you were Nikki's age?"

"We baked. We did crafts. We tie-dyed stuff— T-shirts and fabrics that we could make stuff out of. Mom taught me to macramé. Oh, and how to spin yarn from wool. That was cool." Cara smiled at the memory.

"I had to ask," Allie muttered, and got up and started to pace again.

"This week is going to be a total disaster. I bet she'll never want to spend time with me again. And she's so excited about coming! She can't wait to see the house and the town and the theater and meet her new aunts and Barney. . . ."

"So that's good, right? She's looking forward to being here," Des pointed out.

"There's nothing here, Des. No cute shops, no cute little restaurants. . . ."

"Did you tell her there were?" Des raised an eyebrow.

"I might have intimated it."

"I had lunch at the Good Bye Café today," Cara piped up. "It's kind of cute."

"What were you doing there?" Des paused. "Wait.

Let me guess. Joe took you to lunch to talk about the reno plans."

"That's right."

"I hope you talked about more than work," Des said.

"The restaurant has some great photos of the theater on the walls. Joe's going to see if the owner will let us make copies."

"Oh, speaking of photos of the theater," Des said excitedly, "wait till you hear this great idea I had today."

"That's nice. Joe has the hots for Cara. Des had a great idea. Now can we get back to *my* problem? My kid will be here in a couple of hours."

"Okay, first ask Barney if it's okay if she stays here. I'm sure it is, but give her the courtesy. Then see if there are any girls her age in the neighborhood that she might be able to hang out with. I think Barney's still out back gardening," Des suggested.

Allie stopped pacing long enough to hang over the back of one of the kitchen chairs. "Look, I know you mean well, but Nik is not a small-town country girl. She's L.A. and she's private school and . . . well, she's used to a totally different way of life. Different kids." Allie made a face and whispered, "And I'm afraid I sort of built up Hidden Falls a little to make it sound more exciting than it really is."

"Ah, now we're getting down to it."

"Shut up, Des."

"What exactly did you tell her?" Cara stood and walked to the sink. "Coffee?"

"Yes, please." Des raised a hand.

Allie sighed. "Guys, could you focus?"

"Okay, so you told her . . . what?" Cara drained the dregs of the morning's coffee into the sink and rinsed the pot.

"That our family home was a mansion, and that—"

"Wait a minute," Des interrupted. "It sort of is. I mean for Hidden Falls, this place is almost palatial. It is the biggest house in town."

"Yes. But we're in the sticks. There are garages in sections of L.A. that are bigger than this place."

"We're not in L.A.," Cara reminded her.

"That's exactly my point." Allie blew out one long, exasperated breath.

"Why is that necessarily bad? Why does every place have to be the same? This is a great country, Allie. It's time she saw more of it."

"Des is right," Cara said. "Nikki should know that everyone doesn't live the same way, that every town doesn't look alike. Honestly, I think you're making too big a deal out of this."

"I think she'll hate it here," Allie blurted. "And she'll hate me for bringing her here."

"I think you're underestimating your daughter," Cara said. "And her father sent her here, not you."

"All the same, she'll be here and she'll have nothing to do and she'll blame me."

"I think you're being very shortsighted and snobby," Des declared. "So fine, there are no fancy stores here. No fancy restaurants. Take her to the places that *are* here, let her see where her family came from. The town is absolutely charming."

"I'm sure that'll impress the hell out of her."

Des turned to Allie. "Why are you worried about impressing your daughter? You're her mother, Al. You shouldn't have to impress her. And you shouldn't want to."

"You don't understand." Allie sighed, and started for the back door.

"Where are you going?" Des asked.

"To ask Barney how long it takes to get to Scranton, and then I'm going to download one of those GPS apps onto my phone so I can find the damned airport. . . ."

It was close to nine before Cara heard tires crunching over stones in the driveway. She grabbed a flashlight and headed toward the front door. A storm had blown the power out around seven thirty, and there was no sign it'd be coming back on soon. She met Barney and Des in the hall; Des armed with a flashlight, Barney with a fat white candle.

Dragging a huge suitcase, Allie threw open the door, and she and her daughter, pushed by the wind, all but fell inside. "You could've at least left the porch lights on."

Des held up the flashlight. "No power. The electricity has been off for a while. But here's my beautiful niece and she's much more important." Des opened her arms and hugged the girl.

"I swear, Nikki, you are going to be the tallest woman ever in this family. Not to mention the most beautiful."

"I'm as tall as my mom." Nikki embraced Des. "But you're still a peanut, Aunt Des."

"I haven't grown since fifth grade." Des held Nikki at arm's length. "Now, say hello to your great-aunt Barney—"

"Bonnie," Allie corrected her.

"No one ever calls me that." Barney handed her candle to Des and stepped forward to bear-hug the girl.

"What do I call you?" Nikki pulled off her hat, and her blond hair spilled over her shoulders.

"Aunt Barney will do just fine."

"Thanks for letting me stay in your house this week, Aunt Barney." Nikki's eyes flitted around the darkened hall. "Wow. Mom said this was a great Victorian house, but this is even cooler than I thought it'd be. And it's just a little creepy. Like one of those old movies? The ones where someone is hiding behind these hidden panels so they can creep around the house at night and spy on everyone?"

"There's a visual I'll take with me tonight," Cara said. "Nikki, I'm Cara. I'm your mother's—"

"The secret sister." Nikki's eyes were wide in the dim light. "My mom told me all about you and your mother and how my grandpa had two families. It's so cool, don't you think? Don't you want to know that story? Of course, with my gramma and grampa dead, we'll never know everything, right? I told Mom I'd love to have a secret sister, but she said no chance of that happening."

"Well, she would know. And I'm not sure how cool it is, but it's certainly been interesting. And look—besides two sisters and an aunt, I got a niece out of it." Cara offered Nikki a hug. "Win, win, win."

The lights played off the portraits hanging on the walls and bounced off the stained glass windows in the front doors.

"Was your plane late?" Barney asked. "We thought you'd be back hours ago."

"A little late, and we stopped in Scranton for dinner." Allie rolled Nikki's suitcase to the bottom of the stairs, where she left it.

"I can't wait to see the rest of your house, Aunt Barney." Nikki still appeared slightly starstruck.

"As soon as the lights are back on. And it isn't just my house, you know. It belongs to all of us. And I can't tell you what it means to me to have you all here." In the odd light, Barney looked as if she were almost about to cry.

Cara dismissed the thought. Barney was made of solid steel.

"So how about we take you upstairs and get you settled." Allie struggled to get the suitcase up the first step.

"Here, let me help," Des said.

"I've put Nikki in my old room." Barney turned to lock the front door.

"Which room is that?" Allie and Des had gotten as far as the third step.

"The room next to your dad's old room," Barney said. "The turret room."

"That's all the way in the front of the house." Allie stopped mid-step.

"That's right. It's the nicest room for a young girl," Barney replied. "It has such a pretty view out the side windows and a cushy chair where you can sit and enjoy the scenery."

"But it's so far from my room . . ." Allie began.

"Mom, I'm not a baby. I don't have to sleep next door to you," Nikki reminded her.

"You don't have to sleep alone in another part of the house, either," Allie protested.

"I'm right across the hall, so she's not alone," Barney assured her.

"Let's go see." Nikki took Cara's hand so that they could climb the steps together, led by Cara's flashlight. "I can't wait to see everything here. Mom told me that you all were having such a fun adventure. I think it's so cool that I got to come. I read all about Art Deco theaters online, and I can't believe how lucky we are to own one. I can't wait to see it and be part of it. I want to help. I'll show you what I found online. . . ."

Nikki continued to chatter as they made their way up the stairs. They had just arrived at the second-floor landing when the lights began to flicker on and off.

"OMG, does this place have ghosts?" a breathless Nikki asked. "Wouldn't that be the coolest thing ever? Maybe we could communicate with our ancestors' spirits."

"No ghosts, honey, sorry. But apparently we do have electricity once again," Barney said as all the lights came back on.

"Wow, for a minute there, it was like that TV show—actually it may have been a made-for-TV movie. Anyway, there were these kids in this old house and there was no electricity at all, so everyone was in the dark? And one of the boys was an ax murderer but nobody knew, and . . ."

Nikki's voice faded into the bedroom Barney had prepared for her.

"What do you think?" Des whispered to Cara.

"OMG, I think this is going to go better than, like, you know, Allie thought it would?"

Des laughed.

"Seriously, Nikki is adorable," Cara said. "She's not at all what I expected after listening to Allie earlier. I thought she'd be a spoiled little brat who'd be put off by the lack of glitter and flash."

"I think Nik is more levelheaded than her mother is sometimes. She's certainly more open to the experience here than Allie was."

"Let's hope the enthusiasm lasts, or it could be a very long week." Des pushed open the bedroom door. "Come on, let's help Nikki search the walls for hidden panels and then we can take her on a tour. . . ."

Cara and Barney were already in the kitchen when Nikki came downstairs the next morning. She was dressed in leggings, hot-pink sneakers, and a long sweater knitted in shades of purple and green.

"How'd you sleep, sugar?" Cara asked.

"Pretty good. It's so quiet here, though. I didn't hear one car go by all night." Nikki looked at the kitchen table where fruit, yogurt, and cereal had yet to be put away. "Could I have some yogurt?"

"Of course. You may have whatever you like." Barney got up from the table and went to the refrigerator. "Juice, Nikki? Toast? What do you usually have?"

"Yes, juice, please. I usually have a Pop-Tart and a glass of milk," she admitted, "but don't tell my mom."

"Don't tell your mom what?" Allie yawned as she and Des came into the room. She was dressed in a similar fashion to her daughter, but her eyes had none of Nikki's sparkle and her skin was pale.

"Mom, are you okay?" Nikki frowned. "You look . . . I don't know, sick or something."

"I've had better mornings." Allie poured herself a cup of coffee. "Now what isn't anyone supposed to tell me?"

"That sometimes I have Pop-Tarts for breakfast." Before Allie could respond, Nikki went on the defense. "Dad doesn't care, and I can eat in the car on my way to school. Courtney's mom doesn't mind if we eat in her car as long as we don't make a mess."

"Your dad doesn't drive you to school anymore?" Allie took a seat at the table.

"Sometimes, but some mornings he goes to work

early so Court's mom picks me up." Nikki smiled as she reached for the orange juice Barney had poured for her. "Thank you, Aunt Barney."

"You're very welcome, Nikki." Barney's smile was pure joy. It was easy to see she was delighted to have all her family here with her, and especially thrilled to find the youngest member such a sweetheart.

"So you and Courtney are very close friends, I gather." Allie took a banana from the bowl and began to peel it.

Nikki nodded. "She's my BFF. Like, for real. We're like sisters."

"I guess her dad works a lot, too, or he'd drive you guys to school once in a while." Allie took a bite of the banana.

"Oh no. Her dad lives near Malibu. Her parents are divorced." Nikki sat across the table from her mother and scooped some yogurt into a bowl. "Aunt Barney, is this yogurt organic? Just asking. It's okay if it isn't," she hastened to add.

"Cara bought it, and Cara's all about organics," Barney told her. "That's a definitive yes."

"Cool, Aunt Cara. Courtney's mom is all organic, too. She even got my dad to start buying organic."

"I guess your dad and Courtney's mom must see a lot of each other." Allie took a harder bite of the banana.

"Well, yeah. I mean, they just live three houses away, and sometimes we all have to go to school for stuff so we all go together." Nikki turned to Cara. "Did you ever have almond milk ice cream? Well, I guess it's not really ice cream since there's no real cow cream in it. . . ."

"I have. I love it." Cara had been watching the exchange between Allie and Nikki as it developed, and she was glad when Nikki changed the subject. Everyone in the room—except Nikki, apparently— saw where the conversation was going, and Cara was hoping it'd end before Nikki caught on as well.

"Me too." Nikki went back to her yogurt.

"Write down the brand name of the yogurt you like and I'll see if they have it at the market." Barney handed Nikki the growing grocery list for the week. "This is how we shop for food, by the way. If there is something you want, you have to write it on the list, which hangs on the side of the refrigerator door until market day. If it isn't written down, I don't buy it."

"Cool. I'll remember." Nikki finished her yogurt and rinsed the bowl without being told. "So, what's everyone doing today?" Her eyes were shining with anticipation. "I can't wait to see the theater. Can we go?"

"Right now you can't see much until the electrician gets all the circuits working again, but that could happen anytime now." Cara slipped her arms into the sleeves of her jacket. "I had the electric company turn the power back on yesterday. It's been off for a long time."

"What else is there to do while we're waiting for electricity?" Nikki asked.

"Oh. I started to tell you all yesterday about the idea I had." Des told them about her plans to put together a book with photos of the theater, then and now. "I thought we could use it not only as publicity, but as a fund-raiser."

"Where are the photos?" Cara asked.

"I haven't found them yet. I started to look in the attic, but I didn't find anything. I thought maybe we could all take some time today to look," Des said.

"Oh, cool. I love old attics. Court's gramma's attic has these cool old Christmas ornaments in dusty old boxes, and she has lights for the tree that are bigger than my thumb."

"I'm sure there are plenty of those up there, too," Barney said, "and you're welcome to look for them. But if you're looking for the theater photos, you'll find them in one of the filing cabinets in the office."

"Can we see them?" Nikki jumped up.

"Certainly. And maybe you could help us decide which ones would be best in Des's book." Barney led the way into the office and opened a file drawer.

"I should've waited until you got home yesterday before I started looking," Des said to Barney.

"Well, no doubt you uncovered some things upstairs that one of us will be looking for, sooner or later." Barney pulled a thick stack of files from the cabinet and set them on the desk. "Here we are. Let's see what we have."

Nikki leaned over Barney's shoulder. "Oh my God, it's gorgeous! It looks just like the theaters I looked up on my laptop."

"Oh, wow. It really was an Art Deco treasure," Des said.

"That's the outside. I know there were photos of the inside as well." Barney shuffled through the stack. "Ah, here we are. The grand staircase. It leads up to the balcony."

"We need to go see that right now." Nikki was almost jumping out of her skin.

"We didn't see that the other day," Cara noted. "It must have been on the other side of that center wall. But since the lights aren't on yet, we'll be using flashlights again."

"Then that's what we'll do. But Nikki's right. We need to check it out." Des looked over the top of Nikki's head to where Allie stood in the doorway. "Let's get our jackets and we'll all walk down together."

"I'm so there." Nikki raced out of the room.

Cara's phone pinged and she pulled it from her pocket to check out the incoming text. "Oh, wait. Scratch that last part. We have light in the lobby!" She held up her phone to show the others the photo Joe had texted her. "He said Mack has most of the first floor wired and he and his guys are working in the basement. Hallelujah!"

She sent a return text: *Thanks! We're on our way!*

"Fabulous. We'll be able to actually see all the mice and bugs and any other creepy-crawly thing in there." Allie made a face.

Barney turned to her. "Allie, that is the most delightful child I have ever met. I'm so glad she's here."

"And you were afraid she'd be bored." Cara chuckled. "We'll be lucky to keep up with her."

"But Al, if I could say one thing. Make one little suggestion?" Des said softly. "Don't put Nik on the spot where Clint and Courtney's mother are concerned. If there's something going on and she hasn't figured it out yet, don't put that in her head. Let her find that out on her own. If there is nothing going on, all you'll accomplish is making her suspicious when she shouldn't be. Let it go, Al."

"Easy for you to say," Allie snapped. "She isn't your daughter and he wasn't your husband. When you've walked in my shoes, then you get to tell me what I should do. Stay out of it, Des."

Allie turned her laser gaze to Cara and Barney.

"Everyone—stay out of it."

Nikki all but flew back into the room. "So we're going now, right? All of us?" She turned to Barney. "Will you come, too?"

"Sweet pea," Barney told her, "I wouldn't miss this for the world."

Des glanced at her watch. "I can only spend about an hour there. I have the name and number of a woman who runs a shelter near Clarks Summit that I wanted to talk to. We've emailed, and she said she'll only be available until one this afternoon. I don't want to miss her."

"What kind of shelter? Like a homeless shelter?" Nikki asked.

"Yes, but for dogs, not people. I worked with one back in Montana. I miss it," Des admitted. "I was hoping I could find a group I could work with while I'm here. And if there isn't one . . ."

"Let me guess. You'll start one yourself." Allie slipped into a heavy dark blue cardigan.

"That's right." Des turned to Barney. "That is, of course, if you have no objection."

"Why would I object?" Barney asked.

"Because sometimes a dog needs to be rehabilitated because it's been abused or has trust issues. I have a talent for putting animals at ease."

"So you mean you'd bring these needy dogs into the house, here?" Allie asked. "What if they bite? Or have fleas?"

"If there is no one else to do it, yes, they would stay with me. If they are known biters, they wouldn't be sent to foster care. And there's such a thing as flea baths." Des took her suede jacket from the closet.

"You know what Mom always said. Dogs are wild animals and should stay outside in the wild."

"And, Allie, you know Dad always said that was a bunch of BS because Mom didn't want to take care of it." Des forced a smile and put on the jacket. "Hell, Mom didn't want to take care of us."

"Nora always was a bit . . . self-centered." Barney wrapped her scarf around her neck and opened the front door and held it until everyone had filed out. She turned and locked the house.

"It'd be cool to help homeless dogs, Aunt Des. I'd help you," Nikki volunteered as she hopped down the steps. "And I want to help on your photo book, too."

"I think your mother might want to be in on that." Des looked pointedly at Allie.

"If nothing else, I can use the photos to guide the restoration," Allie said.

"Mom, what do you mean?" Nikki's curiosity apparently demanded that she know everything about everything.

"The three of us agreed that we'd each take an area of responsibility for the theater. Mine is the interior design."

Cara noted that as much as Allie initially had protested any involvement in the restoration, there was a touch of pride in her voice.

"So your job is, like, being an interior designer?" Nikki looped an arm through her mother's.

"Sort of. I'm going to have to do some research, though. Authentic paint colors, fabrics for the stage drapes and seats."

"All the pretty stuff. Right up your alley, Mom." Nikki turned to Cara. "What's your part, Aunt Cara?"

"I guess you could call me the construction liaison. I'm going to be working along with the project manager so that we know what's being done and when."

"Cool. Do you get to wear one of those, you know, helmets?"

"Hard hats? Not yet."

"And Aunt Des . . ."

"Show me the money." Des grinned. "I hold the checkbook."

"You guys are so together," Nikki declared. "Oh! I know! I can be, like, your intern."

"That's exactly what we need," Des told her. "An intern."

"I can help with whatever you have to do. I'm really good at research," Nikki said excitedly. "My English teacher said I write the best papers in my class because I always look up the extra stuff. Maybe I could help you. And I love history. It's my new favorite subject." Nikki looked over her shoulder to Cara. "And I can help you with . . . whatever it is that you're doing."

"I can't think of anyone I'd rather have as my assistant," Cara told her.

"I'm so glad Daddy had to go to London so I got to come here. I'm the luckiest girl ever," Nikki all but sang as they headed for the theater.

"Oh, wow, is that it?" Nikki pointed to the boarded-up building on the opposite corner.

"That's it," Cara said.

"Nik, I know it doesn't look like much now, but . . ." Allie began.

"It's awesome! Just think of what we're going to find when all that wood comes off the front! It'll be just like in those pictures that Aunt Barney showed us. We're, like, archaeologists, finding old stuff and figuring out how to put it back together." Nikki broke free from her mother and raced across the street. Not bothering to wait for anyone, she went through the open door.

"If only there were a way to bottle that enthusiasm," Barney said. "I have a feeling that child is going to keep all four of us going for the rest of the week."

They followed Nikki into the theater and found her in the lobby.

"Oh my God, Mom!" she exclaimed. "This place is amazing."

"It is." Allie glanced around at the walls they were all seeing in good light for the first time. She inspected the decorative painting that surrounded the arches. "The paint appears to be in good condition, but there are a few places where it's flaked a little. I wonder if it's worth it to try to fix it or if it's more historically correct to leave it as is."

"That's something we can research together, Mom," Nikki said before she took off to explore the other side of the arches.

"How gorgeous is this place now that we can finally see it?" Cara looked up at the ceiling. "I see the chandelier isn't lit yet."

"It probably needs all new bulbs," Barney said. "And they may not be easy to find."

"They aren't," Joe said as he came into the lobby. "And who's the kid I just saw racing up to the balcony?"

"Allie's daughter, Nikki," Des told him.

"She shot past me like a rocket."

"As she's been doing to all of us since she arrived. Let's see if we can catch up to her." Barney headed in the direction that Joe had come from.

"So what's the story with the electricity? Is all the wiring completed?" Cara asked Joe.

He shook his head. "They're still working in the basement. Mack said he probably needs about three more days. They haven't done anything around the stage yet. But since you're not going to be putting on any shows for a while, the stage is probably the last area we need to worry about."

"True." Cara walked into the auditorium, where the overhead lights had been turned on. "It looks so much bigger now that I can see it in its entirety."

"They used to pack the house, from what my grandmother told me. You'd have to buy tickets in advance for whatever was happening here on weekends," Joe said. "They'd sell out all twelve hundred seats."

"It would be so great if we could make that happen again," Cara murmured.

"Hey, Aunt Cara! You have to come up here! It's so cool," Nikki called down from the balcony.

"I'm on my way." Cara turned to Joe. "How do I get up there? Around this corner?"

"The stairs are right over there. You can reach them from in here, or through the lobby." Joe pointed toward the stairwell. "Listen, I have to run back to a jobsite. Mack and his crew are in the basement if you need them, Eddie has been and gone, and the plumber is supposed to be here in about an hour. I'll try to get back in time for that meeting."

"If not, it's okay. I can handle the walk-through," Cara told him.

"Of course you can. But I want it understood that we'll both be on the job."

"Got it. Maybe we'll see you later." Cara walked toward the stairwell.

She knew what Joe really meant was that the plumber needed to know that Joe'd be on the job breathing down his neck, but she appreciated that he didn't come out and say it. Eventually, the subs would realize that she was the owner on-site, and that Joe worked for her. She'd educate herself as much as she could, but right now, she needed Joe's experience and his reputation as one who tolerated no nonsense on the work site. She didn't expect to learn everything there was to know, but she could learn the basics. It would take time, and she was grateful to have Joe there to walk her through things.

The stairwell came into view and she stopped for a moment to admire the workmanship. It was wide enough for two people and covered with the same carpet as the lobby. As Cara climbed to the balcony, she checked out the condition of the carpet on every riser.

"Carpet looks pretty good," she announced when she joined the others. "Which is a blessing, since it'd be a lot of carpet to replace."

"We can do a closer inspection when the lighting up here is better, and then decide," Des said, "but you're right. It doesn't look too bad. And the seats are the same as downstairs."

"With the same layer of dust on them." Cara paused to examine one of the wooden seats. "They're in pretty good condition, actually, but we can do a complete inventory later."

"Great view from here." Cara looked down to the first level, then up to the ceiling. "It looks even better, the closer we get to it. The chandelier is gorgeous."

"It's awesome, Aunt Cara. I'll bet it was the coolest thing back when they did plays here. Like when my gramma and grampa were in them?" Nikki stood behind the back row of seats. "Can't you just see it?"

"I can. And remember, this was a film theater, as well. We found posters in the basement for some of the pictures they showed here. One was an early film of your grandmother's." The words were barely out of Cara's mouth before Nikki took off.

"Where in the basement? I want to see. Mom, come on." Nikki waited for her mother at the bottom of the steps.

"We'll all be so much thinner at the end of this week," Allie muttered as she hurried to catch up with her daughter.

"It's been such a long time since I was in this building." Barney came down from the upper level of the balcony.

"I'll bet it brings back a lot of memories," Cara said.

Barney nodded but didn't respond.

"Were you in any of the plays?" Des had followed Barney down the steps, a camera in her hand. She'd been taking pictures of the balcony from every angle and taking notes in her small notebook.

"One or two, but only when they needed someone for a crowd scene," Barney replied. "One actor in the family was plenty."

"Let's catch up with Nikki and Allie," Des said. "Barney, you're going to want to see the posters we found."

"There might be some freestanding display cases in one of the closets. I know there were display cases outside, under the marquee," Barney said, "but they were built into the wall and covered with glass. I imagine they're still there, under those boards, but it may not be the right time to uncover those."

"I agree. I think I'd rather wait until we're almost ready to reopen," Cara said. "It'd be better to finish the exterior and then put the posters back up."

"Have you thought about reopening?" Barney followed Cara through an arch and into the hallway that led to the basement steps.

"Dad's will just said we had to complete the renovations," Cara said carefully. "He didn't specify what we were to do once we were finished."

"So anything's on the table? Reopen it? Sell it?"

Cara shrugged. "I guess. I know Allie's said she's out of here once the job is done, and I can't blame her, really, because she does have Nikki to consider. Other than Des's involvement with the rescue shelter, she doesn't talk about her life in Montana very much."

"And you?" Barney paused at the top of the steps.

"I miss my yoga studio. I miss my friends and my students. I know it's in good hands. I've been texting with my assistant, who's running it for me, and I know she's been doing a great job."

"Hmmm." Barney started to descend to the basement.

"What was that 'hmmm' for?"

"Just thinking. Oh, I hear Nikki. They must've found something that she's excited about."

Cara laughed. "Nikki gets excited about everything. It makes me wonder if her life with her father is as wonderful as Allie seems to think."

As they neared the office, they heard Nikki's laughter.

"God, how I love having that child here," Barney murmured as she went into the office. "What have we found, Miss Nik?"

"Oh, Aunt Barney, check out these movie posters! They're so old! They're even older than—" Nikki stopped. "Than Mom and Aunt Des."

"Way older than they are, and I appreciate you not stating the obvious. Though they are even older than I am. Well, some of them, anyway." Barney walked around the desk to look at the posters.

"These are in such great shape," Allie said as she held up a 1939 poster. "*Wuthering Heights.*" She held up another. "*Gone with the Wind.* Could you just die looking at the smoldering look on Clark Gable's face as he gazes into Vivien Leigh's eyes?" She carefully placed the poster on the desk and held up a third. "*The Wizard of Oz.*" She turned to Des. "Hey, if we run out of money and that grant doesn't look promising, we can always sell some of these. I'll bet they're worth a fortune."

"I don't know about a fortune," Barney said as she looked through the stack of posters, "but certainly worth a respectable amount. I'm sure there are people who collect old movie posters, and some of these are absolute gems." She pulled one from the stack. "*My Man Godfrey.* Carole Lombard and William Powell."

"Look here." Cara joined in. "*A Farewell to Arms.* Gary Cooper and Helen Hayes."

"I read that book last summer," Nikki told them.

"Isn't that a little old for you?" Allie frowned.

"Mom. I'm fourteen." Nikki sighed, and continued going through the cabinet. "Who's Andy Hardy?" she asked. "There are a bunch of movie posters here with his name on them."

"Andy Hardy was a character played by Mickey Rooney. They did make several movies based on that character," Barney explained.

"Just like *The Hunger Games.* I guess people have always liked stories that are connected to other stories," Nikki said.

"Be still my heart." Cara sighed. "One of my all-time favorite movies. *The Philadelphia Story.* Katharine Hepburn, Jimmy Stewart, and Cary Grant. If I thought I could get away with it, I'd smuggle this home for my yoga studio."

"Well, you can't, so put it back." Allie pointed to the cabinet. "We should include a few of these in the promo items we're going to do." Allie slid another stack of posters onto the already crowded desk. "And if we ever do that fund-raising book, we can use some of these. If we have duplicates, we could auction them off."

"Good point," Des said. "Let's look through them and see if there are any dupes."

"While you're doing that, I'm going to look for the restrooms. The plumber should be here now, and I should know where to direct him. We also need to look for some display stands that might have been used for the posters."

"First things first," Des said. "Let's help Cara find the bathrooms."

"Good idea." Barney followed Cara out of the office.

"Wait for me," Nikki called.

It took them almost fifteen minutes, but they found the staff bathroom in the basement, which consisted of a toilet and a sink, both old, cracked, and dirty, and on the first floor, the bathrooms intended for the use of the patrons.

"These are really small and disgusting," Nikki said. "The ladies' room is even uglier than the men's room, even though it does have this nice mirror and the long vanity and these cute little stools." She pulled one of the stools out from under the vanity. "Okay, not so cute."

"We could have new seat cushions made for them." Des took a closer look. "Or maybe not."

"I'd toss 'em and have something nicer made," Barney said.

"I'm with Barney." Allie nodded. "And toss that big cushy chair there in the corner as well. I bet it's got bugs. Cara, are we going to get a Dumpster anytime soon? There's nothing in here we can even consider keeping."

"I guess we'll have to look into having a Dumpster delivered as soon as we identify what's going to be scrapped." Cara looked around the small room. "This space is going to have to be enlarged, more stalls added, a separate lounge area. Maybe a closet for supplies. Same with the men's room. We're going to have to take some square footage from one side or the other."

"I have never seen so many cobwebs," Allie said as she brushed one off her shoulder.

"We'll need handicapped facilities," Des noted.

"You're right." Cara started to say something else when she heard someone call, "Hello?" from the lobby.

"That's probably the plumber," she said. "I'll go check."

"Let's look in all the closets," Nikki said brightly. "Maybe we can find some of those display stands Aunt Cara talked about."

A woman in her early forties wearing baggy jeans and a well-fitting University of Scranton sweatshirt stood in the lobby.

"Can I help you?" Cara said as she came into the lobby.

"I'm looking for Joe Domanski. I was supposed to meet him here this afternoon to take a look at the plumbing," the woman said.

"You're the plumber?" Cara asked.

The woman nodded. "Liz Fox. Fox for Plumbing. You are . . . ?"

"Cara McCann. I'm one of the owners. Joe had to run back to one of his jobs."

"I can wait for him in my truck," Liz said.

"I'll be happy to show you around. The bathrooms are right off this hall." Cara gestured to the arches.

"I'll wait for Joe." The woman turned to go.

"Just so you know, Joe's my project manager." Cara straightened her back, annoyed at being dismissed. "But the final decision on who to hire is mine."

She could see the plumber weighing her options, and knew exactly when the message hit home.

"Fine. Let's start with the basement." Liz gestured for Cara to lead the way.

Once in the basement, Liz began to inspect the exposed pipes.

"You have all lead pipes?" Liz asked as she shined a flashlight overhead.

"I'm not sure. I know there were some renovations completed before we took over the project. Some of the electric was replaced, but I don't know if anything was done with the plumbing."

"I'm going to take that as a yes, most of your pipes are lead. And I wouldn't be surprised to find at least some of them are wrapped in asbestos." Liz turned off the flashlight. "Let's see what else you have. Restrooms?"

They'd finished going through the basement and were into the first-floor ladies' room when Joe returned.

"Oh, there you are." Liz smiled. "We were just doing a preliminary walk-through. Looks to me like you have all lead throughout the building, and the restrooms here are too small."

"I was just about to tell Liz that—" Cara began, but Liz cut her off.

"So I'm thinking you're going to want to expand this room by taking space from the utility area behind it."

Joe looked at Cara. "What do you think, Cara?"

"We'd already decided that the restrooms needed to be enlarged, and of course we need handicapped facilities," Cara said.

Joe rubbed his chin, listening attentively as Cara ran through their wants for the bathrooms.

"Pretty much the same for the men's room, with a few modifications," Cara said. "But I do think we could take more space from the area offstage where the actors would gather before they were called. So the bathroom would be larger than if we cut into the utility area."

"But if you took the space from the utility room, you'd save some money because you wouldn't have to move the pipes as far."

"I'd rather have the additional space," Cara said. "I want the restrooms larger."

Joe nodded. "Whatever the boss wants, the boss gets."

"But . . ." Liz clearly wanted to continue to make her case.

"Besides, I agree that the rooms should be larger." Joe turned to Cara. "I could see this building being used for a variety of things someday, maybe fund-raisers where you'll try to bring in some big players. They'll expect super amenities. Good idea."

Cara nodded.

Joe turned to Liz. "You're going to need the original mechanical plans for the building. I have an idea where they might be. I can get a copy of the plans to you so you can work up an estimate. Assuming you're interested in the job."

"Of course I'm interested. Call me and I'll come pick up whatever you find." Liz started toward the door.

"Great. Once all the estimates are in, Cara and I will look them over and she'll make her decision." Joe gave Cara a push to propel her toward the front of the theater.

"All what estimates?" Liz looked confused.

"We're looking for three or four bids." Joe smiled. "It's a big project, Liz. The Hudsons want to keep things competitive."

"But you've always used Fox for Plumbing." Liz frowned.

"On my jobs, yes. On this job, I'm just a consultant." He shrugged. "Cara and her two sisters are the owners. I serve at their pleasure."

Cara stepped forward. "It was nice meeting you, Liz. We'll be in touch."

Liz nodded and took the hand Cara offered. "I'll look forward to getting a copy of those plans." Having obviously adjusted her attitude, she added, "It was a pleasure meeting you. I'd love to work with you on this." Liz's eyes raised to the ceiling. "This would be the coolest job in town. But of course, it's your call. Thanks for your time."

"I'll walk you out, Liz," Joe told her.

"No need. I found my way in. I'll find my way out." Liz's voice faded as she left the lobby.

"Thanks for coming back," Cara said to Joe. "She really didn't want to talk to me."

"You'll run into some of that. People are used to me and they don't know you. Word will get around that you're Fritz's daughter, and that will smooth the way for most people."

"Are we getting three more estimates?" she asked.

"Only if you want them. Fox is the best plumber around and the most reasonable. I threw that out there because Liz needed some manners put on her." Joe stood with his hands in his pockets. "She wasn't taking you seriously. We both know I'll be doing the heavy lifting around here, but at the same time, the subs can't dismiss you."

"Well, thanks for taking my side. I appreciate the backup."

"I sided with you because I think you're right, not because I wanted to suck up to you."

"Either way, it was appreciated. Moving on . . ." Cara was happy to change the subject. "You really think you know where the original plans are?"

Joe nodded. "I have a damned good idea. I'll let you know."

"Great." She looked around. "When will the engineers be here?"

"Toby Cartwright said he'd stop in on his way back from another job this afternoon. He's going to give me a call when he gets here."

"And you'll let me know when?"

"If you want to be here."

"I want to be here for all the inspections from

now on. I learned my lesson this morning, meeting with Liz. No one is going to take me seriously if I'm not here at their first walk-through."

"Fake it till you make it?"

"I'm not going to pretend to know what you know. How could I? But I can learn enough to understand what needs to be done so that I know what's really happening in this building," she said. "I know that you're the point man when it comes to the work, but if I don't understand the problems, I can't have an intelligent conversation with you or my sisters or anyone else. Part of my role in this is to be the bridge between the project and my sisters. I can't explain what I don't understand."

"Then I'll expect you to ask a lot of questions," Joe said.

"Don't worry, I will. Now, as far as the engineer is concerned, his report could be the most important, right? He's going to look at the structural integrity of the building as a whole?"

"Yes. He'll be able to tell if we have any problems."

"Then it wouldn't make much sense to have Liz start ripping out the plumbing to replace it if the building is about to fall down."

"I don't think there's a danger of that happening, but you make a good point. Toby's assessment will be key to where we go from here."

"Cara, come quick!" Nikki dashed into the lobby.

"Where's the fire?" Cara turned.

"Upstairs. Aunt Des and I found the projection

room! You have to come see! There are round tins with film still inside! I have to find Mom and Aunt Barney."

"Wait. Say hello to our friend Joe." Cara tried to slow her down.

"Hello, Joe." Nikki waved and was off, calling her mother's name.

Amused, Joe turned to Cara. "You sure she's Allie's kid?"

CHAPTER ELEVEN

"**H**ow did you find this?" Cara stood in the doorway of the projection room, where the rest of her family had gathered. The room was half a floor up from the balcony level, tucked away all by itself.

"I remembered it was here." Barney stood behind a table upon which the old projector stood. "I started looking at those old posters, and it made me think about some of the movies I'd seen when I was younger." She smiled. "My dad used to let me bring friends in for free, and we'd sit up here in the balcony and eat popcorn."

"What was the first movie you ever saw here, Aunt Barney?" Nikki leaned on the table, her chin in the palm of her hand.

"Oh, it would have been a cartoon, for sure. Bugs Bunny or Tom and Jerry. I had my sixth birthday party here and I know we watched a bunch of cartoons and drank a lot of soda and ate a lot of candy."

"Didn't you watch cartoons on your TV?" Nikki asked.

"Honey, we're talking about the dark ages. I was born in 1942, so I would have been six in 1948. We didn't have a TV in our house until the 1950s. My parents thought it was a fad and that the only real entertainment that mattered was right here, on the big screen."

"Did you always have birthday parties here?" Des asked.

"I did. And I remember every one of my birthday films." Barney grinned. "Go ahead. Test me."

"When you were eight . . ." Des said.

"*Madeline*," Barney replied without hesitating.

"When you were twelve?" Allie asked.

"*Brigadoon*."

"How 'bout when you were fifteen?"

Barney laughed. "I told my mother we were going to see Pat Boone in *April Love*, but I talked the projector operator into showing us *Jailhouse Rock*. We all had a crush on Elvis." Her eyes sparkled. "Oh, the fun we had here back then. For a time, science-fiction films were all the rage. Looking back now, they were so corny, but when you're fifteen or sixteen and you're watching *Attack of the Crab Monsters* or *The Deadly Mantis* with your girlfriends, you are expected to scream and cringe at the appropriate times."

"How 'bout when you were with a boy?" Nikki teased.

"Oh, then you'd scream twice as loudly." Barney laughed again.

Allie stood in front of the open cabinet looking over the large round metal tins that held films.

"Well, if we knew how to run that projector, you could see one of your favorites right now." Allie held up a container. "*Brigadoon.*"

"I wonder if that thing still works?" Cara said.

"It hasn't been run since . . . I'm not even sure." Barney shook her head. "The 1980s, I think."

"Barney, I think we need to interview you," Des said. "We've been talking about doing a book about the theater. At first I was thinking it would be good promo for the project, but we've also talked about a fund-raising project. You know, in case we run short."

"If you run short, you're going to have to sell a lot of books, but we'll worry about that later," Barney said. "There are a number of people still in town who would remember the theater. I'll give it some thought, come up with a list of people you should talk to."

"That would be great. Thanks, Barney."

"Wow, did you ever see so many cobwebs in your life?" Nikki went to her mother's side and pulled a web from Allie's hair. "They're, like, everywhere. You could have an epic Halloween party in here."

"That would be fun," Cara agreed. "Maybe some of those old spooky sci-fi films Barney talked about are still around."

"There are a lot of those reels in here," Allie said.

"Oh, I could inventory the films," Nikki said excitedly. "That could be my first job as your intern."

"That's an excellent idea, Nik." Des picked up

a metal container and was disappointed to find it empty. "At some point, we'll have to decide what to do with them. We could sell them, or—"

"No!" Nikki protested. "We should show them here in the theater."

"What are the chances the projector still works?" Cara asked.

"It can be fixed, right, Aunt Barney?" Nikki looked to her great-aunt. "And when we show them, you can run the projector. Maybe you could even teach me how." Nikki grinned. "How cool would that be?"

"Very cool, I'm sure," Barney told her. "Keep that thought on the back burner for now. There's a long way to go before you can even think about showing films here."

"Right now, I'm thinking about lunch," Cara said. "I'll be coming back later to meet with Joe and the structural engineer, so I'm ready to head back to the house if anyone else is."

"Oh, look at the time." Barney hoisted her bag higher on her shoulder. "One of my high school friends invited me and some others for lunch today. Unless I leave now, I won't have time to get cleaned up." She held up her hands, which were dirty from the projector.

"I wanted to see more." Nikki frowned.

"We can come back," her mother said, "but I've had enough for one day. I've inhaled so much dust my throat is dry."

Nikki reluctantly returned the film cases to the

closet. "I'm coming back with a notebook to make that list."

"Later." Allie steered her toward the door, and they all followed.

By the time lunch was over, Cara had little more than an hour before she expected to return to the theater. She cleaned up and changed her clothes in anticipation of the meeting with the engineer, and when she came back downstairs, she heard voices in the living room. She peered in to find Nikki and Allie on the sofa, Nikki's iPad open in front of them.

"What's going on?" Cara asked.

"We're looking at the interiors of other old theaters. There are a number of them around the country of the same era as ours, though not many are still being used," Allie said.

"I saw that one when I looked up stuff. It's in Kansas. It has a fancy marquee out front. Oh, and that one, I remember that one. It's the Saenger Theater in New Orleans. Hurricane Katrina destroyed it, but it was rebuilt." Nikki reached past Allie to scroll the tablet's screen. "Some of these were already restored, and they use them for concerts and stuff. I think that's the coolest thing. Like this one? It's in Fort Wayne, Indiana. Their orchestra plays there. See the floor? It's like mosaic. Will ours be used for anything?"

"I don't know. I guess that will be decided by someone else." Allie shrugged.

"Like who? You and Aunt Des and Aunt Cara own it, right? So you should decide." Nikki looked first to her mother, then to Cara.

Before Cara could respond, Allie said, "Nikki, your grandfather's will only called for us to renovate it. Nothing else. Nobody's talking about using it for anything."

"But what's the point in doing all that work if the theater just sits there?" Nikki made a face. "That seems pretty stupid to me."

"Not our problem." Allie went back to her tablet.

Cara watched the interplay between mother and daughter with interest.

"That would be the biggest bummer ever." Nikki was still frowning. "Did you see the ceiling in the lobby? It's like . . . gorgeous. I was at this theater once, in Hollywood? It was brand-new and the ceiling was all painted like that? But it was a *copy*, and this is the *real thing*."

"Honey, no decisions have been made about anything concerning the theater," Cara said. "We're still figuring out what work has to be done to make it safe and bring all the systems up to code and working again. Those things take time."

"It would just stink to do all this work and then just close it up again."

"Too soon to worry about it, like Cara just told you," Allie said. "We'll worry about what to do with it when the time comes."

"I think you know you're not going to do anything with it," Nikki said as she started out of the room, "except sell it. Which would stink."

"Nikki, when it's finished, we're all going back to our lives," Allie told her. "I'm coming back to California and Des is going back to Montana and Cara is going back to New Jersey. We're only here to renovate the theater."

"That's so dumb. Why did Grampa make such a stupid will? Why would he want you to fix it up and then just leave it?" Nikki stood in the doorway, her hands on her hips, her face flushed. "And what about Aunt Barney? You're just going to leave her by herself?"

Allie shrugged. "Nik, Aunt Barney has lived here by herself for a long time. I'm sure she'll be fine."

"*I'm* sure she'll be lonely." Nikki stomped out of the room. Seconds later, Cara heard her footsteps overhead and the slamming of a door.

"Teenagers," Allie mumbled. She looked at Cara. "Want a kid?"

When Cara arrived at the theater, Joe was outside talking to the electrician.

"Mack has good news," Joe told her.

"Great. I love good news." Cara joined them under the marquee.

"All the circuits are now on the control panel. We still need to figure out what's on which circuit, but we're working on that. The wiring was already replaced, as you know, so if all goes well, we might be finished by the end of next week."

"Everything?" Cara asked. "The stage lights, the chandelier . . . ?"

"Well, not those," Mack said. "You're going to have to find special bulbs for the chandelier, and it should be rewired. You'll probably have to send it away to have that done, unless you can find someone locally who has worked with things like that in the past. Me, I'd be afraid of breaking it, and besides, rewiring old fixtures is not my thing. You're going to want to replace the stage lights with newer ones. I can do that once you decide."

"You'll have to come back later anyway," Cara said. "The marquee is going to need work, and there'll be new fixtures in the bathrooms once those are completed." She thought for a moment. "And the office and the hall and the projection room . . ."

"You just let me know when you have all that together, and I'll send a crew over." Mack handed Joe an envelope. "Invoice for the past week."

Joe handed it to Cara without opening it. "Here you go."

"Thanks." Cara slipped it into her bag. "Mack, would you be able to rewire some of the fixtures from the lobby? I love the sconces on the wall, but I imagine they'll need some updating."

Mack nodded. "If I can't, my son can. I'll be back tomorrow and we can take a look at them." Mack started toward his truck, waving as he walked away.

Cara turned to Joe. "Is the engineer here?"

"Not yet."

She took the envelope out of her bag. "Did you already see this?"

He shook his head no.

"Still trying to show the subs who's in charge?" she asked.

"Sort of," Joe said. "A job this size, I want them to know that I'm looking over their shoulders, but someone is looking over mine as well."

"Got it. And once again, appreciated." She handed him Mack's bill. "But I don't know how to tell if we're being overcharged."

He handed it back. "I'll show you."

"When?"

"Tomorrow. Meet me here around one," he said. "Oh, and now that we have light, the HVAC people can come in. I'll give them a call tonight. The roofer comes in on Thursday."

"You've been busy."

"You betcha." Joe made no effort to hide the fact that he was feeling pretty smug. "Give me a title and I'm all in."

"How many hours did all that take?" Cara knew hiring him on as project manager had nothing to do with his diligence. He'd been working on lining up contractors for the past week.

"Fewer than you might think."

An SUV pulled up out front and parked. Seconds later, a man with a full head of dark hair and wearing dark glasses hopped out.

"That's Tom Allen, the engineer." Joe waved a greeting, then said softly to Cara, "He's a tough nut, doesn't miss much, but that's what we need here. If the structure is bad, if there are cracks in the foundation, we have serious problems."

Joe made the introductions; then he and Cara accompanied the engineer into the building and watched as Tom examined the foundation inside and out, inspected the walls, and tested the ceiling joints. After almost two hours, Tom told them he'd have a report for them by the following Monday.

"But I can tell you that I didn't see anything that alarmed me. There is that hole in the back wall, but that's not affecting the building's structure. The foundation is solid—a couple of insignificant cracks here and there that you can fill. All in all, she's in remarkable condition for a building her age. Maybe having her boarded up for so many years has helped preserve her."

"We'll look forward to your report," Joe told him as the three of them walked out.

Once the engineer drove away, Cara exhaled. "That couldn't have gone better. I can't wait to tell Des and Allie. They'll be as relieved as I am."

"We're not out of the woods yet. I don't know for sure, but I won't be surprised if the roofer tells us the entire thing needs to be replaced. It's old and it's already been roofed over two or possibly three times."

"And I guess the heating and air-conditioning will be a big ticket."

Joe nodded. "There is some duct work, but there's never been AC in here. And we're going to have to decide what type of heat will be most efficient. Those will be big items."

"Speaking of big tickets, we still don't know what you're charging us to be our project manager."

He took a small pad from his back pocket and wrote a number on it, then handed it to Cara.

"That's your number?" It was less than she'd have thought, but it was still a lot of money.

"I told you I'd be reasonable. That's a reasonable number for the amount of time I have to spend here and all the meetings I'm going to have to go to."

"I'll run it past the others and let you know." Cara tucked the slip of paper into her pocket.

"You do that."

"I guess we can talk about it tomorrow. I'll see you at one."

"Right. I'll be here."

Cara could feel his eyes following her as she walked to her car. She hated knowing that someone— anyone—was staring at her rear.

All the same, she hoped he was enjoying the view.

After dinner, they all met in the living room for what Nikki called a "state of the theater" meeting.

"Joe wants a hundred grand to be our project manager," Cara said, opening the meeting.

"What?" Allie frowned. "I hope you told him we'd have to negotiate that number."

Des tapped her pen on her notebook. "I don't know. He has a lot of responsibility. And he's been there every day."

"Joe's the guy you were talking to this morning, right?" Nikki asked.

Cara nodded.

"Aunt Cara, he is hot. Boy, if I were old, like you? I'd be there, if you know what I mean."

"I get the gist." Cara smiled. "Old as I am."

"We all agree he's hot, sweetie," Des said to Nikki. "Right now we're talking about how much to pay him, which has nothing to do with where he lands on the hotness scale."

"He does spend a lot of time there. He's lined up all the subs and he's got all of them writing up estimates for their work. The exterminator is almost finished and the electrical work is nearing completion. At least, as much as can be done right now," Cara said. "He's going to be supervising the entire job."

"Then what are *you* doing?" Allie asked.

"I'm trying to learn as much as I can from him. Obviously, I'm in no position to do what he's doing, but he's willing to teach me enough that I can converse with the subs and I can come back and report to you with some semblance of understanding." Cara turned to Allie. "You don't really expect him to do all that for nothing, do you?"

"All things considered, I think he's giving us a break on the price." Des looked at Barney. "What do you think?"

Barney shrugged. "I don't have a vote."

"But you have an opinion." Des grinned. "And you know you're dying to express it."

"Well, from my experience at the bank, I think he's undercharging you by a good third."

"Really?" Cara frowned.

"Really." Barney nodded.

"So we should pay him more," Des said. "It's only fair."

"I agree. So we raise Joe's overall compensation to one hundred fifty thousand dollars. Any objections?" Cara looked directly at Allie, who merely shrugged.

"One fifty it is." Des made a note in her book, then glanced up at Cara. "Anything else to report?"

Cara shook her head no.

"So, Allie?" Des gestured for her to begin.

"Nikki and I have spent the afternoon doing research. We have a list of companies that reproduce paint colors. I'm hoping it's historically acceptable to touch up here and there on the walls in the lobby. At some point, we might want to contact one of the universities that have an art conservation department to take a look at the ceiling," Allie said. "We also have a list of companies that sell theater drapes and seats. We're going to go seat by seat and see what needs to be replaced."

"Maybe some of them only need repair," Des noted.

"We'll look them all over carefully. If we have to replace them all with the same type of velvet, it could cost us. Today's theater seats are smaller, narrower, and nowhere near as cushy. We'd probably have to have them custom-made, in which case we're going to have to decide between cost and authenticity."

"I'm going to help Mom with that," Nikki told them proudly. "This is so seriously cool. I can't believe I have the chance to do something *important* like this."

"Like what, Nik?" Des asked.

"Like, you know, help restore a historic building.

That's like, epic, you know? I mean, how many kids get the chance to do that? How many kids' families *own* a historic theater? Court was so jealous when I told her. Like, she's sending me pictures of her on the beach, and I'm going to send her pictures of our theater. You just can't compare the experiences, you know?"

"I do know." Nikki was so sincere, so enthralled by the idea of the theater, so eager and determined to be a part of it, Cara couldn't help but smile.

"Oh, and that stained glass? The little theater masks? That would make the coolest tattoo *ever*." Nikki's voice was reverent.

"No tattoos," Allie said without looking up from her notebook.

"Mom, lots of kids have tats, but this would be *meaningful*. Like, it's my *heritage*, you know? Like, the theater is in my blood," Nikki said dramatically.

"We're lucky you had this time to spend here, Nik," Des told her. "There's going to be a lot of work involved. We want everything to be authentic, and we want to preserve as much as we can."

The four adults in the room suppressed smiles.

"So in keeping with that thought, I have a list of books about renovating historic theaters. I'm going to order a few—Des, you can reimburse me for those—and I can see if the local library has some of the others, though I doubt it. Maybe one of the local colleges would have more. I'm also going to contact an organization that can give us tons of information. It's called . . ." Allie looked through her notes. "The League of Historic American Theatres."

"I'm going to take pictures every day. I can't wait to send them to Courtney so she can see. She's going to be so jealous." Nikki appeared to be thinking out loud.

"What's Courtney doing this week?" Allie asked.

"Mostly she's surfing, but I just got a text from her. She has to babysit her dad's girlfriend's five-year-old. Court said he's a total brat and she hates him and she hates her father's girlfriend because she's a bitch."

"Watch your language, miss," Allie said.

"Sorry, Mom."

"Where's Courtney's mother?" Allie tried to appear casual.

"Oh, she went to London for some conference. I forget what it's about, but she got told at the last minute that she had to go, so that's why Court got shipped off to her dad."

The silence in the room could not have been thicker.

"London. What a coincidence. Isn't your father in London?" Allie asked casually.

"Yes, but he's not going to be in the same part of the city, he said."

"Oh. Pity." Allie rolled her eyes. Cara could see the steam rising behind them.

"Yeah. That would've been fun for them, but I guess they'll both be busy."

"I just bet they will," Allie muttered.

"Lucky for me, though, right? If Dad didn't have to go on this trip, Court would be at her dad's place and I'd be home alone."

"Don't you have other friends?" Allie asked.

"Yeah, but I have the most fun with her. But I'd rather be here than home even if Court didn't go away. I get to spend some time with you, Mom." Nikki stood behind Allie's chair and wrapped her arms around her mother. "I missed you. And I got to meet all my aunts and see your theater and I get to be part of it. I'm so happy to be here with you guys."

Cara watched as Allie's expression completely changed. In less than a few seconds, she went from being totally pissed off to near tears as her daughter embraced her. In the glow of Nikki's simple declaration, Allie's façade dropped, and for just a few moments, she was a mother feeling the pure love of her child. The hard edges, the sarcasm, the snarkiness all fell away, replaced with a gentleness, a tenderness Cara had never suspected was there.

She knew it wouldn't last, but for those few seconds, it was a lovely sight to see. Cara's oldest sister was human, after all.

Another storm blew through that night, but the power held. Des was searching the town ordinances online to see what was on the books as far as keeping animals was concerned. Allie and Nikki were at the kitchen table, shopping online for books about the Art Deco period and searching for a pair of boots or hiking shoes for Nikki that'd be more suitable for trekking up to the falls than her pretty pink sneakers. Once Barney told Nikki that there were indeed hidden falls, and that they were on Hudson property, Nikki had to see them firsthand. It would take two days for her purchase to arrive, but she assured her mother she could find other things to do. Barney had offered to call a friend of hers who had a grand-daughter Nikki's age who was also on break that week, but Nikki declined.

"I'm only here for a week," Nikki reminded her. "I want to spend time with my family. I want to know everything I can about the Hudsons. Did my great-great-grandfather really own coal mines? We read about the Molly Maguires in history. Are the mines still here? Can we go? Who are all those people whose portraits are hanging in the front hall? Am I related to them . . . ?"

There was seemingly no limit to Nikki's curiosity, or her questions.

Cara found Barney in her favorite chair in the library, with her glasses perched on the end of her nose, and that nose in a book.

"Barney, do you have a minute?" Cara asked as she tapped lightly on the door.

Barney looked up and smiled. "Of course I do. Come on in, Cara. You don't have to knock."

"You looked so engrossed, I hated to disturb you."

Barney held up the book. "I can read anytime. I don't have forever with you." She closed the book and with characteristic directness asked, "Something on your mind?"

"A couple of things, actually. I guess I'm confused about some things that Joe told me."

"What was it he said?" Barney put the book aside.

"Stuff about my dad and Pete and Pete's brother."

"Start with what bothers you the most." Barney sat back in her chair, her legs crossed, a wary look in her eyes. "I'll tell you whatever I know. *If* I know."

Cara repeated what Joe had said about Fritz leaving with Nora right after Gil died.

"Are you wondering why I didn't tell you Pete's brother and I were going to be married?"

"No. That's your business. It's not like I have a right to know everything about your life."

"It's not a matter of it being 'my business.' It was a long time ago, Cara. I don't dwell on what was or what might have been. You can't change the past." Barney stared out the window at the rain. "Gil asked me to marry him right after I graduated from college. We'd always been a couple, from the time we were kids. We both knew that we were meant for each other." She smiled wryly. "Of course, we thought it would be in this life, not the next."

"You must have loved him very much."

"I did. He was the love of my life. There never was anyone who even came close to being the man he was in my eyes. I tried dating sometime after he died, but it was a big fat waste of my time. He was the only man I ever wanted, and he was gone. Why should I settle for second best? I've had a very good life, child. I loved a good man who truly loved me. I've lived exactly the way I wanted. I had a wonderful career, one that permitted me to help people, to really be there when the people in this town needed me. I have no real regrets." That wry smile returned to her lips. "Other than Gil dying, of course."

"Did you ever talk to my dad about it? Joe said Dad and Pete were with Gil when he fell."

Barney shook her head very slowly. "I couldn't. For the first couple of weeks after Gil passed, I was in shock. I couldn't believe he was gone. For so long, I had a hard time believing that he was really gone for good. He was so full of life, you see—smart and funny and such wonderful company. Oh, the times we had together." For a moment, a tiny bit of lost joy danced in her eyes—then it was gone. "I knew that Fritz and Pete had been up at the falls with him, I knew they said he got too close to the edge of the rock and fell, but I never asked for details. By the time I started to come around, Pete was away at law school and Fritz had headed to California."

"Eddie said he knew Dad in school and that he used to watch him in plays. He said Dad was a really, really good actor—that he was better than Nora would ever be."

"All that's true. Fritz could've been a star. Everyone knew it. What's your question?"

"Why would he give up something he loved that much? Was he so crazy in love with Nora that he'd give up everything for her, and why would he have to?"

"I don't have all the answers, but I know he loved her more than he loved anything else, and that he believed she was the one destined to have the career. He didn't think he could be her manager and promote himself at the same time, and felt he needed to devote his focus and energy to making her a star. Did I think that was strange?" She nodded. "For one thing, I'd watched my brother come alive on the stage. I could feel what it meant to him."

"Did she love him as much?"

"You know, when you see two people who are truly in love, you can feel it. It infects you, and it's a happy thing. I never felt that love coming from her the way it came from him. I think he was dazzled by her. She was very beautiful, you know. I also thought she was manipulative and self-centered, but maybe that was just me. Though the self-centered part certainly was true when it came to her children."

"What do you mean?"

"I think she had them because it softened her image with the public. I'm not saying she didn't love them—she did. At least, I want to believe she did. I know Fritz loved those girls till his dying day, though he wasn't always the best at showing them. I understand your experience with him was different, but I suspect that could've been because his relationship with your mother was so different from his relationship with Nora."

"I guess I'm puzzled by the fact that he left Hidden Falls with her when you needed him. It seems so uncharacteristic of a man who always seemed so caring."

"The bottom had fallen out of my life. My brother couldn't fix that." Barney shook her head. "I was glad he left. I wanted to be alone."

"I can't imagine how painful that time was for you."

"It was. Sometimes it still is."

"Barney, I'm sorry I brought it up."

Barney shrugged. "It is what it is. Now, as far as your father quitting acting is concerned, my own personal feeling? I believe Nora couldn't stand the thought of the competition. He was always going to be better than her, more successful. If he kept acting, might he not get the bigger roles, the lion's share of the attention? Awards that she could only dream about winning?"

"But they wouldn't have competed for the same roles."

"No, but he'd have been a much bigger star than she could ever hope to be. I don't think Nora's ego could've handled that. I could be wrong. As I said, I always thought he loved her more than she loved him."

"Why couldn't he see that?" Cara wondered aloud.

"Ahhh, well, you know, love is blind, Cara. Nora just didn't seem his type to me. For one thing, she wasn't a very warm person—please don't repeat that to Des and Allie, but it's true. First I heard she was taking off to Hollywood on her own, and the next thing I knew, Fritz was going with her to be her agent and manager. They got married as soon as they got to California, and that was that. I'm not saying I didn't care, but it was right after Gil died, and I was a lot more upset about that than about my brother's elopement. I've always felt there was more to the story, but

I've never been able to figure it out. Too bad there's no one left alive who might have the answer."

"Did you ever talk to Pete about all this?"

"Not really. I've tried, but he either ignores me or says something like, 'It's all in the past, and bringing it up now will serve no purpose except to make you sad.' As if I'm not sad about it unless I'm talking about it. But I don't push him too much. Remember, he lost his only brother that day, and very soon after, his best friend eloped with a woman he couldn't stand."

"Pete didn't like Nora?"

"He never did. I asked him once and all he said was that she wasn't good enough for Fritz. I think it might have been more that she took his best friend to the opposite side of the country and Pete had to find someone else to hang out with."

"How did your parents take my dad's elopement?"

Barney grimaced. "My father was apoplectic over the whole thing. Fritz was our generation's designated bank president, and here he'd taken off with a girl my parents didn't really know. My mother was just starting to show the first signs of Alzheimer's, and she was mostly concerned about who Nora was in terms of Hidden Falls. She kept asking, 'Tell me again who her people are.'" Barney shook her head. "As if that mattered at that point."

Cara sat quietly, mulling over all she'd heard.

"Cara, I can see something is bothering you. What is it?"

"I guess it's just that the main reason I decided to

come here and to do what my dad asked was to understand *why* he did the things he did. I thought I'd find something of him here that would help me know the real Fritz Hudson."

Barney met Cara's eyes straight on and said, "I'm not so sure that any of us ever saw *all* of Fritz. I think he showed a different side of himself to you than he did to Allie and Des, but both sides were the real man, if you follow. I guess the three of you are going to have to piece all that together if you want to know the whole man." Barney smiled. "God knows you'll have plenty of time to do that before your work on the theater is done."

CHAPTER TWELVE

Cara's phone pinged with an incoming text.

Can we change our meet-up time to two? read the text from Joe.

Sure—see you then, she replied.

The house was quiet. Barney was off at one of her committee meetings, Des was upstairs making phone calls, and Allie and Nikki had taken Cara's car to go into Wilkes-Barre to tour the old Comerford Theater, which had, at one time, rivaled the Sugarhouse for first-run films. Through her research, Nikki had found that the old Art Deco theater had been damaged during Hurricane Agnes, then renovated, and its name changed to the F. M. Kirby Center for the Performing Arts.

"It's not far from here," Nikki had pointed out over breakfast that morning, "and it'd be good to see firsthand what someone else has done. Of course, the Comerford was so much larger than the Sugarhouse, but I'll bet a lot of the detailing inside is similar since it's from the same era. Maybe we'll get lucky and we can talk to someone who actually worked on the renovation. How cool would that be?"

Even Allie agreed that could be worthwhile. When Cara offered her car for the trip and Nikki had let out a whoop, Allie had no choice but to go.

At one forty-five, Cara walked the block to the theater. Joe was already out front talking to two men dressed in work clothes. His attention was diverted from them as he watched her walk across the street.

"Cara, meet Larry Masters and Rick Sennett. They just finished their inspection of the roof. Cara," he told them, "is one of the owners of the theater and is working with me on the renovation."

She shook hands with both men.

"How'd it look up there?" she asked.

"Not so good. You have shingles over shingles over badly broken tile," Larry told her.

"Tile? On the roof?" Cara's only experience with roofs was limited to shingles or cedar shakes.

"The style of the building is what some called Hollywood Moroccan," he explained. "They put red clay tiles up there. I can't believe anyone expected them to last for more than a few years. Then, instead of removing them, they simply put shingles over the tiles, and later, when that began to leak, they shingled over the whole thing."

"So in other words, it's a hot mess," she said.

Rick nodded. "And some of the wood under the tile has to be replaced as well."

"So if the roof leaked, where did the water go once it got inside the building?" Cara asked.

"Judging from the condition of the roof, I'd say the point of entry was the back wall of the building. The water would have run down between the exterior and the interior walls."

Cara turned to Joe. "You can handle that, if the wall needs to be replaced?"

He nodded. "But let's not get ahead of ourselves. Larry, when can we expect your estimate for the replacement of the roof?"

"Friday at the earliest," the roofer told him. "But remember, it's going to be a tear-off of three layers and off the top of my head, I don't know how many Dumpsters it'll take."

"Let us know. We'll wait to hear from you." Joe watched the two men head for their truck.

"This isn't encouraging," Cara said after the roofers had left. "Ripping off three layers of roof, water damage to the back of the building . . ."

"Yesterday the engineer said he thought there might be some damage behind that back wall, but he didn't think it was structural. That's the good news. If we have to take a wall down, we take it down. There's lath underneath the plaster, and if water seeped into it, we'll have to replace it. Then we'll replaster. All very doable."

"But a lot of money, right?"

"Well, you knew you were going to have to spend it. The roof will be one of the big tickets. There's no getting around that, so let's accept it and move on."

"Move on to what?"

"Move on to what I had planned for the afternoon." He took her by the elbow, walked her to his truck, and opened the passenger door.

"Where are we going?" she asked.

"You'll see." He slammed her door and went around to the driver's side.

"You said you had something for me," Cara said after Joe got behind the wheel and started the truck.

"I do. Let's just get to where we're going."

He looked across the seat and smiled at her, and the only thought in her mind was, to quote Nikki, *OMG*. He wore a burgundy waffle-knit henley, khaki pants, and dimples.

If I were looking for someone, if I were ready for someone, if I were in a better place . . . if I . . .

"Hey. You look cold." He turned on the heater, then grabbed her hand. "You *are* cold. There are these things you wear on your hands when it's cold out. They're called gloves. You might look into getting a pair."

"I left them in my car, which right now is somewhere between here and Wilkes-Barre." She stretched her legs in front of her, hoping to reach the heat that blasted from under the dashboard, and told him about Allie and Nikki's excursion.

"That's a great idea." Joe put the truck in gear and pulled away from the curb. "I might want to talk to some of their contractors myself."

"It was Nikki's idea. I swear, no one has more enthusiasm for this project than that girl. She wants to know everything about the place, wants in on everything we say or do that has anything to do with the Sugarhouse."

"It's great to see the next generation show some interest. If the young people around here don't start to do the same, this town is going to curl up and die."

"I didn't say she was staying. I only said she's thrilled we have the theater. By Sunday night, she'll be back in California, and we probably won't see her again until the summer."

"Allie's all right with that?"

"I don't think so. You know, she's such an odd duck. She plays such hardball sometimes with people. Like she's sarcastic and smart-mouthed—then you see her with her daughter and you see who she really is."

"Who do you think she is?"

"A woman who desperately loves her kid and would do anything for her. I think Nikki is the only real thing in her life. The rest of it strikes me as being superficial. Nothing means anything to Allie, except Nik."

Cara looked out the window. "I probably shouldn't say that. I don't really know her well enough to pass judgment."

"That wasn't passing judgment. That was making an observation."

"One of my goals before I leave Hidden Falls is to get to know my sisters. Whether or not they want to know me is not the same thing, but that's my goal."

"What are your others? Besides getting the theater renovated."

"I want to get to know my dad better."

"I would think that might've been easier while he was still alive."

"I know everything he wanted me to know, everything he wanted me to see, but there was so much he kept hidden. So much I know nothing about. That's what I want to learn."

"Maybe he kept things hidden for a reason."

"There's no reason good enough, as far as I'm concerned."

"Now who's playing hardball?"

"I talked to Barney about Gil Wheeler and the day he fell, and about my dad and his first wife and why he gave up acting. Something doesn't add up. So another of my goals while I'm here is to figure it out."

"In the meantime, grab that briefcase behind my seat."

She reached around behind him and pulled the brown case to her.

"Open it. There's a large envelope right inside."

She opened it to find a thin stack of photos.

"The theater! Where did you find these?" she exclaimed.

"My grandmother had them. When I told her I was going to be working with you all, she started looking for them. She said Barney has a ton of them, but 'knowing Barney, she has no idea where they are.'"

Cara studied the photos. "These are lovely. Look at that lobby. It's exquisite. The paintings and the frescoes and the ceiling . . . It's so wonderful to see it as it was back then."

"These were taken when the place first opened. My great-granddad did some of the stucco work when it was first built, so he was always given VIP passes for whatever was going on." He braked at a stop sign and selected a photo from the stack. He put his finger on a couple dressed in what must have been the fashion of the day. "Here are your great-grandparents . . ."

"The woman with the long fur dangling over her shoulder?"

He nodded. "And the man in the hat they're talking to . . . that's my great-grandfather."

"Do you think I could borrow these, just to show Des and Allie?"

"Keep 'em. I scanned and printed copies for you. I knew you'd want them."

They approached an intersection where the light had turned yellow. Joe slowed to a stop behind a mail truck.

"Thank you, Joe. That's so thoughtful." She held the photos in one hand and looked at him. Really looked at him. Saw the way he was looking at her—and deep inside she felt a *zing* she hadn't been sure she'd ever feel again.

She cleared her throat and shifted uncomfortably in her seat. His smile said he knew exactly what she was thinking.

"I . . . ah . . . can't wait to share these with Des and Allie. And Barney."

"You already said that."

"I did?" She frowned. "Sorry. I was so excited. About seeing the photos, I mean."

She wondered if she could get through the rest of the drive without speaking. It seemed every time she opened her mouth, she was in danger of giving herself away. The thought of him was far too new, and she wasn't sure she wanted him to know just how much he'd gotten through to her, past her defenses and around all the resolve.

"When is that idiot ex of yours getting married?" he asked, his eyes still locked on hers.

"Ah . . . the third weekend in the month. A week from Saturday."

He frowned. "No, the third Saturday is this coming weekend."

"What? No. That can't be right."

"Town council meets on the third Wednesday, which is this week. Which would make this Saturday also the third of the month."

"Oh. Well. I guess it is, then."

"How 'bout we go out and celebrate on Saturday night? Say goodbye to that old life of yours. You know, out with the old, in with the new?"

"I don't know. I haven't thought about how I want to spend that night."

"Trust me. You'll never come up with something as cool as what I have planned."

"That almost scares me," she deadpanned.

"Nothing to fear. But I do have the perfect way to celebrate the occasion." The light turned green and he drove through the intersection.

"Dare I ask . . . ?"

"Saturday night is bluegrass night at the gun club." He wiggled his eyebrows. "Go ahead. Top that."

"That's a joke, right?"

He shook his head from side to side. "Nope."

"Bluegrass night at the gun club."

"Best time you'll ever have. Think it over." He made a left turn onto a dirt road. "And the rest of the Hudson girls are welcome to join us. Even the young one. Good opportunity for her to meet other kids her age."

Cara knew she was staring at him, but since he didn't seem to mind, neither did she. "Well. I hardly know what to say. I mean, how does one turn down an invitation like that?"

"One does not. So is it a date?"

"I'm still stuck on the thought of Nikki meeting other kids her age. What kid thinks a night out at the gun club is a cool thing?"

"You'd be surprised." He lowered his voice. "You might have noticed there's not a whole lot for kids to do in Hidden Falls. Especially for kids who aren't old enough to drive. Some weekends, it's the gun club or nothing."

"I may have a difficult time selling that to Allie."

"Date?"

Cara nodded. "Sure. Date."

He pulled into what once was a parking lot but was now a sea of broken concrete and clumps of grass.

"Where are we?" Cara looked around and saw nothing but tall pines.

"Compton Lake. Back when I was a kid, it was the place to go to have a good time." He opened his door and hopped out.

Cara didn't wait for him to come around to her side and met him in front of the truck.

"It's a little . . . Is creepy too strong a word?" Cara frowned. Why would he bring her to such a place? "I don't see a lake. Actually, I don't see much of anything."

"There's plenty to see. Come on." He took her by the hand and led her to a path between the trees.

"If Barney hadn't vouched for you, I'd be worrying about your motives right now," she said. "Did you ever see that movie *So I Married an Axe Murderer*?"

Joe laughed and directed her to a side path to their left.

"Great flick," he told her.

"Figures."

They walked a short distance more before a clearing opened up.

"Compton Lake, as promised."

"It's beautiful," she said, and it was. The lake was the truest of blues and, in the sunlight, seemed to reflect the sky. The surface was perfectly calm, and around the perimeter, tall pines grew straight. The effect was serene, like a painting come to life. "Breathtaking."

"This is as pristine a mountain lake as you'll find in the Poconos. There are a lot of lakes, but most of them are in the areas where there's been the most development. Hidden Falls, as you probably noticed, has no little faux-Alpine cottages or A-frame cabins."

"Why is that?" she asked. "How did Hidden Falls escape the developers?"

"A lot of the land around the outskirts of town belongs to one family, and they always refused to sell. I heard they've turned down millions in the past." He nodded toward the lake. "The lake and the surrounding woods belong to them, too."

"So they didn't sell because they didn't need the money, or because they thought they weren't offered enough?"

"I think it was because they liked things the way they were, but you can ask Barney. I'm sure her father told her why he decided against selling."

"The Hudsons own this?" Cara frowned. Barney hadn't mentioned owning land outside of town. Then again, the subject had never come up.

Joe nodded. "Right down to the boathouse and the dock where that canoe is tied up. Come on."

She followed him to the end of the dock, wondering what he was up to.

He pulled the rope that held the canoe to move it next to the dock.

"Ever been in a canoe?" he asked.

"Not since I was in high school and a bunch of us decided to explore the Pine Barrens." She watched the canoe bob up and down. "There's no way I'm going to get into that thing without tipping it over."

"Sure there is." Joe lowered himself into the

canoe, then held it steady against the dock. "One foot at a time, or we'll both be in the water."

The sun was sparkling on the lake and warming the air, and Joe was holding out his hand to her, his eyes as bright as the sunlight on the water. She took his hand and stepped gingerly into the canoe.

"Okay, sit right there." He gestured to the seat in front of her.

He sat across from her, then handed Cara an oar.

"You know how this is done, right? We paddle on opposite sides at the same time, then we switch."

Cara nodded. "I remember."

He pushed off from the dock and dipped his oar into the water. It took a few tries before they'd synched their strokes, but soon they were headed across the lake, competently, if not smoothly.

"So you were going to show me how to read an estimate to determine whether we're being over-charged or not," she said.

"Look for the labor charge—it should be on an hourly rate unless we negotiated a flat price—and should clearly show the number of hours."

"How do I know if the hourly rate is too high?"

"Ask me."

Cara laughed. "That's your tutorial? Ask you?"

"I know what everyone should charge. The electricians, for example, charge anywhere from seventy to one hundred dollars an hour. Most trades are in that range."

"Yow."

Joe nodded. "That's why you want to be present

on the jobsite, so that when the bill comes in, you'll know if the time has been exaggerated. And you want to make sure the timing is good. You don't want the plumbers showing up on the job, standing around at that hourly rate while they wait for the electricians to get out of their way."

"Got it."

"What else do you want to know?"

Cara shook her head. "There's a lot about construction that I don't know. However, I do know that you're undercharging us by a considerable amount of money. We've discussed it and we're upping your fee by fifty thousand dollars."

"Look, I owe Barney for—"

"This isn't Barney's project. If you want to show your gratitude to her, take her out to dinner once in a while. Send her flowers. But don't confuse what you feel you owe her with what you're doing at the theater. We want to be fair with everyone who works for us, and paying you way less than what your time is worth simply isn't fair. Whatever you think you owe Barney is between you and her, but has nothing to do with this project." She paused. "Apples and oranges, Joe. Get it?"

He nodded slowly. "Got it."

They paddled quietly for a moment. Then Joe said, "If you have any questions about the work or what any of the contractors are doing, ask me. You have every right to know and every right to ask. Don't let anyone intimidate you, hear? The theater belongs to you and your sisters, so whatever you say goes.

You're the boss. Don't let anyone—even me—try to talk you into anything until you understand exactly what it is that you're agreeing to."

"Thanks, Joe."

"Sure. Oh, by the way, I found the plans for the building."

"Where were they?"

"In my mother's garage. My dad apparently did some work for the guy who'd bought the theater from Fritz. When the guy went under, my dad rolled up the plans and stuck them on a shelf in the garage. I'll have copies made for Liz and save a set for you."

"That would be great, Joe. Thanks."

"So. How 'bout having dinner with me tomorrow night?"

"I can't. I promised Des I'd go to some meeting with her."

"The town council meeting?"

"I guess. She said it was at the police station."

"Why would she want to go to a council meeting?"

Cara shrugged. "Something about dog ordinances."

"Des brought a dog with her?"

"No, but she's thinking about doing some type of rescue, or fostering abused dogs. It's something she did back in Montana, and she misses it."

"Are you sure she isn't going just to see Seth again?"

"Who?"

"Never mind. Well, I might see you there. It might be my month to give the fire report."

"What fire report?"

"Report to the council on how many fires we

had in town over the past thirty days. How many times we took the pumper out. The volunteer fire department—of which I am a member—reports to the council every month. Since we don't really have a chief, we take turns reporting. So if it's my month, I'll see you there."

"Well, aren't you just a jack-of-all-trades. How many fires were there in Hidden Falls last month?"

"Yes, I am." He steered the canoe toward the shoreline. "And there were none. We had the EMTs out twice, once for a suspected heart attack that turned out to be indigestion, and once for a fall in the parking lot behind the diner. Edie Parsons, who is about ninety, slipped on a banana peel and broke her hip."

"I thought the old banana peel thing was just for cartoons."

"She wasn't laughing."

"Are you an EMT also?"

Joe nodded. "I was a medic in the army."

"Were you stateside, or— "

"Or Iraq, yes. I did my time, then got out and came home while I was still in one piece."

"You're lucky," she said.

"You have no idea."

Cara could feel Joe's eyes on her. Finally, he said, "You want to ask, right? What it was like? It was hell."

"I'm sorry," she said softly.

"It's one of those crazy things. On the one hand, I wish to God I'd never gone. That I hadn't seen some of the things I've seen. On the other hand, I wouldn't have missed it. I served with some of the finest human beings I've ever met, men and women. I got to see what true courage is, the kind that makes heroes out of ordinary men. I saw selfless acts that took my breath away, saw men risk their lives to save civilians as well as their buddies. I saw the best in men, and, unfortunately, at times I saw the worst. But I saw that the good guys outnumber the bad by far, and it's the good I want to remember." Joe's oar went still in the water. "And as a medic, I remember everyone we couldn't save."

"Joe, I can't even imagine how difficult it must be to live through that, then to come back and be the same person you were when you left."

"No one's the same, Cara. You can't unsee, you can't undo. But if you're lucky, you'll learn something important from the experience that goes with you when you leave."

"Would I be out of line asking what you learned?"

"Not at all. But I should put it in context." He resumed paddling for a moment, then stopped again, and they drifted on the smooth surface of the lake toward the opposite shore. "I joined the army because I wanted to escape Hidden Falls and I couldn't afford to leave and go anyplace else. Growing up as the son of the town drunk was really tough. My father's shadow followed me everywhere I went. I went to college and it was great having four years where I didn't have to be embarrassed about my family, where there were no whispers when I went to class in the morning because of something my father had done the night before. But college was only four years, and I had the rest of my life ahead of me. I was really torn about where to go, what to do. Of course, my mother wanted me to come back home, but I couldn't face that scene again. So Ben and Seth and I talked it over and decided we'd enlist together right after we graduated. We thought we'd be serving together, but the army had other ideas. Ben got into the military police and stayed in the States. Seth and I were deployed, but not at the same time. He was injured and shipped home within eighteen months, so he was out before Ben or I came home. I think he'd have traded the extra time home for that shot he took in the leg."

"I don't know Seth," she told him.

"He was at the Bullfrog the other night. I saw him talking to Des at the bar. Tall guy, bald, lots of tats?"

"I only saw him from the back," Cara said. "You really chose the army over Hidden Falls?"

"It seemed like a good idea at the time."

"That important thing you learned . . ." she reminded him.

"For so long, I couldn't wait to leave, and after being away, seeing what the world is really like, I learned the only things that really matter are the people in your life. Your family, your friends. It's such a cliché, right? But when you see what we saw over there, it all becomes crystal clear." Joe sighed. "So at the risk of sounding like Dorothy, I learned there really is no place like home."

"So you're planning on staying in Hidden Falls?"

He shrugged. "I'm a lifer."

"It's not a bad place to live. I'm enjoying my time here. I miss my friends and my studio. I miss teaching. But I like the pace here. It suits my temperament."

"It's that laid-back vibe you got from your mother."

"That's probably true."

Joe began to paddle, and Cara followed suit. "Anyway, that's the story of the three amigos who had visions of fighting the enemy together and coming back to a welcome-home parade."

"No parade?"

"Seth got a party at the Frog." He smiled good-naturedly. "Which I missed because I was still dumping sand out of my clothes in the desert. I'm just happy that part of my life is over, and I'm here." He paused. "Actually, I'm glad you're here, too."

Cara nodded slowly. "Me too."

"Let's head for that shady area and get out of the sun." Joe pointed to a section of the lake where the trees grew almost to the waterline. Once out of the direct sunlight, the air was cooler and the scent of the pines was stronger.

"By the way, I emailed my contract to Pete Wheeler for him to look over," Joe said.

"I thought he was going to draw up the contract."

"I wanted to use my own. It seems to me that sometimes lawyers make things more complicated than they need to be. So I typed up my own and sent it to him this morning. I haven't heard back from him yet, but it's early."

"Can I have a copy of what you sent him?"

"It's in my briefcase. It's not that complicated. It

says that I'll act as your project manager from this date until the project is finished, and it says how much I'm charging you."

"Which has to be changed," Cara reminded him, but gestured for him to continue.

"In the event either party wants to void the contract, we can do so with thirty days' notice. That gives either of us a month, me to finish up whatever might be outstanding, you to find someone else. Read it over and tell me if you think we should add anything else."

She continued to paddle and they followed the curve of the lake.

"I included my proof of insurance and asked that I be added as an additional named insured on yours." Joe paused. "You do have insurance, right?"

"I don't know. Maybe for fire, but I'm not really sure."

"Then you need to call your broker as soon as possible and find out. You have people coming and going, you have a liability situation here. Call Jen Welsh. She'll know what you need."

He stopped rowing and pointed toward the shore. Cara turned and saw a doe with two fawns stepping beyond the tree line.

"She's beautiful," Cara whispered. "And her babies are adorable. They're the first I've seen since I've been here."

"I'm surprised you haven't seen them around the house, with all the woods around Hudson Street."

"I run in the woods and I haven't seen anything but a couple of birds."

Joe resumed paddling, and so did she.

"There's all sorts of wildlife here. Raccoons, opossums, skunks . . ."

"Ugh. I'd hate to run into one of those." Cara made a face. "Way to start your morning."

"They don't spray unless they feel threatened. So if you come across one, don't approach it."

"Duh." She rolled her eyes, and Joe laughed.

"The best thing you can do is just turn your back and slowly walk away. Which is not what you should do if you meet up with a bear."

"Right," she scoffed. "Like there're bears behind Barney's house."

"There are bears all around here. You're in their home territory. You don't mess with bears."

"Then why haven't I seen any?"

"Probably because they're just coming out of hibernation. You might want to change your morning route since the weather's warmed up. Last thing you want is to come face-to-face with a grumpy old mama that just rolled out of her den."

"Oh, like *you* have, Daniel Boone?"

He laid the oar across his knees, grabbed the bottom of his shirt, and started to pull it over his head.

"What are you doing?" she demanded.

"Showing you what happens when you get too close to a grumpy bear."

The guy was ripped. There was no other word for it. His chest was well defined with just a sprinkling of dark hair that contrasted with his skin, which still bore the faint remnants of last summer's tan.

Cara's mouth went dry. She tried to remember if she'd ever seen anyone that well built who wasn't on the cover of *Men's Fitness* magazine.

"Right here," he was saying, his fingers splayed on his left side.

"What?"

"This is where she got me." When Cara didn't respond—because she was still staring—he said, "The bear. See the claw marks? She got me good." He pointed to the three long white scars that went from his rib cage toward his back.

Cara cleared her throat. "A bear did that?"

"Yeah. That's what I'm trying to tell you." He pulled his shirt back on and picked up the oar.

"When did that happen?"

"When I was twelve. Julie and I were hiking up behind the falls. The bear came out of nowhere, swinging like a prizefighter. I told Julie to run, and she did, thank God. The damned thing took one big swipe at me, knocked me down, and took off. I was lucky, I know. She could have killed me. As it was, I lost a lot of blood. Jules went home and got our dad. He carried me down to his car and drove me straight to the ER. They gave me blood and a bunch of stitches and sent me home with the advice to stay out of the woods."

"You *were* lucky. She really could have killed you." *And what a total waste that would have been.*

"Tell me about it."

Joe changed direction and pointed the canoe back toward the dock.

"I've seen them out here around the lake, too. Which is why I prefer canoeing to hiking."

"Do you come out here a lot?" she asked.

"When the weather's good, yeah. It's peaceful and beautiful and Barney doesn't mind. She said I'm doing her a favor by keeping an eye on the place for her. Which we both know is a crock, but it's nice of her to say."

"Where do you keep the canoe?"

"In summer, I leave it in the boathouse." He pointed toward the building Cara had noticed earlier. "Through the winter and early spring, I keep it in my garage because I'm not out here often enough to check on things."

"So how did it get here today?"

"I drove out earlier and dropped it in the water."

"I like a man who plans ahead," she said.

"I'll keep that in mind."

They paddled back to the dock, pausing once to watch a flock of geese fly across the surface of the water. When they reached the dock, Joe maneuvered the canoe so Cara could safely climb out. He followed, dragging the canoe to shore, where he stood it up on one end.

"Can you carry the oars?" he asked.

"Sure." She picked them up in both hands. They were long and unwieldy, but she managed to carry them back to the truck without dropping them or smacking Joe in the head.

They reached the truck and Joe loaded the canoe on, then reached for the oars.

"Had enough nature for the afternoon?" he asked as he slid the oars onto the flatbed.

"I had enough after the bear story." She glanced warily at the woods surrounding the parking lot. If a bear came charging out of there right then . . .

"I'd scare it off with an oar."

"What? How did you know what I was thinking?"

Joe laughed. "You had that 'Oh God, what if' look on your face." He opened the passenger door.

"Nice to know I'm so transparent." She climbed into the seat and Joe closed the door.

"I hope I didn't scare you. Showing off my scars, that is." Joe hopped in and started the truck.

"Well, let's call it a new awareness that we're not in Kansas anymore."

He turned on the radio, which was set to a country music station.

Cara looked across the cab and smiled, thinking back to the dance at the Bullfrog the other night.

"Can't get away from that country music," she said.

"There's a station that plays oldies from the fifties and sixties. Maybe you can find it."

"We found a ton of fifties records in Barney's attic and we played them." Cara took over the radio dial. "Barney even taught us how to dance like they did back then."

"You can teach me, next time the VFW has oldies night."

"I'll do that."

Why was it, she wondered, that the trip *back* from someplace always felt faster than the trip *to*? It seemed no time at all before they were pulling up in front of the house.

Cara gathered her bag and the envelope he'd given her.

"Wait," Joe said. "Let me give you that copy of the contract I sent to Pete."

He opened the briefcase and handed her an envelope much like the one that held the photos.

"Let me know if you have any questions, and if you're okay with it, let Pete know."

"I'll do that, thanks."

"And don't forget to check on the insurance for the building."

"Right." She held up the envelopes. "I know everyone is going to love these. Again, that was very thoughtful of you."

"Well, I guess that means I was thinking about you, doesn't it?" He gave her arm a squeeze.

"So maybe I'll see you at the meeting tomorrow night."

For a second she thought he was going to kiss her. He had that look about him as he leaned in and held her gaze for a very long moment. But then the spell was broken and he reached across her to open her door.

"I'll see you there."

Clutching the envelopes holding the photos and Joe's contract to her chest, she jumped out of the truck and headed up the driveway to the house, wondering what she would have done if he had kissed her.

No question. She'd have kissed him back.

CHAPTER THIRTEEN

Cara dreamt of giant bears that chased her up the trail behind Barney's house and onto the rocks, and that when they swiped at her with their big clawed feet, she and the rocks went over the falls and into a pool of fire way below. She awoke with a start, sweating, her heart pounding. Not prone to nightmares, she tried to calm her shallow breathing. Glancing at her phone, she groaned when she saw it was 2:00 a.m. and she was wide awake.

When she was a child and had one of her rare nightmares, Susa would make her a cup of warm milk and it always helped her back to sleep.

She slipped out of bed and tiptoed down the stairs. Once in the hallway, she turned on the lamp near the front door and found her way to the kitchen. She'd taken three steps into the room when she realized the back door was open.

She froze. Had someone broken into the house?

She strained to hear sounds that shouldn't be there, but all was silent. As quietly as she could, she crossed the floor and peered out into the backyard. Her breath caught when she saw a figure seated in one of the Adirondack chairs on the patio. It took a moment for her to realize it was Allie.

Cara opened the door the rest of the way and went outside.

"Oh my God," Allie whispered. "You just scared the crap out of me!"

"Much as I felt when I saw the back door open," Cara whispered back. "What are you doing out here?"

"Enjoying the peace of a lovely spring night, what does it look like?"

Cara took a few steps closer. Allie held a glass in one hand and a bottle in the other.

"Would you like to join me for a drink?" Allie lifted the bottle so Cara could see the label.

"I don't care for vodka, thanks." Cara sat on the edge of the seat next to Allie. "Why . . ."

". . . am I drinking alone in the middle of the night?" Allie took a sip. "Because I couldn't sleep and there was no one to drink with me."

"Do you do this often?"

"Most nights, I have a cocktail or two in my room." Allie met Cara's gaze defiantly. "Don't even think about lecturing me, okay? I'm a big girl. I haven't had an easy time lately, you know."

"Sounds like you're making excuses, but"—Cara held up her hands as if to ward off whatever harsh words Allie might fling at her—"it's your life."

"It is. Thank you." Allie took another drink. "It's been a bitch of a year."

"Oh, please. Can we talk about bad years? My ex is getting married this coming weekend."

"I thought it was the weekend after."

"I did, too, but Joe reminded me that the third weekend in March is this week."

"Ah yes. Joe. He is pretty fine, for a country boy. So you're going to go out with him, right?"

"This weekend." Cara was tempted to tell her about bluegrass night at the gun club, but she thought that might go over better when Allie was sober, and her condition at the moment was questionable.

"I'm sure you'll have a great time. The guy's had the hots for you since he met you."

"I don't know if I'm ready for a relationship yet."

"I must've missed the part where he said he wanted a relationship. I thought he just asked you out for Saturday night."

"Yes, but I'm pretty sure he's not a one-and-done kind of guy. I'd bet money on it."

"What makes you think that?"

"I can't explain it. It's just this feeling I get from him."

"It's perfectly natural for two adults—preferably unattached—who are attracted to gravitate toward each other. It's part of the mating game."

"Yeah, well, I'm not so sure I'm ready to mate with anyone yet."

"The dating part is all foreplay. I can't believe I

have to remind you of all this." Allie turned in her seat as if studying Cara. "He did a job on you, didn't he?" No need to name that particular "he."

Hot tears welled in the corners of Cara's eyes but didn't fall.

"Yes, he did. I trusted Drew. With my life and with my future. And now he's going to share that life and that future with someone else. Someone who used to be my friend. Who used my friendship to get close to my husband and steal him."

"So all this came out of the blue?"

"We'd been arguing for a while."

"Over mostly stupid things, right? You worked too late, the Visa bill was too high, he didn't like the way you had your hair done?"

Cara nodded. "Close enough."

"Been there. Clint just wanted out. He said it wasn't anything in particular, just that he didn't *feel* it anymore."

"Drew said I spent too much time at the studio."

"Didn't you have a business to run?"

"I'd started offering classes at night for people who couldn't come during the day. Classes for men. Mommy and Me yoga, Daddy and Me yoga. That's how you build a successful business, by offering something no one else does."

"And the time you spent at the studio was time you weren't catering to him."

"I never catered—"

"I bet you did. And as soon as you stopped, he had to find someone else to stroke his ego and tell him what a super-duper hot stud he was. When you married Drew, you had no yoga studio—you weren't giving classes, right?"

"I was working in my mom's shop." Cara paused. "But you're right. I had lots of time on my hands and I spent a lot of that time focused on Drew, taking care of the house and all the little details of his life."

"So everything revolved around Drew until you started your business."

"But Drew was supportive of that: He helped me to fix up the studio—"

"Oh, pooh. It was a chance for him to show off whatever skills he had so you and everyone else could tell him what a great guy he was and what a great job he did. Then once the studio was up and running, the picture changed."

"So you're saying he cheated on me because I started my own business?"

"No. I'm saying he cheated on you because he couldn't stand not being the center of your universe."

Cara fell silent.

"What about this chick he's marrying?"

"My friend Darla says Amber was always jealous of me and was happy when she had an opportunity to take something that was mine." Cara sighed. "Though I don't know who started it between the two of them."

"Well, it sounds like they deserve each other."

"You know the worst part? I never saw it coming."

"Same here," Allie said softly. "Well, I hope you're past that."

"I'm getting there. How 'bout you?"

"I was there until I realized how he'd played me."

"There's a special place in hell for men like that."

Allie nodded. "There is."

"But for the record, you've done a wonderful job with Nikki. We all adore her."

"Thank you. I'd love to take the credit, but she's just naturally herself. She's always been this happy-go-lucky, out-there kind of girl." Allie realized her glass was empty, so she picked up the bottle and poured.

"You think Joe is the type who'd be threatened by a woman who can stand on her own?"

Cara laughed. "He gave me a pep talk about not letting any of the contractors walk all over me. Including him. So no, I'd have to say Joe is the last man on earth to back away from a strong woman."

"Well, then, I think I like Joe." Allie sat all the way back in the chair and closed her eyes. "I think your ex was an immature, immoral ass. Don't let the way he made you feel change the way you feel about yourself."

"Thanks, Allie. I needed that. Especially with the wedding this weekend."

"Like I said, your ex and his little honey deserve each other. You can do better." Allie paused. "Are you sure you don't want a drink?"

"I'm positive." Cara stood. "I think I'm going to go in. I'm freezing. It's probably time for you to go in, too."

"Uh-uh." Allie wagged a finger at Cara. "I'll decide when it's time for me to go in."

"I don't want you to fall asleep out here, Allie. What if Nikki finds you in the morning?"

"You mean passed out in an Adirondack chair in Barney's backyard?" Allie seemed to consider that. "You're right. That would be bad." Allie stood and took a deep breath. When Cara reached an arm out to steady her, Allie shook her head. "I'm fine."

She took three steps toward the back porch and stumbled.

"Allie, give me the bottle and the glass. If you fall, you're liable to cut yourself." She managed to get the glass away from her sister but not the bottle.

Allie smacked her hand away. "Stop it. I'm fine," she insisted.

"You're going to hurt yourself, and if you don't lower your voice, you're going to wake everyone up."

The threat of possibly having Barney, Des, and Nikki awakened settled Allie down. She took the steps slowly but deliberately, and Cara got her into the house. Once in the kitchen, she rinsed out Allie's glass.

"Will coffee help?" Cara asked.

"Just sleep."

"Then wait up and I'll give you a hand. We're going to have to be really quiet," Cara reminded her.

Allie nodded and did as she was told. Cara helped her take the steps slowly, and soon they were back in Allie's room.

"Thanks."

"Don't mention it."

"Seriously, don't mention it to Des, okay? She

has this aversion to drinking. Guess 'cause of our mother." Allie lay back against her pillow, her eyes already closed. "Promise?"

Cara hesitated. She and Des were well on their way toward a true friendship. Keeping something important from her seemed like a betrayal.

"Cara? Promise? I don't want Des to know. She'll make a big freaking deal out of it."

"Allie, don't put me between you and Des."

"I'm not. I'm just asking you not to discuss my business with my sister or anyone else."

"All right." Cara sighed. She didn't like keeping secrets, but Allie had a point. It was her business. "I promise."

Cara pulled the quilt over Allie and closed the door. She went back into her room and got into bed, still uncomfortable with the promise she'd made. Eventually she fell asleep, the bears, the falling rocks, and Allie's late-night, one-woman, backyard party forgotten.

Cara was up early the next morning, so she went through her yoga routine and had a good long run through town in the brisk March air before either of her sisters or her niece made it downstairs. Barney was off on her walk, and the house was pleasantly quiet. Cara was trying to decide what to have for breakfast when her phone rang.

"Hey, Cara. It's Joe. I hope it's not too early to call."

"I'm up. What's going on?"

"I'm over at the theater, and . . . well, you need to come down here."

"What's wrong?"

"Remember that hole in the back wall that Eddie said something had been getting into the building through?"

"Yes." Cara held her breath. *Please, God, not a wild animal. Mountain lions. Or bears. Especially bears.*

"Looks like a couple of stray dogs have been using the theater as their home. When we went to board up the hole, they were trying to get out, but once they saw us, they went back inside the building. They don't seem vicious, but I can't get near them. They look pretty ragged, like they've been on the road for a while. I'm not sure what you want me to do, and we don't have an animal control officer. I called Ben to see what he suggested, but he said I should talk to you, since they're in your building."

"I'll be there as soon as I can." She hung up and went straight up the steps to knock on Des's door. "Des. Des, are you up?"

"What?" A sleepy-eyed Des opened the door.

"Joe just called. They found a couple of stray dogs that have been making their home in the theater, and they want to—"

"Five minutes." Des slammed the door in her face.

Cara turned toward the stairs just as Nikki came around the corner.

"What's going on, Aunt Cara?" she asked.

Cara explained Joe's call.

"I'm coming, too. I'll be right back," Nikki told her. "Don't leave without me."

"What the hell is going on out here? Sorority meeting?" Allie's door opened.

Cara told her.

"There are dogs living in the theater?" Allie shook her head. "Call animal control. I'm going back to bed."

"We'll see you when we get back, Mom." Nikki returned, her bag over her shoulder, her phone in her hand. "I'm going to take pictures. I've decided I should be documenting my visit so I can show Dad and Court."

"Great. 'Here's a picture of me chasing mangy dogs down Main Street.' He'll love that." Allie yawned. "If everyone else is going, I might as well go, too. I'm assuming the Dog Whisperer is on the case." Allie pointed to Des's door.

"I heard that." Des emerged, fully dressed. "And we're leaving now. If you want to come, you have three minutes to get dressed. I'm not waiting for you." Des went to the steps. "Actually, I'm not waiting for anyone. I'm going now before some yahoo gets the idea to do something stupid to get the dogs out."

"Something like what?" Nikki was right on her heels.

"Like something that could result in the dogs being injured. Or worse."

"Joe wouldn't let that happen." Cara went into her room and grabbed her bag. She was still dressed in her running clothes, but there was no time for vanity. Cara heard the front door open and close. When she got to the front hall, she saw Des and Nikki sprinting across the wide yard to the sidewalk. They were already crossing the street by the time Cara got outside. Already sweaty, her hair a mess, she figured she couldn't look much worse. She broke into a jog and arrived at the theater in time to see Des shooing everyone away from the hole.

Des sat back on her heels ten feet from the wall and seemed to be observing. Cara started to approach her, but Des held up her hand.

"Get everyone back on the sidewalk, please," Des said in a low voice. "The dogs are getting spooked."

"What are you going to do?" Cara whispered.

"Whatever I need to in order to get them safe. Will you wait back at the sidewalk, please? If I need you, I'll let you know."

Fifteen minutes later, when the restless dogs hadn't emerged from inside the wall—scared off, no doubt, by Allie's arrival in Cara's car—Des asked that someone run across the street to the Bullfrog and get a couple of hamburgers.

"Allie, you go. Tell them no bread, and definitely no onions," Des said.

"Des, I don't think they sell burgers at eight thirty in the morning."

"Actually, they do. At least, they can." Ben pulled up in his cruiser, turned off the engine, and got out of the car. "They've cooked burgers for me after I've worked all night."

"Well, since you apparently have some pull with them, why don't you go?" Allie suggested without looking at him.

"I'll go." Before Allie could react, Nikki was on her way to the bar.

"They're not going to let her in: She's just fourteen." Allie went after her daughter.

"How many dogs are in there, Des?" Cara asked quietly.

"I saw three. Two medium black-and-white dogs and a small white one. At least, I think it's white. It's pretty dirty." Des never took her eyes off the wall. Every few minutes, one of the dogs would check to see if Des and the others were still there; then it would duck back into the hole.

Nikki and Allie returned, Nikki carrying a white bag, which she handed to Des.

"The guy behind the bar said no charge," Nikki whispered to Des. "He wanted to know what was going on, so I told him. He said he's seen the dogs around for about a week and he's been feeding them. He said they come to his Dumpster in the mornings."

"Thanks, Nik. You'd make a great sleuth. Now do me a favor and go into my bag and see if you can find that list of shelters that you made the other day," Des instructed.

Nikki did as she was told and located the list.

"I have it, Aunt Des."

"There's a number there for a woman in Harlow. Maria something."

"I see it."

"Can you call her, tell her what we have here, and ask if she has a couple of loop leashes we can borrow?"

"Will do." Nikki pulled her phone from her pocket and walked to the front of the building to make the call.

In less than three minutes, she was back.

"She'll be here in twenty minutes," Nikki whispered to Des.

"I really appreciate your help, Nik." Des smiled up at her niece. "Now, see how well you can keep everyone back so I can try to coax at least one of these babies out with a burger."

Nikki shooed everyone back onto the sidewalk and asked them all to please be quiet so Des could do her thing.

Cara watched as Des scooted just a little closer to the wall, an unwrapped burger in her outstretched hand. It wasn't long before a black-and-white nose appeared in the opening. It sniffed wildly and grew more restless but didn't venture out. Des began to coo to the dog in a low, calm voice.

"Come on, pup. I know you're hungry and scared. But we're here to help you, I promise. Come on out and get a snack, and let me at least see that you're okay."

The dog's head stuck out from the wall. It appeared to Cara that the dog was actually listening and trying to decide whether or not to trust the voice.

Des kept up her soft chatter, and before long, one dog ventured out tentatively. Warily watching Des, its tail down and its ears flat to its head, the dog crept closer by a step or two at a time, never taking its eyes off Des.

Finally, Des pulled a chunk off the burger and tossed it to the dog, who snatched it and chewed, its eyes now on the rest of the burger. Des threw it several more pieces, each aimed to bring the dog closer to her. All the while, she was speaking in that low, reassuring voice. When the dog had gobbled down the last of the burger, it stood looking at Des for a long moment before turning and jumping back into the hole.

"Oh, he's gone, Aunt Des," Nikki moaned. "You could have caught him."

"He's not ready to be caught yet, honey, and I'm not ready to catch him. Once Maria gets here, we'll try again."

"You're going to need a few more burgers if you're going to get all three of those dogs out." Nikki got up and went to the curb. "I'll get more."

By the time Nikki returned, Maria, a chubby middle-aged woman with short hair and a sweet face, had arrived and was in quiet conversation with Des. Nikki unwrapped the burgers for Des, then sat back with the others on the sidewalk, taking pictures with her phone the whole time. Maria knelt behind Des, a loop in one hand, and Des called to the dogs again. At the sound of her voice, the dog who'd eaten the first burger returned to the opening. After a moment, it jumped out.

"You're such a handsome guy," Des crooned. "Let's get you to the vet and make sure you're okay."

She drew the dog closer with the food. "You're wearing a collar, so you must have belonged to someone. Do you have a tag on?" Des peered closer. "I don't see one. Did you lose it, or did someone take it off before they let you go?"

The dog's tail began to wag, slowly at first, but it came close enough for Maria to get the loop around its neck. To the surprise of everyone except apparently Des, the dog did not struggle but lay down and ate the last bit of burger from Des's hand.

"You're a very smart and good dog," Des told it. "Now let's get your buddies out here and see if we can wrap this up." She turned and looked over her shoulder. "Joe, where's the nearest vet?"

"Dr. Trainor over on Winter Street. You need him?" Joe asked.

"If you could just call him and tell him we have three strays that we'd like to bring over for evaluation and testing, I'd appreciate it."

With Maria's help, all three dogs were soon lured out of their hiding place, leashed, and were sitting in the back of Ben's police car.

"Des, that was amazing," Cara told her. "We really will have to call you the Dog Whisperer from now on."

"Oh, dear God." Allie rolled her eyes. "They're just *dogs*, people."

"They were just scared and hungry. As soon as they realized they were going to be fed and not hurt, they were fine." Des stood up and stretched. "Trust me, it usually isn't this easy."

"I want to go to the vets with the dog," Des told

Cara. "But I doubt I'll be allowed to ride in the police car."

"Since Allie drove my car over, we can drop you off at the vet's, and if you want to stay for a while with the dogs, I can come pick you up later," Cara offered.

"That'd be great, thanks."

"Let me get the keys from Allie and we can go." Cara signaled for Allie to join them. "I'm going to take Des to the vet's office," Cara told her.

Allie handed over the keys. "I'll ride over with you. I don't feel like walking home. I still haven't had breakfast and I'm starving."

"I'm coming, too, Aunt Cara." Nikki headed for the car and jumped into the backseat. "And I'm going to stay with Aunt Des at the vet's." She leaned into the front as Des got into the passenger seat. "You were awesome, Aunt Des. Totally awesome. You saved those dogs. I was so proud of you."

"Well, I'm grateful to you for the part you played. You got the bait that convinced them to leave their shelter." Des turned around, and she and a smiling Nikki high-fived.

"Hey, Cara," Joe called to her. "I'm assuming you want me to board up the wall so that nothing else can make a home in there."

"Yes, please." She reached for the driver's-door handle. "You might want to just check to see if there's anything else in there, but boarding it up is definitely the way to go. Thanks."

"Sure."

She slid behind the wheel and he closed the door for her.

"He's really cute, Aunt Cara." Nikki turned to watch Joe walk away. "And he really does have the hots for you—I can tell."

"Nikki, you're scaring me," Allie told her. "How do you even know what 'the hots' are? Or what it looks like when one person has said hots for another?"

"Mom." Nikki sighed with apparent great patience. "I'm *fourteen*."

"That's the part that scares me." Allie snapped her seat belt as Cara took off.

The vet's office was two blocks down and three over, and they were there in minutes. Des thanked Cara for the ride and got out of the car.

"Wait for me," Nikki called to her. "I want to stay with you."

"Nikki, have you even had breakfast yet?" Allie got out of the car and stood next to it. Nikki was already halfway up the sidewalk.

"I'm not hungry. We'll be back later." Nikki's voice faded as she followed Des inside the clinic.

"Honestly, that child gives me a headache sometimes." Allie slammed the car door and started around to take the front passenger seat.

"I'll bet she says the same thing about you." Allie didn't need to turn around to see who was behind her. "I bet it's not easy being your kid."

"Sheriff, you have a lot of nerve. You don't know my child, you don't know anything about our relationship, and you know nothing about me."

"I know you're a snob from California who likes her vodka." Ben crossed his arms over his chest. "You still have my card?"

"No. I burned it." She got into the car and slammed the door. "After I ripped it into a thousand tiny pieces."

"Allie, what was—" Cara started to ask, but Allie gestured for her to drive.

"Just go."

"What did he mean, he knows—"

"He thinks he's smart and he thinks he knows something but he doesn't. Just drive, will you?"

All the way back to Hudson Street, Cara wondered what in the world was going on between Allie and the police chief. But judging by the death-glare on Allie's face, now wasn't the time to ask.

CHAPTER FOURTEEN

Des brought the little white dog back to the house once it had been given a clean bill of health and a bath by the vet's staff. She'd desperately wanted to foster the dog at least until she could arrange for someone to adopt it, but she knew that'd be up to Barney. She practiced her plea to keep the little dog, but she needn't have bothered. She called home while the dog was being groomed, and Barney picked up on the first ring.

"Cara already told me all about how you rescued those dogs from the theater and got them over to Doc Trainor's to be checked out. When Nikki came back for lunch, she said they were getting ready to give the little white one a bath. Good job, Des." Barney had sounded pleased. "So what's happening now?"

"They're going to keep the two larger dogs at least overnight. But the little white one will be released as soon as they're finished grooming her. She's a really good dog, and she's—"

"So you'd like to bring her home, right? I've always liked dogs. Yes, bring her home and we'll see how she likes living with the Hudsons for a while."

"Thanks, Barney." Des had breathed a sigh of relief. She went back into the clinic and told the vet, "I'll check back with you in the morning about the other two." Des had left the clinic with the little white dog on a new red leash.

Des talked to the dog all the way back to Hudson Street. Once at the house, the dog ran across the yard and squatted once to pee before taking off for the front porch. By the time Des caught up with her, the dog was staring at the front door as if willing it to open.

"Now listen, little one." Des knelt down next to the dog and unsnapped the leash. "Be really nice to Barney. She can send you away if you're not. You have to mind your manners and understand that Barney is in charge. You make nice with her, you've got it made."

Des stood just as the door opened and Barney stepped out onto the porch.

"Oh my, she's just a little thing, isn't she?" Barney sat on one of the rocking chairs and snapped her fingers to get the dog's attention. "No idea what her name might be?"

Des shook her head.

"We'll have to come up with something suitable," Barney told the dog.

Nikki stuck her head out and squealed when she saw the dog. "OMG, she's adorbs!" She sat on the porch deck and the dog climbed into her lap. "Who knew you were so stinking cute under all that dirt?"

"I can't believe you brought it home with you." Allie followed Nikki outside.

"Mom, stop!" Nikki looked horrified. "She'll hear you. You don't want her to feel unwanted." To the dog, Nikki said, "Aunt Allie didn't mean it."

Allie stared at her daughter for a moment. "I'm wondering if this week in Hidden Falls was a good idea after all. You're starting to sound like your Aunt Des."

"I'm going to take that as a compliment," Nikki told her.

"And you're starting to sound like our mother," Des said to Allie. "And that *wasn't* a compliment."

Allie watched her daughter cuddle the dog.

"All right, it's . . . almost cute. Now that it's clean." The dog looked up at her, tail wagging, tongue lolling, and Allie sighed. "Okay, you're cute. You're no Lassie, but you're cute."

"Yep, cute as a button, Mother would've said." Barney rocked back and forth rhythmically in the chair.

"Oh, can we call her that? Buttons?" Nikki laughed as the dog climbed higher to lick her face. "She should have a cute name."

"'Buttons' isn't cute. 'Buttons' is . . . common," Allie said.

"Maybe you'd rather name her after one of the Kardashians?" Des all but cringed.

"No. Her name is Buttons." Nikki turned to her mother. "And it's not common. It suits her."

"I like it." Des sat on the front step, pleased that so far, so good.

"I do, too. Good choice, Nikki." Barney nodded.

"It's hard to believe she's the same dog we dropped off at the clinic." Nikki sat back to take a long look at Buttons. "She was so dirty, she was brown."

While Des was picking up the dog, Barney and Nikki had gone through the old quilts in the closet and found one that had been put away for mending that never happened. Des had placed the quilt in a corner of her bedroom and told the dog, "This is your bed, Buttons."

When the dog looked longingly at Des's bed, Des told her, "Don't press your luck, girlfriend."

The dog slept on the quilt all night and, once Des took her outside, promptly did her business in the yard as soon as she could scamper out.

"She's been well trained," Barney observed as she slipped the dog a tiny bit of bacon at breakfast the following morning. "Someone took the time to teach her manners."

Nikki broke off another piece of bacon and held it up. "Sit, Buttons. Can you sit?"

The dog sat, and was promptly rewarded with not only the bacon, but praise from all the humans in the room. When everyone moved onto the patio to sit in the warm morning sun, the dog followed.

"If you're still planning on going to the town council meeting tonight, I suggest you go early." Barney stood at the top of the steps, on her way back in for a second cup of coffee.

"I was talking to a guy at the Bullfrog on Saturday night, and he said the same thing, that the room filled up really fast. I really do need to find out what the town's position is on rescue shelters." Des was hoping they'd be as open-minded as Barney.

"Who was that?" Barney asked.

"His name was Seth. I never got a last name, but he's tall. Muscular. Bald. Lots of tattoos."

"Oh, Seth MacLeod." Barney leaned against the door frame. "You didn't mention you'd met him."

"We just chatted for a moment at the bar."

"Nice boy, Seth. His daddy was mayor here in Hidden Falls. He passed a couple of years ago. Cancer. Just like Fritz, I guess. Diagnosed one day, gone practically the next." Barney paused. "I don't know which is worse. Having a lot of time but knowing your days are numbered, or having just a month or so and not so much time to think about it. Or just not knowing at all."

"I'd rather know," Des said.

"Not me." Allie shook her head. "Keep me in the dark for as long as possible."

"How 'bout you, Cara?" Des asked.

"I don't think it makes any difference, frankly. You don't have control either way. It is what it is." She turned to Des. "Do you think I could take Buttons out for a walk? It's a beautiful morning. I had my run, but I'd like to explore the town on foot while the weather is so nice. I promise not to wear her out."

"Sure. But keep in mind she's just a little thing

and won't be able to keep up a fast pace with those short little legs. Her leash is on the back of one of the kitchen chairs. And don't make her go too far. It might be too much for her."

"I'll get it." Nikki went into the house.

"Geez, Des, it's a dog, not a child." Allie settled into one of the chairs with her coffee.

"To some people, their dogs are their children," Des told her.

Allie muttered something so low under her breath that no one could hear.

"Aunt Cara, can I go with you?" Nikki returned, leash in hand, and snapped it onto Buttons's collar.

"Sure. Anyone need anything from Main Street?" Cara looked around. Des and Barney both shook their heads. Allie yawned. "Okay, we'll be back in a while."

Nikki held the leash, and she and Cara disappeared around the side of the house.

A few minutes later, Barney went back inside. "I have some paperwork to do," she said.

Ten minutes later, Allie and Des went inside, too. They found Barney at her desk in the office.

She had a stack of envelopes and her checkbook on the desktop and a small calculator in her hand.

"Bill day," she explained. "I have everything set up so that all my bills are due on the same day. That way, I only have to sit down and deal with it once a month." Barney opened an envelope and glanced at the contents. "So do you know what you're going to say at the council meeting?"

"Sort of. But I'm not sure how to approach them.

I mean, I don't know any of these people. I don't even know how to start."

Barney began to write a check. "Just think it out beforehand, because they don't give you much time to speak."

"So you go sometimes?"

Barney laughed. "I go every month, whether I need to or not. I want to know what's going on in town, what people are thinking about, what they're talking about." A smile still on her lips, she signed the check. "I'm a die-hard busybody, Des, and I don't give a damn who knows it."

"Why do you care what the law is, Des?" Allie looked up from the text she'd been typing. "It's not like you live here."

"Actually, right now, I do live here. And even if I didn't, there's a problem and no one seems to know if there's a ready solution. I want to find out."

"So what do you think you're going to do about it? Build your own shelter?" Allie shook her head. "You won't even be here a year from now to run it, so what's the difference?"

"How do you know where I'm going to be in a year when I don't even know?"

"Des, don't tell me you'd consider staying here?" Allie scoffed. "There's nothing for you here."

"Really? There's a long and distinguished family history here, a legacy. Our family did a lot for this town, Al."

"Yeah, well, that was then. This is now." Allie made a face and left the room.

"I'm sorry, Barney."

"About what?"

"That my sister is such an ass."

"Honey, if we were all responsible for the actions of our siblings, every one of us would be in trouble. Allie is who she is. I suppose she has her reasons." Barney tapped her pen on the table. "She was such a sweet little girl. So happy, it made you feel good just to be around her. I can't help but wonder what changed her."

"What was she like back then?"

"She was a darling little girl with all the curiosity in the world and a happy smile. She was actually a lot like Nikki, now that I think about it. We had a great time together."

"Funny she doesn't remember it."

"Not really. She was what, three at the time? There are photos—I forgot to look for them but I'll try to remember to search while you're still here. I won't have time tonight." She grinned at Des. "I'm going with you to the council meeting. You don't think I'd let my niece walk into that den of vipers alone, do you?"

At six thirty, Barney started to round up everyone who was going to the meeting. Des wanted to take Buttons, to make a point about the need for provisions for lost or abandoned animals, but Barney didn't think it was a good idea because there was no way of knowing how long it would be before Des got a chance to speak. Nikki offered to go along and keep Buttons quiet and amused outside in case Des needed her, which meant that Cara would come along as well so she could go out and get Nikki and the dog should the time come. Allie went because there was "nothing else to do in this Podunk town on a Wednesday night."

"I'm driving, girls." Barney grabbed her keys from the hook.

"Are we going in Lucille?" Cara asked.

"Is my name Bonnie Fletcher Hudson?" Barney headed out the door. "Meet me outside."

By the time everyone made it to the driveway, Barney had backed Lucille out of the garage and was idling. Nikki climbed into the backseat with Allie, Des, and Buttons.

"All in? Good." Barney hit the gas.

"Aunt Barney, I still haven't found my seat belt!" Nikki squealed.

"This car didn't come with a middle belt. I think it was an option Mother never thought she'd use. Sorry, honey." Barney looked in the rearview mirror. "Just hold on to something."

They arrived at the police station and Barney pulled up right out front.

"Aunt Barney, the sign says, 'No Parking,'" Nikki pointed out.

"Well, let them try to tow me. I'm not parking out back where some yahoo can swing open their door and smack Lucille on the quarter panel." Barney cut the engine and pulled the key from the ignition. "The parking spots in the lot are so close together, you can't park anything bigger than a Mini Cooper back there. We go home with so much as a scratch on this thing, we'll all be up all night." Barney opened the driver's door and slid the seat up to allow the back-seat passengers to exit.

"Why would we be up?" Nikki wanted to know.

"Because your great-grandmother would be banging on the pipes all night to let us know she wasn't pleased."

Nikki tapped her mother on the shoulder. "Does she mean a ghost?"

"Sounds that way." Allie slid out and held the seat for Nikki.

"That'd be so cool," Nikki said as she got out of the car.

"So Nik, you're going to hold on to Buttons until Cara comes out for you, right?" Des handed Nikki the dog's leash. "And you'll text me if you need us for anything?"

"Right." Nikki shortened the leash to keep Buttons from chasing after someone else who was arriving for the meeting.

"I'll stay outside with you, Nikki," Allie told her.

"You don't have to. I'll be okay out here."

"I don't mind." Allie watched Cara get out of the car, then took her place on the front seat. "I can just sit here and people watch. I'm sure it'll be fascinating."

"Wish us luck," Des said as she, Cara, and Barney went into the building.

They had to pass the reception desk to access the

long, narrow hall that led to the back of the station where the conference room was located. The hall was jammed, and the line to get into the room moved slowly. By the time Des, Barney, and Cara made it inside, there was only one seat left, which Des grabbed for Barney, who was happy to take it.

"You two can stand right there against the wall until the president of the council—that would be Irene Pettibone—asks if anyone has anything to discuss. You raise your hand, and when you're pointed to, they'll pass you the microphone. Identify yourself, and then you begin. Don't let anyone speak over you, by the way. Irene has a bad habit of not letting people finish if she isn't interested. Ross Whalen is another one. He was appointed to the council after someone else passed away or he'd never be up there. No one would vote for him. He's a self-serving, self-important SOB and he's got a mean streak a mile wide."

"Why don't you tell us what you really think of him, Barney?" Cara gave her aunt a nudge.

"There isn't enough time for me to tell you what I really think of that man."

At exactly seven, the six members of the council took their seats at a table that stretched across the front of the room. The meeting was called to order by Irene Pettibone, a woman in her fifties who wore her glasses at the end of her long straight nose, which was just as straight as her mouth. She looked over at the empty seat at the center of the table and said, "It appears the mayor is running late. He knows we start promptly at seven. We're not going to wait for him."

After calling on the treasurer for her report, and the secretary, who read the minutes of the previous month's meeting, she called on the chief of police to give his report. Ben had just stood when the crowd parted to allow a latecomer to enter the room. Des glanced over her shoulder and watched Seth—bald, tattooed Seth—pass behind her and head to the front of the room, where he took his seat behind the nameplate that said MAYOR.

"Apologies to everyone. Chief Haldeman, you were about to give your report?"

"Yes. Once again, we had no major crimes. Seven car stops—six of which resulted in speeding tickets. Three acts of vandalism." Ben paused and looked at the council table. "All underage kids who thought it was funny to puncture tires on Main Street. They'd managed to damage six before they were spotted. Their parents are paying restitution to the car owners, and the boys will be doing community service for the next six months. One month for every tire." He looked back at his notes. "There was an attempted break-in at the Bullfrog, but one of the patrol officers saw the guy." Again he glanced up. "Probably not real smart to try to burglarize a building so close to the police station, especially when the officers are changing shifts. Other than that, it was a pretty quiet four weeks since my last report. Any questions?"

As there were none, Irene said, "Thank you. Is there a report from the fire company?"

Joe stepped forward to take the mic. "No fire calls. Two medical emergencies. No fatalities. Pretty much the same as last month."

"Thank you, Joe." Irene adjusted her glasses. "Now, on to new business. Anyone?"

A man in front raised his hand. After he identified himself, he went on a rant about the traffic light out on the highway malfunctioning. He was cut off and told that since it was a state highway, he should call the state authorities. Two other residents stood, one to announce a fund-raiser for the library, the other to discuss plans to clean up the main park in town. Finally, Irene asked, "Anyone else?"

Des, whose hand had been in the air each time a speaker sat down, raised her hand again. Irene looked directly at her, then looked away.

"If there's no further new business . . ."

"Excuse me, but do you not see this young woman's hand?" Barney called out.

"Do you have something to say?" Irene addressed Barney. "You're going to have to identify yourself if you want to speak."

"Irene, you know damn well . . . Fine. Bonnie Hudson. This young woman has been trying to speak and you keep ignoring her."

"Only residents may bring new business issues." Irene's eyes focused on Des. "Are you a resident of Hidden Falls?"

"Well, no, I—" Des began her reply.

"Well, then . . ." Irene held out her hands as if to say, *So much for that.*

Barney grabbed Des by the arm and whispered in her ear. To the council, Des said, "But I am a property owner, and as such, I believe I have the right to the floor."

Before Irene could respond, Seth said, "That's correct. Someone pass her the mic. Go ahead, give your name and tell us what's on your mind."

The microphone was in Des's hands in seconds. "Thank you, Mayor MacLeod. My name is Desdemona Hudson. My sisters and I inherited the theater across the street from our father, Fritz Hudson." Des cleared her throat. "It's my understanding there are no ordinances that prohibit an animal shelter. Can you confirm that?"

The members of the council all looked at each other blankly. Finally, Seth said, "I don't believe there are any, Miss Hudson."

"So my next question is, how would one go about establishing a rescue shelter?"

Again, there were blank stares all around.

"You mean a kennel?" Ross Whalen—Barney's "friend"—spoke up for the first time. "You need to be licensed to own a kennel."

"I don't mean a kennel. I mean a shelter that would take in stray, abused, or abandoned animals and—" Des started to explain.

"That's not going to happen in Hidden Falls," Whalen told her before she could finish her thought. "We're not going to have our town become a dumping ground for every dog that someone lets out on the highway."

"What do you propose to do with them?" Des asked, earning a long, dark look from Councilman Whalen.

"What we do with them now. We send them to the county SPCA, right, Chief Haldeman?" Whalen turned to Ben.

"Well, my first step is to see if we can find the owner. If I can't, I try to find someone to take the animal, which is usually a dog."

"There, you see? We have a plan in place." Irene dismissed Des by looking over the crowd and asking, "Anyone else tonight?"

"Excuse me, Councilwoman Pettibone," Seth intervened. "Miss Hudson, were you finished?"

"No, I wasn't. Thank you." She turned to face Ben. "So if you can't find anyone to take the dog in, where does it go, Chief?"

Ben stood and faced her. "There have been times when I had to take the animal to the SPCA."

"Do you know what they do with animals that are dropped off there, Chief?" Des asked.

"It's my understanding they keep the animals for ten days before euthanizing them."

"Do you know what means they use to 'euthanize' the dogs?"

Ben shook his head.

"I'm sure they're very humane," an exasperated Irene said. "Now, if I may . . ."

"'Humane'? Shall I describe to you what 'humane' methods are used in most kill shelters, ma'am?" Des crossed her arms over her chest, not conceding the floor.

"What's behind all this?" Whalen all but yelled at Des.

"Today we rescued three stray dogs that had managed to get into our theater. We took them to Doctor Trainor's clinic and he's keeping two of them overnight. We're keeping the third one at my aunt's house until we can find a permanent home for it, but the others probably will be released in the morning. If we had a shelter in town, I could take them there. But in the absence of such a place, I need to know what to do with them."

"Well, I suppose you could turn them over to Chief Haldeman and he'll find homes for them." Irene addressed the crowd, an empty smile on her face. "Anyone here want a dog?"

There were no takers.

"As I said, you can turn them over to the chief tomorrow and he can see if he can place them, and if not, he'll take them to the SPCA."

"Where they'll be 'humanely' euthanized if no one claims them." Des tried but failed to keep the emotion from her voice.

"This is not the council's problem, Miss Hudson," Irene snapped. "Now, if we could—"

"What kind of dogs are they, Miss Hudson?" Seth asked.

"I believe they're border collies," Des told him.

"Those are the dogs that are supposed to be the smartest, right?"

"Yes, Mayor." Des nodded.

"Male or female?" he asked.

Irene Pettibone shifted in her seat, making no attempt to hide her annoyance. "Mayor MacLeod—"

"One of each," Des told him. "What we need immediately are foster homes for them. Just someplace safe where they'll be cared for until we can find permanent homes."

"I'll take the male," Seth announced. Before Des could react, he looked over the crowd, his eyes settling on Ben. "Anyone else willing to step up?" The room was silent, and he continued to stare directly at Ben.

"Oh, hell, fine." Ben raised a hand.

Seth turned his attention back to Des. "Understand that this doesn't solve the problem long-term. In the future, the council may want to consider what is involved in establishing such a facility. So if you have something specific in mind, write it up and bring it to the next meeting."

"I understand." Des nodded. "Thank you."

"The chief and I will speak to you after the meeting about when to pick up our new companions."

Des thanked him again and passed the microphone back to the front of the room. Ten minutes later, the meeting was adjourned, and Des waited at the side of the room for Seth and Ben to finish their conversations with other residents.

"How 'bout we walk outside and talk this over," Seth said when he finally approached her. To Barney, he said, "Way to make friends on the council."

"Like tonight should be different from any other night. Your daddy would've been proud of you," Barney told him. "He never let that old sourpuss push him around, either."

"Now, now, Barney. She's our esteemed council president." Seth suppressed a smile.

"Whose big fat idea was that?" Barney frowned.

"No one else wanted the job. Guys, Ben's going to catch up with us outside," Seth said, "so let's head on out."

"Thank you again," Des said as they followed the hall to the front door. "I was really starting to get annoyed with that woman."

Seth towered over her, so he leaned down as he lowered his voice. "Irene annoys everyone. Having her on the council is our cross to bear."

"One has to wonder what the people of this town did to warrant such a punishment." Barney shook her head and went through the door Seth was holding open for her.

"Lucille's looking good, Barney." Joe came up behind the group.

"She's loved and well cared for." Barney nodded. "And yes, looking good for her age."

Joe touched Cara's back. "I have some estimates for you in the car. How 'bout we walk next door to the Bullfrog, grab a beer, and go over them?"

"Sure. We've been waiting to start adding up what this venture is going to cost us." Cara smiled and turned to Barney. "I'm going to have a drink with Joe and—"

"I heard. Go on." Barney wagged a finger at Joe. "Just get her home before the bar closes."

"Hey, did you forget about us?" Nikki stood next to Lucille, Buttons sitting patiently at her feet.

"We didn't need to bring Buttons in, but thank you for being on call." Des knelt down and picked up the dog. "Seth, meet Buttons."

Des held the dog up to him, then turned to Nikki and Allie. "Seth is going to foster one of the border collies. Isn't that great?"

"Really? Oh, that's so cool." Nikki beamed at him approvingly. "Which one?"

"The male." Seth turned as Ben came down the sidewalk. "Ben here is taking the other one."

"She's a real sweetheart, Ben. You'll love her," Des promised.

"Right, the bitch," Ben said, his eyes on Allie.

Allie looked as if she was dying to comment, but she stood and pushed the front seat forward so she could climb into the back. "So mission accomplished, right? All the dogs have homes and everyone's going to live happily ever after. Once again, Des does it all. So can we please leave now . . . ?"

CHAPTER FIFTEEN

The lighting inside the bar wasn't great, but Joe found a table near the front of the room directly under a sconce. Cara noticed that some others who'd been at the meeting were clustered here and there throughout the room.

"What can I get you from the bar?" Joe asked.

"Beer is fine."

"I'll be right back."

Joe returned with two beers in one hand and a bowl of munchies in the other. He handed one of the beers to Cara and placed the bowl in the middle of the table.

"Yum. Peanuts and pretzels," she said, reaching for the snacks.

"Unhand my dinner." Joe sat across from Cara. When she raised an eyebrow, he said, "Okay, you can have a pretzel. One of the broken ones."

She laughed. "Why didn't you have dinner?"

"I got held up on a job, and the next thing I knew, it was almost seven."

"Were you held up because you were at the theater?"

"Eddie came back to check the traps, so I had to let him in. I'm thinking about having a key made for him, unless you object. That way he can come and go and the traps will be working overtime."

"That's fine with me. You shouldn't be on call every time someone wants into the building."

"Actually, as project manager, I should be."

"Is this going to be a problem for you, once the actual work begins?"

"At times, maybe. But, as I told you before, I have great crews. I don't have to be hanging over them eight hours a day. Besides, I *want* to be part of the theater's comeback. People in town are very excited about it. Older people who were there as kids are nostalgic: They have great memories of the place and want to see it reopen. Younger people are just happy there might actually be someplace to go once it's up and running."

A waitress passed their table. "How're you doing, Joey?"

Cara smiled. "I don't think of you as a 'Joey.'"

"Old habits die hard, I guess." He took a drink. "My dad started bringing me here from the time I was about four years old. He always called me Joey. Sue—the waitress—has been here longer than that, so she remembers."

"Your sister mentioned that your dad passed away a few years ago. I'm sorry."

He picked at the label on his beer. "Everybody's sorry. Not so much that he passed away, but that he took others with him. If he'd hit the tree first, he wouldn't have hit the car coming the other way." He took a long sip, then lowered the bottle and added, "And Ben would still have his wife and son."

Cara's mouth dropped open.

"You didn't know that? Yeah, my father was responsible for killing Sarah Haldeman and her and Ben's two-year-old son."

Cara couldn't find the right words, so she shook her head.

"I told you my father was the town drunk. Ran his father's business into the ground until it was worthless. Bankrupted our family." His voice was filled with both anger and regret. "And killed my best friend's family."

"But you and Ben are still friends."

"Ben has never held it against me, or my mom, or my sister. That should tell you exactly what kind of man we have running our police department."

"It's hard to imagine anyone being that forgiving."

"He hasn't *forgiven* my father," Joe said pointedly. "He just doesn't blame anyone *but* my father."

"Still . . ." It was almost unimaginable to Cara that someone could take your family away and you'd still be okay with anyone or anything connected to that person.

"I know. But we're as tight as we ever were. I was there for him, and he's been there for me. It's what friendship's all about, right? You're there for each other when it counts the most. You support each other, hold each other up when things are rough." His mouth curved into a barely there smile. "I guess that's what love is, too."

"I always hear women talk about how much they love their friends—I certainly love mine dearly—but I've never heard a man say he loves his friends. It's nice to know."

Joe's smile grew just a little. "Yeah, we make each other as miserable as possible every chance we get and we're competitive as hell. But there's love there. I know they have my back, and they know I have theirs."

"Still, it's remarkable that Ben has stayed so close to you after . . . after the accident."

"Ben knew my family had a loss as well. What my mother went through . . ." He shook his head. "It's been very tough for her to go on after all that happened. She's always been a sort of second mother to Ben. His mother left his father a long time ago, took his younger brother and sister with her. After his father died, Ben lived with us. As far as my mom was concerned, he wasn't allowed to go anywhere else."

"So it's almost as if you're brothers."

"We were like brothers before that, but yeah, that sort of sealed the deal. My mother adored Ben's wife, always teased that if it weren't for his son, she'd have no grandkids at all. So she took the accident the hardest, I think. Yes, she lost her husband but she felt that Sarah and Finn were part of our family.

I think she mourned them more than she mourned my dad."

"Wow." Cara took a drink to give herself time to sort through all that Joe had just shared.

"That's why Ben is so tough on anyone who drinks and drives. There's been many a night he's taken keys from people who have been in here and stumbled out. He'll drive them home but keeps the keys at the police station. You want your car back, you have to go into his office to get them." Joe picked some peanuts out of the bowl. "And that's why there is zero tolerance for driving impaired in Hidden Falls."

"If you don't mind my saying so, I'm surprised that you drink at all."

"I'm a one-beer-a-night man. Maybe two if it's a really special occasion. Once in a blue moon, maybe a glass of wine. But I don't drive if I've had more than one, and I give myself an hour to make sure I'm not buzzed. Not that one beer ever buzzed me, but yeah, I'm sensitive to the issue." He tossed the peanuts into his mouth. "I'm lucky that despite the fact that my father was an alcoholic, I never had much of a desire to drink. But that's enough about me. How are you doing in your search for Fritz Hudson?"

"I'm putting bits and pieces together, but I'm still looking. Just being in Hidden Falls and living in the house my dad lived in makes me feel closer to him. But I can't say I've had any *aha* moments. Though I did learn that he was quite the athlete when he was a young man."

"Does that surprise you?"

"A little. He never mentioned having played sports."

"How are you getting along with your sisters?"

"Des and I have gotten along almost since day one. Allie's been a tougher nut. There's a lot of baggage between her and Des, and sometimes that surfaces. The short version is Des had her own TV show when she was a kid, and Allie didn't." Cara thought back to her 2:00 a.m. chat with Allie on the patio. "Actually, Allie has a lot of issues she needs to deal with."

"What's going on between her and Ben, do you know? Man, she just about snarls every time she sees him."

"I noticed that, too. Maybe he reminds her of her ex-husband."

Joe nodded. "Maybe. Ben's such a good guy, so easy to get along with, it's hard to imagine anyone not liking him."

"She's never really said why he annoys her so much. I just hope she tones down the sniping or we're all in for a very rocky year."

"You think you're going to be here for a year?"

"We're hoping it doesn't take longer than that. I guess that's up to you."

"It'll be up to the subs and how quickly they work. Which doesn't mean I'm above dragging things out if it keeps you around longer," Joe replied with a wink. "But be prepared for everything to take longer than you plan. Which reminds me . . . I have some estimates and a few invoices for you." Joe took an envelope from his inner jacket pocket and handed it to Cara.

"Here's Eddie's bill for the first week. You can take a look at it and let me know if you have any questions."

Cara read through the invoice, noting how many times Eddie stopped to empty the traps.

"I sure can't argue with this. He's doing the job we asked him to do. I'll give it to Des to pay." She folded the invoice and dropped it into her bag. "What else?"

"These are the estimates from Mack for the electrical, and from the plumber." He placed both on the table. "I expected to get the estimate from the roofers today, but it didn't come in. I'll check my office in the morning."

"I didn't expect the plumbing work to be this high." Cara frowned.

"You can see what Liz is saying has to be done. Because you can't use lead pipes in town anymore, and that's mostly what you have, everything has to be replaced with PVC, which means she has to replace all the fixtures, too. You need handicap-accessible facilities on both sides of the theater, and a new bathroom downstairs near the office. All in all, it's a lot of work."

"All right." She sighed. "I guess there's nothing we can do about it."

"Not if you ever expect to get the building open again."

"I hope we can reopen. I mean, what's the point

of doing all this if it isn't going to be used." She blew out a long breath. "I sound like Nikki. She said the same thing to Allie. I guess in the end we'll have to sell it."

"Why?"

"Allie won't stick around. Des might. I know she does a lot of rescue work out in Montana, but she could just as easily do that here."

"And you?"

"I have a business back in Devlin's Light. I love my yoga studio. It'd be really hard to give it up."

"You couldn't have a studio here?"

"I could. I've thought about it, actually. I miss it so much. I still practice every day, but I miss the camaraderie of the people who come in for classes. First I'd have to find a place." Her mind briefly went back to the first floor of the carriage house.

"Barney would be your first student. She loves anything new."

He glanced at her unfinished beer. "That must be warm by now. Want a cold one?"

"No, thanks."

Joe went to the bar to settle their tab, and Cara watched as he exchanged teasing but polite banter with one of the waitresses. Her mind went back to an evening about a year ago, when she and Drew were in a busy restaurant just outside of Devlin's Light. The restaurant had been terribly understaffed that night, with two waitstaff to serve a packed house. Drew had berated their waitress because his steak was overcooked. Then he'd given her a hard time because she hadn't brought him a drink refill when he'd wanted it.

"For crying out loud, Drew, the woman is moving as fast as she can," an embarrassed Cara had protested.

"That's her job," he'd snapped, and she'd let it drop until he gave the poor woman an insultingly low tip.

"I should use the ladies' room before we leave," Cara had told him on their way out the door. "You go get the car. I'll just be a minute."

She'd gone back to the table and tripled the tip he'd left. "Sorry," she said to the waitress who was clearing the table. "We had to get change."

The waitress had thanked her, but it was clear that she knew exactly what Cara was doing. "Thanks again," she'd said in a weary voice. "It's been a rough night."

There'd never be a need to clean up after Joe like that, Cara thought as he took her hand as they walked out into the cool March evening.

She shivered as a breeze blew against her bare arms.

He put an arm around her all the way to his car.

"Now, I realize she's not as fancy as Lucille," Joe said as they reached his old Jeep, "but she's a big step up from my truck."

"She has a name?"

"A car has no name." He parodied a line from *Game of Thrones*.

"Oh God, not you, too." She laughed as she

climbed into the front seat. "We had a conversation about the show not too long ago, and Barney was appalled at some of the goings-on."

"Yeah, my mom won't watch it either, so my sister comes to my place to watch." He climbed behind the wheel and backed out.

It took less than three minutes to arrive at the house. Joe pulled all the way up in the driveway and stopped next to the carriage house.

"You know, I peeked inside the—"

Joe leaned over the console and took her face in his hands and kissed her. She hadn't been expecting it, but she found herself responding as if she'd planned it all along. His lips seemed to know their way around hers the same way his tongue seemed to know her mouth.

It'd been years since Cara had been kissed by anyone except Drew, and she would've expected it to feel unnatural. But surprise, surprise, kissing Joe seemed like the most natural thing in the world, and she gave herself over to the feeling that washed through her. She felt a slight stab of disappointment when he pulled back and whispered, "So, you ready to make your debut at the gun club Saturday night?"

His lips were close enough to her ear that she felt the softness of his breath on her skin. The light touch sent goose bumps up both her arms.

"Saturday night?" She forced her eyes open, told her brain to focus. "Right. Saturday night. The gun club thing."

"Bluegrass. You'll like it." He kissed the tip of her nose and got out of the Jeep.

He opened her car door for her and took her hand as they walked to the back steps. She stopped at the bottom of the stairs.

"Thanks again for the estimates and the advice and the drink and the—"

He kissed her again and she forgot whatever else it was she had to thank him for.

"See you on Saturday," he said. "Go on in. It's getting cold."

"Hey, just for the record, how many girls have you taken to the gun club on bluegrass night?"

"You're the first."

"Really?"

"Really. That oughta tell you how special I think you are."

She wasn't sure if he was kidding, but then he kissed the side of her cheek before he went to the car.

Grateful that no one else was in the kitchen, Cara poured herself a glass of water and drank it down. She sat on the window seat and looked out at the dark woods and thought about the evening. The touch of Joe's hand on her back as he'd passed behind her. The haunted look in his eyes as he told her about his father's death and the deaths of those much-loved souls his father had taken with him into the next world. The depth of a friendship that had remained strong even under the most terrible of circumstances. The way Joe's mouth had claimed hers, as if she'd been his all along. The way his arms felt around her, the warmth and the strength of his hands, the touch of his fingers, as he'd held her face.

Somehow, she'd thought moving on would have been harder, would have stirred up much more angst and almost a kind of guilt, but Cara felt none of those things. Instead, she felt wanted and cared for, desired.

For the first time since Drew had walked out on her, Cara felt like she was enough.

"You were out late last night." Des looked up as Cara came in from her run.

"Not so late," Cara said as she pulled off her gloves. The temperature had dropped overnight and was barely into the thirties. She poured a cup of coffee and tried to ignore the questions on Des's face. "Joe gave me some estimates we need to go over. He gave me his opinions, but I don't feel comfortable giving my okay without everyone knowing what's going on. Oh, and Eddie the exterminator handed in his first bill."

"Why don't we take our coffee into the library and talk there." Des stood and grabbed her mug. "I need a refill."

"Why do we even have to talk about it?" Allie complained. "Cara's in charge of getting the building redone, right? It's her decision."

"We're talking about a lot of money, Allie. I don't

feel comfortable spending it without you and Des knowing where it's going."

"I agree. We all need to be on the same page." Des started for the door. "Move your butt, Allie. It's showtime."

Grumbling, Allie followed her sisters down the hall.

"Where are Barney and Nikki?" Cara asked as they settled into cozy chairs.

"They went on a hike about fifteen minutes ago. Nikki wanted to see the falls, and Barney took her. Can you imagine, in this freezing cold?" Allie shifted and pulled her legs up under her.

"Oh God, I hope there are no bears," Cara said.

"Bears?" Allie scoffed. "Yogi? Boo-Boo? Smokey?"

"It's not a joke, Allie. There are bears all around here," Cara said. "Joe told me."

"Oh, *Joe* told you. Well, then, that makes it true." Allie rolled her eyes.

"He was attacked right up there on the path where Barney and your daughter are walking."

"Attacked by a bear. Right."

"He was. He has these scars that run from here to here." Cara demonstrated the location of Joe's scars.

"Is this secondhand information, or did you see these scars with your own eyes?" Allie pressed.

"I saw them."

"So he must have taken his shirt off. . . ." Allie's eyes danced with humor.

"Yes, he did. And I don't mind saying it was a fine

sight to see. The guy is sculpted like a god, but that doesn't change the fact that there are bears in these woods."

"I'm willing to bet that Barney knows when it's safe," Des said. "Besides, bears hibernate, and it's really cold out."

"It was warm most of the week," Cara reminded them. "They might have awakened."

"Okay, now you're freaking me out." Allie grabbed Cara's arm. "Swear you're not lying."

"Cross my heart," Cara told her. "I saw the scars."

"I should go tell them to come back." Allie stood.

"If they're not back in ten minutes, we'll all go tell them," Cara said.

"I really think Barney's lived here long enough to know when the bears wake up," Des said, then paused. "I need to take some notes. Let me get my pad and a pen. My bag's in the kitchen."

Des was back in a minute. "I'm expecting to hear from Dr. Trainor's office anytime after nine, so we may be interrupted. I'm not sure if both dogs will be released this morning, but I'll need to call their fosters and let them know."

"You mean Tattoo Guy and the sheriff." Allie rested against the arm of the wingback chair.

"Seth and Ben. You know their names," Des said.

"I know the sheriff, but I didn't actually meet the other guy. Tattoo Guy. He looks like he belongs on *Sons of Anarchy*. I bet he rides a Harley," Allie said. "Go on, Cara. Throw some big numbers at us."

"Let's start with the bill from the exterminator."

Cara passed the bill to Allie, who barely looked at it before passing it on to Des.

"This is for one week?" Des asked.

"Yeah. Hopefully, as time goes on and more and more of the rodent populations are removed, he'll need to make fewer stops at the theater," Cara said, "but in the meantime, the mice and rats have got to go."

"Agreed." Des was still looking at the bill. "I don't see where we have a choice."

"Unless we want small, hairy things dashing across our feet," Allie noted.

"Speaking of small, hairy things, where's Buttons?" Cara asked.

"Hiking with Barney and Nikki. I told Barney to . . ."

". . . carry her if she started to look tired." Allie rolled her eyes. "Des, we get it. You're like a helicopter mom for dogs."

"Allie . . ." Des stared at her, then shook her head. "Never mind."

"Nikki's going to miss that dog when she leaves on Sunday," Cara said.

"I think the dog is going to miss her, too." Des tapped her pen. "They've spent a lot of time together. Last night Nikki moved Buttons's quilt into her room so they could sleep together."

"Maybe she'll start bugging Clint for a dog when she gets back home. That'd drive him crazy," Allie said with a smile.

"Why would that make him crazy?" Cara asked.

"He's allergic to dogs."

"Well, make sure Nikki washes everything before

she leaves," Des cautioned. "The dander will travel home on her clothes."

"Oh, that would be too bad." Allie's smile never faded.

"Yeah, poor Clint. All that sneezing and scratching," Cara said.

"He'd be so miserable," Allie agreed.

"So much for Clint and his allergies. Do we all agree to pay the exterminator as Cara suggested?" Des held up the bill.

Allie and Cara nodded, and Des put the bill in the checkbook. "I'll take care of it today. Next item . . ."

They'd just finished talking about the plumber's bill when they heard the back door open and the sound of little feet running down the hall. Seconds later, a white ball flew into the room and, panting, flung itself onto Des.

"Well, someone had a good walk." Des laughed.

"She had a good carry, mostly," Barney told them as she and Nikki followed the dog into the library. "She pooped out about halfway up the trail."

"Mom, you have to make the climb with me." Nikki sat on the love seat across from Allie. "The waterfall is so beautiful. The way the water tumbles over the rocks—you have to see it, Mom. It's, like, a mystical experience."

"Doubtful, pumpkin. I hear it's a long way up," Allie told her. "And there are those bears."

"What bears?" Nikki asked.

"Joe told Cara he was mauled by a bear up on that very trail," Allie told her.

"Oh, for heaven's sake." Barney dismissed her with a wave of her hand. "That was so long ago. Joe was just a kid. And the bear had cubs. Besides, it's too early for them to be out of their caves." She turned to Cara. "When did Joe tell you this?"

"The other day. Oh, the lake. I forgot to tell you about the lake," Cara said excitedly. "He took me to Compton Lake and we took a canoe—"

"You had a date with Joe and you forgot to tell us?" Allie poked her. "What's wrong with you? Stop holding out on us."

"There was so much excitement with the dogs, it slipped my mind." Cara turned to Barney. "But speaking of holding out on us, why didn't you tell us you owned a lake?"

"A lake?" Des asked. "An entire lake?"

Cara nodded. "A beautiful pristine lake surrounded by woods."

"Is that when Joe showed you his 'scars'?" Allie's fingers made quotation marks.

"Yes. And before you ask, he pulled his shirt up to show me the scars only because I didn't believe he was attacked by a bear."

"So how was the view?" Des asked.

"Pretty amazing," Cara replied.

"Girls, please," Allie deadpanned. "Not in front of the *k-i-d*."

Nikki laughed. "I know she's talking about the view of Joe's chest and not the woods. I'll bet he looked fine, Aunt Cara."

Cara gave her a wink.

"Okay, let's get back to business here," Allie said, then whispered to her daughter, "You're too young to be noticing such things."

"I'm not blind," Nikki muttered.

"How did this conversation even begin?" Allie moaned.

"We were talking about the falls," Cara said. "And I agree with Nik. They really are something to see."

Des nodded in agreement.

"Wait, Mom, are you the only person here who hasn't seen the falls?" Nikki frowned. "Seriously? Everyone but you? *The hidden falls of Hidden Falls?*"

"Yes, everyone but me. I'll do it. Someday. Maybe."

"Mom, besides being a mystical experience, it's great exercise." Nikki leaned closer. "Something you don't seem to be getting much of."

"What are you talking about?" Allie protested. "I walked all the way to the theater."

"Mom, you don't get enough exercise. It's not healthy."

"That's because there's no spin class. I'll bet there's no personal trainer within at least a hundred miles of this outpost," Allie grumbled.

Nikki took out her phone and sat on her mother's lap. "These are the pictures I took this morning. Let me show you what you're missing. . . ."

Cara looked at the clock on the mantel. It was time to call Meredith and see how things were going back at her studio in Devlin's Light. She knew Meredith was a highly capable assistant, and she was sure things were fine, but she wanted to be brought up-to-date on the business.

Thinking back to last night and her conversation with Joe, she thought it might not be a bad idea to check into the possibility of opening a studio in Hidden Falls, even if only for the time she was here. After she made her call, maybe she'd check out the inside of the carriage house. It couldn't hurt to take a look— just for the fun of it—and see if it could be suitable.

Des and Nikki had taken Buttons to the park, Allie was taking a nap, and Barney was off with her friends. Cara had tried every door—from the big double doors in the front to each of the side doors and the back door—but all were locked. On a whim, she checked the hooks near the back door, and there was the key, clearly marked CARRIAGE HOUSE. Certain that Barney wouldn't mind, Cara took it and began to try the locks, but it didn't fit the lock on the front or back doors.

"Third time's the charm," she murmured as the side door swung open. She stepped inside and looked around.

There were marks on the floor where carriages had stood who knew how many years ago. Cara wondered what happened to them. Had they been sold along with the horses once the horseless carriage came to Hidden Falls? All that was left from the carriage era was a discarded wheel that stood against the back wall. There were windows across the back and both sides, but they were covered with dust and cobwebs, and little light passed into the space.

She walked through the large, empty room, trying to picture it completely redone. The floor, being concrete, was hard as, well, cement. Hardwood or a thick pad under wall-to-wall carpet could rectify that. The walls could be painted white—actually, she thought, they might *be* white, but years of dust and dirt had darkened them. So white paint—or at the least, something light—and a more comfortable floor. Lights along the sides of the room rather than overhead to soften the effect. It could be done, if that was what she wanted to do. She had so much on her plate now with the theater, she wasn't sure she was up to yet another renovation project. Still, she missed teaching. Maybe once the theater was further along she could seriously consider opening a studio here. It was a dream she wasn't about to give up—she'd just shelve it for the time being.

A narrow stairwell rose from the side wall, and Cara climbed the steps tentatively. Once upstairs, she found the second floor divided into several rooms, all much brighter than the carriage room below. Though the air still held a dusty chill, the sun spilled brightly through the tall windows. The room at the top of the steps was one large rectangle that clearly revealed that someone had once called this home. The kitchen took up the back wall, and the placement of furniture on strategically situated area rugs defined the other spaces. The living room furniture, arranged around a brick fireplace, was covered with sheets, but a peek underneath revealed a 1950s-style sofa and two chairs. The dining area was little more than a long farmhouse table that stood between the kitchen and the living room. A partially opened door on Cara's left led to a bedroom, beyond which was a bathroom. Another bedroom was off the kitchen and a powder room off a small pantry. The apartment could be charming, she thought as she completed a second tour. Cara wondered who had lived here, and when.

She opened a desk drawer in the living room, but found it empty except for a few paper clips and a yellow pencil that someone had anxiously gnawed. The wooden kitchen cabinets held two chipped yellow cups and a broken saucer. The door of a small refrigerator stood open, and a single glass stood upside down on the dull Formica counter next to the sink. A copper teakettle had been left atop the electric stove. Bookcases on either side of the fireplace were built into the wall, the books long gone except for a worn copy of *Twenty Thousand Leagues Under the Sea*.

Cara went into the first bedroom and ran a finger over the top of the dresser where the dust was thickest, and wondered how long the apartment had been unoccupied. The bed was covered with a faded green spread that matched drapes bleached by the sun. She opened the door to the closet, but it was totally empty. The bathroom sink had rust stains and the plastic shower curtain stuck to the wall. The remnants of a white bar of soap had been left in the soap dish on the side of the tub next to a neatly folded hand towel.

The second bedroom was bare of furniture, but

there was a built-in window seat covered with a thick cushion. Cara sat and parted the checked curtains and looked out onto the woods. She shifted slightly on the cushion and felt something hard jab into her hip. She shifted again, but it was still there. She got up and turned the cushion over, expecting to find something on the seat, but nothing was there, so she unzipped the cushion and stuck her hand inside. Her fingers closed around a wooden object, and she pulled it through the opening.

The box was made of rough pine, unpainted, smaller, but the same shape as a tissue box. There was no closure, so the lid opened easily. Inside Cara found a thick envelope and a handful of yellowed newspaper clippings folded together.

She unfolded the clippings, articles dated over a series of days, all relating to the death of Gil Wheeler. She read through the unemotional recounting of the incident as the reporter had written it.

> Gilbert Jefferson Wheeler, age 25, fell to his death from the rocks overlooking the falls for which this town—Wheeler's hometown—was named. According to two witnesses, Wheeler had been sitting close to the edge of one of the largest rocks, and it appeared when he stood up, he misjudged his distance and slipped before either of his companions could reach out to save him.

"It all happened so fast," said Peter Wheeler, 22, brother of the deceased. "We just couldn't get to him in time."

The second witness, Franklin Hudson, also 22, could not be reached for comment.

Another clipping was the obituary, which was glowing in its praise of the young man, listing his accomplishments—academic and athletic—as a bragging parent might do.

Cara was surrounded by an overwhelming sense of sadness for the Wheeler family as well as for Barney. It occurred to her that Fritz must've been mourning Gil's death as much as Pete, if he'd been too upset to speak with the reporters.

But then off he went to California with Nora, just a few days later. How odd was that?

She opened the envelope and found several letters wrapped inside another. She unfolded the top one and began to read:

F. ~

I'm sending back your letter. I don't ever want to see you or hear from you again. Not that I would anyway, since you're leaving Hidden Falls with her. You're just a liar and a cheat and I will always hate you for what you've done to me. I never should have believed you when you said you and she were just friends. It was just another lie, like "You're the only girl for me."

I should have listened to my sister.

J.

"Whoa," Cara said aloud. *Looks like Dad did someone wrong.* Curious, she opened the letter that had been folded inside the one from "J."

J. ~

It's really hard for me to write this letter. I don't know how else to say it, so I'll just say that I'm leaving for California on Tuesday morning with Nora. I know you will hate me now and that is the worst thing about this. I know you will think I lied to you, but every word was true. You are the best girl I ever knew. I'm sorry I can't stay and be with you.

F.

Cara read both letters twice more. So Fritz had a girlfriend he'd cheated on with Nora. Cara understood the anger and hurt in the letter from J. to her father. But something about her dad's letter seemed off. For one thing, where was his declaration of love for Nora? If a guy was writing a letter to a girl telling her he was going away with someone else, wouldn't he justify that by saying how much he loved the girl he was leaving with? Wouldn't he say, *I'm sorry, but I've fallen head over heels in love with her and I can't live without her?* Hadn't Drew said those words to her when he told her he was leaving her for Amber?

And yet here was Fritz telling J. that he cared about her but was leaving anyway.

What, she wondered, was wrong with this picture?

Cara sat on the window seat with the letters in her hand, unsure what she should do with them. If she shared them with Des and Allie, would they pick up on that same lack of feeling for Nora? She wasn't sure, and her uncertainty led her to return the letters to the box. She needed to think this through before sharing her findings with the others.

"Cara?" Des called from the first floor.

"Up here." Cara stuffed the box back into the cushion and zipped up the cover, then walked into the living area of the apartment.

"What are you . . . ?" Des stood at the top of the steps. "Oh, how cool is this? Did you know this was here?"

Cara shook her head. "I was just doing a little exploring and came upstairs to see what was here."

Des walked through the entire second floor. "This is a great apartment." She looked out the window. "Great views. I wonder who lived here?"

"I have no idea, but when they left, they took everything that might have identified them. There's nothing in any of the drawers or on the counter with a name."

"We'll ask Barney. I'm sure there's a story here." Des returned to the steps. "Coming?"

"I am." Cara pulled the key from her pocket and once outside, she locked the door.

Barney was just returning from her afternoon out as Cara and Des walked across the driveway to the patio. They waited for their aunt to park Lucille in the garage.

"What are you two up to?" Barney asked after closing the garage door.

"We were wondering who lived in the apartment over the carriage house," Cara said. "I hope you don't mind, but I wanted to see what was in there, and once inside, I saw the steps and . . ."

". . . had to see what was upstairs. I'd have done the same thing." Barney twirled her keys on her index finger as she walked.

"Who lived up there?" Cara asked.

"Mr. and Mrs. Allen. They worked for my grandparents. Mr. took care of the grounds and the cars, and Mrs. took care of the house. Mr. died before she did, and Mrs. lived here until she passed on. She was in her eighties then, I think." Barney dropped her keys and bent to pick them up. "Mr. Allen had his first stroke when he was in his sixties; the one that killed him happened a few years later."

"And your grandparents let them stay?" Des held the door for Barney. "Even after they couldn't work for them?"

"Of course. Where would they have gone?"

"They didn't have children?" Des asked.

"A son," Barney said.

"Why didn't they live with him?" Cara wondered.

"This was their home," Barney said simply.

Cara returned the key to the hook near the door, still undecided as to whether she should tell the others about the letters. It seemed there was always an underlying tension between Des and Allie whenever their mother's name was brought up, Des speaking what she believed was the truth about Nora, and Allie defending her.

Not that Cara really understood just what Fritz's letter had meant. She felt that she'd stumbled onto something that was important, a piece of a greater truth she'd yet to find. She decided for the time being to keep it to herself. For now, it would be her secret, hers and Fritz's. Later that night she realized that by keeping his secret, she'd found one more thing about him that she hadn't known before.

"Your secret's safe with me, Dad," she told him before she turned over to fall asleep. "At least until I understand what it all means."

Chapter Sixteen

Cara followed the voices into Des's room, where she found her sisters seated on the bed. She carried a big bowl of popcorn and a couple of bottles of water. Not exactly what a single woman in her thirties might consider a hot time for a Friday night, but the ferocious storm blowing rain across the back of the house had other plans. Downstairs, Barney had a fire going in the library, where she sat with Nikki, who couldn't get enough of the stories about the family members in the portraits hanging in the hallway. Cara had poked her head in momentarily before she'd headed upstairs, long enough to catch the end of the story about how the first Reynolds Hudson had avoided a strike of his coal miners by paying fair wages and taking care of anyone injured while in his employ.

". . . and he's never had a dog before, so I had to go over and show him what to do. You know, things like how to let the dog know what you expect of it.

When and what to feed it. When to let it out . . ." Des chattered away about her successful placement of the male border collie with Seth.

"You know, Des, your eyes are all shiny right now. Is that because of the dog or because of Seth?" Allie leaned back against the headboard.

"It's definitely because of the dog." Des laughed. "I'm just so happy that this sweet dog found a great home."

"Isn't this dog a foster?" Cara asked.

Des reached for the popcorn and Cara passed the bowl before she took a seat in the room's only chair.

"Well, yeah, but I think he'll keep him. They bonded really well. I felt really badly about the fact that the vet decided to keep the dog an extra day because of the infection in his foot, but it seems fine now. He was sent home with some antibiotics."

"Honestly, if I didn't know better, I'd think we were talking about a child." Allie leaned over and grabbed a handful of popcorn.

Ignoring her, Des asked, "What are Nikki's flight arrangements on Sunday?"

"Eleven in the morning. Clint is supposed to pick her up at LAX at four." Allie tossed a few kernels into her mouth. "I hope he and Mrs. Courtney's Mom had a fun time in London."

"Why do you care?" Des held up both hands so Cara could toss her a bottle of water.

"What do you mean, why do I care?" Allie poked at Des with her foot. "He lied to me about her. He's been lying about her all along."

"So what?" Cara sat with her legs over the arm of the chair, a favorite position when she was a child. She could almost hear her mother scolding her.

"So *what*? He lied to me about his motives for moving away and enrolling Nikki in Pine Hill. Because of *him*, I don't have my daughter with me except for weekends, and sometimes that time is cut short because of school or sports or her social life. Because of *him*, I've been paying tuition I can't afford and I almost lost my house. Nothing he did was for Nikki's benefit. It wasn't about putting her into a better academic environment," Allie said indignantly. "It was all about him pursuing this woman."

"At least he didn't cheat on you when you were married."

"Not that I know of," Allie conceded. "As far as I know, he didn't meet her until after the divorce was final."

"Well, I *was* cheated on. Now he's marrying one of my former best friends." Cara paused as she shoved in a mouthful of popcorn. "Tomorrow night," she mumbled.

"What's tomorrow night?" Allie asked.

"Tomorrow night, my ex is getting married," Cara announced with a smile on her face.

"Why does that make you happy?" Allie made one of her faces that seemed to mock whomever she was addressing.

"Amber is marrying a man who cheated on his wife to be with her—and we all know that old saying that goes something like, 'If he cheated on me to be with you, he'll cheat on you to be with someone else.'"

"I don't think that's how it goes, actually, but go on," Des said.

"So while she's marrying my cheating ex, I'm going to be celebrating with a man who makes me feel really good about myself and who would never cheat on me."

"I'll bet that's what you thought when you married what's-his-name." Allie went back for more popcorn.

"I never thought about it when I married Drew. Why would I? I'd never been cheated on before. I'd never even been in a serious relationship before. It wasn't something I'd ever had to think about."

"So what makes you so sure Joe would be Mr. Fidelity?" Allie asked.

"I get a completely different vibe from him."

"Different how?" Des wanted to know.

"With Drew, I always felt insecure about myself and how he felt about me. I never felt like I was enough for him. When he left me for Amber, it only proved to me that I was right. I wasn't enough." Cara took a deep breath. The admission hadn't been an easy one to make. "When I'm with Joe, I feel like it's okay to be myself. Like he isn't judging me or wanting me to be something or someone I'm not. He makes me feel like I'm enough for him, just the way I am."

"Wow. That's really heavy, Aunt Cara." Nikki stood in the doorway, Buttons at her feet.

"That's a lesson I should've learned a long time ago, honey. No guy is worth the time of day if he doesn't like you for who you really are. Your mom and Aunt Des will tell you the same thing."

"Yeah, even all the magazine articles say that, and it always sounds so corny. But when you say it, it sounds true."

"So what does that mean to you, Nik?" Allie patted the edge of the bed and motioned for her daughter to sit with them. Buttons followed and jumped up onto her lap.

"That if you like a guy, but say, he likes piercings and you don't want to get, like, your eyebrow or your lip or your . . . you know, *down there* pierced, you shouldn't do it."

The room fell silent, and Nikki's gaze went from one face to the next. "Not like that ever happened to me . . ."

Cara cleared her throat. "Well, then. Who's up for *Game of Thrones*?"

"The new season doesn't start for a couple of months," Nikki reminded her.

Cara held up her laptop. "We can still get us some Westeros love. Anyone have a favorite episode?"

"'The Battle of the Bastards,' for sure," Nikki said.

Everyone nodded in agreement.

"'The Battle of the Bastards' it is." Cara found the episode and they all settled in around the laptop.

Nikki snuggled next to her mother, a happy smile on her face. "Jon Snow has a man-bun in this one, and he totally rocks it. And there are dragons. I love the dragons." Nikki sighed. "If they were real, I'd want one, for sure."

"I think you'd have a better chance talking your father into getting a dog, allergies aside," Allie told her. "What's Barney watching?"

"*Downton Abbey*."

"She doesn't know what she's missing," Allie replied as the show began and Jon Snow—man-bun and all—appeared on the screen.

"Amen," Des said.

"Barney, what exactly is bluegrass music?" Cara stopped raking for a moment.

Barney paused and leaned on the rake she was using to clear the bed where she wanted to set out early vegetables. "It's sort of like country, maybe what some would consider hillbilly style. There were a lot of folk songs brought to this country from Ireland and Scotland a couple of hundred years ago. A lot of those early immigrants settled in the Carolinas and Tennessee and Kentucky. Over the years, the songs took on a different sound as they were passed down through families. Like folktales, you know? That's sort of the way I understand how bluegrass music evolved from, say, a centuries-old Scottish ballad to something that had a distinct sound. There are a lot of banjos, guitars, mandolins. The voices sometimes sound out of sync with each other, and the music from different regions will differ."

"Gosh, it sounds wonderful. Discordant singing." Allie had been listening from her perch on the back steps. "I can hardly wait."

Barney laughed good-naturedly. "You go on and pull up some music app on your phone, search for some bluegrass tunes."

"I'll do it." Nikki sat on the step above her mother. A few moments later, she said, "Listen to the names of some of these songs. 'Little Rosewood Casket' . . ."

"I bet that's an uplifting tune." Allie turned to get a better look at Nikki's phone.

"'Girl I Left in Sunny Tennessee.'

"'Down in the Willow Garden.' That's another. . . ."

Nikki continued to scroll through the titles. "Oh, here's one that might be good. 'On My Mind.'" She tapped the screen and the song began to play. They all listened for a few moments.

"Well. That's . . . different," Cara said once the music ended.

"Not exactly the Temptations," Barney said.

"Who are the Temptations?" Nikki asked.

"Who are the . . . Oh hell, look them up on your phone." Barney attacked the garden soil with a hoe, muttering, "Who are the Temptations . . ."

"It's a generational thing, Barney," Cara pointed out. "What do you think of Kesha?"

"Who?" Barney frowned.

"Point proven." Cara went back to work.

Moments later, Nikki held up her phone. "Here you go, Aunt Barney."

"My Girl" began to play. Within seconds of the opening chords, Barney, Cara, and Des were singing harmony. By the second verse, Allie had joined them.

"Oh, it's nice," Nikki said when the song—and their singing—was over. "It's a quiet song."

"The world could use a few more quiet songs, if you ask me. All that boom boom boom and that nonsense I hear on the radio sometimes." Barney shook her head.

"But back to bluegrass," Cara reminded her. "Specifically, bluegrass at the gun club."

"The Hidden Falls Gun Club," Barney corrected her.

"I've been looking forward to this all week." The touch of snark in Allie's voice was unmistakable.

"As have a lot of people around here, missy." Barney's eyes narrowed. "Don't knock it till you've tried it."

"Well, looks like we're all going to be trying it tonight." Allie turned to look up at her daughter, who was now reading her texts. "I understand you're coming with us?"

Nikki nodded and, still looking at her phone, told her mother, "Courtney's going home tomorrow, too. Her mom's plane gets in tonight."

"When is your father coming back?" Allie asked casually.

"Wait, there's a text from him." Nikki read silently for a moment. "He's just reminding me that he'll arrive sometime tonight and he'll pick me up on Sunday at the airport. Hey, maybe his plane and Court's mom's plane will get in around the same time. They could share a ride going back to town."

"Oh, what are the odds?" Allie rolled her eyes.

Nikki put her phone down. "I want to go home to see Court and Dad and all. And I can't wait to go back to school and tell everyone about the theater and the coal mines and the emerald necklace and everything. But I kinda hate to leave. I've had a really good time." She looked directly at Barney. "I'm so glad you let me stay."

"Oh, honey, I've been delighted to have you here. You're a joy to be around. I hope you'll come back for a longer stay." Barney blew her a kiss.

"I want to come back in the summer, for sure." Nikki blew a kiss back.

"Let's see what your father has to say about . . . Wait, what about the emerald necklace?" Allie turned to her daughter.

"The one Great-great-great-grandmother Althea is wearing in that painting in the front hall. I asked Barney if it was real and she said it was, but nobody knows what happened to it." Nikki's eyes danced. "And it used to belong to some Spanish princess! How cool is that?"

"The necklace was actually given to Althea's mother, Lydia, when she was on a grand tour of Europe when she was eighteen," Barney said. "The story goes, she met a Spanish prince who fell madly in love with her and gave her the necklace. Her parents were not amused—they thought the prince only had seduction on his mind—so they whisked Lydia home. They told her she couldn't accept such an expensive gift and demanded she return it. She told them she did—but she kept it. She came back to Pennsylvania, married Jefferson Hudson, and wore that necklace every chance she got. It was the talk of Hidden Falls, back in the day, or so I've been told."

"Go back to the part where no one knows what happened to it," Cara urged.

"It was passed down through the family, and my mother had it at one time. She kept it in the bottom drawer of her dresser in a purple velvet box that had a white satin lining. Oh, when you opened that box, believe me, you knew you were looking at the real thing. The emeralds were gorgeous."

"But how did it disappear?" Cara wanted to know.

Barney shrugged. "As I said, my mother kept the box in her dresser. She used to take it out from time to time and look at it; then she'd put it back. Well, one day it occurred to me that I hadn't seen her do that in a long time, so I asked her about it. She said it was in the drawer where she'd left it. I looked, but it wasn't there. It wasn't in any drawer in any room in the house. I asked her if she'd moved it and she said she didn't think she had." A shadow fell across Barney's face. "My mother was already in the early stages of Alzheimer's at the time, but I wasn't aware of it. She never left the house in those days, so I know she didn't take it somewhere. I checked the bank's safety-deposit box, of course, but it wasn't there, either."

"What do you think happened to it?" Cara asked, intrigued.

"The only thing I can think of is that she took it up into the attic. I think she saw it one day and thought, 'Well, I don't wear this anymore.' You know how she took everything she had no use for up to the third floor." Barney shrugged. "Maybe someday when one of us is looking for something else, we'll find it. Or when I'm gone, and you girls have the task of cleaning out this house, one of you will find it." She smiled. "I'll go on record right now—finders, keepers."

"You mean, whoever finds it can keep it?" Nikki's eyes widened.

"That's what I said." Barney nodded, and resumed hoeing the last row of the garden bed.

"Mom, let's go." Nikki stood and pulled her mother's hand.

"I'm with you, girl." Allie took Nikki's hand and followed her into the house. "Last one up to the third floor is a . . . well, I guess they're a loser."

"Not fair to Des and me," Cara called back to her.

"Don't worry, Cara," Barney said. "The chances of them finding it today are pretty slim. I've been through a lot of that stuff for one reason or another over the years, and I've never found it. I think Mother found some obscure place to tuck that box into. But go on and join them if you like. We're pretty much done here anyway."

"Maybe I will. If for no other reason than to make the day go a little faster." Cara returned her rake to the shed.

"Why would you want the day to move faster?" Barney asked when Cara headed for the house.

Cara flashed a smile over her shoulder. "I have a big date tonight, remember?"

*   *   *

The Hidden Falls Gun Club sat at the end of a long, winding, narrow road in the woods just at the edge of town. The building itself was one story constructed of weathered logs, and had a long covered porch out front. Inside, the log walls were lined with photographs of current and previous club officers, shooting competitions, and stuffed animal heads, mostly antlered deer, though a few foxes and a moose from someone's Maine hunting trip were in the mix.

There were rows of folding chairs set up, audience style, and a bar ran along one side of the room.

"Does anyone really think it's a good idea to drink and shoot?" Cara whispered to Joe when they first arrived.

"The bar is only open for special events, like tonight. And the shooting range is closed, so you don't have to worry that some yahoo is going to get drunk and go out and start taking shots at the targets."

The club, he'd told her, was established as a place where gentlemen could come and test their skill.

"Remember, back when this area was being settled, people hunted, and ate what they brought home. As time went by and the area became more 'civilized,' fewer people depended upon hunting for their survival, but skill with a rifle or pistol was still admired. Competitive shooting became a big thing. Guys would bring their weapons out and practice on the shooting range, and then there'd be these competitions to see who could outshoot everyone else. I don't know about your dad, but I do know that your grandfather and great-grandfather were members."

"How do you know that?"

"They're both on President's Row." Joe pointed to a row of photos. "Want to see?"

"I do." Cara followed Joe to the photos.

"Here you go. Here's Reynolds One, and here's Reynolds Two."

Cara stared at the photos, a smile on her face. She could see a resemblance to Fritz in his father's face, but not in his grandfather's. They were both distinguished-looking gentlemen even in their sporting clothes—white shirts worn under buttoned hunting jackets, and trousers that looked a bit like riding pants. They had each been photographed holding a long rifle, standing in front of the building.

"Handsome guys," Cara said. Still smiling, she turned to Joe. "Funny how you never know where you're going to find family."

"In Hidden Falls, you should expect just about anything, if you're a Hudson."

"I guess so. It seems they had their hands in everything."

"They did," Joe told her.

"Do you come here to shoot?"

"I've used the range from time to time, but I'm not a member. I don't shoot that often, just enough to keep my eye and hand sharp."

"Why would you need to?"

"Because we're in an area that has vast, uninhabited forests; because we have bears and cougars and other wild things living very close to us. Just about everyone around here shoots. Because we're in a town that's sparsely populated and sometimes things happen and you have to rely on yourself for protection."

"Protection from what?" she persisted.

"The aforementioned bears and cougars." Joe looked around. "How 'bout if we get our seats now before the place fills up? That way we can save room for Barney and everyone."

"How about right over here?" She pointed to an area to the left of the space where the musicians were setting up.

Joe took her hand and led her to the seats she had her eye on.

The seats behind them began to fill, and Cara spent a few moments people watching while Joe got something from the bar. It didn't take long for her to realize her denim skirt and white sweater had been the right choice, since so many other women wore denim with tops that ranged from nice sweaters to sweatshirts. Barney arrived in nice pants and a matching top in dark green that flattered her coloring and hair. Des and Allie both looked fashionably casual, as did Nikki, in tights, a long tunic, and high boots. Watching her family drift through the crowd to join her, Cara felt a little tug at her heart.

It wasn't so long ago that she'd walked into Pete Wheeler's law office and her life had totally changed. She now had sisters she'd never known existed and an aunt whom she had come to love. A niece who made them all smile and who'd found her own place in Cara's heart. Allie wouldn't be the only one to shed tears when Nikki left tomorrow morning. Who knew these women would come to mean so much to her in so short a time? Who would have guessed how much richer her life would be after less than a month in Hidden Falls?

"Hey, this place is so cool." Nikki grinned as she and the others took the chairs Cara had saved for them.

"Yes, nothing says 'fun family outing' like a trip to the local gun club." Allie deposited her bag on the ground.

"I think it's way cool, Mom." Nikki took her phone from her pocket and began to take pictures.

"What are you doing?" her mother asked.

"Taking pictures so that when I get back to school and we have to talk about what we did this week, I'll have some killer photos."

"I'm sure your friends will be impressed. Especially the ones who went to Cancún and Puerto Rico and the Caribbean over their breaks."

"Are you kidding? Mom, anyone can go to those places. Everyone *has* gone to those places. Same old same old. But no one gets to see places like this. And who else has a theater like ours? Or has a real mystery like the missing emeralds? I mean, that's like Nancy Drew."

"I'm surprised you know who Nancy Drew is." Barney took the seat next to Nikki.

"Courtney's mom had a whole bunch of the books and we took turns reading them last summer."

"Somewhere on the third floor is a box with the entire set of Nancy Drews, first editions," Barney told her. "If you're here next summer, you can go up and search for them."

"Maybe I'll find the emeralds, too," Nikki said, clearly taken with the possibility.

"We'll have to work on your father to make sure he doesn't make other plans," Allie said.

"I asked him about going to camp, and he said okay. But that was before I came here. I'd rather be here. I want to work with you guys on the theater." She paused. "I need to take some pictures there, too."

"I doubt there'll be time before you leave tomorrow," Cara told her. "We can take some for you as the renovations progress, so you can keep up with what's being done."

"Thanks. I want to do more reading about theaters from that time. I'm going to write a kick-a . . . a kick-*butt* paper about it. Maybe I'll even do an article for the school paper." She appeared to think that over. "Yeah, that would be epic."

Joe returned from the bar with two beers and handed one to Cara.

"What can I get for you all?" Joe asked.

"You sit. I'm going to head over there and I'll bring back drinks," Barney said. "I see some friends of mine at the bar."

Barney took orders, then made her way through the ever-growing crowd. Cara watched as Barney joined a group at one end of the bar and was welcomed with friendly hugs.

A moment later, Allie said, "I think I'll head off to the ladies' room. I'll be back in a few."

Nikki chatted with Joe about the photos on the walls, and before long, the two of them were off to get a closer look at her ancestors. Cara glanced at the bar and saw a flash of red closing in on the far end. She watched Allie, in her red sweater, maneuver her way through the crowd until she was close enough to the bar to lean on it.

Cara watched Allie get the attention of the bartender, then lean forward to give her order. A moment later, the bartender placed something in front of Allie, who tossed back one, then a second, of something in a very small glass.

She's doing shots. Cara grimaced inwardly. *What happened to "I don't drink when I'm around Nikki"?*

Nikki and Joe were heading back to their seats.

The musicians arrived and began to warm up. Barney wasn't kidding when she said there were a lot of strings—guitars and banjos, in particular—and the voices weren't exactly in harmony with one another.

Barney returned with everyone else's drinks and passed them out. "There are a couple of kids around your age here, Nik. My friend Flora's grandsons and granddaughter are here, and Seth's cousin's son and daughter are here as well."

"Where?" Nikki craned her neck to take a look.

"Over by the side door. I suspect that they'll go on out to the porch once the music starts." Barney settled into her seat. "You could go introduce yourself."

"I don't know . . ." Nikki stared at the group. "Aunt Barney, who's the boy in the white sweater?"

"Oh, that's Seth's cousin's boy, Mark."

Cara glanced over at the group of two girls and three boys. She could have guessed exactly which of the boys had caught Nikki's eye, even without the description of his clothing. He was tall, dark, and handsome. Any young girl would have been interested.

"I know Mark really well. He's a junior volunteer fireman. Nik, want me to introduce you?" Joe stood.

"Ummm. Okay." Nikki got up, but Allie grabbed her by the arm to hold her back.

"I'm not so sure you should—"

"Oh, for the love of Pete, Allie," Barney said. "Leave the kid alone. It will be good for her to make friends here if she's coming back over the summer. You can't expect her to hang out with her mother and her aunts all the time."

"I agree with Barney," Des spoke up.

"Me too," Cara chimed in.

"I don't remember putting this to a vote." Allie sighed. "Fine. Just be careful and don't leave the grounds. And if anyone starts shooting, get your butt back inside."

"No one shoots on Saturday nights, Allie," Barney informed her.

"Okay, then. You've been cleared." Joe draped an arm over Nikki's shoulder and led her to the outside aisle.

Allie and the aunts all watched as the small group of kids made room for Joe and Nikki. A few minutes later, Joe returned alone.

"Mission accomplished," he said as he sat next to Cara.

"I forgot to tell her to meet up with us back here." Allie started to stand and Des pulled her back down.

"Allie, don't embarrass her. She knows where we're sitting and she knows where Barney's car is."

"So Barney, did you drive Lucille tonight?" Joe turned around in his seat.

"No, I'd never bring her out here. That dirt road has so many potholes in it. I drove Cara's car." Barney sat up straight in her chair. "Oh, they're going to start. Looks like Bruce is ready to introduce the band."

The president of the Hidden Falls Gun Club, Bruce Oliver, took the microphone and introduced the Pennsylvania Mountain Boys.

The first song was one Nikki had named when she'd been searching online for bluegrass, "Little Rosewood Casket."

"Oh my God, it's even more of a downer than I'd thought it'd be." Allie scooted to the end of the row, past Nikki's vacated seat. "I'm getting a drink."

"Bring me a club soda?" Cara turned around and whispered.

"Sure."

Afterward, Cara wasn't able to say for certain that she actually liked what she'd heard—to her, some of the songs were depressing, and she preferred more real harmony. But still, she had to admit she'd enjoyed the experience.

"Never hurts to try something new," Barney had said.

For Cara, one of the evening's highlights had come when Allie returned from the bar with a beer in one hand and Cara's club soda in the other to find Ben Haldeman in her seat.

"You again." Allie's eyes blazed. "That seat is taken."

Ben had patted the seat next to him and said, "You could sit right here."

"My daughter is sitting there."

"No, actually, your daughter is outside sitting on the top step. Beautiful girl, by the way. And polite."

"Thank you. Now you can go."

"Not gonna happen." He looked directly at the beer in her hand, then at her face, but said nothing further. Allie elected to stand against the wall rather than sit next to Ben.

A ping from Cara's phone drew her attention from the minor drama behind her.

The deed is done, read the text from Darla.

Cara sat back in her seat, the words stuck in her brain. *The deed is done. The deed is done.*

"You okay?" Joe whispered.

"I'm fine." A feeling of lightness came over her. She hadn't expected to feel this happy, but she did. "Excuse me for a minute."

Cara found her way to an exit, opened the door, and stepped outside. She took a deep breath of air drenched with the scent of pine and exhaled, a smile on her face.

Free. I'm free.

She looked up into a sky dotted with stars and a big moon that had risen behind the trees, and knew she was going to be fine. When she heard the door open behind her, she knew who it would be, and turned to Joe with the smile still on her face.

"Are you okay?" he asked.

"I just got a text from my friend Darla."

Joe looked puzzled. Cara held up the phone so he could read the text.

"Drew and Amber are now officially man and wife."

"Congratulations. How do you feel?"

She'd been dreading this night for months and had had great anxiety over it. But that was before she'd come to Hidden Falls—more accurately, before she'd met Joe and started to feel like her old self again. Her pre–Drew McCann self. She focused on the moment the way she did when she was going through her yoga workout, and she felt *cleansed*. Drew had started down a path that didn't include her, and she was relieved to find that *that* no longer brought her pain.

I have my own path, she told herself, *and there is no place for him on it.*

"I feel good." She gazed up into Joe's blue eyes, eyes that always seemed happy to see her. "Actually, I feel very good."

He squeezed her hand. "I'm happy for you."

A small group of young people came around the corner and took seats on the porch steps.

"Hey, Aunt Cara, what are you doing out here?" Nikki called.

"Just getting some air. We were just about to go back in," Cara told her. "How 'bout you?"

"In a while. We're just, you know, chilling."

"See you inside," Cara said.

Joe opened the door and music rushed out.

"Didn't they already play this one?" Cara whispered as they returned to their seats.

"Just one that sounded the same," he replied.

Cara looked around for Allie, who'd been standing next to the wall in an attempt to avoid conversation with Ben, but she wasn't there. Her eyes swept the room and found a red sweater at the end of the bar.

Cara started out of her seat, and when Joe looked up, she whispered, "Ladies' room."

She went straight to the bar, where Allie had just downed another shot.

"What are you doing?" Cara whispered, and poked Allie in the back.

"What does it look like?" Allie barely glanced at Cara.

"I thought you didn't drink around Nikki."

Allie made a show of looking around. "Nikki's not around. She's outside making new friends."

"What is wrong with you?"

"I was thirsty." Allie gestured for the bartender.

"If you order one more shot, I'm telling Des and Nikki."

Allie's eyes flashed with anger. "You're such a Girl Scout, you know that?"

The bartender pointed to the empty shot glass and looked at Allie. "Another?"

She sighed deeply. "Make it two club sodas with

lime." She turned to Cara. "Why are you being such a pain in my ass? Why can't you just mind your own business?"

"Maybe because, against my better judgment, you're starting to grow on me."

The bartender set the two glasses on the counter. Allie handed one to Cara and said, "Yeah, well, you're growing on me, too. Like a hangnail. An annoying little hangnail."

Allie picked up her glass and headed back to their row. Moments later, Cara followed.

When she took her seat next to Joe, he whispered, "What was that all about?"

Cara shook her head. "Just girl talk."

Nikki rejoined them just as the band completed their last set, without anyone having to go looking for her, and while it took them almost twenty minutes to leave—Barney had to have "just a quick word" with a number of people—soon they were all headed to the parking lot. Once outside, Barney, Des, Allie, and Nikki went in one direction, Joe and Cara in the other.

"So what did you really think?" Joe asked after they left the parking lot.

"Of the show? Interesting. I can't say I loved it, but it had a very distinct flavor. Not like anything I've ever heard before." She shifted so she could see him better. "I guess it's an acquired taste."

"I have some CDs you can borrow if you like."

"That's okay. I've had my fill for a while." She looked out the window and suddenly realized nothing looked familiar.

"Where are we?" she asked.

"The other side of town." He turned a corner, then stopped across the street from a small ranch-style house. "That's where I grew up. My mom and my sister still live there. When my father died, he left us with a big financial mess. The mortgage company had been threatening to foreclose on our house, a fact he'd kept hidden from my mother. When the worst happened, and she got that notice, she just crumbled. She'd already lost so much, she couldn't take one more thing. I don't know how Barney found out about it, but she arranged for my mother to get a mortgage through the bank here in town." He rested both arms on the steering wheel. "I didn't know about that until this morning. I told my mom I was taking you out tonight, and she told me about the mortgage. 'Don't mess with Barney's girl, Joe. Promise me you'll behave yourself.'"

He reached over and took her hand. "I couldn't make that promise. I've been wanting to 'mess' with you from the minute I saw you at the gas station. You were so proper, so polite. Too polite to lay on your horn to get our attention. Too polite to call me a jerk when I clearly was being one." He paused. "Of course, you made up for that the morning I met you at the theater."

She nodded slowly. "I did call you a jerk. At the time, I thought you were."

"And now?"

"Now I think you're the guy I'd like to 'mess' with a little."

He leaned over and kissed her, not with the fervor of the night before, but with a promise of all the things she'd stopped believing in.

Joe pulled away from the curb and drove four blocks farther, then made a right and a quick left. He slowed after the first stop sign and pulled into a long driveway that ran alongside a white Cape Cod–style house.

"This is it," he told her. "It's not exactly Hudson Street. . . ."

She peered out the window. The house was small and had a front porch that begged for a rocking chair and a big pot of flowers that spilled over the sides. "It's adorable. I love houses that have those alcove-y things on the second floor."

"Dormers," he said as he got out. He was at the passenger door before Cara was free of her seat belt.

"Right. Dormers. I don't know why I can never remember that word." Her nerves began to sneak up on her, and soon she was babbling as they walked to the front door. "Does that ever happen to you? There's maybe one word you can never remember? And it's usually something simple. Not like some technical term for some obscure medical procedure. It's like those simple words you can never remember how to spell. One time I had to look up 'soon.' Who can't remember how to spell 'soon'?"

"Probably someone who has second thoughts about messing with a guy."

He pushed the door open and held it for her, kicked it closed quickly behind him, and pinned

Cara to it with his body. He kissed her, long and hard, in a way that both asked and answered. Finally, he pulled back and, looking into her eyes, said, "Spell 'soon.'"

Cara laughed. "S-o-o-n."

"You passed. You may have champagne." He led her by the hand into the small kitchen, where he turned on the light and opened the refrigerator door.

"You bought champagne just for tonight?"

Joe nodded and took two juice glasses from a cupboard and opened the bottle. The cork popped with a loud bang and flew across the room.

He poured the bubbly wine into the glasses and handed one to Cara.

"What's the occasion?" she asked.

"Your ex got married tonight."

"You bought champagne to celebrate Drew's wedding?" she asked.

"No. I bought champagne to celebrate you. He doesn't matter. You matter." Joe leaned over and kissed her. "*We* matter. We deserve a chance, and this is where we begin." He kissed her again. "You in?"

"I'm in," she whispered.

He touched the rim of her glass with his, and they both drank. Joe set his glass on the counter and took hers to place it next to his. With his hands on her face, he kissed her again with so much heat and emotion her knees began to wobble.

He took her by the hand and led her into the living room, which was comfortably furnished with a sofa over which a knitted afghan had been tossed, and a wingback chair that had an open book face-down on the seat. Across the mantel of the red-brick fireplace stood a line of fat white candles. Joe took a long wooden match from a box on the mantel and lit the candles, one by one.

He fumbled in his pocket and took out his phone and scrolled on the screen until he found what he was looking for. When the music started, he took her in his arms and began to dance with her. It took a minute for her to recognize the song.

"This played when we were in the Bullfrog that night," she said. "We danced to this."

"That's right. Johnny Rivers." He cocked his head for a moment. "It's coming up in a minute." He started to sway again, humming for a moment, then whispered along with the song, "'You're the one I thought I'd never find.'"

She sighed. "Dancing by candlelight to a pretty song. Champagne. You're pushing all the right buttons."

"I'm trying. I *am* a pretty romantic guy."

"It makes me wonder what else you have up your sleeve."

The song ended and he sat her on the sofa, then picked up the TV remote control. He turned on the television, sought the On Demand feature, and selected a movie.

"What did you just do?" she asked when Joe sat and put an arm around her.

"Movie time."

"What movie?" she asked with some trepidation. *Oh please, not porn . . .*

"*Love Actually.*"

"That's a chick flick."

Joe nodded. "I'm trying to get in touch with my softer side."

Cara laughed. "You put this on because you thought I'd like it?"

Joe nodded again.

"Even though you'll probably hate it."

"'Hate' may be too harsh a word," he said.

She took the remote and returned to the movie selections, then scrolled through a number of films before clicking on an image.

"I'm not a chick-flick kind of girl," she explained.

The theme song from the movie she chose began to play.

"Seriously?" he asked.

"My all-time favorite movie."

"No kidding? Mine, too." Joe grinned from ear to ear. "The original *Ghostbusters*. Best cast *ever* . . ."

Joe went into the kitchen, retrieved the champagne, and refilled their glasses. As the candles continued to flicker, he proposed one more toast.

"To everything we have to learn about each other—and to taking our time along the way."

CHAPTER SEVENTEEN

Cara awoke the next morning slightly disoriented. She wasn't sure where she was, but she knew she wasn't where she was supposed to be. When she looked around the unfamiliar room, it all started to come back to her: starting the night at the gun club and ending it at Joe's house.

She sat up and stretched her legs, which were cramped from having been curled up on the sofa. The afghan that had been thrown over the back of the sofa had been tossed over her at some point during the night.

Joe came into the room, sweatpants hanging on his hips. The sight of him—blond hair tossed this way and that, his bare chest—sent her reawakened libido into overdrive.

"I made coffee," he said, "but I'm not sure how you take it."

"You made coffee?" *Sweet*, she thought.

"You strike me as a girl who can't do anything until she's properly caffeinated."

"You're correct," she told him. "Caffeine makes the world go round."

"Where did you sleep?" she asked.

Joe pointed to the floor next to the sofa.

"You slept on the floor?" She frowned. "Why didn't you just get into your bed?"

"I didn't want to leave you out here alone. I thought about carrying you into my bedroom but I figured you wouldn't appreciate finding yourself in my bed this morning." He was, she thought, only half kidding.

"Thank you. The last thing I remember, you were putting in a DVD."

"*Caddyshack,*" he told her.

"Damn. Another of my favorites."

"Next time."

Cara followed him into the kitchen, a square room with counters and cabinets around two sides. He poured coffee into a mug and handed it to her.

"Milk and sugar on the counter if you want it."

"Thanks." She added a bit of each to the mug and took a sip. "Very nice. And I like your kitchen."

"I bought this as a fixer-upper," Joe told her. "As you can see, I haven't gotten around to fixing it up yet. I thought it had real possibilities, but I'm not sure what I want to do with it."

"This could be so pretty," she told him as she walked around the room. "You have great light in here. You could do granite or quartz for counters, though concrete is very in right now. The windows are lovely, and you have a great view of your backyard. Those wooden cabinets could be really cool if you painted them white, or maybe gray, and replaced some of the solid doors with glass. Maybe leave a few of the doors off so you'd have open shelves."

He looked at the cabinets as if seeing them for the first time.

"Wow. That could be very cool. I never would've thought to do any of that. My inclination is to rip it all out and put up something new."

"Ah, I see. You subscribe to the caveman approach to home renovation." She nodded solemnly.

"It's not that I lack vision—it's just that I . . ." He paused to reflect. "I guess I lack vision. I like your ideas a lot. I'd thought I'd just buy some stock cabinets from one of the big-box stores and put 'em up, but what you described is so much cooler. When I finally get around to redoing the room, I will definitely consult with you."

"I'd be happy to toss in my two cents." She stood at the back window looking out. "The yard is really big. I could see a patio out there and maybe a pergola. Some flower beds, a tree or two."

"That's pretty much how I see it, too. I just need to find the time to make it happen."

"I guess taking on the theater project has taken a bite out of your free time."

Joe nodded. "But it's totally worth it. I figure I've gained more than I lost."

She opened her mouth to speak but her gaze fell to the clock on the wall above the table.

"Is that the right time?"

"Might be a minute off, but—"

"I have to go. I have to go. . . ." The words came out in a rush as she panicked.

"Whoa, what's going on?"

"Nikki leaves for California this morning. I don't want to miss her." She flew into the living room and put on her shoes, tears in her eyes at the thought that her niece might leave before Cara could let her know how much she cared. "I have to be there to say goodbye, Joe."

"I'll get you there."

He disappeared into the hall, then returned a minute later, pulling a sweatshirt over his head. Five minutes later they were in his car, headed to Hudson Street.

"I'd like to come in," Joe told her when they arrived at Hudson Street.

"Won't that be a little obvious?" She paused, her hand on the door handle. "You know. You and me . . ."

"I think that cat's out of the bag. Besides, you're wearing the same thing you wore last night." He lowered his voice. "Dead giveaway. Time for your walk of shame."

"But we didn't . . ." She jumped out of the car. "Crap."

"Damn, if you aren't the most romantic, sentimental woman I've ever met." He followed her up the back steps.

She turned and planted a quick kiss on his lips. "We have time, you and me. But Nikki . . . I'd really like to be with her and my sisters and Barney right now. I hope you understand I'm not trying to—"

"I do understand. Go."

"You're sure you don't mind not coming in?"

"Positive. I should get going anyway. I need to take my mom to church." He kissed the side of her face. "Tell Barney and Des I said 'bye, and give Nikki a hug for me. Try not to cry too much, the three of you."

"I don't think it'll be seriously bad until Allie gets home."

"Give me a call if you run out of tissues." He pushed the door open for her.

Only Des was in the kitchen, sitting in the window seat, Buttons on her lap, tears in her eyes.

"Oh no. I'm too late." Cara could have cried.

"They haven't left yet. I was just thinking about how much I'm going to miss that kid. You know—and I've said this before—as wacky as Allie is, she somehow managed to raise a remarkable child."

"She is, and she did." Cara grabbed the box of tissues from the counter and shared the contents with Des.

"I'm going to run up and change my clothes real fast."

"Oh, like no one will realize you didn't come home last night?"

"It's not the way it looks," Cara protested. "We didn't—"

"Well, then, other than that, how was it?" Des asked pointedly. "Did you have a good time?"

Cara thought back to the candlelight, the champagne, the laughs they'd shared when they both recited the same movie lines at the same time. The heavy make-out session between *Ghostbusters* and *Forrest Gump*.

"I had the best time. Joe is . . ." She tried to find the right words, then smiled. "The one I thought I'd never find."

With that, Cara went into her room and started pulling the sweater over her head and unbuttoning her skirt. She washed her face, brushed her teeth, and tried to comb her hair, but it was all over the place. She tamed it, then pulled on jeans and a soft sweater. She glanced in the mirror and told herself that was as good as it was going to get for a while. The last thing she wanted was to miss what time she had with Nikki because she was preening.

How had that kid come to mean so much to her in so short a time?

She went into the hall, where she ran into Allie, who was just emerging from her bedroom.

"Oh, you made it home. Now, if I'd had to bet, I would have put money on you not coming back last night. I'm not sure I would have, if I'd had a guy like Joe to cuddle up with all night. Or did you already change, lest the rest of us witness your walk of shame?"

"I changed, but it's not what you think. Nothing happened. And for the record, Joe's not up for grabs. But I think you'd stand a good chance with the chief of police if you made nice."

"Don't even mention that man to me. He's an ass." Allie got to the end of the hall and called her daughter. "Nikki, we have about twenty minutes before we have to leave."

"I'm almost ready, Mom. I'll meet you downstairs."

"I can't even look at that man without having homicidal thoughts." Allie started down the steps, Ben Haldeman still apparently on her mind. When they came into the kitchen, Buttons greeted her with a wagging tail but Des was weepy. "What's your problem?" Allie asked.

"Really, Allie? You think you're the only one who's going to miss Nikki like crazy?"

The topic of conversation came into the room, accompanied by Barney. "Mom, I left my stuff in the hall. Hi, Aunt Cara. Morning, Aunt Des. Where's Buttons?"

At the sound of her name, the dog leaped to Nikki, who knelt on the floor and let it kiss her face for as long as she wanted. "I'm going to miss you, pup. If I could find a way to get you into my suitcase, I would."

"She'll be waiting here for you when you come back this summer," Barney assured her.

"We have to make Dad let me come back." Nikki looked up at her mother. "This has been the best week ever, Mom. I wish I could stay with you."

"I know, sweetie." Allie opened her arms and Nikki ran into them, the dog still held against her chest.

"It's so unfair. I hate that I can't be in both places."

"A lot of people would like that magical ability." Barney patted Nikki on the back as she passed by.

"I can't believe I didn't know any of you till now." Nikki wiped her eyes as she looked from one face to the other. "I have the coolest aunts in the world. It's so hard to say goodbye. I feel like I've known you all forever, and I love you guys."

"We love you, too, Nikki," Des told her.

Allie teared up then, and Des handed her a tissue.

"I'm going to do so much reading and research. Mom, I'm going to be your design assistant."

"I can't think of anyone I'd rather work with." Allie kissed her daughter's head. "Now get some juice, we have to go. You need to be at the airport early before your flight, so we'll have to grab breakfast there."

Within minutes, everyone was filing out the back door to say goodbye and load Nikki's suitcase into the back of Cara's car.

Kisses and hugs all around, one last hug for Buttons, then Nikki was in the car, and they were disappearing down the driveway.

"It's going to take me a few days to get used to the quiet," Barney said as they all stared down the now-empty street. "She brought so much life into this old house."

"She did." Des sniffed.

"Gonna miss the kid."

"Me too."

"Let's all go inside and have a good cry." Barney went up the steps slowly and held the door for Des and Cara.

Cara'd told Joe she thought things wouldn't be too bad until Allie returned from the airport, but she had no idea just how bad it would get.

Allie got back around two and went straight up to her room. Des, Cara, and Barney decided to give her space. After all, Nikki was her only child, and she wouldn't see her for at least three months, maybe more, depending on what Allie could work out with Clint.

No one was too concerned when Allie didn't show for dinner, but by the next morning, Cara was concerned enough to knock on her door.

"Allie?" she said softly. "Allie? Are you awake?"

When there was no answer, Cara pushed open the door and peeked inside the room. It wasn't quite dawn, and the room lay in shadows, but even in the dark, Cara sensed that something wasn't right. She stepped into the room and approached the bed.

Allie was on her back, her head turned to one side. Cara's breath caught in her throat and for a moment, she thought Allie wasn't breathing. She felt for a pulse and exhaled when she found one. But then Cara saw the bottle on the floor. The empty bottle. Allie had apparently drunk however much had been in the bottle during the night.

Cara tried to wake her, but Allie was dead to the

world. Cara thought about going back to her room, but she was afraid to leave Allie alone. What if she choked or needed help? Cara sat in the chair by the window and watched the sun come up over the woods. After a while, she went into her room, picked up her mat, brought it back to Allie's, and unrolled it. She did twenty minutes of yoga with one eye always on the figure on the bed. Allie never even made a sound.

Cara heard Des talking to Buttons in the hall as they went down the stairs for the dog's early walk, and she heard the steps creak as Barney made her way downstairs. Cara kept checking Allie's pulse, but finally wondered if she shouldn't call in Des and Barney. Maybe the thing to do would be to tell them, then call 911. She'd promised to keep Allie's secret, but was she bound to that if she thought Allie's life was in danger?

No, she decided. Life trumped everything.

Allie groaned and rolled over. A minute later, her eyes opened. She looked around the room as if trying to focus. A few minutes more, another groan or three, and Allie's gaze finally fell on Cara.

"What're you doing here?" Allie grumbled.

"Trying to make sure you don't die from alcohol poisoning or, God forbid, that you don't choke on your own vomit and die like a rock star."

"What difference would it make to you?" Allie half sat up. "You don't really like me. And that wouldn't be such a bad way to go. Messy and un-glamorous, but out with a bang."

"You're right. I don't like you, especially right now." Cara picked up the empty bottle and held it in Allie's face.

"I don't like you right now because Nikki deserves better than this." Cara felt her anger rise in her chest. She tossed the bottle into the trash can next to the bed and pointed to it. "I don't like you right now because you owe Nikki better than to lose yourself in *that*. You're lucky to be the mother of absolutely the greatest kid on the planet, and yet you do this."

Allie opened her mouth to speak, but Cara cut her off. "Don't say anything, all right? I get it. You love your child with all your heart, more than anything in this world, and it killed you to put her on that plane yesterday and you can't stand missing her. It hurts like hell. I get that. But I don't get the part where you drink yourself into such a stupor that I almost called nine-one-one. There is no reason, no excuse good enough to do this to yourself. At least we don't have to call that child today and tell her you drank yourself to death last night."

Cara picked up her mat and left the room, her anger at Allie still hot. She put on her walking shoes and went downstairs, debating whether she should tell Des and Barney. But Barney was off on her morning walk, and Des was deep into the morning news, which she watched every day. There'd be time enough to decide the best way to deal with Allie and her problem.

"Okay if I take Buttons out for a walk?" she asked Des.

"Sure. She's been out, but she'd love a good walk with her aunt Cara."

She snapped the leash onto the dog's collar and slipped her phone into her pocket, but not before reading the last text she'd gotten from Joe the night before.

Thinking of you. Wish you were here.

She'd fallen asleep with a smile on her face. That he thought about her made her happy. She'd still been feeling lucky when she woke a little while ago. At least she had been, until she checked on Allie.

Cara slipped out the back door and paused in front of the carriage house. It might have been un-occupied for years, but her father had clearly spent time there. The first floor could be a perfect place for a studio—it was certainly big enough. She was still thinking about that possibility. It was something she'd discuss with Barney, when the time was right. She just had to decide if she wanted to put that much of herself into Hidden Falls. What would be the point, if she were to leave in a year? On the other hand, it would be a year of doing something she loved and could share with others.

On a whim, she ducked back into the house and grabbed the key from the rack.

"Come on, Buttons. I just want to take another look around." Cara unlocked the side door of the carriage house, and she and the dog went inside.

The morning was bright and cheery, despite the gloom inside the Hudson house. Everyone was still feeling the absence of Nikki and the energy she'd brought with her. While only she had been a witness to Allie's drama, the tension still hung over Cara like a storm cloud. Had she done the right thing by not calling an ambulance? Allie appeared to be fine, if hungover, and had been coherent once she'd awakened. But the question of telling or not telling weighed on Cara. She'd promised Allie that she wouldn't tell Des, but that had been before Cara understood just how serious the problem was. Was she her sister's keeper?

She rubbed the windowpanes with a tissue she had in her pocket in an effort to remove enough of the dross to permit a little more light, but it was hopeless. She stuffed the tissue back into her pocket. She brushed leaves and debris from the bottom step of the staircase that led to the second floor, and sat, dropping the leash so that Buttons could explore on her own.

It really was a great space, and with proper lighting, a wood floor, heat in the winter, and air-conditioning in the summer, it could be a charming studio. The Hudson property sat well off the street and was surrounded by tall trees. Already the songbirds were gathering in the morning. A studio here could offer a naturally serene setting.

Definitely something to think about, if they could figure out how long the theater renovations would take. Of course, if she opened a studio here, how would her students feel—how would *she* feel?—once the work on the theater was completed and she was free to close up shop and return to Devlin's Light? And how would Barney feel about such a venture?

Why, she sighed, did life have to be so complicated?

She watched Buttons pounce on a leaf and toss it into the air, leaping on it again when it hit the floor.

"There's nothing complicated about your life, is there, pup? Sleep, eat, play. Love your humans. Be loved in return. A couple of treats, a squeaky toy, and all is good, right?" At the sound of Cara's voice, Buttons trotted over and curled up at her feet. Cara leaned over to scratch behind the dog's ears. "I guess we're both in places we never thought we'd be," she said softly. "Where did you come from, pup? Who were your people? Is someone looking for you?"

Selfishly, Cara hoped no one was. The dog had fit into the Hudson family as if she'd been made for them, and they all loved her. Even Barney had been overheard on the phone telling a friend she'd never seen herself as a dog owner, but now that Buttons was there, she couldn't imagine their home without her.

How much more would Barney miss her nieces when the time came? Cara tucked away the thought. On the heels of Nikki's departure, there'd been enough goodbyes for one day.

She wished there was someone she could talk to about Allie. She wished she'd never made that damned promise. There was no question that Allie would have to get her drinking under control, but the only one who could do that was Allie. No amount of shaming would make it happen if she didn't want it for herself and for her daughter.

And then there was that promise Cara'd recently made to her father, out loud, in the apartment overhead. There had to have been a reason why Fritz had hidden those letters between himself and the mysterious J., and the clippings about Gil Wheeler's death. Would showing Barney the clippings just make the tragedy new for her once again? Cara wasn't sure.

Was that to be her role—the keeper of secrets? Cara's natural inclination to tell the truth rebelled against the thought.

Allie was more of an immediate problem, but the longer Cara sat on the step, the more her anger toward Allie dissipated and she began to feel sorry for her sister.

Her sister.

She had a sister. *Two* sisters.

After a lifetime of being an only child, the fact that she had sisters still stunned her. She'd always wanted a sibling, but had long ago accepted the fact that it wasn't to be. And then there they were, the two strangers in Pete Wheeler's office, learning the truth about their father, and each other.

Her once familiar life in Devlin's Light seemed far away now. Who would have suspected how quickly things could change, how unpredictable life could be? There'd been so many changes in so short a time, and she was still sorting it all out.

She'd come to Hidden Falls to find something of her father that might explain why he'd led the life he had, why he'd left one family in favor of another, why he'd hidden so much that mattered deeply to him from the people he'd loved most. Pete Wheeler had called Fritz a coward. Was that all there was to it? Cara wondered. So far, she'd found no answers.

Then again, wasn't it unrealistic to think you could find, overnight, what had been hidden for a lifetime?

But then she considered all she *had* found, things she hadn't even known she'd needed.

Her sisters. She might not always like them, but she was starting to love them. Even Allie.

Her niece had turned out to be an incredible bonus, a smart kid who saw only good and whose heart was an open book.

And Barney—Cara wished she'd known her aunt sooner, wished with all her heart that Susa and Barney had met. They were so different, yet so alike in the ways that mattered. They both loved freely, opened their hearts and treated everyone with kindness and compassion. They would've been friends, Cara thought. They would have loved each other.

She thought about the legacy in Hidden Falls that belonged to her, to Allie and Des and to Nikki. There were generations of people who'd made a difference in the lives of those around them, and it was humbling to know what her ancestors had accomplished. If not for the terms of Fritz's will, she'd never have discovered any of it.

Fritz had been wrong not to tell them the truth sooner, but he was right, in the end, to make sure it happened. In that alone, she realized, she'd learned something about him after all: While he hadn't been able to bring himself to risk alienating his daughters in life, in death, he'd loved them enough to take that chance. There were still so many questions, but there'd be time to seek the answers.

Cara would stay in Hidden Falls until her father's wishes had been fulfilled. Who knew what she'd find between now and then? She already knew she was a better person for having come here, a happier person who'd been gifted with so much more than she could ever have imagined.

And oddly, she found herself more at peace about her father's double life, because while she hadn't found answers to the questions that had brought her here, her sisters were becoming more important to her with each passing day. They were pieces of Fritz, just as she was.

And then there was Joe.

Just thinking about Joe brought a smile to her face.

Susa would've liked this place. She would have liked the town and she would've been totally in love with the theater and the plans to renovate it. She would have seen and embraced the magic in the old building.

Wherever Susa was at that moment, Cara was certain she was happy her daughter had found so much even after all she'd lost. She'd tell Cara there would still be love and happiness and joy to be found. That it might not look like the love and joy she used to know, but it would still be love and joy, all the same. She'd tell Cara to trust in the magic and to open her heart, to greet each new day as an opportunity to bring fresh joy into her life. And knowing Susa, she'd tell Cara to look beyond today and to trust the universe to bring her what she needed.

"I trust, Mom," she said aloud.

Cara got up from the step and brushed off her pants. She grabbed the dog's leash, and together she and Buttons left the carriage house. She locked the door and set off on their walk.

Hidden Falls at eight in the morning was a peaceful place. Most of the residents who commuted to work left around seven, and those who did rarely came down Hudson Street. It was so quiet, Cara could almost believe she had the town to herself. She walked past the park and stopped to read the plaque at the entrance: REYNOLDS E. HUDSON PARK, DEDICATED 1972.

Her great-grandfather, the one who'd built the theater. The same Reynolds Hudson who'd built a hospital, given land for a school, started a college, and avoided strikes in his coal mines by paying his workers well and treating them fairly. That was quite a legacy, she thought as they passed the children's playground.

Buttons spotted a squirrel and pleaded to be taken off her leash, but Cara held firm and the squirrel retreated to the safety of a nearby tree. She and Buttons made their way around the block and ended up on Main Street.

Up ahead she could see the theater, the big old boarded-up edifice they'd be sinking so much time and money into. It was a magnificent building, and it deserved to be restored to its former glory. Her father had been right about wanting to bring it back to life.

She was grateful the task had been left to them, despite the cockamamie means their father had used to make it happen. She, Des, and Allie would see the renovations through to the end. Together, just like Fritz had wanted, however long it took.

POCKET READERS GROUP GUIDE

THE LAST CHANCE MATINEE

MARIAH
STEWART

This reading group guide for **The Last Chance Matinee** includes an introduction, discussion questions, ideas for enhancing your book club, and a Q&A with author **Mariah Stewart**. The suggested questions are intended to help your reading group find new and interesting angles and topics for your discussion. We hope that these ideas will enrich your conversation and increase your enjoyment of the book.

INTRODUCTION

When celebrated and respected agent Fritz Hudson passes away, he leaves a trail of Hollywood glory in his wake—and two separate families who never knew the other existed. There's Allie and Des Hudson—sisters who are products of Fritz's first marriage to Honora, a beautiful but troubled starlet. Then there's Cara, Fritz's daughter with New Age hippie Susa. While Fritz loved Susa and Cara, he never quite managed to tell them about his West Coast family.

Now Fritz is gone, and the three sisters meet all together for the first time. As if that shock isn't enough, there are the strange stipulations surrounding their inheritance. Each sister stands to gain a large share—but only if they work together to restore a decrepit theater that was Fritz's obsession growing up in his small hometown of Hidden Falls.

As the sisters reluctantly set out to fulfill their father's dying wish, they find not only themselves but the father they only thought they knew.

TOPICS & QUESTIONS
FOR DISCUSSION

1. Discuss the book's title. Why do you think Mariah Stewart chose it? Whose last chance is it? Explain your answer.

2. When Darla asks Cara what she hopes to find by going to Hidden Falls, Cara answers, "My dad. I want to find out who my father really was, because he obviously wasn't the man I thought I knew." (page 61) What does Cara learn about her father? Does Cara have other motivations for complying with her father's will and visiting Hidden Falls? If so, what are they? Discuss her motivations along with those of Allie and Des.

3. Allie calls Hidden Falls "strictly Small Town USA." (page 195) Describe Hidden Falls. Do you agree with Allie or do you, like Cara, find Hidden Falls charming? Could you make a place like Hidden Falls your home? What did you like about it?

4. What was your initial impression of Barney? She is beloved by the residents of Hidden Falls—why do they hold her in such high esteem? Do you think their admiration is warranted?

5. When Nikki asks if the family's theater will be used once the restoration is complete, Allie tells her "[Y]our grandfather's will only called for us to renovate it. Nothing else. Nobody's talking about using it for anything." (page 313) Why is Allie reluctant to commit to using the restored theater in any way? Compare her attitude about the theater with that of the rest of her family. What would you do if you were in Allie's position?

6. Do you think Honora was a good mother to Allie and Des? Explain your answer. Compare Honora's parenting style with Susa's.

7. Why is Allie nervous about Nikki's visit? Given Allie's fears, did Nikki behave as you expected? What do you think of her? Were you surprised by Nikki's enthusiasm for the restoration project? Why, or why not?

8. Of the theater restoration, Nikki says, "This is so seriously cool. I can't believe I have the chance to do something *important* like this." (page 320) Do you agree with Nikki that restor-

ing the Sugarhouse is important? What role has the theater played in the community? Are there any historic buildings in your hometown that have similar importance?

9. Early on in the novel, the reader learns that Cara's husband, Drew, has left Cara for her best friend. Given what you learn about Drew, were you surprised by his actions? Why, or why not? How would you describe his character?

10. When Cara finds Allie drinking alone on the patio in the middle of the night, she reluctantly agrees not to tell anyone, particularly Des. How does this promise come back to haunt Cara later in the book? What would you have done? Do you think Cara should have broken her promise to keep silent after finding Allie passed out in her room?

11. When Allie chastises Nikki because she's "starting to sound like [her] Aunt Des," Nikki responds by telling her, "I'm going to take that as a compliment." (page 375) Describe Allie's relationship with Des. Why does she see "sounding like Des" as worthy of disdain? Do you? Which of Des's traits does Nikki admire? What do you think of Des?

12. Were you surprised by Cara's discovery in the carriage house? Do you agree with Cara's deci-

sion to keep the letters a secret? Would you have shared them with Barney and/or your sisters? Does it lead to more questions about Fritz for you? If so, what were they?

13. As Cara watches her family at the Hidden Falls Gun Club, she "felt a little tug at her heart. . . . Who would have guessed how much richer her life would be after less than a month in Hidden Falls?" (pages 432–33) How has Cara's life been changed by her time spent in Hidden Falls? Compare Cara's frame of mind at the end of *The Last Chance Matinee* with that as the book begins. What do you think will happen for Cara in the book's sequel?

ENHANCE YOUR BOOK CLUB

1. As Allie, Des, and Cara discuss their father, Allie reveals that one of her favorite memories was the birthday trip to New York City that she took with their father, and she tells how she "stayed for an entire week in a big suite at the Plaza because I loved *Eloise* when I was younger." (page 160) Are there characters from books that you read in your childhood that you loved as much as Allie loved Eloise? Discuss your favorite children's books and characters with your book club.

2. In preparation for bluegrass night at the Hidden Falls Gun Club, the Hudson sisters listen to bluegrass music with Barney, who describes it as "sort of like country, maybe what some would consider hillbilly style." (page 424) Listen to bluegrass music with your book club. Do you like it? Or do you find the music "different," as Cara does? Discuss your reaction to

the music. If you're already a lover of bluegrass music, share some of your favorite songs with your book club.

3. Cara grew up in Devlin's Light, the setting for Mariah Stewart's wildly popular Enright series. Read one of the books in this series (*Devlin's Light*, *Wonderful You*, *Moon Dance*) with your book club and discuss it. What do you think of Devlin's Light based on Cara's descriptions of it in *The Last Chance Matinee*? Were you surprised by anything?

4. Practicing yoga and teaching it to others provides Cara with a sense of calm, and she "loved that she could teach others how to obtain that same sense of peace and well-being." (page 5) Try yoga with your book club. Are you able to focus and find a sense of inner peace? Talk about your experiences with your book club.

5. Make Susa's granola recipe for your book club!

INGREDIENTS:

5 cups organic rolled oats

1 cup each of:

   wheat germ

   sesame seeds

sunflower seeds

chopped almonds

brown rice flour

coconut oil (heated to liquefy)

honey

1 tablespoon cinnamon

1 tablespoon vanilla

DIRECTIONS:

- Mix all the dry ingredients together in a large bowl.

- Mix the honey and melted coconut oil together, then add to the dry mix.

- Stir the mixture until evenly dispersed.

- Spread onto two large jelly roll pans (17" x 11" or 19" x 12").

- Bake at 275°F for 20 minutes.

- Let cool for about 15 minutes, then scrape granola off the pans with a spatula and store in an airtight container. (The granola will be chunky.)

A CONVERSATION
WITH MARIAH STEWART

You've written more than forty books throughout your career. How did the writing and publication process for *The Last Chance Matinee* compare?

I don't plot things out before I start writing, so the process is always one of discovery—the characters reveal themselves and from there the story settles around them. The first hundred pages are always agonizing, because while I know the basic story, I'm not sure how it's going to play out; I'm still getting to know the characters and hearing their voices. If I can make it through those first hundred pages, I'm probably going to make it to the end of the book. That being said, this book was a little different for me because I had more of a clear understanding of where I was going right from the start.

In the book's preface, you write that *The Last Chance Matinee* is loosely based on something that happened in your family. How much of your

family's story influenced the story of the Hudson sisters? Did your family have any objections to you using your own history as source material?

When my mother was in her mid-forties, she discovered that her father had had another family in another state, and that the person she thought was her cousin was actually her half brother. He'd been adopted as a toddler by my great-aunt Bess, my grandfather's sister, and she and her husband raised him as their own son. He died not knowing that the man he called "uncle" was actually his father. After the "cousin" passed away, my mother received a letter from his widow, who laid out the truth. My mother also discovered that she had a half sister, and that another half sister had died shortly after being born, along with the child's mother. Since the story I wrote is far from the truth of what actually happened, I didn't expect anyone to object. My mother and her siblings have all passed away, but I think my mother might have been amused by my version.

Many of your novels have been *New York Times* and *USA Today* bestsellers, and you've been the recipient of many awards, including the Romantic Times Reviewers' Choice Award. Given the success of your earlier books, did you feel any added pressure when writing *The Last Chance Matinee*? If so, how did you deal with it?

There's always pressure when I start a new book. I can't say that writing this one was any more stressful than any other! A lot of whining and angst goes into writing every book, because it's never easy. There's always a moment when I ask myself why I thought this story was a good idea. The only thing you can do to get past that is to keep writing.

As an award-winning novelist, do you have any advice for aspiring writers? Is there anything that you wish you had been told at the start of your writing career?

Read. Read often. Read everything. Read thrillers and romances and literary works, fiction and nonfiction.

And write. Write every day, even when you think what you're writing is dreck. There's a great quote from Nora Roberts that goes something like, "You can fix a bad page, but you can't fix a blank one."

I wish I'd known that this is never easy, regardless of where you are in your career. Writing a book is hard work. Yes, sometimes the words come easily and the writing flows, but don't be fooled. Sooner or later—usually just when you start thinking, *Hey, this book could write itself*—you'll round the corner and come to a screeching halt, and you will have no idea where you're going. You just have to keep banging away at it until it comes out right.

***The Last Chance Matinee* marks the beginning of a new series for you. Can you tell us a little about your writing process? How do you decide which story lines to leave unfinished so that you can address them in future novels within the series? Do you know how the entire series will conclude?**

My writing process is always the same: I sit in front of my computer every morning and hope my characters are speaking to me that day!

Every series is different, and sometimes the story arcs overlap more than in others. The most difficult part of writing this series was deciding how much of the story to give the reader in this first book and how much to hold back. Because I have three lead characters, each having their own book, the first thing I had to decide was whose story to reveal first. Each of these women are in different stages of their lives, and they each have issues to deal with. Some will be resolved earlier than others. It's a balancing act, and I don't mind saying that my editor has been very helpful. She has a really good feel for such things!

There are so many threads that cross each other in these books, from the first to the last—from Cara's search to find out who her father really was, to Des's commitment issues, to Allie's alcoholism—but I can say I do know how the series concludes!

Have you found anything particularly rewarding about publishing *The Last Chance Matinee*? If so, what?

The most rewarding thing about publishing any book is connecting with the readers. This book is no different in that regard. I did enjoy putting a different spin on the story my mother was told, imagining how it might have all played out, and I came to love all five of the women—from Nikki, who turned out to be the total opposite of what I expected, to the three sisters, to Barney, who is a great character herself. And yes, I do see a bit of my great-aunt Bess in her.

You describe the community of Hidden Falls so vividly. How did you come up with it? Is it based on a real place? If so, can you tell us more about it?
Hidden Falls is a product of my imagination. The town developed in my head around the story. I knew it had to have the theater, of course, and a few restaurants, and the usual police department, pharmacy, that sort of thing. It needed to be small, and it needed to be one of those Poconos towns that never fed into the tourist thing. So I had the Hudson family carefully control how the town developed over the years so that it could stay small and maintain its character and rich history.

I should add, my mother's brother and his family lived on one of the Poconos mountains, and we visited at least once every year when I was growing up. I remember how the roads twisted and turned, and I remember seeing the gouges in the earth left from strip-mining the coal. But I also remember the beauty of the mountains and the ponds and lakes and forests around my uncle's home. If you're from the area and are familiar with Cummings Pond (we called it "the lake" back then), you'll recognize it in Compton Lake. It's the only thing in the book that I took from memory.

Your descriptions of the Sugarhouse Theater really bring it to life. What kind of research did you conduct in order to get all the Art Deco details correct?

For many years we lived in Lansdowne, Pennsylvania, a small town outside Philadelphia, where a 1927 theater is being restored. I'd been inside it several times and remember how my jaw dropped the first time I looked up at the magnificent ceiling. I borrowed elements of this lovely building for the Sugarhouse. If you've seen the movie *Silver Linings Playbook*, you saw the outside of the theater in the scene where Bradley Cooper and Jennifer Lawrence are running down the middle of a street—they run past the Lansdowne Theater and stop in front of it and argue (the memorable "He's harassing me!" scene). You'll find pictures of the interior of the Lansdowne Theater here: www.lansdownetheater.org and www.abandonedamerica.us/historic-lansdowne-theater.

I also studied the restoration process of other historic theaters in different parts of the country.

What would you like your readers to take away from *The Last Chance Matinee*?

That sometimes life tosses you a curve, and it's how you react to the circumstances that determines the way your life—your journey—plays out. That in the end, it all comes down to the relationships you have with the people who mean the most to you. That family is where you find it. That sometimes we have to take that unexpected step to end up where we're supposed to be, or as Cara imagined her mother, Susa, saying, *"[G]reet each new day as an opportunity to bring fresh joy into your life. Look beyond today to the future and trust the universe to bring you what you truly need."* (page 5)

Fritz left his daughters a great deal of money, but it came with strings attached. For all his shortcomings as a father, he knew the only way these women would get to really know each other would be by living together and working toward a common goal, and becoming part of each other's journey. By agreeing to go somewhere they didn't want to be, with people they didn't want to be with, in the end, they each found something they didn't know they were looking for, and all their lives were so much richer for the experience.

Can you tell us about the sequels to *The Last Chance Matinee*?

From the beginning, I'd planned three books in this series, one from the point of view of each of the Hudson sisters. *The Last Chance Matinee* tells the story mainly through Cara's eyes. The second book, *The Sugarhouse Blues*, continues the story from Des's point of view, and was released in May 2018. The third book, *The Goodbye Café*, will follow Allie's journey as she learns how to balance her new relationships—as sister and niece—and find her own place in "this family of amazing women" (thank you, Robyn Carr). She's also navigating being part of a larger community—something new for her, because she's always avoided anything beyond the superficial in her dealings with others, except for her daughter. Living with her sisters and her aunt will challenge Allie in ways she'd never dreamed.

The Goodbye Café will be published in the spring of 2019.